I0820009

SHADOWS

CHARLIZE K. KELLY

Cover design by Betthina Eriella
Interior design by Natalia Junqueria
Editing by Agatha Whitechapel

Paperback ISBN: 978-0-6457-3352-5
Hardback ISBN: 978-0-6457335-1-8
Ebook ISBN: 978-1-4452-9952-5

To DL—the band I love,

whose music was always playing in the background.

I never would've written half of this book without you, thank you.

Author's Note

Before you re-indulge in the world of Celacali, it's important to understand that *Shadows of Vengeance* isn't for the faint of heart and shouldn't be read without reading *Shadows of the Night* (Book One) first. Warning: this is a *dark romance.* I don't condone the behaviour depicted on these pages or the actions of my characters, I just find writing about the darkness … enthralling.

Shadows of Vengeance contains:

Alcohol and drug usage, assault, blood, death, divorce, emotional and physical abuse, fire, gore, hallucinations, flashbacks, hostage and kidnapping situations, murder, profanity, PTSD, anxiety attacks, loss of a loved one (grief), drowning, religious metaphors, sexism, sexual harassment, sexually explicit scenes, torture, violence, child death, vampirism, bloodsucking, polyamory, BDSM themes, stalking, voyeurism, corruption, size kink, exhibitionism, degradation, character and animal deaths, threesomes, group and M/M scenes, knives, consensual and non-consensual biting.

Still here? Welcome back to the malignant city of Celacali. It awaits your return eagerly. And, if you're family or friends … *strap in* because if you thought Book One was 'full on,' *this* might make you question my sanity once and for all (don't worry, there's a straitjacket with my name on it somewhere).

Welcome to the club, little doves.

—Charlize K. Kelly

"You are a killer."

—David - Kiefer Sutherland - The Lost Boys.

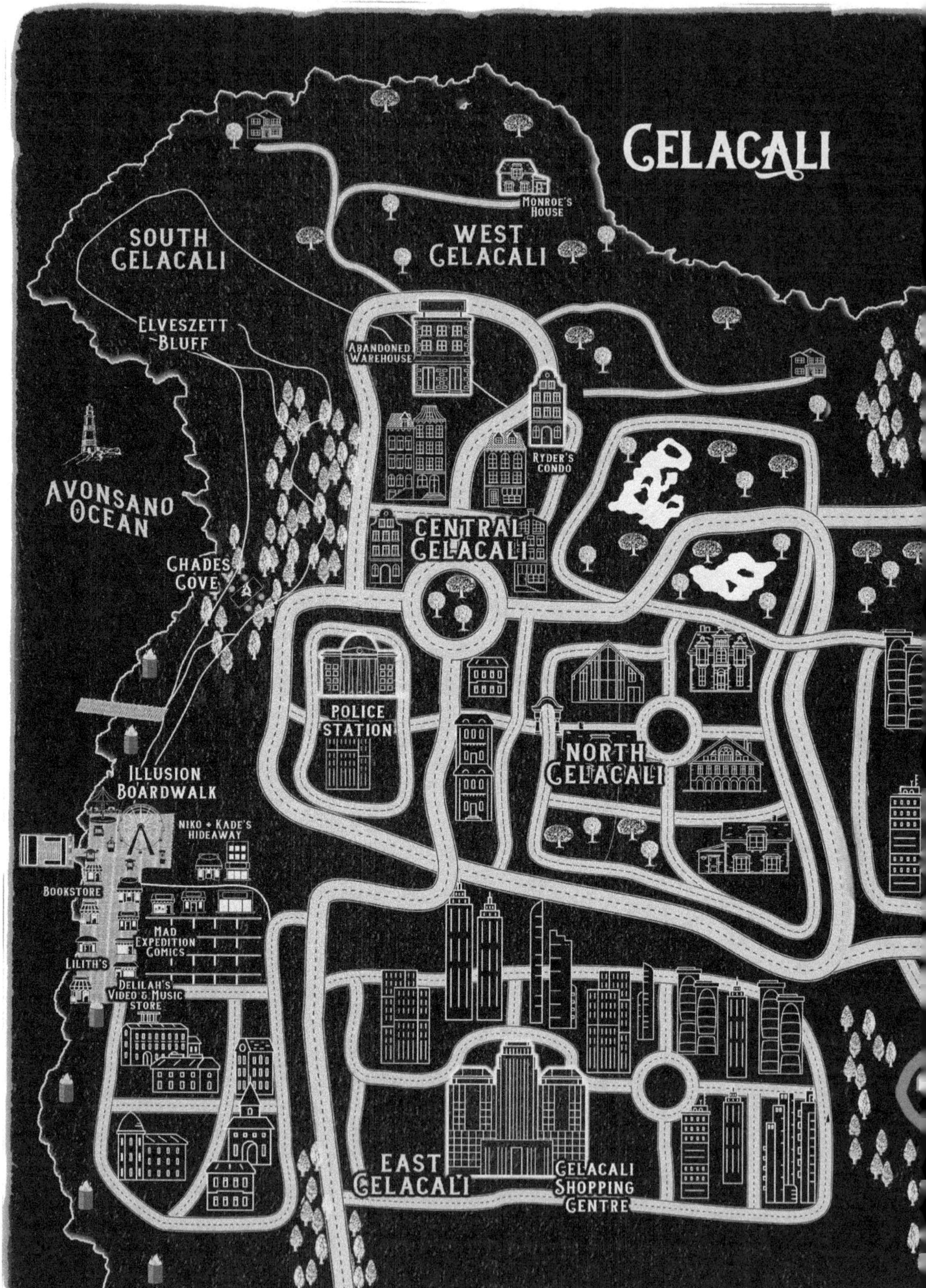

CELACALI

Monroe's House
South Celacali
West Celacali
Elveszett Bluff
Abandoned Warehouse
Ryder's Condo
Avonsano Ocean
Central Celacali
Ghades Cove
Police Station
North Celacali
Illusion Boardwalk
Niko + Kade's Hideaway
Bookstore
Mad Expedition Comics
Lilith's
Delilah's Video & Music Store
East Celacali
Celacali Shopping Centre

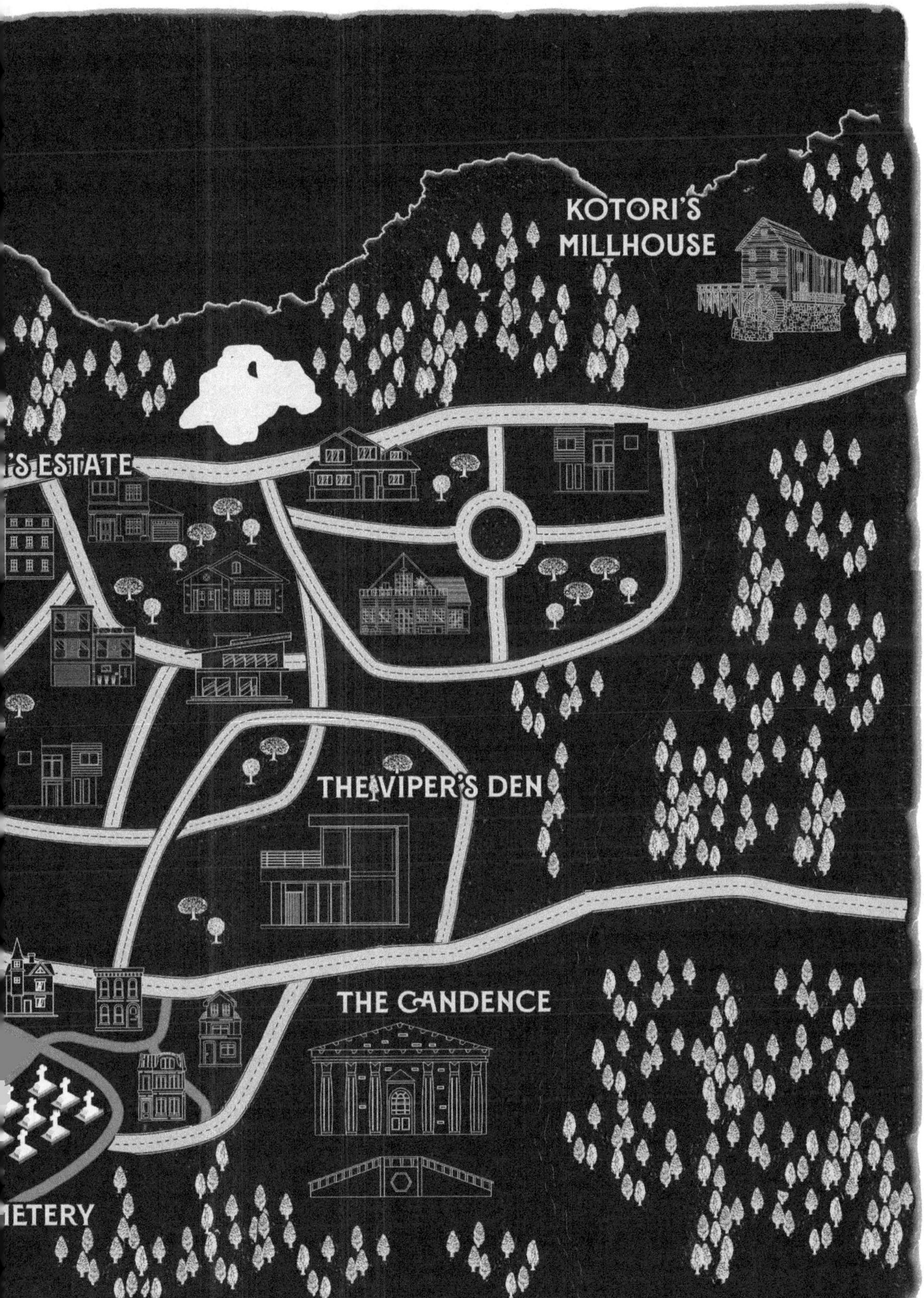

KOTORI'S
MILLHOUSE

'S ESTATE

THE VIPER'S DEN

THE CANDENCE

ETERY

O

October, 2037.

Screams of elation perforated the star-flecked sky as brewing storm clouds cusped the horizon. A thousand scents blustered his senses as neon lights glared holes into his eyes through the large windows of a store's second-storey, one-way glass where he sat, obscured from the bustling stretch of fairground below. The pages of a lined notebook perched on his lap as he read in a cushioned armchair.

It's been too long. I left my sons too long, Leon thought, drumming his fingers upon the blocky scrawl of his handwriting—his notes and plans. *Their loyalty has been bent by* her *influence and it must be restored before she corrupts them completely.*

He knew he would break a vampiric law by ridding his bloodline of the halfling—whether it was direct or by his sons' hands—but he didn't care. He *needed* her gone before her blood tainted his pack. *Needed* the information Asher Monroe had possessed before he'd died so it could be destroyed, finally, and he knew one person would have it since Azeil had fled the city to save his life. Nyx. After all, Asher had entrusted his leatherbound tome to the Stone family—trusted friends he'd found in Wildegulf while he was alive, and he'd planned ahead … *if* he died, it was to be returned to the Monroes.

Leon would be double-damned now if he was going to let Nyx keep it, and show it to his sons. *I haven't spent centuries keeping the truth from them for a halfling* blood bag *to ruin it all*, he thought, tracing the name written on the page, underlined.

Emilia Stone had returned from Elveszett Bluff—a rocky cliffside to the shoreline's south—hours ago and he'd followed her back to Illusion Boardwalk. He'd continued to watch her from the building he'd easily slipped into, knowing the hidden walkways and tunnel systems of Celacali like the back of his hand. His sharp eyes followed her now as she led her younger brother to a food stall, the boy's blond curls bathed in glittering lights.

Footsteps echoed off the tiled floor and wrenched his attention from the Stone siblings to two women in the doorway, his head angling toward them as his fingers plucked at a speck of lint. He sniffed disdainfully as the dark blot, now purged from his white dress shirt, drifted to the floor. "Do you have Asher's journal?" he murmured, eyeing his eldest daughter, Qadira, and then his youngest, Phaelyn, expectantly.

"No," Phaelyn admitted, dropping her silvered gaze to the tiles.

"Why not?" he said, rage flickering in his eyes.

"Because it wasn't at the Bluff. Emilia left *nothing*," Qadira said, stepping forward to block Phaelyn from his fury.

A laugh lacking humour lashed the silent room, the clatter of the rollercoaster wheels background noise to his mounting anger. "*Nothing?*" he repeated, a cold warning in his desolate tone.

"Nothing," Qadira confirmed, crystalline irises etched with candour.

He rose from the armchair with an agitated tick at the corner of his eye, slack-clad legs closing the distance between his daughter in a burst of unnatural speed until he towered over both women. "*Find it*," he ordered, an otherworldly command in his voice.

Qadira and Phaelyn straightened as a sharpness entered their eyes.

He felt pleased. He was *proud* of his daughters and their loyalty while their brothers lashed out like cornered wolves who'd tasted freedom. Orion, Kotori, Niko and Kade were growing unruly and bared their teeth at him, but his girls obeyed with blood-thirsty grins. *My vipers will find Asher's journal,* he thought, assuring himself as he stepped closer, brushing his fingers affectionately across Phaelyn's cheek before he stooped and pressed a fatherly kiss to Qadira's forehead. "Go," he said, inclining his head toward the store's staircase, dropping his hand to his side. "Find Asher's journal."

"Of course," Phaelyn said, dipping her head as she started toward the exit, Qadira at her side.

A sharp, bubbling squeal pierced the night sky and drew Leon's attention to the boardwalk—to the Stone siblings he'd watched for too long. A thought crossed his mind. A low sound came from the depths of his chest, halting his daughters' retreat.

"Leon?" Qadira asked, unsurety palpable in her voice.

Leon turned to Qadira with an itch he couldn't shake—an itch that had plagued him for centuries since he'd woken as a halfling in a creek bed and stumbled to the nearest village. He couldn't remember much of *how* he'd found himself by the water or why he'd lurked like a monster in the shadows before his instincts—*new* and *unnatural*—had latched a hold of his mind and he had struck, dragging a young girl into the darkness. She'd smelled of lilies and sheep's wool. And, before he knew it, he'd drained her and shunted himself head-first into vampirism with a nasty side effect. One he couldn't shake, purge, quell, or soothe.

"Get rid of Emilia Stone," he said.

Leon wandered back to his seat by the window, distracted by his thoughts as he sank into the armchair and rested his notebook back upon his knee, focus once more on the Stone siblings.

Phaelyn and Qadira's stares prickled across his shoulders. He felt the weight of them but he *couldn't* tear his eyes from the delighted look on Emilia's brother—*Jesse's* face as Emilia led him to the Ferris wheel, passing a new ride part-way to completion barricaded off by its side. The eager tugging on her hand was impossible to miss. Fixated, Leon *couldn't* rid himself of the itch trickling into his bloodstream. *Couldn't* forget the decadent taste of a child's blood, how their innocence and malleable natures gifted him indelibly with an ambrosia and euphoria unlike any other.

"And … the boy?" Qadira pressed, dragging him from his thoughts, a knowing edge to her voice. She was aware of her sire's habits—his *addictions*.

"Bring the boy to me," Leon said, dismissing them with a flick of his wrist.

"But he's a child," Phaelyn said, glancing at Qadira with a troubled frown.

A humourless chuckle echoed in the room as Leon rose from his chair. *Sweet Phaelyn,* he thought as he moved in a burst of preternatural speed and his hand curled around her throat, dragging her to his chest with a sneer curling his lips. *How your morals* try *to arise at the most* ... inconvenient *of times.* "And?" he drawled, arching a blond brow as Phaelyn's heart raced beneath his fingertips.

"You can't—he's so young. *Too* young," she spluttered, eyes staring into his.

"Blood is blood, or have you forgotten *what* completed your transition? You're as damned as I," he said lowly.

"Leon—" Qadira started, her words dying with the look he sent her.

His grasp tightened on Phaelyn's throat.

"He's just a boy," Phaelyn murmured, pleading.

"I told you to *fetch him* and you *will* obey," he commanded.

Something caught in his words as he uttered them. They were just words but they pierced Phaelyn like knives, catching, cutting, slicing. In their wake they caused a pain that became her will. Qadira watched her sister as a glazed sheen obscured Phaelyn's eyes and her protests ceased, rendering her defenceless to his commands.

"Now, *bring the boy to me*," Leon said, smiling.

PART ONE

Nyctophilia (n);

an attraction to darkness or night;

finding relaxation or comfort in the darkness.

I

Nyx

"*A local woman, Emilia Stone was found murdered at Chades Cove this morning, and officials are urging residents to be alert and to stay indoors after nightfall. Chief of Police Issac Silvia is asking anyone to come forward with information on Emilia Stone's six year-old younger brother, Jesse Stone's whereabouts. He has not been seen in over twenty-four hours,*" the reporter's voice twanged over the airwaves with heartfelt precision as she concluded her harrowing mid-morning report.

A gentle, saline breeze glided through the open doors of the comic bookstore, Mad Expedition, ruffling the sleek comics clipped upon the display wire above the sage-green, three-tiered tables. The morbid news break echoed in Nyx's ears as her gaze lifted from a newspaper on the countertop containing the same article. Murder headlines were splayed across the cover, and the twins watched her from beside the display tables. Cardboard boxes filled with new comics were cradled in their arms, and the silence of the empty store seemed suddenly, inexplicably greater.

A jolt of excitement and hope darted through her, her hands brushing a fine sheen of dust from her black halter top before she grasped her sunglasses and perched them atop her head. "Do you think it was them?" Nyx mused, breaking the silence. Her nose screwed up as a sharpness throbbed across her temples, her altered sight struggling to adjust to the sunlight.

Alexander's fingers carded his mouse-brown curls, hazel eyes flickering between Nyx and Tobias as he propped the cardboard box against the table. "It *could* be an animal attack, Night," he said.

Nyx scoffed, disbelieving as Alexander toyed with the hem of his shirt, boots crossed at the laces. "*Animal attack?*" She winced as a clamour of screams and laughter rushed past the store, children's footsteps pounding the wooden planks in pursuit of the neon-lit rides. "When has there e*ver* been an animal attack in Celacali?"

"It could be," Alexander offered lamely.

Nyx nodded with feigned consideration before she breathed a laugh and held the newspaper up, shaking it to garner their attention. "So, *animals* kidnap kids now?"

Tobias sighed, rubbing his palms down his jeans, coffee-brown irises sombre. "That's not the point, Nyx. Don't start chasing ghosts," he said, joining his brother in seriousness.

A pang of anguish rippled across her chest, sharp and biting as she turned her head toward the open doorway. "I'm not chasing ghosts, Bias ... *they* promised." It wasn't like she could forget, or that she'd want to. And much like Tobias's urging, Nyx couldn't stomach giving up. She knew it'd been three months since she'd seen them, a crudely sharpened stake jutting from her stomach, blood wetting her hands as oceanic shrubbery pressed her skin and the crashing of waves filled her ears. But some part of her—a foolish sliver—clutched at their whispered promises. *They'd come back for her.*

Then where were they?

Nyx's fingertips drummed against the tabletop, mind swirling with blurry memories of the twins' faces when they'd found her, on the cusp of death on Elveszett Bluff, mere hours after they'd been discharged from the nearest hospital and her father had skipped town; as per Nyx's urging. As she refocused on the room around her, she couldn't have been more grateful for the twins she called her brothers.

Despite their father's and uncle's deaths being partially at her hands, Alexander and Tobias hadn't faltered in their brother-like statures, opening their shared apartment to her in the months that'd passed. Although she continued to flit between their apartment, her family's house and the cave nestled into the cliff face of Elveszett Bluff—seeking security, Nyx couldn't settle. Like a wolf without its pack, one moment she'd be content in the cavernous hideaway tucked away from the liveliness of Celacali, and the next, she'd be fleeing the cave and the tide of memories it evoked. No matter how hard she tried or the sleepless nights that seemed to pile atop the others, she couldn't linger in one place for too long.

Alexander's voice ghosted her ear, tinged with sympathy. "Nyx—" he began.

She reared up from the stool she'd been perched on so fast it made her stumble. Cutting him off, she clicked her fingers to garner the attention of the black and white-pelted Malamute lolling beside the tiered tables.

"Don't say you know," she said as she rounded the counter, pushing her sunglasses onto the bridge of her nose. Ares dutifully meandered to her side, ears inches above her mid-thigh. "Because you don't. How could you know?"

Tobias opened his mouth to speak, to correct himself maybe, but Nyx wasn't having any of it. Her onyx irises glinted with anguish as she shook her head and strode toward the sun-bathed doorway, Ares at her side.

"Nyx," called Tobias, her exit faltering as she paused on the threshold.

"It's not your fault, Bias," she said, then glanced at Alexander, "or yours, Alex. But I have to live with the memories, I can't … *escape* them." She chuckled bitterly, urging Ares through the door. "Trust me, I've tried."

* * *

Blades of grass swayed in the summery breeze, tangling the loose tresses of Nyx's hair as she sat cross-legged, the sun warming her skin. Sweet-smelling narcissi dotted the desolate graveyard and Ares' head was propped against her jean-clad thighs, dozing.

Silence was hard to come by in Celacali, normality harder still and so it was within the eerie quiet of the city's cemetery that Nyx found her calm. It was like the eye of the storm, motionless and silent, but peaceful. And for someone like her, caught between the grasp of vampirism and mortality, it served as a retreat where she could re-establish her footing and just be in the world without her altered senses rioting.

She had returned to the graveyard every other day to sit beside the ornately designed, ash-grey tombstone. The name 'Asher Monroe' was etched into the shiny marble in a sprawling font. Flashes of blood and crystalline-blue eyes filled with adoration filled her memories. A twisted shard of her being latched onto the pain that jarred her senses with the onslaught of memories, convincing her she *needed* to feel the anguish of losing Asher. Like her turbulent nightmares and memories weren't torment enough. And as much as she knew it wasn't her fault, some part of her needed the reminder. The shifting tide of normality and *the waning* of her mortality left her on shaky footing. Some days it was all she could do just to hang on.

"It hasn't been the same without you, Ash," she said, a watery chuckle bubbling from her lips. Her fingers toyed with the yellow petals of the roses she'd brought with her as a lump formed in her throat. The bright foliage reminded her of her uncle's vibrant and gentle personality, of nights and days spent on the boardwalk with him or hunting for comics, of his failed attempts at babysitting her. "Nothing has been," she continued.

Silence answered when she paused, fighting away the images of his lifeless body from her mind. Like she'd done for the past three months, lost in a daze of grief and the longing for her father's presence. It'd gotten easier as the days had turned into weeks and then months, but she often felt like she'd died herself with her body left to drift. Detached but always angry. Something about sitting beside Asher's tombstone brought her comfort. It was as though, if she sat there long enough, she'd be able to see him again. To feel the warmth of his embrace and hear his easy laugh, convince herself it'd all been a cruel dream dredged up by Ryder and Amir. But she knew it wasn't. As she reached out and brushed her fingertips across the cold stone and the carving of her uncle's name, she knew none of it had been.

A sharp snap of bone echoed in her eardrums; a phantom sound dredged from the caverns of her memories. Like the flickers of firelight, the wet *squelch* of a heart being torn from someone's chest and that baleful grin stretching across a certain tattooed blond's face plummeted Nyx's memories into a black chasm. Mocking applause crashed in her mind, a tawny-blond man in an immaculate suit. Leon.

She wondered what would've happened if he hadn't appeared and swept her legs from under her, tossing her thinly veiled understanding of the world to the waves of the Avonsano Ocean. It seemed foolish to reminisce over a past she couldn't change, to fight the onslaught of time that kept on passing and fill the vacancy of the quartet who'd traipsed into her life with such predatory ease. Where *were* they?

Despite everything they'd done, Nyx missed them. She missed Niko's eyes sparking like lightning in a storm and his grin that dared her to not smile or indulge in a little mischief. She missed Kade's concern and eerie attentiveness like he was more in tune with her senses and emotions than she could ever really understand. She missed Kotori's silent and intimidating presence, his quiet so different from his platinum blond counterpart. He, who still haunted her dreams. Orion.

Perhaps, it was strangest of all, that she missed Orion. The safety of knowing he got whatever he wanted and that his word was law amongst his companions. Those pale blue eyes … She knew she didn't need them, despite longing for them, but some part of her had found comfort in them and the ease with which the four navigated the world's darkness. It was at the precipice of this darkness that Nyx now found herself. It was one she wasn't sure she'd be able to cross. Not alone.

Nyx's silvery-toned voice drifted across the cloud-flecked sky, Ares' ears pricking up as his tail thumped softly against the grass. "I haven't seen Dad since you died … or them. Dad's been sending possible leads, helping me to find them." A soft laugh spilled from her lips, gaze fixed on Asher's headstone as she tipped her head back. "So far, they've all been dead ends." She winced. "And if vampire media or folklore is anything to go by, I'm officially a halfling." Her smile slipped as she turned back to her uncle's tombstone, traitorous tears finally spilling, voice wavering and plunged with anguish, "*Not quite human. Not quite a vampire.*"

Her fingers caressed the soft fur along Ares's back while she wiped at her face. Flickers of her uncle's excited grin and a smaller Ares spectered her foresight, the Malamute's delighted tail wagging, Asher waiting eagerly for her response after he'd handed her the sled dog. A happy laugh as Ares' wet nose tickled her collarbone, his open-faced markings gazing up at her, almond-brown eyes alight, charcoal black coat, and snow-white undercoat glossy as the five-month-old pup raised his head from her lap and she gazed down at him.

Keep him close, alright?

Her teeth sank into her bottom lip as she ruffled Ares' fur and remembered what Uncle Asher had said. Her voice whispered soft, laced with agonised nostalgia as she talked with ghosts, "I promise."

II

Nyx

Neon light pulsed and flickered with the guitar riffs and drumbeats clamouring in Nyx's eardrums, a cornucopia of sound intended to capture and contain the attention of tourists and locals alike. It was a feat the rock band performing on Illusion Boardwalk's stage had mastered, garnering the interest of patrons with their glam-rock attire and incandescent presence.

Nyx watched the band from the top of the stands splayed in a J-shape around the stage, her forearms pressing into the barricade at her back, boots crossed at the ankles. A serene smile crawled across her face, her eyes empty. The crowd danced, screamed, and sang along to their heart's content, lost within the siren's thrall of Celacali.

Just like those months ago, when Nyx had first wandered the boardwalk, she now pondered the allure of Celacali, turning every suspicion and factor over in her head. With a huff of dismissal, she pushed off the railing and started down the metallic staircase, fingers on the chilled handrail. She could count on one hand the number of times she'd been on the boardwalk in the past months, choosing to avoid anything that'd remind her of her uncle and the agony of his death. But, in a decision nurtured by Alexander and Tobias, she'd ventured out into the nightlife of the city to try to forget the past and live in the present. Like Asher had always urged her to, re-establishing herself in the night's embrace. She passed barrel fire pits, slipping between them and weaving through the boardwalk-goers, dodging sugar-hyped children the closer she got to the amusement park sector. She avoided a section of bunted off fairground to her right where construction for two rides was underway.

Nostalgia clawed at her chest when she squeezed between two food carts and the white halo of the carousel gleamed before her, twirling whimsically to calliope music.

Its intricate swirls and arches were bathed in shining silver, lights dotting the canopy and beams, the horses of various colours raising then lowering as the ride turned. As Nyx stopped before it and gazed up at the ornate ride at the boardwalk's heart, ignoring the disgruntled sneers of passers-by who sidestepped her, her mind dragged up memories of teasing blondes and an imposing brunette. A scuffle. Beneath the neon-lit umbrella, it felt like nothing had changed.

But Nyx knew it had, could feel it in her every atom. It had all changed. The difference hung over her head like a guillotine. The disgusted tone of Ryder's voice, the square-shaped scars on her abdomen burrowed the memory deeper into her skull like a jigger flea. *Blood-sucker.* Though Nyx knew she wasn't a vampire—she was stuck in a limbo of mortality and immortality, life, and death. Even if every one of her newfound instincts urged her to act on bloodstained desires, to complete the irreversible transition from halfling to fledgling and take one life to begin her immortal one, she wouldn't act on it. Not now. Though she'd never admit it out loud, Nyx was afraid of delving into the world's darkness without a tether or sense of direction, *terrified* of the person she might become.

Sharp, ear-splitting wolf whistles punctuated her train of thought, shunting her from her silent musings as a calloused hand wrapped around her bicep and she turned to peer up into the mossy-green gaze of a dark-haired Ivory Skull. Her gaze darted to the duo accompanying him and her tongue pressed into the soft flesh of her cheek, irritation bubbling in her chest as his companions crept closer and huddled around her. *What is it with these men*—boys—*and ganging up on women*? she thought, onyx stare darkening as she arched an unimpressed brow.

"Yes?" she prompted, reaching up and removing the man's hand from her arm.

The man's auburn-haired companion grinned, raising his hand to skitter his fingers down her other arm. "What's a pretty little thing like you doing all alone?" he asked.

She eyed the man and each of his friends in turn with disdain, features devoid of emotion. "Enjoying my night *alone*. *Without* harassment." She pursed her lips, looking the men up and down, "But it seems I don't get that either."

Mossy-green chuckled, tossing a wicked look to his blond friend who watched, leering. "Aw, don't be like that. *We* can show you a good time."

"I'm not interested in your *good time*. Thanks, but no," she said calmly.

"I'm sure we could persuade you into saying yes," he said, licking his lower lip.

She squinted up at the man like he'd grown three heads, a bitter scoff tumbling from her lips with the displeased shake of her head. "No means no."

The Ivory Skull scoffed back, stepping forward before he roughly grasped both her arms this time. "Don't be a bitch. You're free game."

"You want to know what I am?" Nyx drawled, leaning closer to him as her lips curled with the faintest sneer. "*Not interested.*"

It never ceased to amaze her how quickly men bristled at a firm rejection, and the three Ivory Skulls huddled around her were no different. Unable to handle the simplicity of a two-letter word, let alone a two-worded phrase, it seemed they'd resort to getting physical. But she knew in the eyes of society that it wouldn't be their fault, it'd be hers. They'd blame it on what she wore, the way she acted, the things she said—or the lies they'd create. That she didn't say anything to stop them, that she'd flirted. It was like a whirlpool, ever turning and relentlessly tugging you into its current. Nyx wasn't naïve enough to believe that women didn't play the system, they did, but the extensive brawls and harassment cases her father had to work were always there as a majority reminder—dominated by the male population.

So, when the Ivory Skull's hands latched upon her, she didn't think about the consequences of her actions. She plunged her elbow into the flesh of his stomach, waiting for him to stagger back with a pained groan and for his hands to leave her before she whirled on his friend. Bringing her knee into the sensitive junction of his groin, she watched him sink to his knees, a smug smirk pulled at her lips. Slowly, she turned to the last man, seemingly deaf to the pained exclamations of his compadres as his lips twisted into a nasty snarl and he lunged, Nyx narrowly dodging his approach. A sharp pain zinged across her scalp when the man's fingers caught in her hair, and he yanked her toward him. Through gritted teeth, she threw her head back into his face, whirling around before she curled her hand into a fist and swung. Her knuckles collided with his nose before a sickening *crunch* sounded and a gush of blood bathed his upper lip and chin crimson.

She froze as the coppery scent of blood permeated her nose, eyes widening as a dark instinct of her awaiting immortality sidled forward, beckoning her to act—to kill. First it whispered, then it bellowed its wants, dragging its talons through her mind until she forced herself back several paces, hands trembling at her sides, the knuckles of her right hand stained red. *That smell, I want more*, an almost unshakeable thought as she fought against every fibre of her new, split being. *No.*

Ignoring the desperation and fierceness of her body's wants she turned and hurriedly ducked, shoving through the boardwalkers to put distance between herself and the bleeding man. It did little to quell the turn her senses had taken, this new urge to complete her months-long transition from human to vampire, was strong.

Kill him, it crooned, trailing clawed fingers down the base of her skull. Taste *his blood. Feed.* The night seemed to turn on her and her vision clouded. Panic rose in her gorge.

Then …

A familiar scent of sandalwood, cigarettes and leather washed over Nyx's senses with her next inhale, her bloodstained thoughts stuttering as leather-clad fingers dragged down her left bicep and an orotund voice sliced through her turmoil.

"Breathe, little dove."

Her heart jolted, kickstarted before she whirled at the ghostly caress and came face-to-face with … nothing. Nyx's gaze raked across the passers-by, searching for the owner of that voice she knew so well. They caught on a flash of platinum blond hair disappearing around the corner of a shadow-blanketed alleyway. Nyx started through the crowd, pushing, and shoving past people, now gripped by a different urge, until her footsteps echoed off close-bricked walls. Like Alice chasing the white rabbit in the waistcoat as it muttered about being late, the deeper she ran down the dimly lit alleyway, the more mad she felt. Because who chased after a figment of their own imagination?

A startled scream tore from her chest when gloved hands clamped around her arms once more, pinning her to a broad chest so she couldn't turn and peer up at her captor's diamond-shaped face or glimpse the glacier-like blue of his eyes.

She *knew* who it was. The unmistakable smell of him sent a traitorous pang to her heart. She'd missed him. *So much.* "You're here," she croaked, betraying herself, her voice echoing off the alleyway walls. *Wasn't he?* "Like, this isn't a dream?"

A honeyed chuckle answered her, "Oh, sweetheart. You know I'm more like a nightmare."

Nyx shifted, trying to turn and face him but his grasp tightened, holding her in place.

"I've always been here, Nyx. You've just been looking in the wrong places."

She felt dazed. She almost didn't care what she said, what *he* said, as long as he was talking. The feel of his arms around her was like … home. "But—" She couldn't *think* with him this close to her, mind tumbling over itself as she tried to decide whether she was relieved or shocked. *He'd* never *left*, she thought, heart racing its odd rhythm in her chest. *He was back … just like he promised.*

Orion cut her jumble sale of thoughts off, rooting her in the present. His words calm but somehow stilted, "It's never been the right … time."

She frowned, puzzled. "And now it is?"

A dark chuckle tumbled from his mouth. "Almost," he paused, dipping his head to press a kiss to the crook of her throat—upon the scarring of *his* bite mark, made so long ago, it seemed. "I'll be coming back for you, soon."

"No, Orion, I—" but before she could question him further, he was gone.

His departure was quicker than her senses could comprehend, leaving her alone in the alleyway with only the moon for company and his words ricocheting in her mind. It was almost worse than if he had never been there. Like a sucker punch, his sudden absence was like the dangling of a drug that she needed, only to have it whisked away. He was like crutches for her broken soul. And he'd left her … without them.

Nyx sobbed. Her chest felt like a crater and the brief comfort of knowing he was here, that he'd never left her, that she wasn't alone, was replaced by a sinking nothingness. She flailed, going down in the elevator of herself. *Stop.* Orion was many things, most malicious, but he'd never been above breaking promises. So, as she stared into the darkness with only the memory of his touch, she wondered not if it'd be the last time she'd see him or if he really would be back, but *when*.

He always called her his *little dove*. Would it be to set her free or trap her in the confines of a glass-domed prison? Nyx steadied. She didn't know the answers yet but something told her she was going to find out, whether she liked it or not.

III

Orion

The coppery tang of blood addled Orion's senses, weaving through his veins like the poison of a venomous snake. He raised his head from the crook of the dark-haired Ivory Skull's throat and emotionlessly released the fabric of the man's T-shirt, dropping the corpse to the wet pavement of the alleyway with a sickening *thump*.

Orion stared down at the body for a moment, his upper lip twitching with disgust before he rolled his shoulders and adjusted the cuffs of his obsidian trench coat, starting down the moonlit labyrinth of alleyways without a second thought. He paid the music and screams from the boardwalk at his back no mind, continuing down the back streets as he lifted his gloved hand to his face and wiped blood from his chin. He focused instead upon the plan unravelling in his mind and the woman it concerned.

Some part of him didn't understand his never-ending plotting or determination to return to Celacali, but the darker and warped shard of his being recognised his intent, cocooning it in a blanket of darkness until he was ready to act on it. Not that Orion thought he'd *ever* be able to act on it, not after everything he'd done—would continue to do—or the things he hadn't … yet. His brothers might've been open to the gut-wrenching thought of being vulnerable, but Orion wasn't. Not after the betrayal that stained his mortal memories or the bloodied aftermath that'd led him into the waiting arms of immortality. Instead, Orion opted to keep Nyx at an arm's length. He would do everything in his capabilities to make her hate his existence, if only to protect himself from the ghosts of his past. Or because that's what Leon *wanted*, the hooks of his sire commands … were *irritatingly* hard to shake no matter how Orion *tried* to dispel them from his mind.

Was it better to be hated than loved by her? he silently mused as he reached up and pulled a cigarette from the confines of his jacket pocket. *Or would Leon get his wish if I can't fight*—get rid of—*the command?* He paused, lighting the cigarette as he was reminded of his companions' gaping absence. It smarted like a jolt of electricity, lancing his steely indifference as he held the smoke in his lungs. A muscle in his jaw feathered, the tension releasing after he exhaled. Orion forced himself to continue to the boardwalk's carpark, ignoring the sting at the reminder of Kotori, Niko and Kade. They should be here, but they weren't.

It was maddening—hysteria-inducing—as Orion waited for the perfect moment. A lion poised as it waited for the wildebeest to draw closer. But as the months drew on, Orion wasn't sure he'd find the *right* time to act, to send Leon's plans to ruins, freeing his companions from their sire's clutches. Not that it mattered, because Orion *needed* Nyx first, otherwise those plans would crumble to dust. Without Nyx, he'd lose his brothers forever. And he hadn't lived with the trio for decades, growing accustomed to their every thought, desire and need, for their sire to send it all toppling. Not when he still had so much to fix, or before he could ensure they'd never be harmed again—the memory of his vow all those years ago to protect them after Azeil, Asher, Ryder and Amir had almost killed them all, now flitted across his mind—even if he had to die trying. He'd come too far to stop now, lost too much before he'd found his footing in the comfort of darkness.

Orion hadn't *chosen* this path of immortality. Like Nyx, he'd been thrust head-first into a vampiric world. Leon had dragged him to it and Orion knew he wasn't much better after he'd started Nyx's transition, saving *her* life without her knowledge.

But he couldn't take it back.

Would I if I could? He dismissed the thought with a shake of his head, no one could change the past. But the present and the future … now those were very different matters. He could *try* to help Nyx now. Even if his actions made him the villain in every one of her memories to come.

* * *

The smell of wisteria permeated the crispness of Celacali's normally oceanic breeze. It was a headiness of tuberose, the sultriness of jasmine and the spice of freesia and it assaulted Orion as his boots thudded against the pristine brick pavers of Leon's compound estate to the north of Celacali.

His once spiky mullet brushed the tops of his shoulders now, longer. He strode across the courtyard to a pair of lavish french doors, latched open to allow the perfumed breeze in, to waft through the two-storey estate made of stone. Intricate wrought iron balconies and stair balustrades were an afterthought as Orion rounded the shaded veranda and slipped inside, footfall silent as he passed ornately decorated hallways, pausing before the well-lit estate's large dining room. His ears trained on the conversation that echoed in the silent halls.

"If Nyx's blood taints your … bloodline. Why is she still alive?" came Phaelyn's voice, laced with an undertone of puzzlement.

A frustrated sigh of Leon's thinly veiled irritation. "Because I *need* Asher's journal before she has the chance to show it to the boys. They don't need to know what's in it, or I'll lose them to *her* forever," Leon said.

What did Asher find that Leon wants hidden? Orion thought, chewing over the conversation before Qadira spoke and his blood froze in his veins.

"So, then we kill her. Get rid of the problem before it arises," Qadira said as if it should have been obvious.

"Not yet," Leon said. "Nyx must give me the answers … I—she is required. I *need* to know what they are, first."

"But—" Phaelyn started.

"*No.*"

Before they could sense his lingering presence, Orion stepped around the doorway to the room that opened before him, halting on its marble steps. Three sets of eyes were suddenly drawn to his darkly clothed form.

His gaze narrowed on Phaelyn and Qadira who bracketed Leon's shoulders. They were sat at the head of a mahogany twelve-seater table, overhung by two monstrous chandeliers, dripping with crystals. Wooden floor-to-ceiling bookshelves bracketed the wall at the trio's back. Which was *odd,* he thought, and not for the first time. *Who puts bookshelves in a dining room?*

Dark floor tiles gave the room a claustrophobic tone, despite its size. A muscle ticked along the underside of Orion's jaw, the barest sign of resentment of the tawny-blond man in the immaculate suit and the bounty hunters at his side. Both women were dressed in similar outfits of leather and halter tops, and both had the appearance of dangerous pets.

Orion arched a prompting eyebrow, gaze flickering pointedly to the women before Leon gestured at them to leave. He noticed the brisk flick of his wrist dismissal was heeded but not appreciated. The light from beyond the windowpanes fell into the room, only to be swallowed by the tiles, leaving Leon ominously untouched by the glare. Orion waited, poised for the scolding he knew was coming.

"What took you so long?" Leon questioned, drumming his fingertips upon the table as he stared across the room at Orion.

Orion shrugged dismissively, striding further into the room until he stood at the table's opposing end. "The chase before the kill."

In an alarmingly single, fluid motion, Leon rose, rounding the carved back of his chair until he stood suddenly beside Orion, his eyes flaming with irritation. "*Where* were you?" he demanded.

Orion stilled his heartbeat and surveyed his sire, tucking his unease away into the depths of his mind. "Exactly where you *wanted* me to be."

A sharp *crack* echoed across the dining room, ringing in Orion's ears as the back of Leon's hand collided with the right side of his face. "Don't *lie* to me."

Orion's chin knocked his shoulder when his head snapped to the side, his tongue pressing angrily against his cheek as he turned to face Leon. Orion hated him, his blue irises lit like cold fire, smouldering amongst the ashes of his patience and his lip twitched into a sneer as he straightened. The press of his elongated fangs brushed against his lips and he exercised control.

"I didn't. Your little *loose end* ran to the boardwalk. I just cleaned it up," he spat.

Leon inhaled a frustrated breath through his nose, raking his hand down his face. "When will you start obeying me, Orion? It's been centuries, and you s*till* fight for a life that was stripped from you when I found you half-dead."

"I don't follow orders well," Orion said pointedly, memories of his mortal life and the command he couldn't shake flickering through his mind. "I never have. You know this."

A bitter chuckle reverberated off the room's walls as Leon's gaze brimmed with a condescending edge. "Maybe that's why your siblings plotted your assassination in 1643."

"At least they never got to live out their twisted goals."

"Oh, Orion, don't you see?" Leon crooned, stepping closer to his eldest protégé. "Everything I'm doing to Niko, Kade and Kotori is *for us. My goal isn't twisted, it's ... family.*"

IV

Nyx

Nyx pressed the pad of her finger to the metallic buttons of the phonebooth, stringing together a memorised number before the droning dial tone reverberated in her ear and she leaned into the hard plastic at her back. Her mind wandered like her gaze, dredging up her recent interaction with Orion as she drummed her fingers against the plastic panes of the booth.

Ares's ears pricked at the rapping noise, the Malamute's fluffy head rising from the pavement outside. He huffed softly.

I'll be coming back for you soon, resonated in her head, paired with the press of Orion's lips against her throat as she wondered about the seriousness of his words. An impatient sigh tumbled from her mouth as she dismissed the thought, instead, focusing on the phone. It was a haven of bright in the dankly lit space with a flickering lamppost and sea spray slick ground.

Brr, brr, brr.

Nyx's onyx gaze dropped to Ares. "You know, for someone who says he's concerned about my safety, Ares, he sure has a weird sense of punctuality whenever I call."

Ares angled his head toward her when she uttered his name, almond-coloured eyes alert and brimming with adoration as his bushy tail thumped against the pavers. It never ceased to amaze her—the unending loyalty of a dog to its owner—when he adhered to every command she gave, sitting when she told him to, staying outside a shop's doorway while she wandered into pet-free facilities or watching passers-by for danger if she wasn't paying attention to her surroundings. It seemed easy for the Malamute, like he enjoyed every tiny fragment of Nyx's hectic and grief-plagued day-to-day life, and she couldn't have been more grateful.

Brr, brr, brr—

The mechanical click of the phoneline connecting jarred Nyx from her thoughts, a stray curl tumbling into her vision as she waited with bated breath, clinging to the phone like it was a lifeline, anxiously waiting for her father's levelled voice to emit through the faded speakers.

"Night?"

"It's me, Dad." She chuckled when she remembered she was the only person with her father's phone number since he'd fled Celacali to keep his life. She remembered what it had taken to get him to leave, and the laugh died on her lips. He almost hadn't. *Blood, pain, death ... Asher.* Their family, as estranged as it was, was still around to bitch about it. Nyx breathed in. If he hadn't left then, she wouldn't have a father on the phone now. She breathed out. The thought was sobering and she swallowed, hard, before continuing, "I'm sorry if you were expecting someone else, but I'm okay."

Azeil Monroe chortled through the phone's speakers. "You're not just saying that to comfort me, are you? Because I *can* tell when you're lying."

She arched a disbelieving eyebrow even though she knew he couldn't see her, a playful upward tilt. "On the phone?"

"An ocean could be separating us, Nyx and I'd still know your tells," he said.

"Would you?" her voice wavered, fingers toying with the springy cord as playfulness was replaced by fear. "Or am I too monstrous for you to recognise?"

"*Nyx—*"

"No," she uttered firmly, breathing a sigh before turning her attention to the neon lights of the boardwalk at the alleyway's entrance. "I called because of the leads you'd have, not because I wanted to start a fight."

An exasperated sigh crackled down the phone, and Nyx knew that if her father had stood before her, he'd be scrubbing his palm down his face, slate-grey irises aggrieved with muddled sympathy.

"It's been three months, Night," he said. "He wouldn't want you to be stuck in the past, he'd want you to live your life to the fullest … like he always wanted you to."

"But he's not here now, is he?" she quipped, swallowing that familiar lump suddenly clogging her throat. "He's *never* coming back."

"We can't change the past, Nyx, but we can *try* to make the future better," her father said and, like he couldn't—or wouldn't—entertain further reminiscence of his brother's memory, he cleared his throat and redirected their conversation.

Once a detective, always a detective, Nyx thought.

"There's a club in Celacali's east, called the Candence and for the past … weeks there's been some unusual injuries and unexplainable disturbances reported. Donovan says the chief believes it's a gang-related crime but it's worth checking it out. Just … be careful."

She chuckled with bad humour as the call's warning tone droned against the background of static, announcing the timeslot's impending expiration. "You know me, Dad. Careful is my middle name."

"I know for a fact that's not what your birth certificate says … Nyx *Alyvia* Monroe."

"Stay safe, old man. I'll call again soon, I promise."

"*Nyx*, I mean it. *Be careful*."

Careful, she thought with a humourless chuckle. *Like using his connections in the police force to find four* vampires *could be.*

The phone's warning tone grew louder, and she hurried in a response before the automatic voice announced cut off. "I always am," she got in as the defiant *click* of the call ending sounded, leaving her with nothing but the weight of her words and the ominous path of her father's lead.

*   *   *

"No, no, no." Nyx's hands trembled with anguish, caught between a swell of disbelief and the jarring reality before her. "Wake up!"

The dimly lit room around her shifted, its wooden floorboards pressing unpleasantly into her knees as she clutched at the colourful fabric of her uncle's T-shirt and shook him. Like it'd be enough to wake him from Death's embrace. But it wasn't, and Nyx knew it. It was a gesture of sheer agony that elicited her actions, blood staining her hands when she pressed them to the gaping tear across Asher's throat; a tear tracked down her cheek. As Asher lay cradled across Nyx's thighs, his gaze glassy and unseeing, a sound, part sob, part scream spilled from her lips.

As useless as Nyx knew her actions to be, she shook her uncle's cooling shoulder. Her bottom lip trembled when he didn't blink or jolt up as if from sleep, and a pain like a thousand razors sliced her heart. "Asher, wake up," she tried again, but there was nothing. She rested her head upon his chest. No beat. "C'mon ... please, *I can't do this without you."*

"Nyx, hey. Nyx," Azeil murmured, coming up behind her and gingerly removing her from her uncle's chest. His hands cupped her face, forcibly tearing her gaze from Asher. "Breathe, okay?"

"I ... can't—"

A wet nose pressed into Nyx's arm before a deeply toned bark sounded, jarring her from her dreams as she jolted up from the lodge house's, three-seater-couch and appraised the moonlit room around her. She sucked in a shaky breath, scrubbing a trembling hand across her sweat-slick brow before her gaze darted to Ares at the couch's edge, the Malamute peering up at her alertly. Nyx extended her hand out and stroked him, seeking comfort in his constant presence. For a moment, the action soothed the ache her dreams left behind. Her stare skittered across the wooden floorboards she'd once been dragged across, the Tibetan rug a dagger had clattered toward still there, lounge chairs she'd darted around in a desperate lunge for freedom and survival still standing. It didn't matter now, the homey feeling of the cream-coloured walls no longer settled her frayed nerves, the ghostly creak of the staircase and the groaned protests of the floorboards in the bedrooms on the second floor were rooms, besides her own, she hadn't dared to enter. They were the moans of an old house. They grated and ached like old insults, still there.

Her heart pounded in her chest, ringing in her eardrums like a bell tolling. Ares's silky fur brushed her fingers as she continued her idle caresses, her gaze dragging from the lounge room to the darkened entranceway of the dining room, lingering on its shadowed threshold. *It's been three months. It's just a room,* she thought, trying to convince herself. But the logic didn't stick, as Asher's gaping presence flickered to the forefront of her mind and the longing for her father gripped her. Despite her rational mind's scolding, she wished for the golden-eyed men with monstrous natures.

It was morning, early but not too early, and with a jitter, she reached for the glass-screened phone lying face down on the coffee table, her eyes unmoving from the dining room doorway while her fingers numbly pressed the call button.

It rang twice before noises echoed down the connected line and Tobias's concerned voice sounded, "Is everything okay? Are you okay?"

Silence hung thickly between them, the younger twin awaiting her answer while she gazed toward the room of her nightmares. As he waited, she wondered if … if she'd done something differently, would it have led to the inevitable anguish she couldn't shake or the memories she wished to forget—to tear from her skull? As futile as she knew it was, she couldn't stop herself from scrambling over every scenario, every what-if, every path she could've taken. *But none had felt right,* she reminded herself. *How could I have chosen what I knew was wrong?* It was an endless torture, and she was drowning in it.

"Nyx?" came Tobias's uncertain prompt.

She pushed herself up from the couch and crossed the room to the door. "I'm going to the Bluff, Bias," she said as she paused, leaning into the wall as she slipped her jeans and then sneakers on and her gaze darted to Ares, who shadowed her. "I need to clear my head … *please*, would you keep an eye on Ares for me?"

She stepped around Ares, opening the flyscreen door before the main one without letting him slip past her. She couldn't stand being in the veranda-wrapped house any longer, and Ares no longer fit on the back of her motorbike. She knew Tobias would look after Ares. It wasn't the first time she'd called him in a cold sweat, and she knew it wouldn't be the last. She just wanted to let someone know where she was going.

"'Course," he said. "Be safe, Night."

"Thanks, Bias." She pulled her phone away from her ear and ended the call.

Striding down the stone steps and across the gravelled driveway, fingers shuffling through the pockets of her jeans for her keys, she slipped one into the ignition and started the engine. Almost immediately, the thunderous rumble and thrumming vibrations of the bike comforted her. A soft smile upturned the edges of her mouth as she tossed a reminiscent glance over her shoulder to the house at her back and sped out of the front yard for the road, leaving the world behind.

V

Nyx

Sunlight dappled the sheen of sand coating the floor through glass-patched holes, refracting off glinting crystals cinched to the askew chandeliers hanging from the cavernous ceiling. The crashing of white-capped waves lulled the shadow-blanketed tunnelways, and dancing tangerine fires in the pits placed throughout the living space bathed the room in warm, comforting hues. Nyx paid the flickering flames and yellow lighting of little hidden globes scant attention. Instead, her nose was buried in the pages of an antique book she'd found hidden between others on a shelf by the forgotten bedroom with gauzy curtains.

Despite the niggling whispers of memories and nightmares that'd led her to the cavernous home, she was entranced by the vampiric folklore she now read. *Had Kotori collected these?* she wondered, thumbing the ancient-looking paper. *Why would he need them as a vampire with firsthand knowledge?* Though the pages crinkled with every turn, she greedily absorbed the lore within, delighting in the smell of old parchment. She catalogued the information she read, cancelling some myths, and speculating over others. She knew the basics of her impending vampirism, but others, like the clarifications and the process from mortal to immortal stumped her. Some pieces of folklore she scoffed at, like the common myths of garlic and crosses, and others made her wonder what truth lay beneath. With each new titbit she hadn't heard of came a swell of questions, and where she'd once been able to turn to the men whose home she currently lounged in, now she was met only with silence and crackling firelight.

It frustrated her—scared her—whenever their presence was required because part of her was terrified of the truth in Ryder and Amir's goading taunts. Even before their deaths, Ryder—Alexander and Tobias' father—had been rash and fuelled by his desire to kill vampires while Amir, the twins' uncle, had been an awaiting disaster; silent and cruelly effective. Snippets of their words jostled her memory, 'Bloodsucker … 'Worse than them … Driven mad without a pack.' *Would she be?* Nyx thought, distractedly. *Is that what I would become? Some wild creature with no restraint? Alien to myself?*

Anguish and rage, honed like a knife edge, carved her insides in a cruel recollection of past events. She wanted to wield her emotions like a blade of reckoning upon Leon who'd strode into her life, unwanted.

She jolted up from the grey couch when the skittering of small stones echoed off the walls, alerting her to the entranceways of each tunnel as her skin prickled with goosebumps. The yellowed pages of the book were lowered from her gaze as she strained her ears to hear something—*anything*—that would convince her she'd been imagining things. *No one knows I am here. Except Tobias.* When nothing happened, she sat back carefully into the cushions and tried to refocus.

Aloys, Kade's beloved pet, chattered softly, the partial albino plumaged hawk's feathers ruffling as he shifted on his driftwood perch. The carcass of a field mouse lay pinned beneath his talons as the cooing of doves high up in the alcoves of rocks soothed her nerves and complemented the gentle rustle of turning pages. The fire in the standing barrels danced as a breeze glided across the room, carrying a faint narcissus fragrance through the cave. Gradually, an eerie silence slunk from the shadows. Bit by bit, it claimed more presence until the hair upon Nyx's neck rose and she paused her reading once more, angling her head as her gaze flicked to the shadowed entrance. She knew immediately that something was wrong, that something—somebody—was there. The knowing crawled across her skin like a thousand ants, eliciting a trickle of fear down her spine. She straightened, squaring her shoulders while she waited for something to confirm her suspicions. She somehow sensed it wasn't someone she knew. Dealing with Orion had successfully ensured she wouldn't trust blindly. Though she'd never admit it to him, she was grateful for his persistence in quashing her naivety. She knew there was a chance it'd save her in the long run.

Apprehension rankled across her forearms, crawling up past her elbow, bicep, and shoulder until it seemed to settle behind her—in line with one of the tunnelways shrouded in darkness. As much as she didn't want to turn around, to glimpse whatever lurked at her back, she wasn't going to sit still and hope the unnerving feeling would just disappear. So, she turned. Ever-so-slowly to the tunnel behind her, staring into the blackness that gaped back at her. The longer she stared, the more unsettled she felt. Something shifted and the birds occupying the living space startled, flying in a mass of beating wings.

Nyx waited, poised on the edge of the couch as she carefully placed the ageing book flat upon the seat. A purposeful tread of footsteps drifted to her ears. At once, the hidden lighting system shut off with a defiant *click,* and the firepits extinguished, plunging the cavernous room into shifting darkness. The sudden black was potholed only by the sunlit ceiling shafts. She watched as a shadow crossed the elaborate map sprawled on the wall behind Orion's chair. Her heightened senses were steepled with budding hysteria, but she refused to be intimidated. Swallowing, she pushed herself up and moved to the centre of the room.

A feminine voice traipsed to Nyx's ears from the shadows, seeming to come from every direction as she turned in a slow circle, "You're *her,* aren't you? The mortal, the *fledgling* the boys became too … enthralled with. *Too invested* in."

Nyx's brow furrowed as she continued to turn. "Depends on who's asking."

A gravelly chuckle rippled from the direction of the forgotten bedroom, a sound tinged with zealous amusement. "Feisty little thing isn't she, Qadira?"

The first voice, Qadira's, chuckled with malevolent pleasure. "She is, Phaelyn." Then, silence before, "I think we'll enjoy this more than we anticipated."

Nyx tamped down a tide of unease that clawed at her chest. She wouldn't let it take hold, forcing it away as she focused on the two unfamiliar presences. She reminded herself of Tobias and Alexander's impending arrival, knowing the pair were on their way to the Bluff. They had been eagerly awaiting new comic editions, making them stay late at the shop, and then they had wanted to plan their next course of action with the possible lead Azeil had given her, to find Orion, Niko, Kotori and Kade. Either that or come face-to-face with another dead end.

For a moment, Nyx found the similarities of Qadira and Phaelyn's dramatics amusing, the duo's actions reminding her of Orion. *Immortals and their love for theatrics,* she mused, a faint grin cracking the tension.

Suddenly, the vampire Phaelyn shifted, and Nyx turned toward the rustling of fabric in the same moment a metallic glint caught her eye. A sharp burst of white-hot pain flared across her face, smarting from her cheek and past her right eyebrow. She gasped and stumbled back, her hand lifting to brush a gushing wound on her face. Blood was already staining her chin and throat.

Despite the throbbing pain, she knew the wound would be gone by dusk. One of the perks of her transition from human to vampire. She didn't have to worry about it. Nyx's lips curled into a sneer, suddenly angry. A dark laugh tumbled from her mouth. "What is it with you immortals and hiding behind your shadows? Are you scared to face a *fledgling*?"

"Scared?" came Qadira's murmur, a dry titter echoing through the room before Nyx's senses picked up the movement of the hidden woman. "Not in the slightest, Nyx."

Surprise stung as a knife blade dragged across Nyx's back with unearthly precision, eliciting a pained groan, before a brunette traipsed into a sun patch, silver dagger clasped in her hand. Her attire was purely business and when a blonde stepped from the shadows beside the bookshelf, dressed similarly to her other in black leather pants and a darkly toned T-shirt with boots, Nyx recoiled at the blonde's gaze. So surgical.

"Qadira," she said in a sing-song lilt, smiling unpleasantly with a slight bow.

With a flick of her wrist, the second woman darted forward, slicing Nyx's arm, a malignant glint to her silvery gaze as she play-curtseyed. "Phaelyn!" she sang, "The pleasure's all mine!"

Nyx hissed in anguish as the blue-eyed blonde grinned, her tongue tracing her teeth before she moved in a motion too fast to comprehend and grasped Nyx's throat, dragging her closer with a vice-like tug. Up close, Nyx could see there was no song in her eyes. Startled by the directness of Qadira's attack, Nyx clawed at the blonde's fingers, her eyes wide at the lack of oxygen before she paused, whirling, and plunged her elbow into the vampire's stomach. It did little to free herself from Qadira's grasp, a pale eyebrow-raising as if she'd known Nyx would lash out.

"Are you done?" Qadira quipped, digging her fingertips into the soft skin of Nyx's throat before she loosened her grasp and oxygen flooded Nyx's lungs. "Because we have a message to deliver, and as much as I'd like to kill you, that's not what he wants."

"Well—" Nyx started, coughing as her tender windpipe grated from the harsh grip. "Deliver it."

Qadira's lips curled and she tutted, disparagingly as her gaze darted to Phaelyn over Nyx's shoulder. Her profile was elegant, her nose a tapered ski-jump, unlike Phaelyn whose features were heavier set. "Stop looking, *fledgling*," she said. "Bad things happen to those who look for things they shouldn't." She stared at Nyx, her eyes button-like.

A bitter chuckle reverberated from Nyx's sternum, sounding ragged through her shaky breaths. The noise seemed to anger Phaelyn as she drew closer, trailing her knife across Nyx's cheeks until the blade caught on the torn flesh near her eyebrow. Phaelyn hummed, pressing the hilt so the blade sliced into the bleeding wound, dragging it down her jawline until Nyx could smell the tang of her own blood and feel the pain of her flesh being torn into. Blood poured into her eyes, marring her vision.

"The same could be said for those that stand in *my* way," she drawled, voice devoid of emotion but laced with promise.

"And what could *you* possibly do to us? You're nothing to us," Phaelyn dipped her head, lips brushing Nyx's ear. "Or *them*."

Qadira grinned, grasp tightening on Nyx's windpipe. "You're nothing but a blip in their immortal lifespans, girly."

Phaelyn dragged the blade of her knife down further, down Nyx's throat, avoiding Qadira's fingers. "A fleeting glimpse. There one moment and gone the next."

The sound of crunching stones drifted to Nyx's ears as Qadira's fingertips dug into her throat. Then, the sound of a car ignition cutting out. And before Nyx could muster up the nerve to draw Alexander and Tobias's attention to her, Qadira and Phaelyn released her, shoving her to the sand-covered floor.

In a breath, they were gone.

Nyx pushed herself up from the floor, dusting her hands down the front of her jeans before the twins hurried into the cavernous home, Ares at their heels with his hackles raised. The Malamute's deafening growl boomed across the rock walls, comforting Nyx as she attempted to staunch the flow of blood with her T-shirt. Both boys approached her with worried looks, surveying the room like they expected someone to leap from the nearest shadow.

Alexander reached her first and turned her face carefully, his eyebrows screwing together as he tried to mask a grimace. "What the hell happened?"

She blinked up at him, feeling as shocked as he looked. Her gaze darted to Tobias, who eyed the nasty gashes across her flesh with obvious anger. "I don't know, Alex."

"You don't know?" Alexander repeated, unconvinced.

Tobias interjected before Nyx could speak. "She *knows*, Alex. She just doesn't understand why. I don't care about the why right now. I just want to know *who* did this."

"It was two women, Qadira and Phaelyn." Nyx winced against the burn of her wounds when she spoke. "They were sent to deliver a message."

"A message?" Alexander parroted while Tobias rubbed his palms agitatedly against his forehead.

"What message, Night?" Tobias asked, his dark gaze darting to her bleeding face.

"To stop looking," she answered, a fissure of anguish slicing her sternum.

Understanding seemed to douse Tobias as if he knew the answer to his next question before he spoke it, "For …?"

"*Them*," she said, her head lowering to her palms as if the weight of her admission tugged it down. *Leon knows I'm looking for them,* she thought with dread as blood trailed down her chin to her throat. Her shoulders trembled as her body was racked with silent sobs. If Leon knew she was looking, he knew she was alive. *What was stopping him from killing her?*

VI

Leon

Quietude blanketed a pristine white study, the afternoon's light spilling through arched windows to the right of a grey desk spotlighting Leon's actions. His grasp tightened on the boy in his lap as he drew languid mouthfuls of blood across his tastebuds, elongated fangs sunk in the soft flesh of the boy's throat. His eyes were clamped shut to revel in this liquid euphoria. *Jesse Stone,* he thought, reminding himself of the boy's name in the muddled rush of his mind as copper and something so … *virtuous* coated his senses.

His grip on Jesse's arms was sure to leave a mark but every pained whimper and terrified struggle only fed the dark beast beneath his skin—a part of his soul—and he couldn't find it within himself to stop. Not if it took away the heady aftermath a child's blood gave him. It was a headrush like no other, the excited kick of a heart as adrenaline settled in their bones. It intoxicated him like an addict chasing their next hit but, more than that, it *thrilled* him to hold so much power; to control another's life and decide when it was time for them to take their final breath. And he wasn't going to give it up, not in this lifetime … or the next.

Certainly *not* for humanity which was nothing more than a means to an end. Humans were *nothing* more than food to quench his thirst or dispose of once they'd reached the end of their useful tether. A species *unfit* to walk alongside vampires as anything more than sustenance and, as he waited for his Ivory Skull pawns, it was time—*overdue*—for him to remind *his* city of its place in the hierarchy; *starting* with his disobedient sons and the human they'd corrupted his bloodline with.

An uncertain cough splintered the room from the doorway to his right as if the mortal who'd made the sound wished they hadn't. His eyes snapped open, and a feeble whine tumbled from Jesse's lips, drawing the trio of Ivory Skulls' attention to the blond-haired boy with matted curls and dark bruises littering his throat, wrists, and arms.

White-gold irises pinned the three men in place as Leon retracted his fangs from Jesse's throat and raised his head, blood smearing his lips like a bad omen. "Do you have something to say?" Leon prompted as the auburn-haired Skull's gaze continued to flicker between Jesse and him.

"Is that—" the Skull began before another cut him off sharply.

"Mire, *don't*," a brunette Skull warned.

Mire shook his head with unfiltered disbelief, tongue tracing his teeth as his eyes narrowed on his companion. "So what? You want me to pretend like there's not an innocent *boy* being used as a Tropicana grab-n-go, Viliaris?" he spat, gesturing to Jesse in Leon's lap in a way that crinkled his leather jacket. "He can barely keep his eyes open for fuck's sake."

Viliaris opened his mouth to reply when the third Skull, Kyree, a man with brown skin and raven-black curls, levelled him with a pointed look and his smoky voice trailed across the room, "It's not like we can go against Leon and win, Mire," he said.

A bemused chuckle rumbled from Leon's chest as he watched the display, plucking a handkerchief from his dress shirt pocket and wiping away Jesse's blood. He sent a mental command for Phaelyn to collect the boy through the bond they shared. Aloud, his voice, plumier than usual, struck the room in a heavy drawl, "I'd love to see you try, but it would be a *futile* endeavour. After all … *you* don't call the shots in this city. *I* do. You're alive because you're useful to me and the moment that ends, your mundane lives *will* end."

"Then why bother with us at all?" Mire said, voice tinged with unbridled distaste.

"Because you are *useful* … at the moment," Leon said, ears pricking as a tell-tale *thump* of boots filled his senses, echoing off the marble tiles.

Mire shook his head as he strode across the room and settled on the window ledge, eyes narrowed with distrust. "Until our purpose is served, correct?"

"Correct," Leon confirmed, tearing his gaze from the auburn-haired Skull to the doorway as Phaelyn's presence—like static and crackling fire—skittered across his skin.

The sweetness of the boy's blood still soaked his tongue, and he savoured it. Pride bloomed in his chest as Phaelyn cut a path across the room and he felt Mire's heart jack-hammering in his chest as he watched her. Leon knew his youngest daughter was unruly and driven by her plentiful personality, but she was *devoted* and answered to his every whim no matter the carnage. She was one side to a double-edged sword, shrouded in his commands while Qadira was the other, silently lethal and steel willed. *His* beautiful vipers whose loyalty had never wavered, not in the decades he'd spent grooming them, they'd never wandered, never strayed—finding comfort in the family he'd built. Grateful, doting daughters … *unlike* his sons.

My boys are confused. Tainted *by a mortal*—fledgling's *blood,* he thought with disgust, loathing the truth as he recalled Nyx and the trouble she'd caused him. *How had they let a mortal into their pack? What was different from their decades of contentment?*

Leon's train of thought was broken as three men's hearts lurched and Phaelyn's shoulders brushed theirs on her way past, knife holsters woven over the dark fabric of her long-sleeved shirt, metallic hilts glinting sharply in the light. Phaelyn's silvered irises softened as she rounded the desk and lifted Jesse from his grasp, a betraying flicker of sympathy in her eyes.

"*Phaelyn,*" Leon warned, an unuttered command in his voice weaving across her senses, settling in the glazed sheen of her eyes. "He is *nothing* to us. He is *food.*"

"Yes, Father," she murmured, a far-off quality to her voice, cradling the young boy's head before she dipped her own in deference and disappeared through the doorway. "I understand."

Leon rested his elbows on the desk and steepled his fingers, mossy irises flitting between the trio. "From now on, you are in charge of the Skulls—*all* of you," he said, the order in his voice.

"Us?" Viliaris parroted, eyebrows arched in disbelief.

"Yes," Leon confirmed, resisting the urge to pinch the bridge of his nose.

"Why?" Mire pressed, glancing to Kyree and Viliaris with unveiled distrust.

"Because I require my eyes and ears once more," Leon said, tone bathed in boredom. He grew so tired of mortal questions. Endless clarification. So little *do.*

"What do you need?" Kyree pressed, appearing to note the shift in the room.

"Watch Nyx Monroe," Leon said, gaze trailing to each Skull in turn as he retrieved a folder from his desk drawer and placed a photograph of Nyx on its surface, pushing it toward its edge in their direction and reaching for another of a leatherbound book. "And … this book," he continued, "belonged to Asher Monroe, her uncle. I want to know when she has it, what she does with it. Who she is with."

"And if we don't do as you ask?" Mire prompted, plucking Nyx's photo off the desk.

Leon's gaze locked on Mire's as he leaned back into his chair, lips curling. "Then you'll find yourselves … *removed* from the living realm."

VII

Nyx

"Just as we thought everything was going back to normal, these two show up," Tobias scoffed, bouncing his linen-clad thigh with pent-up energy. Firelight dappled his face as he lounged upon the couch nearest to the large Cerberus statue, the cave illuminated once more. "And we know what that means."

Alexander exhaled deeply through his nose, before he side-eyed Nyx with a faint twitch to his upper lip. "*Okay*, doom and gloom. We get it."

"Do you?" Tobias challenged, gesturing to his older brother's ring-clad hands. "Because all you've been doing is fiddling with your rings."

"Tobias, you need to relax," Nyx urged, eyeing the twins on their opposing couches.

"Relax?" he countered.

She arched her eyebrows, widening her eyes with mock puzzlement. "Yes, *relax*. Because I can't see when any of this was going to be … *normal.*"

Tobias's coffee-brown irises studied her from the grey cushioned couch, his fingertips drumming rhythmically upon the backing like he knew something she didn't. His suspicious gaze lingered on her face as she glanced down at Ares, her diligent guard dog. She couldn't shake the prickling omission of the full truth. It persisted like the throbbing wounds on her arm, back and face, oozing beneath the cloth she now pressed to her forehead.

She winced when she shifted, trying to get comfortable. Nyx knew Tobias was right, that nothing but trouble would follow Qadira and Phaelyn's appearance. She longed for the time when she'd wandered Celacali and enjoyed the night, soaking in the live music and lifeful nature of the city with eager anticipation, desperate to see what it offered. But now that she'd stumbled into its possessive darkness, she wished for a moment of peace within the churning and shifting depths of her life.

Some sliver of Nyx's being *knew* there was no coming back from the path she wandered, reminding her sharply of Orion and the honeyed drawl of his promise. An encounter she hadn't mentioned to either of the brothers. Because how could she lightly mention Orion's reappearance? Or the confident truths he'd spoken; that he'd never truly been gone. How would she explain?

She worried her bottom lip between her teeth, gingerly pulling the bloodstained cloth from her forehead with a deep sigh. "You're right though, Bias. Qadira and Phaelyn don't intend to be civil."

The younger twin hummed, adjusting the hem of his graphic T-shirt—Godzilla towering over buildings—as he leaned forward, resting his elbows upon his knees. "Besides the obvious, what else did they say?"

"Nothing important," she said, chuckling dryly. "They did a lot of dramatic dancing."

Alexander quirked his brows. "Dramatic?"

"It's just … every interaction I've had with a vampire always seems so … planned. So scripted. It's like they revel in the suspense of their actions."

"Are you saying vampires are drama queens?" Tobias questioned, amused.

She shrugged, onyx irises glinting with zeal. "If the shoe fits."

"I think you're stalling, Night," Tobias drawled, angling his head in a way that prompted Nyx to disagree with him. "What'd Azeil have to say?"

Nyx's fingers twitched at her sides at the use of her nickname—garnered by her love of the night and the ties her name held to the Greek Goddess Nyx—an agitated flare of discontent settled in her chest before she started to tell the twins about her conversation with her father. She told them of Azeil's suspicions about the Candence in Celacali's cast and Donovan, who she explained was one of Azeil's co-workers, who had overheard the chief's interaction with a police officer about the recent, grisly disturbances in the city, when Alexander interrupted with a puzzled frown, laying out the pieces of information.

It took immense patience on Nyx's part to dutifully answer their questions, halting her explanations and beginning anew on something they wanted answered. She indulged them with the grisly details that'd elicited Donovan's interest and fortified her father's suspicion, recounting the disturbances and unexplainable injuries in a light neither questioned. Knowing the darkness of Celacali as well as she did, as well as its monsters—personally, she had insights that they, perhaps, did not.

Alexander and Tobias tossed glances and bandied questions before one would answer an unspoken theory with a swift shake of his head or a not-so-subtle put down, in that annoying way some twins have. Nyx didn't have to be privy to know their thoughts when she'd explained the police's 'gang-related' notion, their displeased faces said it all.

"All in all," she began again, drawing her explanations to a close, "he said it was worth checking out … even *if* it is another dead end."

"*And?*" Tobias prompted.

She huffed, rising from the couch, and childishly scuffing the toe of her shoe against the stone floor. "*And* to be careful."

Alexander chuckled mirthlessly. "Did he say anything about why he suspects it might not be Orion, Niko, Kotori and Kade?"

"No, he didn't. You know him," Nyx uttered airily, waving her hand dismissively.

Tobias shook his head, lips contorted in an amused grin. "You didn't ask, did you?"

For the second time that night, Tobias was right. His attention to Nyx and her habits was comforting but frustrating, making it almost impossible for her to slip beneath his radar. She was grateful for his attentive and diligent loyalty, but also longed for a sense of opacity. Somewhere to hide. She knew it was the twinging pulse of pain her actions enticed and her bitter memories that were pulling her down, submerging her. She thought of her father's harshly snapped words during their last terrible fight. *'Just get out. I don't want you here, just ... leave.* ' Nyx straightened against the swell of her thoughts, pain smouldering to coals of anger. "What would I have done with that information, Tobias? What *good* would it do?"

Before either twin could answer, the burning tear of flesh dragged across her forearm and her left hand rushed to grasp her right.

A hissed curse tumbled from her lips as she cradled the unmarred skin while her gaze darted to the twins with panic splayed across her irises. *What the hell*, she thought as her eyes dropped to the reddened slash spreading across her arm, other angry blots blooming on her wrists like bindings before a distant anguish-filled cry that sounded like Kade echoed through her mind. *Kade? Could it be?*

"What is this?" she breathed, almost to herself as her stare lingered on the darkening livid marks.

"I … don't know," Tobias said, a cautious edge to his voice.

"Alex?" Nyx said, turning to him in panic.

Alexander's expression twisted with some complicated flight of emotion. He looked embarrassed? "It could be something to do with your ties … your *bond* to them," he said. "Didn't Azeil once *almost* transition to a vampire? You could ask him—"

"*No,*" she said, cutting him off with a dark gleam to her eyes. She would handle this. Alone. Anger and sadness seemed to balance each other out on some internally warring scale. *My bond*, she thought.

Alexander glanced tersely in his brother's direction before he tried again, "Nyx—"

"He already thinks I'm a monster," she spat the words out. Distasteful even to her.

A mocking tut, the sound a dead ringer to Orion's whenever he'd clicked his tongue in that same way. "No. I don't owe you, Tobias, him, or anyone else an apology. That'd mean I *regretted* my decisions. This is *my* burden to bear," she said.

Tobias and Alexander shared an unsure look before Tobias cleared his throat, straightening as Ares raised his head from his paws and meandered over to them.

"Do you …" he began, "regret your decisions, Night?"

"I don't, and I don't think I ever will … Hell, I'm not sure I ever did, to begin with. It's not the path we take that makes us *good* or *bad.* It's the actions that lead us there that'll condemn or free us," she said as she tipped her head to the hidden glass panes of the hole-dotted ceiling. Her voice was silvered and sure, wreathed in a knowledge that outweighed her time upon the earth. "For better … or w*orse.*"

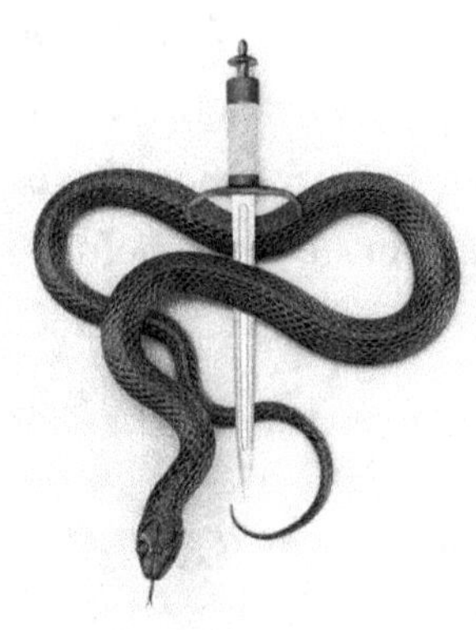

VIII

Kade

The long light glared into the darkened depths of Kade's pupil, lightening his fuscous irises while he stared up at the stone ceiling and tried to ignore the frigid press of the bindings clamped around his wrists. Or the mis-matched duo who silently watched him from the heavy metal door of the compound's lowest levels, their malevolent gazes trained on him as they waited … before they began anew on his torture. Before they reopened the pinkish scarring upon his tattoo-embellished skin, until the scent of his own blood cloyed in his nostrils and he was forced to relive the blazing agony of knives carving flesh, bright pain smothering him like a pillow pressed into his face.

Kade stood in silence as Qadira and Phaelyn watched him from beside the door, anticipating the falter of their hearts when he tore his gaze from the ceiling to them. The sandy-blond tresses of his curls wiped the nape of his neck, a predatory roll of his shoulders twinging as he shifted against the bindings pinning his arms above his head. The metal restraints were secured to the ceiling by a reinforced bolt, immovable, he had tried. His eyebrows arched tauntingly, eyeing the two women with unrestrained disdain, a wince obstructing his features when his movement tugged at a wound from his left hip to below his right pectoral. The waistband of his jeans ghosted the edges of the scar, tender but still healing before it'd fade away to nothing. Only the memory of the laceration was left like a stain. Like the one his blood left, darkening the fabric of his pants and the concrete beneath his boots.

Kade's thoughts were of Nyx in the silence. He wondered what had become of her since Celacali and interfering with Leon's plans. Nyx. She was a loose end to whatever secrets the head vampire intended to keep tucked away, not that they mattered to Kade. His focus was on setting his pack's plans in motion and his companions' well-being since they'd been separated after interfering with Emilia's disposal, and Leon's *lessons* had begun.

Each day had been the same, like a perfectly tuned grandfather clock set to strike at midnight when the moon was at its crested peak. And like the scheduled tolling of the bell, Kade waited for the heavy-set door to swing open and reveal Qadira and Phaelyn, their knives glinting in their hands or the holsters at their hips and thighs. He knew they itched to shed blood after Leon ordered it three months ago, tasked with dishing out their sire's teachings to himself, Niko, and Kotori. It hadn't surprised Kade when Orion had remained unharmed by those orders. Orion, the illusive and frustratingly unbreakable protégé who tested their sire endlessly. And while Orion might have seemed *free,* Kade knew his punishment was in the absence of his brothers; himself, Kotori and Niko—in the slimy grasp of failure to protect them. He also knew—like Niko and Kotori knew—that Orion waited to tip the scales beneath their sire's nose, to topple the foundations of his prestigious estate and decimate the hold he had over the four of them. Forever.

Leon's lessons were like never-ending stretches of road to nowhere, drawn out and agonisingly long. They had started as taunts and goads intended to prod at the fissure of Kade's control but when he'd given them no reaction, their 'lessons' had shifted. Phaelyn and Qadira descending upon him like a pair of lionesses, their knives of varying sizes and blades of myriad sharpness seeming to mock him. Even if their tools could never *truly* mar the intricate detailing of his patchwork tattoos, Kade suffered. Teeth gritted against the meticulous slicing of flesh and wet patter of blood, its warmth clinging to his skin.

"What's it going to be today, girls?" he drawled, his irises devoid of emotion, forcing himself from his thoughts. "Because I *think* you might've missed a spot since we started this back and forth."

Qadira chuckled with dry amusement, her gaze honed on the blood crusting the bare expanse of his chest. "It's funny you should say that, Kade, because we didn't miss Nyx's face when we paid her a visit earlier today."

Kade's heart jolted in his chest, the muscles along his spine locking as he shifted the weight of his body to his opposing foot. "What did you say?"

"I said, we didn't miss—" Qadira began before Phaelyn interrupted her.

"He heard you. Look at him." A sneer curled her lips as Phaelyn toyed with the tip of her dagger before she disappeared behind Kade's shoulder.

And, like a flick of a switch, something in him shifted. A gold tinge lightened the depths of his hazel eyes before his teeth elongated past his lower lip, and he angled his head to the fluorescent lights, fighting to tamp down the burning fuse of his temper.

His voice echoed hauntingly across the room, imbued with a dark, silvery undertone, "You're *dead* when I get out of here." He clicked his teeth shut, head tipping forward as he refocused on the women before him. "And you know I'll enjoy ripping you to pieces until the only thing left in this room is the memory of your screams."

Qadira clucked with mock disappointment, straightening the hem of her blue-toned blouse. "As … *lovely* as that sounds, Leon's enlisted a new method of torment today, especially for you."

He waited.

Phaelyn shifted and something white captured his attention. His stare seared into hers as her fingers clasped a familiar cream and white hawk. *Tha…thump, tha…thump.* Soft screeches emitted from the bird's throat as its beak tore at her hands, feathers ruffling with its movement. *Aloys,* he thought as time seemed to press on his shoulders and a sickening blend of dread fell over him, tightening his chest.

His bindings groaned as he pulled and seconds fell like sand, tugging at them, suddenly frantic. Leon's *lessons* pinpointed the torment of his victims. And it didn't take much for Kade to realise *why* he'd chosen Aloys; it was a simple but devastating truth. Nothing good was coming.

He grappled at the bindings around his wrists, ignoring the aching sting and the warm, wetness of his blood weeping beneath the cuffs. "Don't do this … *please,"* he begged, the change from his confident disinterest, gone. "You don't have to do this. You can fight his orders."

Qadira surveyed him with slitted irises, her lips pursing before she gestured swiftly to Phaelyn who adjusted her grasp on Aloys. His gaze tracked her path as she carried the bird of prey toward Kade until she paused, centimetres away, and crouched on the floor, flicking her gaze to his.

"I'm afraid it's too late for that," Phaelyn breathed with crafted indifference.

Kade's throat worked to rid himself of the lump clogging it. "*No.* Don't do this. Torture me … not Aloys. *Please.*"

"We can't do that, Kade," Qadira said, glancing side-long to Phaelyn, a strange flicker of guilt plunging her irises. "Phaelyn, you know what to do."

Something irreparable shattered in the depths of Kade's chest when Phaelyn dropped her gaze to the screeching hawk in her grasp. Her stare was wiped of emotion. There was nothing there when Aloys' talons ripped again into the bloody mess that was her palm. Like she felt no pain. But he did and something tore open the bond tying Kade to Nyx as sick dread flew into his chest.

Kade loved the cream and white plumed hawk. He knew those feathers like the fine details of his tattoos and the plunging bird of prey etched into his skin; a testament to Aloys and what he symbolised. With a harrowing bellow of rage, Kade thrashed at the confines keeping him in the middle of the room.

The sharp *crack* of a bone breaking beneath pressure rang in his skull. The sight of the distorted angle of Aloys' wing carved into his heart and Kade's bottom lip trembled.

A burning swell of emotion surged his senses, the keen of pain from the hawk replaying in his ears as he ripped at the cuffs. It did little to plunge his senses free of the dread Phaelyn's blade enticed, the silvered edge glinting off the fluorescent lights. Nor would it rid him of the white-hot bite of Qadira's knife as it dug into the flesh of his right forearm, marring the descending hawk sketched with the allure of the paintings of old. He welcomed the pain they gave. It was nothing compared to the other. The panicked pounding of Aloys' heart, there one moment, gone the next, snuffed out beneath Phaelyn's vile, crimson-stained hands.

His thrashing stilled as his irises bled white-gold and a bellow of pure, untapped torment ripped from Kade's throat, the *thump* of Aloys' body falling to the floor ringing in his eardrums. The scent of his own blood punctuated Kade's senses as the bindings around his wrists tore already shredded skin. He kept his eyes trained on Aloys as Qadira drew intricate designs into his flesh.

"I think he understands now … or at least, he got the message," Phaelyn murmured.

Qadira hummed, rounding Kade's shoulder. "The bird of prey reduced to a flightless mess," she drawled. She appraised his features, searing the side of his face as he struggled to rein in his anguish. "It seems fitting that Leon refers to you as such. Considering yours is, well … *dead.*"

Phaelyn rose from the concrete floor in a fluid movement, dusting her palms down her leather-clad thighs before the pair wandered to the entrance of Kade's prison. The brunette's fingers wrapped around the doorframe when she paused and turned back to him, Qadira bracketing her shoulder outside the room. "You can't have both things you care about, Kade. There's one or the other, but never both," she said.

Kade stared at the ceiling, focusing on the light colouring of the stone as the duo pulled the door closed with a loud *thud*. Then, when nothing but silence and the stench of blood hung in the room, his control slipped.

The first tremor of grief racked his body, his shoulders shaking with gut-wrenching sobs that left him gasping for breath. His beloved hawk's final moments replayed in his mind like a terrible, broken record. He wished to tear Phaelyn, Qadira, and Leon to shreds, drawing out their deaths until they begged him to cease their suffering.

Despite the hurt haunting his every breath, Kade knew—like he'd known before—why Leon had chosen Aloys. His sire knew Aloys' significance. He knew how much the hawk had meant to him, what it symbolised whenever Kade ran his fingers over the white and cream plumage. With Aloys' death, Leon had shattered what little humanity Kade possessed. Where Aloys was nothing to some, he'd meant *everything* to Kade. The last sliver of right in the world amassed by wrong when he'd turned all those years ago and slaughtered a dozen partygoers. A love for a beast unfettered by human judgement—the best part of his immortal life. The one good thing.

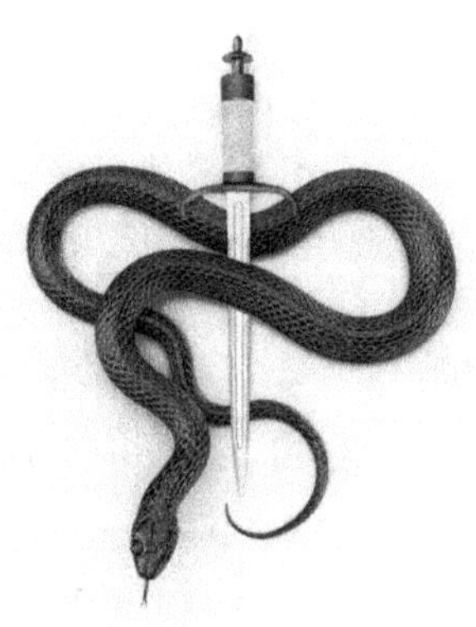

IX

Nyx

The soft rise and fall of Ares's breaths echoed through the cavernous living space, lulling Nyx's anxious thoughts with the constant and methodical crashing of waves crawling in through the dankly lit entranceway while she wandered the Victorian-styled area spliced with something ancient. It was as if Rome's monuments and Italy's rich culture had found itself wreathed in the crumbling statues of the Greek Olympian gods.

As she passed the obsidian statue of Cerberus bracketing the grey couch and Orion's hulking black-iron throne, backdropped by a vast empire on yellowing canvas, her senses honed upon the softest screech originating from down the first tunnelway to the left of the cave. Staring across the room to the darkened tunnel, she waited for it to resume, and when it did, she strode to the natural corridor and disappeared.

Her fingers skittered over the coarse walls as her eyes adjusted to the low light, guiding her further down the tunnel and past the first opening toward the keening screeches coming from Kade's room. Sketch pads, pencils and paintbrushes covered much of a handmade workbench. Containers stained with dirty paint water and others filled with pencils cluttered the natural ledges. She surveyed the space, illuminated by strategically placed golden-plunged lamps, Kade's striking signature decorating the corners of the canvases propped against the walls, and she understood how it all reflected his personality.

Where the golden lighting and soft tones of Kade's room adhered to his gentle qualities, the grotesquely beautiful details of his artwork whispered of the wildness and that darker side of him, bowing to the malignant instincts of his vampirism. Standing there amongst his prized possessions, these observations prickled Nyx's skin like a lover's caress, luring her deeper into his room until her fingers ghosted the driftwood bird stand tucked in an alcove and her gaze darted at the soft keening. She paused for a moment, fingers twitching at her sides before she pushed herself onto the tips of her toes and her stare locked on two, lightly feathered hawk chicks hidden in the cave walls.

The chicks keened hungrily from their nest, shoving against each other when Nyx's brow furrowed, and her tracksuit-clad knee bumped the wall. The rockface scraped against her back as she strained to reach the duo, deftly plucking first one chick and then the other from their hidden nest, cradling them in her T-shirt as she carefully backed up and perched herself on the edge of Kade's neatly made bed.

While one chick resembled the cream and white colouring of Aloys, who Nyx now assumed *wasn't* a male like Kade had thought—or its partner had died weeks ago, the other sooty-grey chick with black patches looked nothing like Kade's beloved hawk as it nudged her thumb with its head. And if Nyx had to guess, she assumed the youngsters were almost ready to fly their nest, judging by how steadily they perched upon her fingers when she freed them from the confines of her shirt.

Peering down at the hawk chicks, a gentle smile pulled at her lips. "Now, what am I going to do with you two?" she murmured.

As if in response, the fledglings ruffled their feathers as Nyx wandered from the room. They warbled with gently timbred chirps, gazing up at her with yellowed irises. With her attention focused solely on the hawks perched in her hands, Nyx didn't register the looming presence lounging regally on his steel throne until he cleared his throat and she jolted, startled.

Orion's lips tugged into a riveted smirk, his ethereal irises alight with blue-fire, eyebrows arched tauntingly as his stare flickered to the chicks within her hands. "Aware of our surroundings, I see," he said.

Nyx glanced around the cavernous room, heart pounding against her ribcage before she moved to the abandoned bedroom barricaded by gauzy curtains and deposited the hawks upon the bedding, adjusting the sheets and pillows into a makeshift nest. With a fortifying inhalation of breath, she turned back to Orion whose stare seared into her skin. He leaned further into the chair's backing and draped his gloved hands upon the armrests, grey-white wisps of smoke slinking from the cigarette in his right hand.

"What the hell are you doing here?" she exclaimed, gesturing hazardously.

He frowned, eyeing her like it should have been obvious. "I live here. This is *my* home."

"That's not what I meant, and you know it."

Orion chuckled, bringing his cigarette to his lips, taking a drag, as his opposing fingers drummed against the chair's armrest. "Aw, little dove. I thought you'd miss me."

Nyx screwed up her nose, ignoring the salacious whispers trailing their fingers across her skin, seeing the dangerous man before her. "Why would I've missed *you*? *You've* put me through hell since the night I met you."

"I'm hurt, Nyx. I really am." His glacier irises seemed to flare with a playful quality she had never seen before. "I thought we had something … *meaningful*."

"If murder and hostage is your definition of meaningful; I'm officially concerned for your sanity."

"Sanity?" Orion theatrically glanced around the throne's backing as if he was looking for something before turning back to her. "Never heard of it."

She tipped her head up to the ceiling with a deft shake of her head, ignoring his laughter. "Why am I not surprised?" she mused, almost to herself.

"Because, despite everything you tell yourself, you *understand* me. And dare I say it, you relate to the atrocities I've committed because some part of you," Orion said, rising from his chair and coming to stand before her in a movement faster than she could fathom, "no matter how small that piece is, wants this." He indicated himself and then, as if in afterthought, the cavern.

"I don't want this," she snapped, stepping back to put distance between herself and the vampire whose words probed too close for comfort.

Orion arched his pale brows, that all-knowing glint in his eyes. "Don't you? Because we both know that vampirism doesn't work like that. At least, not this kind."

"I *don't* want this," she uttered lowly, glaring up at the serpent-like man.

He hummed, trailing his gaze across her oblong features before his lips twitched like he was fighting the urge to grin. "It sounds, to me, like you're trying to convince yourself."

"I hate you," she seethed, pivoting and making for the tunnel leading to her room.

Orion tsked playfully before the rustle of fabric tickled her senses and he appeared in the doorway, barring her entrance. His lips curled into a dangerous smirk, showcasing his love for their game of cat and mouse. "And I love it when you throw insults at me."

Rubbing her palms down her face, Nyx wondered what she'd done in a past life to garner Orion's attentions, his malicious gaze and sudden light-heartedness so off balancing. Her instincts cautioned her, reminding her of the beast with white-gold irises and razor-sharp fangs that lurked inches beneath his skin, waiting for the moment he wished to remove one mask before revealing the trueness of his soul—of all their souls. She knew it should've frightened her, that she should've fought harder to be free of him and his companions. But, as much as she hated to acknowledge it, he was right about the likeness of their personalities. The unspoken desires she craved were masked behind a barricade of finely crafted wrought iron gates set deep within her skull. Because she *wanted* their lives of blood, adrenaline, and mayhem, like she needed her next inhalation of oxygen. But she couldn't—wouldn't—admit that to Orion. Not ever.

So, with an unphased air, she lazily gestured to the open-planned living room before dropping into a cushioned couch. "What do you want, Orion? *Truly*?" she said.

Orion pushed off from the tunnel's entrance, sitting astride his chair before she could blink, his imposing irises analysing her. "Would you believe me if I said *you*?"

Nyx held Orion's gaze, breath caught in her throat, refusing to show her emotions besides doubt. "No, I wouldn't. It'd take a miracle for me to believe that, and you have a *long* road to travel before I would even *consider* you like that."

"Seriously? Do you have a checklist or something?" he spluttered, genuine surprise dappling his diamond-shaped face.

"Would you like me to make one?"

"Did Kade and Niko need one?"

"No."

"Then why do I need one?" he questioned, almost childlike.

She huffed out a laugh tinged with disbelief. "You're unbelievable."

"I'm determined, not unbelievable. I always have been." Orion's eyes glazed with a swell of memories, his posture relaxing into his chair, like he belonged on a throne. "When I set my sights on something, nine out of ten times … I get it."

"What about the tenth time when you don't?" Nyx prompted.

His stare weighed heavily upon her, the honeyed tone of his voice solemn and tinged with dark honesty. "Somebody dies."

* * *

Orion glanced unsurely at the Malamute beside his chair, surveying Ares who'd propped his dark-coloured muzzle on the armrest, gazing up at him with canine interest. Nyx pretended not to notice, her gaze alternating between stealing glances at Orion to the book in her hands. She dropped her gaze to the yellowed pages and half-feigned interest in whatever folklore she'd been reading.

A slight twitch betrayed her amusement when Orion scoffed and she slowly lifted her eyes to his, finding immense satisfaction in having made him sit in utter silence for hours—the sun now cresting the ocean—before she acknowledged his presence.

"Do you have something stuck in your throat?" she quipped with a patronising grin. "Or are you trying to be annoying?"

"Annoying?" he parroted, leaning forward so his elbows rested upon his knees. "Annoying is sitting in silence for *hours* while someone *pretends* to read."

"You're being dramatic."

Orion shook his head with a zealous glint to his irises. "*Anyway* ... what's your plan, Nyx? Are you going to chase up that lead Daddy Dearest found for you?"

"How do you—" she cut herself off with a brisk shake of her head, reminding herself that he'd never left Celacali in the months she believed he had. "We are."

"*We*? As in plural? Like more than one?"

"I know what plural means, Orion," Nyx uttered dryly, closing the book she'd been reading and placing it beside her. "And we, not the royal, are going to look into it."

Orion raised his brows, prompting her to continue before Ares nudged his gloved hand. His gaze flickered at the low canine whine, bushy tail brushing the floor as Ares shifted impatiently. "There's something wrong with your mutt," he said.

"There's nothing wrong with *Ares*," she said drily.

"Then why's he harassing me?"

"Are you serious?"

"Do I look like I'm joking?" he uttered, gesturing to himself with a lazy flick of his wrist.

"He wants affection or some kind of attention."

Orion's voice dropped several octaves as he turned to the Malamute and trailed his fingers between Ares' ears, looking every bit the imposing man he was. "Don't we all?" he drawled, holding her stare, and continuing idle caresses upon Ares's head. "It's just … some of us are deemed *unworthy* of it."

It was Nyx's turn to sigh with unveiled irritation. "*Anyway*. We're heading to this club, the Candence, at the end of the week. We'll drop in, sus it out and then leave."

"That's it? That's your plan?" he pressed.

She bristled at the naturally goading edge to his tone, eyes narrowing upon him. "Do you have a better idea?"

Orion eyed her silently, removing his hand from Ares' head before he rubbed the underside of his stubbled jaw. Something she couldn't place shifted behind his eyes. Like he wanted to say more but couldn't.

"Not right now, I don't. But Nyx … what if this is a trap? Have you considered that?"

She gazed back at him with clean-cut transparency, trying to shake the burrowing truth of his words. It had been the first thing that had crossed her mind, followed by the bitter reminder of everything Orion and his companions had done. Dragging her through a series of bloodstained trails intended to reconnect her with that warped and splintered shard of herself—a feat they'd successfully commandeered. Nyx knew she wanted their unorthodox lifestyle, revelling in the bloodshed and violence with agathokakological ease. But she also knew it was more than that, that it couldn't have been so simple. Because nothing about her life since she'd moved to Celacali was.

In the span of a few months, Nyx had managed to stumble head-first into the vampiric quartet's plan for revenge, almost die—on more than one occasion—skew a pair of vigilante vampire hunter's plans, been thrust into the arms of immortality, and come face-to-face with a narcissist head vampire who was supposed to be dead, well, dead*est*. And, throughout that entire shamble of events, she'd been buffered back and forth between the right and the wrong of the world, driven to the point where she'd realised nobody decided her fate but herself. But her uncle had died … horribly, her father had gone AWOL, and she'd been left alone to deal with metamorphosis beyond any female capacity for physical flexibility, it was all too much. And here she was, again, faltering.

As she pondered Orion's question, she realised there hadn't been a moment of peace since she'd arrived in the coastal city because *they* had never intended for her arrival to be smooth. A thought she couldn't help but agree with, knowing that, despite the turmoil they had caused—and continued to cause—she'd found comfort, and dare she admit it, companionship, with them. A surprise to both sides. It could've been the lifeful and welcoming nature of Niko and Kade or the chaos they caused, enticing her to live her life despite the judgement of others. It could've been Kotori's steadfast persona and wisdom she'd benefited from with every interaction they'd shared. And, as much as she dreaded to acknowledge Orion's presence in her life, it could've been his malignant approach to her acceptance of her past and the dark reminder that she *couldn't* let it control her. It was all of it, all of *them.*

Suddenly, Nyx knew with a piercing, unbreakable certainty that she wouldn't let her past control her or anyone dictate her life, not after the gruelling events that'd led her to this moment and the people she'd lost along the way. Fear was the mind-killer, after all. And she was done with that.

"I have considered it," she admitted, watching as his eyes flashed with something that might have been pride. "But I'm still going to investigate it. Fear isn't a good enough reason to not seek answers."

"And if there aren't any answers at the Candence?" Orion prompted, appraising her with that same intrigued glimmer.

"Then I'll start from scratch again," she said resolutely. "It's not the first time I've been disappointed by a false lead." As she said it, she felt it; determined.

Orion seemed to mull over her words for a moment, bringing his cigarette up to his lips so he could take another drag. Releasing the smoke, his gaze bored into her through white-grey wisps, a frown dappling his forehead. "If only they could see you now, little dove. They'd be proud," he murmured.

She ignored the sudden, flip of her heart at his words, conveying a genuineness she'd never seen from him before. Her voice carried quieter than usual, sombre in her disbelief. "It's nothing, really."

She knew she was lying, that the days since she'd almost died on Elveszett Bluff had been filled with a constant whirl of thoughts and worries about Orion, Kotori, Niko and Kade, but still, she couldn't find it in herself to acknowledge it out loud. *What good would it do?* she thought, recalling the makeshift pinboard covered in news articles, sticky notes of various leads and pins marking the dead ends across the city in the twins' apartment. *It wasn't like I found them.*

"That's where you're wrong," Orion interjected, cutting through the rushing of her thoughts.

She pushed herself up from the couch and began toward the tunnelway to her unofficial bedroom, drawing her gaze to him from over her shoulder.

"It's everything, Nyx. Everything they never had—that *we* never had. So, don't downplay it or try to be humble because *nothing* will change their gratitude, or mine, when they find out what you've done for them."

A slow nod replaced the words Nyx couldn't seem to find, choosing to round the side of the couch instead of answering him before her foot snagged a book stack tucked beside the seating and Orion appeared in front of her. Grasping her forearms between gloved hands and righting her before she could fall, his stare blazed a salacious path across her face while she ignored the traitorous palpitations of her heart. It was as Orion seemed to open his mouth to speak that his gaze narrowed upon the reddened line decorating her face, his fingers grasping her chin as he angled her head so he could better see it. His glacier irises seared the left side of her face, trailing from her eyebrow and down her jawline. A faint tick of muscle across his jaw as he gently gripped her chin between his pointer finger and thumb. He towered above her, waiting for her to say something, gaze trailing lower and nestling upon the angry mark across her arm.

Something shifted in the air when he lifted his eyes to hers, his tongue tracing the edge of his canines. "Who did this to you?"

She squirmed in his grasp. "Nobody that matters."

Orion hummed, the sound bordering on something dangerous. "I think I'll be the judge of that. *Who*?"

"I don't know," she breathed out. "Just a pair of vampires with a message. Phaelyn and Qadira, but that doesn't—"

"Stay here," Orion ordered, cutting her off as he released her and started toward the cave's entrance.

Nyx frowned, whirling as he ascended the marble steps. "Where are you going?"

"To kick someone's ass."

"As much as they might deserve it. You can't kill everyone who threatens me," she exclaimed, hoping it'd deter the serpent-like man on a war path.

"Who said anything about hurting them?" he called back.

"So, what are you going to do? Talk?" she called up at his disappearing feet.

"Conversation. Lesson. It's all the same," he called, disappearing in a trail of words.

"And what *lesson* will you teach them?" she demanded, striding after him, catching up.

Orion whirled to face her, his voice carrying the calamity and ferocity of a cyclone, "The consequences of touching something they shouldn't have."

X

Orion

"Where are they?" Orion said, gritting the words out through his teeth as he shouldered his way into Leon's estate and locked eyes with a hazel-eyed housemaid dusting a vase.

His coat tails billowed after him like a cloud of smoke as he appeared before the woman in a burst of lightning speed, glacial gaze surveying her navy uniform and diamond-shaped features. His unblinking eyes saw the purple-blue bruise bloom across her cheekbone and angry red bite mark peeking out from beneath the neckline of her dress in one all-encompassing glance. The jackhammering of the maid's heart thundered in his ears as he prompted her to speak with a flick of his wrist. She gaped at him with glazed eyes before he shook his head and started down the corridor, leaving her to her dusting.

Mortals had always been considered scum in Leon's eyes and it failed to surprise Orion when his sire—alongside Phaelyn and Qadira—continued to treat them as such, hitting, feeding and disposing of them whenever their usefulness expired. *It's not new,* he thought as he resumed his search for Phaelyn and Qadira. *Leon will never see humanity as anything* less *than vampires.*

So, why did it bother him so much? He'd slaughtered mortals as surely as they had and he'd enjoyed it, repeating patterns like a machine wired to kill. What had changed in the decades of his existence? *Could it be?* he wondered before he shook his head, dismissing the thought quicker than it had come. *No, of course not.*

China vases and abstract art lined the walls of Leon's estate as Orion's boots thudded against the marble floor and he strained to pinpoint Phaelyn and Qadira's heartbeats, knowing the sounds as surely as he knew Celacali's backroads and hideouts. A four-tiered chandelier hung from a glass ceiling as he rounded a corner and entered a gaudy, yet elegant foyer-like room, a grand staircase leading to the second floor situated where a doorway *should have* been … if Leon knew anything about architecture.

Orion's heart stalled in his chest when his gaze swept the room and locked on Leon at the staircase's apex, dread weaving itself into the marrow of his bones as he realised he wouldn't slip from the estate undetected now. Not if the sharp, millenniums-old gleam to his sire's eyes was anything to go by. That life-long tell that oozed untold torments. The images came unbidden and Orion flinched: *A girl with raven hair. The thudding of a terror-filled heart. Fury-born promises amid an otherworldly command.*

"If you cannot enter my home silently and without demands, then I'd advise you to walk back out the door you came through," Leon drawled, wandering down the black-tiled staircase, adjusting the sleeves of his dress shirt. His blond hair was perfectly styled like the creaseless fabric of his navy slacks.

With a displeased sneer, Orion halted at the staircase end and peered up at his sire, gaze flitting over Leon's shoulder to the women he'd been searching for. Phaelyn and Qadira stood shoulder-to-shoulder, the former lifting her hand in a patronising little wave, brunette tresses fixed in a braid while the latter stared down at him without emotion, crystalline gaze as frigid as the ice lands her bloodline descended from.

"As opposed to what? Being a mindless puppet who scrambles to fulfil your commands?" Orion said, resting a gloved hand upon the ebony-wooded, newel post, slack-clad hip brushing the carved beams.

"Your sisters understand *loyalty* unlike you and your brothers … my sons," Leon said, pausing.

"*Sons?*" Orion parroted, eyebrows arching with unabashed disgust. "Three of your sons are *prisoners* in your sublevels. *You* torture them—"

"I—"

"*No,*" Orion interjected, lifting a hand in a slicing motion. "I know what you do to them. You make me feel it! *You* are scum, Leon. The furthest thing from what a sire, what a *father* should be."

A low laugh tumbled from Leon's lips as he descended three steps, sleek black brogues echoing on the tiles. He peered down his nose at Orion, something reptilian lurking in his stare. "Do as I say, Orion, not as I do. Kotori, Kade and Niko wouldn't be in the sublevels if it wasn't for your meddling in Emilia's death. If you'd considered your *brothers* before you'd led them to Chades Cove, they'd be with you now. Instead, you are free … to suffer the consequences of your actions, of theirs too. If you'd thought about them, you wouldn't have *failed* to protect them … once again," he said, scathingly. "Does it hurt?"

The knife met its mark as Orion straightened, fury nestling in his bones. "You—" Orion began before Qadira cut him off.

"You acted on *foolish* feelings, Orion. You—and Kotori, Niko and Kade—acted because of the connection Emilia's family had to Asher, and fear for Nyx's life made you act," Qadira said, long-sleeved shirt rippling as she stalked down the steps where she rested her hand on Leon's shoulder. Now she peered down at him too.

"We did the right thing. Emilia deserved better than what you would have done to her," Orion said, dropping his gaze to the dark tiles as the *crunch* of bones and Emilia's desperate pleas—for a quick death she knew wouldn't come at the hands of Leon—echoed in his ears. "It was a mercy."

Laughter tinged with biting bemusement echoed through the corridors of the estate as Phaelyn skittered down the steps, lithe grace bringing her centimetres from him, silvered eyes alight.

Orion's stare dragged lazily from her knee-length laced boots, up her leather-clad thighs and white singlet to the planes of her face. His eyes questioned promptingly, irked. "Something amuse you?" he crooned, holding Phaelyn's stare as she crept closer to him. Her scent filled his senses.

"Humanity corrupts you," Phaelyn murmured, tiptoeing out of reach when he feigned a step in her direction, a brilliantly mad grin across his face. "While freedom remains out of your grasp."

"It doesn't," he said, eyeing her with distrust as she climbed the stairs and settled on the step beside Leon, propping her head in her hands.

"So, you didn't come here looking for Qadira and me after we'd visited Nyx?" Phaelyn sing-songed as she cocked her head.

Orion's stare lingered on Phaelyn before it flitted to Qadira, holding each of their gazes as his orotund voice slithered across the room, "Watch yourselves."

"Ooo, we're *terrified,*" Phaelyn quipped, waggling the fingers of her raised hands.

"I mean it. You have no business in *my* city," Orion said, daring a step toward Phaelyn.

"Are you threatening my girls?" Leon said, tone laced with feigned bewilderment as his gaze fixed on Orion.

"Of course not," Orion said, pushing himself off the railing. "Just *warning* them."

"You have a lot of nerve for a *boy* with *nothing* to his name," Leon said, eerily calm.

"Remind me why that is," Orion drawled.

"Because I gave you a gift."

"And if there is an alternate universe … I hope there's one you're not in," Orion murmured, a centuries-old ire in his voice.

Leon appeared to prickle at Orion's tone, straightening as a desolate aura ghosted the room. "Ungrateful brat. I gave you everything," he spat.

"I didn't ask for it!" Orion bellowed, starting toward the staircase. His booted foot eclipsed the first step, and he gazed up at his sire. "You stole my mortality and the simplicity of death. *You* took the last thing I found comfort in when death registered in my future … you took my *choice* to die and yet, you want me to *thank you.* For what? Granting me a life I didn't want?"

Silence descended like a hawk as he held Leon's gaze and ignored the searing weight of Phaelyn and Qadira's eyes on his face. It wasn't like he wanted to take back his words because why would he? It was the truth, and it was time they heard it, from him. He hadn't chosen this life of bloodshed and immortality; it'd been forced upon him on the precipice of his death in the guise of false promises.

Leon had promised him many things in his lifetime, but none clung to his skin like those he had breathed into his ear as he'd lain dying, '*Live for your birthright, Orion. It's yours if you want it, but you* need *to want it.*' Though he'd refuse to admit it, some nights Leon's voice kept him up with everything he *should have* left behind and all that he *shouldn't have* wanted. It had been his feeble desire for his promised birthright that had unknowingly manifested his own vampirism. If only he'd known the truth then—that to claim his birthright, he'd *needed* to want to live … even if he hadn't wanted it to be for a lifetime.

Leon's measured tone, gutted of emotion tore into the room, "Then, you'll do well to remember this when you leave," he said.

"And what's that?" Orion prompted, shuddering disdain for his sire.

"When you leave *my* property, *you'll forget how to find it. You will stay away from your brothers but you'll feel their pain as if it were your own,*" Leon ordered, voice bathed in an otherworldly command. Smiling, satisfied, he turned and left.

Blood vessels lining Orion's scalp broke and reformed as he gritted his teeth against Leon's command, connective tissues prickling as if a thousand white-hot pins were being wedged into his head. He fought to shunt the words from his mind, willing himself to find the strength to free himself from this third command. *Three,* he thought with a bitter fever as he struggled to recall them, the effort leaving an acidic aftertaste. *One: Forget and tell Nyx* nothing *of Leon's plans ... Nnrgh!* Pain flared behind his eyeballs as a thin ribbon of blood threaded from one nostril. He blinked, fighting focus. The commands lay buried but he could still find them. *Two: Forget how to find my property.* They were pills he wished he didn't have to swallow, longing to be free of them and the sire they tied him to but, he mustn't forget, there were three.

Leon's command came as a whisper, embedding steel tendrils that drilled their way through Orion's senses, entangling them, miring them, trying to overpower … him.

His mind wrestled. *Three: Stay* away *from your brothers but feel their pain ... as if it were your own.* He exhaled, some of the pain fading. As long as he remembered them, he would know them for what they were: Rules.

Except, rules weren't made to be followed … they were made to be *broken.*

XI

Kotori

Footsteps clamoured in Kotori's eardrums. The incessant pacing of dress shoes upon concrete, irksome as he watched Leon's agitated movement from the confines of a metallic chair, reinforced steel bindings were woven around his wrists, waist, and ankles. Kotori's senses rioted at the constant echoing of footfalls, wishing for the silence of his cell that he'd grown to yearn for, despite the ache in his bones from constant unrest. Though the room itself was comfortless, he prospered in the silence, the loneliness since Leon had tossed his 'sons' into their cells, was a balm, scoured off every time Leon reappeared to *gift* the Levenloos man with his presence and inevitable torment. His dark gaze dragged up from the drab floor, trailing slowly up Leon's slack-clad legs and dress shirt to the older man's mossy irises oozing annoyance and disappointment.

"Did you hear a single thing I said? Or were you too busy staring at the floor?" snapped Leon, a muscle twitching beside his right eye.

"I'm sorry, did you say something important?" Kotori snarked, glaring at the sire who provided little freedom in his prisoner-keeping duties, permitting each of his sons to bathe and attend to mundane needs selectively.

Leon scoffed, pursing his lips at the anger dappling his features. "I see Orion's rubbed off on you."

"Aw, does my warped moral compass bother you?"

"What bothers me, Kotori, is how you all seem to have forgotten *my* rules," Leon stated. "Orion *is not* your sire."

Kotori hummed, the charms on his tribal necklace shifting with the taunting dip of his head. "He might not be our sire, *Leon*, but he's always been there for us, no matter what.

He is dedicated to us, his brothers," Kotori said, gaze raking. "And no manipulations of yours will change that or our bond. Nor will you get in our way when we have Nyx back."

A mocking chuckle rumbled from the depths of Leon's chest, his eyes crinkling at their edges as he shook his head. "Do you really believe that I'll let *any* of you have Nyx in your lives?"

"Well, you see ... we don't give a shit about what you think," Kotori murmured in a dangerously low timbre.

Silence descended as Leon surveyed Kotori in crumpled disarray. An air of defiance seemed to cling to his skin like oil, sticky and impossible to remove. Kotori knew Leon could sense it. When he shifted toward a black metal table beside the steel door, Kotori tracked him, noting every gesture and inhalation of breath until metal scraped on metal and he froze. A pair of scissors were clutched in Leon's right hand, the silvered blades flashing in the fluorescent lights.

A part of Kotori suspected Leon's path before he took it, knowing—like Leon knew—the significance of the ebony-brown tresses of his hair. The realisation smarted like blistering-hot iron on skin. He supposed it wouldn't have mattered, had the culture of his origins not believed their hair and its flowing length was something of prestige. A type of respect found in the tribe of the Levenloos people that governed all—women, children, and men. But Kotori knew it meant more than that, it wasn't about something as simplistic as the length of one's hair.

The dark lock of his hair that was shorter than the rest was a constant reminder of the traditions his tribe upheld—that he continued to uphold—cutting a strand of their hair once they reached the threshold of adulthood and until the day they died to leave placed in the forest as a token to the Levenloos wolf—their protector and bad omen. It was easy to miss the darkened section that was shorter than the rest, continuously cut whenever it grew longer than four inches, kept tucked to the nape of his neck beside his tribal necklace.

But Leon knew.

With a displeased tut, he grasped a handful of Kotori's hair, shifting it until he found the shorter strand before measuring the rest to the same length. "I always thought you were the responsible one, the one of reason, Kotori. And yet, here we are," Leon said, gesturing to the grey walls of the cell with the scissors. "I wouldn't have to do this if you'd just obey me. It'd be painless and you wouldn't have to give up your beliefs for a *mortal*."

Kotori chuckled without humour. "I shouldn't *have* to give up my beliefs for anyone. Nyx doesn't bombard us with ulterior motives like you do."

Leon stilled at Kotori's jab, his teeth chewing the inside of his cheek before a tell-tale *shh-chink* followed by the wispy descent of ebony locks cascading to the floor at Kotori's bound feet.

The muscles of Kotori's back tensed along his spine, locking up as Leon shifted and grasped another handful of his hair. Something—it was *Leon,* he realised with dread—was tearing open his bond to Nyx as he measured one piece of hair to the same length as the first slice of torment before it too, tumbled to the floor. Kotori's gut recoiled at the sight. It continued that way for several minutes of silent agony as Kotori distilled an emotionless mask across his features, hiding the expression of his pain. He bore the cutting, *snicking* sounds and watched the dark mass on the floor grow.

Through it, Kotori focused on his past. The events that'd led to his *almost* death and rebirth as a vampire. Flickers of being dragged deep into the forest that'd bracketed his tribe's settlement, the echoes of his voice as he urged his tribe to do nothing—despite their fierce protective instincts. The sickening laughter of men delighting in his torment as he was tied to a dying tree. These memories polluted his thoughts. He couldn't shake them, instead, he welcomed the tide. The ripping of his skin along his left hip and lower abdomen, the haunting wet sounds of wolves fighting over their food rang in his ears as their canines shredded his skin. He jolted as Leon's polished brogues clicked. Before him was the drawn and lined face of a man appraising him apathetically before his stare snagged on the tribal necklace around Kotori's throat and he stepped forward.

With a sigh of disappointment, Leon grasped the middle of Kotori's necklace and tugged, shattering the tribal charms and hand-crafted thread before he carelessly tossed it atop the pile of ebony hair. "If you'd just … complied, this never would've happened," he said, his hand delving into his pants pocket before he retrieved a lighter and sparked the small flame. "It would've been perfect. My boys … and my empire."

Kotori leaned forward, ignoring the absence of hair not brushing his shoulders. "I don't want a single thing to do with your empire or you. I can promise you that you'll never have it," he paused, recalling the Latin dialect Nyx had uttered before she'd slit Kai's throat in the warehouse. "*Dii te acriter.*"

It seemed to lodge a knife, hitting its mark. Leon dropped the lighter to the pile of hair and shattered necklace but his mossy gaze was bleak. Tangerine flames reflected in the darkness of his eyes and the stench of singed hair struck the room. For a moment, the smugness had slipped. Leon left the cell without a backwards glance.

Kotori remained sitting with his festering anger. A promise of reckoning began to build, sharpening like the blade of a long sword, honed and perfected with the function of spilling blood. For Kotori, the promise of his sire's blood coating his tastebuds as he ripped his jugular from his throat, was sweet. *The future was bright*, he thought. *Bright red.* The baying call of wolves echoed in his eardrums alongside the imagery of their muzzles stained red and an empire crumbling to its knees in a crimson flood. The wolves, once more, *free* to reclaim what was theirs.

XII

Nyx

Children's laughter glided across a candy floss sky alongside the mechanical whirring of rollercoasters, disturbing the silence in the twins' apartment as Alexander rolled a whiteboard littered with assorted news clippings away from the wall to the centre of the lounge room. And now, in the moments after he'd situated it before them, after they'd decided Elveszett Bluff wasn't the safest place, Nyx realised how ghastly Celacali's recent deaths and missing persons list was.

Article after article tied together by a red twine—the '*Leon factor*' as Tobias called it—that branched from the eastern suburbs to the western hills. Women and children had disappeared in a swell so great, Nyx wondered *why* the police hadn't hunted harder. If they could see it here in the comfort of a living room, there was no way the police could have possibly missed it. And through all the innocents missing or found dead, the toll on the Ivory Skulls was unmistakable—countless members of the notorious gang appeared dead in alleyways or nailed for crimes they couldn't escape.

What did the Skulls have to do with Leon? she thought, gaze flickering to Ares, who lounged beside the black leather couch, dozing as Tobias perched on its armrest. *Why had so many children gone missing since his return?*

"What do we know of Emilia Stone?" Nyx said, gesturing to the newest article, unrelated to the Ivory Skulls as her mind drifted to the girl's brother—Jesse—who was still missing.

"I did some digging because I heard she was from Wildegulf," Tobias admitted, pushing off the couch and wandering to the whiteboard, tapping Emilia's article before he turned to face them, gaze straying to Alexander for a moment. "And, imagine my surprise when I found a connection to the Stones and Asher from an old news article."

"Asher knew Emilia's family?" Alexander asked, surprised as he glanced at Nyx.

Nyx's eyes narrowed on Tobias. "*How* did he know them?"

"The article says he helped them reclaim a stolen artefact from their museum," Tobias said.

"*But?*" she prompted knowingly, sensing there was more.

"*But* if you dig a *little* deeper, you'll find that they knew," he paused, locking eyes with Alexander, "our father first. It gets hazy the further you look and eventually Ryder's name is forgotten."

"Is there anything to suggest they were fellow … *mythographers*?" Nyx said, arms folding over her maroon T-shirt.

"What are you thinking, Night?" Alexander said, as his eyes searched her face.

"I'm trying to understand how your father and Asher knew the Stones, *and* why Emilia is dead because of that connection. If anyone should be dead, it's her parents. They knew Asher and Ryder, not her," she said, trying to explain her rushing thoughts.

"Even then, it doesn't explain the logic behind Leon wanting her dead," Alexander interjected. "Because if we've learned anything from following the leads Azeil gave us, and the articles before, it's that Leon doesn't kill randoms. They're all linked so, what did Emilia know that she shouldn't?" He started towards the coffee table, his gaze roving over the sticky notes and news headlines.

Something shifted in the air that Nyx couldn't place. Was it anticipation raising the hairs on the nape of her neck? Or fear of learning the truth that tied Asher to Emilia? Nyx was about to follow Alexander when a sudden, stabbing ache lanced her temples and she stumbled, flashes of dark hair cascading to the floor assaulted her vision, and a bone-deep agony. It was *Kotori?* She thought, no, she knew it, as her heart jolted in her chest.

"You okay, Nyx?" came Tobias' voice.

She nodded, waving him off as she sank into the couch with a pained sigh, her jeans digging into her thighs as she shifted to make room for Tobias beside her. "Just a headache. Nothing," she said. "Why would Leon want Emilia dead?" she breathed, tipping her head on the couch's backing.

"My guess?" Tobias murmured, leaning around Alexander to pluck a notepad covered with his handwriting from the coffee table. "Is that Alex is right. She had to have known something she shouldn't."

A shout of success ricocheted across the room, startling Nyx in the same moment Alexander whirled to them, one hand grasping his knee, his dark-washed jeans complimenting his hoodie, while the other hand held a neon-yellow sticky note up like it was the Holy Grail.

His gaze shot between them awaiting understanding … followed by an exasperated huff. "Our father might have known Emilia's parents for a moment, Bias, but you already said how Asher knew them. Except, Asher trusted them enough to leave something in their care," Alexander said, his hazel irises glinting.

"The artefact," Nyx murmured, plucking the sticky note from Alexander's fingers.

Alexander's lips tugged into a bemused grin, nodding as if encouraging her to put the pieces together. "Exactly," he said.

"Eh?" Tobias said, eyeing them with a confused frown as he adjusted his *Scream* T-shirt.

Nyx stared at the paper in her hand, Alexander's looping scrawl etched across its surface as her silvered voice filled the room, "The artefact was a Trojan horse," she said.

"So, it's a gift in disguise … but of what?" Tobias drawled, craning his neck to see.

"I noticed the connection to Wildegulf myself, Bias, but I followed a different train of thought. Like, what artefact would warrant Asher's presence? And then it clicked. Asher *trusted* them with a copy of his research—an artefact in itself because of the priceless knowledge it contained. Knowledge vampires can't *see*," Alexander explained, grabbing a file from the table's surface to retrieve a photo of a leatherbound book.

"What does it contain? *Why* can't vampires see it?" Nyx said, accepting the glossy photo of a museum's catalogue from Alexander.

"From what I understand, it's vampiric lore so old it surpasses *decades* of information. It's *years* of Asher's life research in a book that was historically accurate. So much so, that historians couldn't understand *how* he got it. On the vampiric front, its rumoured to have text written in silver-laced ink and pages steeped in silver halide crystals along with … something else to prevent vampires from learning its contents. But that's what the article addressed anyway," Alexander continued, his voice laced with wonder.

"I think I've seen it. The cover, at least for a moment," Nyx said, her voice a low whisper. "Before … everything."

"Where?" Tobias prompted, eyes flitting over her features.

"At my house."

"You've seen it at *your house*?" Alexander breathed, his eyes widening.

Nyx couldn't blame Alexander for the puzzlement he felt as she surveyed the photo in her hands, equally proud of her uncle for creating a tome three inches thick and shell-shocked that he had gathered research, folklore, myths and modern media together in a way that had stumped historians—and in a form that prevented vampires from finding it. *Silver halide … Silver ink … Something unknown … How much of his life had he given to his research?* she wondered, tracing the leather laces in the photo. *And how had he deciphered myth from reality?*

She knew Asher had travelled as a part of his job and she remembered being excited whenever her father told her he was coming to visit but at the time, it had never occurred to her that his stories of golden-eyed beasts had been anything more than that. She knew now, of course, that the stories held more truth than lies and a part of her wanted to find the information he'd found so she could understand her lingering vampirism. *Could it help me?* she thought, drumming her fingers upon her thigh. *Could I turn without a pack if I had the knowledge?* "Why does no one know about this?" she murmured, voicing a niggling thought as she recalled seeing a similar book tucked in a cupboard of her family's lounge room.

Tobias' dark eyes locked on her, weighted. "Something tells me Asher knew his research was priceless—dangerous maybe, and he didn't want anyone to know he knew the truth. If the rumours are true about its pages, no vampire could find it. Nothing *undead* can unearth its secrets," he said.

"Surely there's a loophole," she said, glancing between the twins.

"None that we know of," Alexander said, offering her an apologetic smile.

Frustrated, Nyx raked her fingers through her curls before she forced her heart to calm its unsteady beat, ignoring the searing burn in her eyes that came and went in fiery flashes; a side effect she'd learned from Kotori's assorted books that was her halfling instincts trying to force her eyes to shift to a familiar, eerie golden-yellow. "I'm starting to think we should be looking into what Asher knew," she mused, a soft smile quirking her lips.

As if in agreement, Ares rose from the ground and wandered to her side, wet snout nudging her hand.

"I think we should," Tobias admitted, ruffling the fur atop Ares' head. "Asher's research might explain Leon's actions or help find his weak spot while we scope out Azeil's new lead."

"On that note," Alexander began, placing his file of papers relating to Asher's leatherbound book on the table to grab another. "We should talk about what we're going to do about Azeil's lead and the recent activity at the Candence."

"Well, first off," Nyx began, "we need to figure out if it's Orion, Kotori, Niko and Kade or if it's Phaelyn and Qadira carrying out Leon's orders. On top of that, we also need to learn *why* Leon is targeting the club. Is it a coincidence that whoever he wants dead is there or is it something else?" There, she'd laid out the components she wanted to focus on. The twins looked at her, impressed.

"Okay, but what do we do when we get there?" Tobias said, taking the blueprints of the Candence from Alexander with a concerned frown.

"I think we should suss out the Candence and try to find whoever or *whatever* Leon wants. If we don't find anything in two hours, we leave. There's no point hanging around for any more dead ends," Alexander said. "No pun intended." He coughed, his giddy excitement unmistakable.

"Alex, how do you even have these blueprints?" Tobias asked.

Alexander's excitement shifted into a sheepish grin, hazel eyes brimming with uncertainty. "I … borrowed them from the county clerk's office," he said.

"Borrowed or stole?" Nyx said knowingly.

"For legal reasons, I *borrowed* them so I could photocopy them," Alexander said, emphasising his words with playfully narrowed eyes.

Tobias chortled as he waved the papers. "You know you can *legally* access these if you go to the library, right?"

"Since when?" Alexander said, disbelief splayed across his face.

"Oh, Alex," Nyx breathed, shaking her head. Sometimes he was just so naïve. "You can access Celacali's blueprints from the library archives. All you had to do was ask and say it was for a university assignment."

"I hate both of you so much right now," Alexander grumbled, disregarding the *borrowed* files onto the coffee table.

"Why? It's not our fault that you didn't know," Tobias goaded.

"Maybe not, but would it have *killed you* to tell me sooner?" Alexander whinged.

"*Anyway,*" Nyx interjected, eyeing the twins with amusement. "The Candence will be our priority *as well as* learning what's so important about Asher's research. If I can't … see it, I'll need your help. You're … *living,* I'm somewhere between."

"Noted," Tobias said, dipping his head with a fond smile. "We need to understand Leon's possible intentions and if it has anything to do with Asher if we want any chance of normality. We *need* to know his weakness … *if* he has one."

"Do we even know what *normality* is?" Alexander said morosely.

"No," she admitted, trailing her fingers through Ares' fur as he propped his head between her leg and Tobias'. "But white lies are the easiest to swallow."

XIII

Nyx

Days passed in a restless blur since Orion had strode from the cave like a god sent to wage war, leaving Nyx to ponder his intentions and everything she'd discussed with Tobias and Alexander.

As deafening rumbles of thunder churned throughout the cavernous home like a bad case of indigestion—rain striking the glass panelling fastened to the holes in the ceiling, filling her eardrums with rhythmic patter—she towelled her curls dry in the cave-turned bathroom at the end of a tunnelway running alongside her room, and the rooms belonging to Kade and Kotori. Her bare feet padded along the smooth stone floor as she meandered into the living space and draped the towel on a hook in the abandoned bedroom. Distracted for a moment, she dressed and then checked on Aloys' chicks before continuing into the main cave with a mental reminder to find some more hawk-safe meat to feed the keening birds. Her thoughts strayed to Orion and she turned his promise over in her mind. Would she ever unravel the tangled threads tying her to him?

She couldn't shake the reminders of everything wrong he'd done to her, every betrayal, every bolt of pain, anguish or terror he'd cultivated with his gloved hands. Her gaze trailed across to the one room she had yet to see, the final point on the map of the home within Elveszett Bluff—the home of monsters who hid behind the masks of men. With a heavy sigh, she shoved thoughts of Orion to one side and started toward the entrance nearest to the left side of the cave's opening, an assortment of ancient and odd trinkets and furniture pieces scattered pointedly about like markers.

Ares's almond gaze surveyed her, his ears pricking toward her as she wandered past him. A dull throb ached in her stomach, like the beginning cramps of a menstrual cycle but paired with a primal craving she had chosen to ignore since the sensation had begun, the day prior. Her fingers skittered down the uneven and jagged walls, pupils expanding to accommodate the poor light before she jolted as immense pain cleaved her insides from heart to navel, sending her to her knees. She clutched her ribcage, winding her arm around her waist in a desperate attempt to quell it, her opposing palm pressing into the tunnel's wall. It was like her insides were trying to get outside, her body seeking to shear in two.

Through the tide of pain, Nyx knew this moment had been building like a storm, reminding herself of the struggle of her strength when Qadira and Phaelyn had appeared—knowing she'd delivered firmer blows to Orion, Kotori, Kade and Niko. She couldn't stop the groan or the bowing of her spine as she pressed her forehead into the cave's wall, seeking the chill of the limestone as her temples pounded. A cold sweat crawled over her skin, sticking her tank top and blue jeans to her body. Ares barked, barrelling into her side, his concern obvious.

Much of her body's weight sat upon her thighs, yet Nyx wished for a reprieve from the agony of the slicing wave across her upper and lower gums. The elongated incisors and canines she'd seen the quartet bare, now pushed to extend and shape her own mortal teeth. For a moment, it seemed the deities above had heeded her pleas, as the crippling pain fled her bloodstream. She blinked and numbly pushed herself up from the floor, sparing a shaking hand for Ares before continuing down the corridor to a cave she instantly remembered as Orion's torture chamber.

She stood trapped in the doorway, gaze trailing over candle-smattered walls and ledges to the straight-link chain swaying eerily from its eyelet bolt before she whirled and re-entered the main tunnelway, scratching her palms upon the rockface the further she walked. The slow *tha ... thump, tha ... thump, tha ... thump* of her heart clamoured in her eardrums as she stumbled, and her palm met nothingness. Before she fell, she pivoted to the man-sized crevice in the wall and slipped between the jagged rock, weak from her ordeal, hands splayed. They found a switch, the tell-tale flick of mod cons. Absurdly, it puzzled her how the quartet managed to have functioning electricity within the cavernous home. But a moment later, all thought fled her mind as she focused on the darkly-lit bedroom before her.

The room was simple but with an edge she couldn't shake. Like something more—someone more—resided under the dark silk sheets of the king-sized bed, or the leather-bound hardbacks and fraying rolls of parchment stacked precisely upon several black metal shelves. An industrial style paired with something medieval, regal. Candelabras perched on darkly stained spruce wood drawers and bedside tables, a pair of leather gloves left forgotten upon the back of an ash-grey settee with wooden armrests, hinting at the owner's identity. A grotesque but tragically beautiful chandelier was secured to the ceiling, the elaborate whorls and craftmanship of the skulls leaving her stunned by the design.

She knew immediately whose room she was in. The remnants of her previous pain scattered, forgotten as she turned in a slow circle and appraised Orion's room. Her eyes took everything in, marvelling before she paused, and her interest snagged on a shelf tucked in a crevice of a reading nook, white lighting refracting off the elaborate craftsmanship of a crown. Nyx walked slowly, aware she was seeing something she wasn't sure she should have.

With little thought, and a deft glance thrown at the room's entrance, she gingerly extended her left hand, fingertips brushing the chilled crown and the coarse parchment tucked beneath its base before she grasped both items in her hands, her lips parting in mute shock when the weight of the metal pressed into her palm. Like the ceiling-mounted lights, intricately designed skulls decorated the band, its fleur-de-lys wrought in black metal connected by smaller pointed arches above the band, obsidian jewels were fastened to the skulls' eye sockets and rose-like flowers wove around the detail. Her thumb traced the grooves of its arches, mind whirling with questions as she swapped the crown for the parchment and nimbly unfurled it.

Bold text splayed across the paper's top, a body-crumpling bolt of pain cleaved her insides before her grasp on the item slipped and it, like her knees, hit the floor. The splitting sensation muddled her thoughts, polluting her nervous system with a rush of agony, trapping her. She sucked in sharp breaths and fought to calm her suddenly sluggishly beating heart. The slowed *tha ... thump, tha ... thump, tha ... thump* scared her, and she forced herself to focus on the unfurled parchment beside her thigh.

'Tragedy finds newly crowned king hours after coronation,' was etched across the page's headline in bold font, a following admission in smaller italics reading: *The royal family was left reeling as the Prince Xensor and Princess Nylora discovered the body of His Majesty, Orion Tyrie ...*

Nyx seemed to forget her pain as her gaze drifted from the headline to the text beneath it. As unnerving as it was, she read the oddly detailed article, which explained how he had been found, bloodstained, throne covered in blood. And that the bejewelled crown, now centimetres from her fingertips, was still upon his head. She thought of Orion's beloved chair in the cave's living space—she'd always thought it had seemed *throne*-like. She read again, officials believed 'foul play.'

"Nyx?" came the uncertain call from Alexander, startling her, his voice seeming so near to her ears. "Are you ready to go?"

Ares woofed immediately and scarpered off in the direction of his voice. *The acoustics in this place will forever remain a mystery*, Nyx thought. For a moment, she couldn't remember why Alexander was here but then she did. Her voice jittered and lilted when she cleared her throat in an attempt to mask her pain—a pain she knew, from the mythology and folklore books she'd been combing, was her body's way of forcing her to complete the transition from human to vampire, ensuring her survival instincts would kick in and she'd be left with one decision: to complete the transition or die trying to prolong it.

She'd rather die first than admit she was terrified of her impending vampirism, haunted by the memories of Ryder and Amir leering about the creature she'd become. Something w*orse* than Orion, Kotori, Niko and Kade without their guidance. After all, it was their world she'd be stepping into … forever. Without them, she didn't want to consider her path as her heightened instincts raged against her mortal subconsciousness, two sides of the same coin. Infernally destined to battle against the other unless … unless she could somehow control her vampiric instincts, *if* she completed the transition before it killed her. *If* she could find guidance in Asher's leatherbound book—*if* it was at her house like she thought it was. *If, if, if.*

"Nyx?" he called again.

"Give me a minute, Alex," she called, glancing around Orion's room, wincing at the slicing burn tearing across her chest. "I'll meet you outside. I've just … got to grab some things first."

"Alright. I'll take Ares since Tobias is *insisting* on using the car harness he bought for him."

She smiled despite the pain, even though she knew he couldn't see her. "Of course, he is," she called. "Be there in a minute."

"Yeah, we'll be outside."

In a harried haze of panic and pain, she scrambled, scooping the news article up and shakily returning the items to their original shelf positions, ignoring the sharp shredding sensation dragging through her lungs and heart as she turned and fled the room. Nyx was grateful Orion hadn't returned, giving her a moment to register the new information and *try* to make sense of it while she slipped through the man-sized crevice and into the dimly lit tunnel. As foolish as trying to understand Orion and his past was, because Nyx knew there wasn't a day where she'd truly understand him, not if she had two-hundred years. Some part of her was ashamed of her actions, feeling as if she'd pried, even after everything he'd done to her.

A jagged breath hitched in her throat, her fingers digging into the grooves of the tunnel's walls as another harrowing tear gouged at her abdomen and chest. *My sanity will leave me soon,* she thought. Her skin prickled with goosebumps as the saline breeze glided through the tunnels and over her sweat-slick arms and face. A brief respite as she forced herself to keep moving toward the living space of the cavernous home. Nyx blearily registered the room, rounding the fire pits and furniture with little thought. She paused beside the marble staircase, gingerly grasping the handrail as she slipped first her socks and then sneakers on. *Ok*, she thought as she straightened, wincing against the pain. *I can do this.*

The tunnel's dank and mould-infused scent permeated her nostrils as she guided herself out of the hidden cave of Elveszett Bluff to the wooden staircase hugging its limestone cliff face, seagulls crying her release. She closed the door behind her before her hands latched hold of the weatherbeaten railing and the stairs creaked and swayed in the salt-fused wind. This was the platform where Kotori had shared a piece of his past, and then his determination to protect his brothers—Orion, Niko and Kade—by draining Nyx of her blood until unconsciousness greeted her. She didn't dwell on it and instead, hurried upwards to the rocky terrain above.

The glossy paintwork of Alexander's car caught her eye for a moment before she turned and stared out across the Avonsano Ocean and its rolling tides white-capped by the wind. Rain on her skin barely registered as she gazed out at the dark grey clouds. With a shaky breath, she mustered the strength to mask the pain. As she turned and started toward them, she saw the brothers who watched her through the wet windscreen of their car.

Slipping into the backseats beside Ares, as purple-white light cascaded across the heavens, wet skin clinging to the leather, she brushed her curls over her shoulders.

"Ready?" she prompted, grinning when Ares nudged her with his nose.

Alexander nodded, eyes alight with devious mirth, "You look like a drowned rat."

"A thoroughly drowned one," Tobias clarified.

"Thank you for that … *wonderful* compliment," she said drily. "Truly."

Tobias shrugged in his favourite hoodie. "You know us, we aim to please," he said.

"Which is why neither of you has girlfriends," she jested, pausing before she clicked her fingers and a wide grin stretched across her features. "Got it."

Choked laughter bubbled from Alexander as Tobias griped, "What's funny about that, Alex?"

"You walked right into that one, Bias," Alexander said, glancing at his brother, and putting the car into drive before he manoeuvred the vehicle into a three-point-turn. "And no amount of backtracking will get you out of it."

"Still!" Tobias protested. "It's bold of her to assume that we don't."

"Is it?" Nyx goaded, squinting with a questioning gleam.

Tobias narrowed his eyes, tossing a glare over his shoulder before he turned back around. "*Anyway—*"

She tutted mockingly, grinning like the Cheshire Cat. "Always changing the subject when he doesn't want to hear it," she said.

"I hate you," the dark-eyed twin grumbled.

"I love you too, Bias," she quipped, leaning forward to ruffle his mousy-brown hair.

"That's not what I said."

"But it's what you meant."

"No, it's not."

The playful bickering ran its course and Tobias turned, choosing the high road. "You ready for tonight?"

She paused, fingers delving into the white-black pelt along Ares' spine. "We're heading to the Candence, right? Because I'm hoping our plan will be a hell of a lot better than your father's ever were."

"It is, at least, in the sense that innocent people won't get hurt," Alexander stated, light heartedly.

Neither twin seemed to care that their father had been murdered at the hands of the men they sought to find … or the one Nyx hadn't told them never left.

"So … we'll be dropping Ares at yours?" she asked.

"Of course," Tobias said. "We're going to the Candence and dogs aren't permitted. Remember we have two hours to scope the place out and if nothing bites, we leave."

"*Point* taken, Bias," Alexander shot back as Nyx rolled her eyes. "We've had enough false leads to last a lifetime and I don't know about you, Night, but I'm sick of hanging around for hours at a place we don't have to," Alexander added, his eyes flicking up to the rear-view mirror.

"I can work with two hours," she said. "Nothing I've experienced had a plan, it was all instinct and working with what I knew." She mulled. "Simple's good." Then as if reading his mind, she added, "No, Alex," holding his stare in the mirror. "You can't start with the what if's, not now. If something is going to go wrong, it will. And nothing you say now will change that."

"How do you know that? You could be wrong."

"I could be … but I have enough scars to suggest otherwise."

Although she knew Alexander and Tobias wanted to protest, neither would. Because they knew she spoke the truth, they'd seen them firsthand or been there when they'd been carved into her skin. Not that it mattered to Nyx, as she turned her head and stared out at the storm-lashed cliffside, because while they worried about the lead they sought to follow, Nyx fought to stifle the pain inside her. It tore and chewed, shredding her insides from her collarbone to her hips, the searing agony of her upper and lower gums a constant lancing reminder of a choice she had to make.

"Nyx," Alexander said, eyeing her with concern. "You don't … *look* so great. Are you okay?"

Biting back a moan, she nodded with a bad caricature of a smile. "I'm fine."

"You—" Tobias started.

"I'm *fine*," she snapped, pain soaring through her nervous system.

Like someone drowning and fighting against a current, Nyx couldn't find her footing in the pain, so she stopped trying. Resting her forehead against the car window, she closed her eyes and let it in. Embracing the burning of her lungs as she breathed, feeling it roll over her, pushing her down below the waves of the Avonsano, drowning her in her own waning mortality. *It's been such a long time coming,* she thought.

The moment she'd met Kade in the bookstore all those months ago, she'd been destined to drown before she could be reborn. Marked for the depths of their dark world, to be forever changed by its tides … for better … or worse.

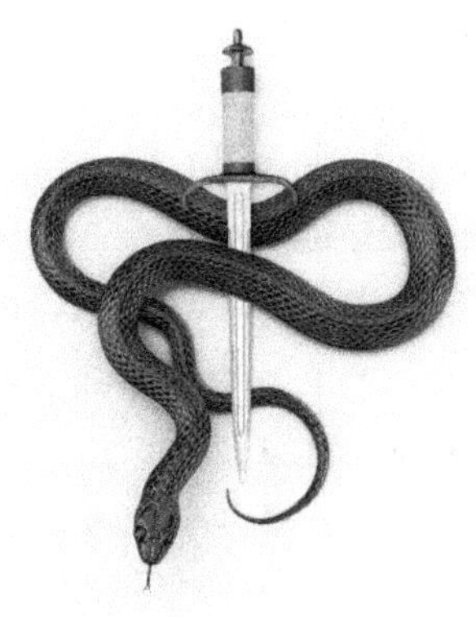

XIV

Niko

A ragged gasp seared a path up and past Niko's lips, the dirty-blond locks of his hair plastered to his face, neck and shoulders as rivulets of water ran off his skin and into the six-metre-deep tank beneath him. The scent of disuse, mould and an unpleasant damp aroma that almost masked a woman's perfume and the biting stench of shoe cleaner assaulted his nostrils. Niko knew, like the many times before, that Leon and Qadira's presence was a minor reprieve from his heart-wrenching terror that clung to him like his sodden jeans and cropped Def Leppard shirt. He knew as his eyes collided with the green of Leon's, why this was *his* carefully planned torture chamber.

Fluorescent-illuminated water sloshed inches below his feet as the unpleasant and harrowing reminder of his past and *almost* death filled his head. But he supposed he had died, at least, some crucial part of his soul had shattered and left him with this trembling of his hands and thumping of his heart. Fear cloyed in his mouth like the zesty juice of a lemon and something rotted, dredging up the memories he wished to forget.

As much as he tried to fight it, he couldn't focus on the room around him as his chest pinched and a panicked tremor shot up his spine. He redoubled his efforts, desperately tugging on the metallic clamps around his wrists and ankles. The tell-tale tearing of his skin didn't stop him. *Even though it should.* He knew he should stop fighting before his accelerated healing failed him like it had failed him in 2012, ingraining the freckle-like smattering of scars etched diagonally across his face.

He could still hear the clamour and life of Celacali's boardwalk in his eardrums just like the day he'd arrived in the coastal city as a runaway with a stripped-down motorcycle and the clothes on his back. His passion for music and his dream of becoming a guitarist had driven him from the four walls of his working-class parent's home without protest from either. And from the moment his boot-clad feet had hit the boardwalk, Niko hadn't looked back. And that might've been why he hadn't noticed the attention from a group of Ivory Skulls. They'd seen the newness of his wandering gaze, which was why he hadn't noticed their silent herding toward the back of the stands bracketing the outdoor stage, not until two of the gang members had pounced, dragging him toward the metal barriers at the boardwalk's ledge.

They had mistaken him for Orion and Kotori's newest companion, unbeknownst to Niko who hadn't yet met them. The Ivory Skulls holding his arms had straightened when their dark-haired ring leader wandered out from beneath the stands, goading Niko about people he'd never met, bearing a grudge for being ushered off Orion and Kotori's turf while they'd stalked the amusement park earlier that night. All that mattered was their anger, coiled to strike. And, like the burst of pain from a serpent's fangs, Niko *felt* the blows the Ivory Skulls had delivered until his blood stained their hands and he could barely hold himself up. They'd bound his wrists and ankles with fraying rope.

Niko tried to shove his memories to a deeper place, almost frantic in his want to go without reliving his past for the hundredth time in the past months. But like all the times before, it was futile.

"I hope your friends know how to swim ..." The dark eyes of the dark-haired man appraised him with a sneer before he leaned forward and the men grasping his arms tightened their grip.

Niko blearily registered the dragging of his feet but, as the barricade of the boardwalk collided with the middle of his spine, he jolted, eyes like a live wire when he whirled out of one gang member's grasp and shunted another with his shoulder, sending him to the floor. Then their ringleader had strode forward and yanked his collar, dragging him to the barricade. His fear had been palpable, wrapping its fingers around his throat the same way the dark-haired man grasped his shirt—he knew they wanted him dead. A terror Niko couldn't see past as the man's lips curled into a dangerous grin, two of his fellow gang members coming to his side before he leaned forward with a patronising look of concern.

"If you want to live, start by keeping your head above *the water," he said.*

As hard as dispelling his memories was, Niko couldn't forget the garbled plea that'd tumbled from his lips before the dark-haired man had gestured to his companions. The phantom press of their fingertips beneath the scrutiny of Leon's gaze, bridged his past with his present as the life-like feeling of falling followed by the icy embrace of the Avonsano Ocean froze his mind.

With a shaky breath, Niko forced himself to refocus on the room and not his memories as his jaw clenched like his hands against the chair's armrests. His cyanic irises churned with the anguish he fought to hide in Leon and Qadira's presence. The blonde-haired women's eerie, steel-blue gaze cut across the room from where she stood behind a three-metre-long control panel with flashing lights, well-greased levers and coloured function buttons. The red light of a button strobed across her squared features, champagne locks secured neatly to the crown of her head in an elaborately twisted braid. Under different circumstances, he might have complimented her on her silvered earring stack.

His eyes narrowed and he turned to Leon, who peered down at him from the raised platform above the tank, the mechanical mechanism of the chair raised and halted by Qadira. If looks could kill, Niko's glare would have put the head vampire six feet under the sub-levels they resided within. His resentment rippled off him, the silver dagger in his left earlobe twinkled. Leon toyed with the cuffs of his sky-blue shirt. He appeared to be in his mid-thirties, but Niko knew better, knew the millenniums under the vampire's belt.

"Are you still *infatuated* with Nyx?" Leon said, tutting mockingly. "Or have you *finally* come to your senses?"

A husky scoff tumbled from Niko's lips, his head shaking as water droplets skittered over the dark ink of the cheetah curling over his right shoulder and pectoral. "Why would I give up on her for *you?* You say you care, that you're doing what's best for us … time and time again. But you're not. You're twisted and corrupt with your *sick* ideals," he snapped.

"My sick ideals? Is that how you all see it?"

"Isn't that what they are? Ideals."

Leon's lips pursed against an unrestrained retort. "When did you become so … disrespectful? Didn't I save your life? Give it a new purpose that wouldn't expire within the lifespan of a mortal?"

Niko's eyebrows raised, a feigned look of surprise on his broad features before a grin bared the upper half of his canines to Leon. "But did *you* do it without ulterior motives? Or were we just pieces of the puzzle you wished to force together?"

The green of Leon's eyes darkened, the triangular planes of his face appearing to tighten with something simmering. He tucked his hands into the pockets of his dark dress pants, the leather of his dress shoes scuff-free. Authority inked his tone, malicious precision in his movement as he turned to Qadira.

With a shake of his head, he directed his words to the silently waiting woman, "It seems like we should've disposed of Nyx sooner … before she took root."

Qadira's steely irises flickered to Niko, who glared at her. "It would appear that way," she said.

Leon hummed his agreement as he appraised his second youngest son and Niko stiffened at his next words, "Don't tell me you've caught feelings for her, Niko, because she won't be around much longer to reciprocate them," he said.

Niko jolted forward in his chair, tugging against the bindings, ignoring reopening wounds as his blood dripped into the water beneath him. The wet tresses of his hair clung to his face, a white-gold glint trickling into his stare before a blood-chilling snarl escaped him. He knew he was always protective toward those he loved but Leon's words were truth, one he'd recognised when Kotori and Kade had dragged him away from Nyx upon Elveszett Bluff, that he couldn't ignore. Those feelings had only grown, like the buds of night-blooming roses.

He leaned as far forward as the bindings would allow him, glaring up at his sire. "You were right to believe Nyx would ruin your control of us—that she'd *taint* your blood, because you can go fuck yourself, Leon. When we're free, we're *never* abiding by your orders again. At least … *I* won't be," he spat.

Leon's smugness fled. In the blink of an eye, that air of all-knowing he carried was replaced by a frigid indifference.

Too slow, poker face, Niko thought. Qadira shot her blue eyes at him, acknowledging the deft flick of Leon's wrist in the same moment Niko tensed. He didn't regret the words he'd spoken or the truths he'd revealed—given to him by Orion after he'd overheard a conversation between Leon, Phaelyn and Qadira. Nothing he'd said had been a lie. It was just a truth Leon didn't want to stomach; a bitter pill the ages-old vampire couldn't accept. But Niko also knew there was no hiding his own terror, flashes of an abandoned warehouse darting to the forefront of his mind, where Leon would see them.

A phantom flare of horror as the stench of the warehouse from his memories polluted his senses, coarse rope around his wrists and the burning agony of a stake through his abdomen filled his mind. Angry murmurs and demands of Ryder and Amir—those wannabe vampire hunters, a blond—Asher Monroe—shadowed by a rust-coloured Malamute with eyes like Orion's. The terror that'd scrambled his mind those twenty-five years ago couldn't be forgotten and paraded before him now as snapping images, his second death. He tried but he could not calm his panicked breaths as Leon's gaze bore into him and the mechanism holding his chair above the water began to sink. As he descended, he felt another violation, the bond connecting him to Nyx as it was forcibly wrenched open beneath Leon's stare.

Bubbling water followed by the disgruntled mutter from whoever shook his shoulder, his heavy eyelids groggily blinking to rid himself of silver-induced unconsciousness—a non-lethal sedative to vampires. Niko wondered how the amateur hunters knew about it, knowing its side effects rendered his heightened senses mute. A shout tore from his throat when a raven-haired man—Amir Montes—doused boiling water over his face, the blue of Niko's eyes flashing white-gold as the sedative residue fled in a slap of pain and the sensation of his own blood trickling down his face.

A deep barking drew Niko's gaze from Amir and Ryder to the blueness of the dog's irises piercing into him as its lips curled back from its teeth and a snarl drifted to his ears.

"Enough, Leo," Asher uttered, scolding the Malamute before Ryder scoffed at him.

"It's not the dog's fault it can sense a bloodsucker when it sees one," Ryder stated with a matter-of-fact tone, his army cadet attire covered with dark patches of dirt.

"They can sense that?" murmured Asher, glancing down at the dog's raised hackles and the way it refused to tear its stare from Niko.

"Of course, they can," Amir drawled, gesturing to Niko with a lazy wave of his hand. "They're unnatural. Abominations *to the earth."*

"I'm sitting right here," Niko crooned, shifting in the chair the trio had tied him to, perched at the edge of a boiling vat of water in the mould-fused warehouse. "And as much as I'd like to hang around and chat, I have places to be ... wannabe vampire hunters to kill."

"And how are you going to do that? You're a little ... tied up," Ryder sneered.

Niko tugged at the binding at his left wrist and a satisfied grin stretched his lips when the rope snapped and fell to the metallic walkway, repeating the action with his left wrist and ankles. The panicked flutter of Amir, Ryder and Asher's hearts burst in his eardrums and a dangerous smirk spread over his throbbing face.

"You were saying?" he said.

"B-but ... how?" Amir stuttered, shuffling back several paces until Asher and Leo stood between himself and Niko.

"Because I'm an abomination, that's how," Niko drawled.

With steps as graceful as a cheetah stalking an antelope in the grassy plains of its territory, he approached the amateur hunters. The planes of his broad facial features sharpened and rutted as his boots thudded against the metal walkway above the bubbling vat of water, the dim lighting doing little to hide the eerie tinge of his irises.

Niko's head titled eerily as a depraved grin stretched his face. "You're dead.*"*

The next step he took was met with a warning growl from the rust-coloured Malamute, the dog's stance changing until its head lowered and its lips peeled back to reveal its teeth. Niko tossed it an uncaring look, taking another step before the dog's head twitched and a spray of saliva accompanied its snarl. Before Niko could register the shift in the animal, the Malamute launched itself at him.

Its paws collided with his chest, jaws snapping at his face as he shoved the sled dog from him, staggering back until his boots bridged the ledge of the walkway. He slipped, hands latching onto the metal grid to stop himself from plunging into the searing water. A jarring sense of helplessness came over him as Kotori's voice split across the room and the Malamute paced agitatedly in front of him, inches from Niko's face. Niko shifted his grasp, the metal grate digging into his fingertips as he dragged his upper body further onto the platform. The clinking of claws against metal echoed in his eardrums, a deathly snarl rumbling from the Malamute as it darted forward with a snap of its jaws.

Niko shouted as he darted backward, loosening his grasp on the walkway before his eyes widened and a harrowing bellow of anguish tumbled from his lips as boiling water engulfed his senses, blazing agony over his skin.

A choked sound—part sob, part shout—escaped Niko's lips now as he tipped his head back, fighting to keep his head above the water while the chair he was strapped to sank further beneath the icy, inky water. It lapped against his chin, torn wrists stinging beneath its surface as he struggled against the bindings. A desperate shout laced with anger and terror rang out across the sub-levels of Leon's estate. Leon's indifferent stare seared into his face as the water washed against the bottom of his nose and a flare of panic clutched his chest. Niko fought against the burn of his lungs when the water hovered above his face like a rippling film of plastic.

Bubbles drifted to the water's surface, sending ripples across his liquid prison as he thrashed. He knew it would do little to free him and he knew this suffocating feel of drowning. But, with a bellow muffled by the water, he blinked back the black spots distorting his vision, clutching to the promise he'd made to Nyx. Even if it'd been a simple reassurance after he'd almost died, he'd meant every word.

"I'm not going anywhere."

A soft smile stretched his lips beneath the burn of his lungs and the choking feeling wrapping its fingers around his throat as his mind perfectly crafted the silvered tone of Nyx's voice and the way her onyx irises flecked with grey peered up at him, her features bathed in the tangerine light of a bonfire.

"Promise?"

"I promise."

Maybe it was the only thing keeping Niko sane or his mind's way of distracting him, but his memories never failed him, never failed to punctuate his senses with Nyx's scent of book pages and coconut. Never failed to recall the feel of his lips against hers in a kiss filled with the weight and conviction of the things he had said and other things he had left unsaid. *"I'm not going anywhere, anytime soon."*

His tortured mind shifted to some point in the universe where he was Eros—the light and Nyx was his Psyche—the darkness to his lifeful allure. He focused on that, on *anything* aside from the terror of drowning.

He focused on her—his everything.

XV

Nyx

"Ryder!" Amir bellowed, his dark gaze brimming with anguish as he broke free of Niko's grasp and hurriedly searched the fabric of his clothes.

*He whirled on Niko and pulled a crudely sharpened stake from the waistband of his pants, plunging it into Niko's chest with a ferocity and rage that resounded in Nyx's ears. Something in her urged her feet to move before she could comprehend her actions. Why hadn't Kotori and Kade moved until she turned her head in search of Orion? Where was he? Nyx's head whipped back to Niko and Amir at the same moment Amir raised his arm to plunge the stake into Niko's chest again. The killing blow registered in her mind as something clicked in her head, and she struggled against Kotori's hold. Her actions were rushed and panic-driven, she had to do something—*anything*—to prevent Amir from killing Niko.*

Everything seemed to move in slow motion, at least in her mind. One minute she was thrashing against Kotori's arms around her waist, desperate to save Niko from Amir's crudely sharpened stake, the absolution in Amir's eyes as his hunter's arm moved and Niko's eyes widened and the next—

An agonised shout escaped Nyx's lips, body jolting upright, senses muddled as she blinked away the dream, the memories, heart racing. Tobias's dark eyes surveyed her, hand outstretched toward her like he was about to wake her. Nyx's eyes widened as she doubled over, hands gripping the leather seats when a burning rushed through her lungs and she struggled to breath, choking on the phantom presence of water, wrists smarting with pain as if her flesh was torn and coated with salt. *Whose memories are these?* she wondered frantically, screwing her eyes shut against the sensations as the twins' muffled voices skirted her ears. Her head lashed from side to side as if to ward off something attacking her. *No, not me*. Him. *Them. What is Leon doing to them?*

It took her a moment to realise where she was—not atop Elveszett Bluff at dusk with her heart lodged in her throat as oxygen flooded her lungs and the swell of sensations fled. Her frantic gaze searched for Ares in the backseat of Alexander's car before she remembered. He was at the twin's shared apartment, the trio having diverted to the home above the comic store before they'd started through the city's suburbs, heading east to the Candence, the club Azeil had informed her about …

As she shoved the last remnants of sleep from her mind, she offered a shaky smile of reassurance to Tobias and Alexander, who leaned upon the car's centre console with concern.

"You're not okay, Night," Tobias murmured, gaze darting to his brother when she jerked her head up, jittering.

"F-fine," she said, cringing internally at the coarseness of her voice and the faint break of the word. "I'll be okay, it was just a dream …"

A memory *you can't shake from your mind,* her subconsciousness crooned, reminding her of a night tinged with bloodshed, anguish and loss that she continued to relive. The cruel dreams starring her uncle and his death, the phantom wet warmth of his blood clinging to her hands plagued her. *A bond set to torment you with another's pain,* another fragment of her mind murmured while she rubbed the back of her neck and tucked her hair behind her ears, Tobias eyed her with an air of doubt before Alexander's car door opened and closed, and he appeared at his brother's shoulder.

"What is it, Nyx? That didn't seem like a dream," Alexander pressed, picking at his T-shirt.

Nyx frowned, instilling a look of calm despite the agony in her body and the sweat dappling the back of her neck and spine. "I'm okay, really. I've just … got a lot on my mind, I … haven't been sleeping," she said. Which was true. *Mostly.*

Alexander hummed doubtfully, leaning into the car's door, ankles crossed. "I don't believe you," he said.

"You don't *have to.* It's the truth."

His brows twisted, head angling before an unamused, huff-like laugh fell from his lips. "It's not, Nyx. You're not okay, but that in itself *is* okay." His voice shifted several octaves, taking on a soothing undertone. "You don't *have to* be okay, not with us."

They're not ok, she thought, and the knowledge seemed to crush her further. She had to find them. *I'm barely coping with my own pain*, her mind swam. *Adding theirs is ... killing me.*

"Nyx?" Tobias nudged her.

Nyx looked at Tobias, at first without really seeing him. In her mind's eye, an endless road of pain stretched ahead, yawning into the distance. She could still choose. *I still have choices*, she thought. *There's still time. I won't be led where I don't want to go.* Slowly, the twin's concerned faces came into focus. Nyx blinked. She straightened her spine and squared her shoulders, plastering a steel-infused wall between herself and the pain. If she hadn't been so distracted by her memories and dodging the twins' concern, she would've noticed the pulsing thrum of music gliding out from beneath the bouncer bracketed doorway. It was sectioned off by rope barricades, clustered with groups of people waiting to get inside the popular club, a sprawling font etched in cherry-red light over the doorway. *Cherry-red, like blood.*

The Candence was a newly opened venue, its marble columns and front steps better suited to a museum or library than a club with its elaborate light fixtures decked in bronze and the gauzy curtains attached to its high ceilings, billowing in the saline breeze as if it wished to free itself from the columns in ethereal arcs.

Nyx jolted, unfastening her seatbelt, and jumping from the backseat before she whacked Tobias's shoulder. "Why didn't you wake me sooner? We're here, aren't we?"

"First off, that hurt," Tobias drawled, rubbing his left bicep. "Second, we thought you could use some sleep and it's not like the club's going anywhere."

"The club might not be, but they could be inside and the longer we wait, the less likely we'll find them!" she almost squealed, a jittery stutter quickening the thudding of her heart. "No more dead ends, remember?"

"Well—"

"Then c'mon, what are we waiting for?" Joining the back of the steadily moving line, Nyx tossed a strained smile over her shoulder. She was going through the motions, but each step felt like wading through sand.

Tobias knocked his shoulder into hers. "What if we don't find anything?"

She sighed, her hand delving into the pockets of her jeans to retrieve the plastic ID card stamped with her face and date of birth. "Then we leave and don't look back." She worried her bottom lip between her teeth, showing the bouncer her ID before the twins. He nodded curtly, dismissing her as the trio climbed the marble steps and passed over the threshold. "Except if—"

"No, Nyx," Alexander interjected, tossing a terse look around the veranda-like outside for those who sought reprieve from the lights, and pulsing music. "We're not chasing after ghosts or what if's. You said—"

"But—" she tried again as Alexander stepped close, Tobias's hand resting against the small of her back, determined not to lose her amid the throng of clubbers.

Tobias's voice, the octave several decibels higher so she'd hear him over the music, carried. "We're *not* wasting time on lost causes, not tonight," he said.

Maybe, she thought with a sweep of the room around her. Her skin felt stretched taut across her cheekbones, her eyes seemed to burn hotly. The slight hallway they wandered down was bracketed with cherry-red lights shaped as squares, built into the walls, ceiling, and floor; spaced evenly every several metres. The sprawling font of the venue's name spanned the hall's end, the screaming red matching her pain. The colours dappled her skin and elicited a shiver down her spine when her hearing noted the sensual opening riffs of a rock song, the rhythmic percussion of the drums kickstarting her heart in the same moment the bass chords layered the song, and the vocalist's distinct voice filled her ears.

She turned to Alexander with an expectant look, ignoring the throbbing pain. "Do you know who's playing here tonight?"

He frowned in concentration, feet thudding against the red-tinged marble floors while they neared the hallway's winding end. "They're a pretty *big* rock band from Fayböurne," he said.

"But *who* are they? What's the band's name?" she pressed, trying to latch on to something to distract from the birthing monster inside her. Quickly, she masked the grimace across her features after a knife-like stabbing sensation punctured her stomach and they rounded the bend of the hallway before it opened out to an enormous area that reminded her of a temple, like the ones depicted in books of old.

Marble pillars, like the ornately carved columns gracing the exterior, decorated the room with large six-metre gaps between them and gauzy curtains bathed in crimson light. Plush, velvet couches the deepest shade of maroon and sleek black, obsidian tables with small but fanciful chandeliers bejewelled with crystals sat nestled between them. The entirety of the club was plunged in crimson that did little to hide the dome-like carving of the ceiling, stunning and intricately designed marble dotted by a circle of orange-red light that poured to the floor like water down a waterfall. At the back of the room, furthest from the entrance, was a stage that spanned much of the back wall. Its light fixtures, metal scaffolding, microphone stands, raised platforms and amps, were decorated however the performing band wished.

Judging by the stage setup with its raised platform for the drummer and incandescent light show with pyrotechnic machinery along the stage's edge, Nyx could see the performing rock band had spared no expense, putting the show in showmen. But she supposed it might not have been the elaborate setup that drew the attention of the dancing and elated screams from the crowd, that it could've been something as simple as being a part of something greater. Even if it only lasted a moment. Or it could've been the glam rock allure of the band, tying rock music eternal to the modern age in a way she wasn't sure she'd seen anyone master. At least, not in her lifetime, but she wondered if Niko had seen anything like this and for a moment, she *almost* turned to Alexander at her side, mistaking his presence for Niko's.

Nyx suddenly wished with all her might that he was Niko. She *wanted* to share *the Candence* with him. Knowing he would love the performing band as much as she did, she could almost picture the sparking of his cyanic irises or the way his calloused fingers would twitch at his sides when a particular guitar riff captured his attention, itching to play the chords on his guitar. Instead, she tamped down the longing in her chest and refocused on the heady sex in the form of lyrics on the stage, wandering away from the twins with a soft murmur for them all to meet back at the entrance in an hour.

She might have been without the sun to her moon, but she wouldn't give up on Niko or Kade and Kotori. They'd saved her life after Ryder had driven a stake through her, mistaking her for a halfling before he'd left her to die on the floor of the cave.

It was only fair that now she save theirs.

A life for a life.

XVI

Nyx

Within the shadows of a crimson-lit booth tucked between the ethereal columns, velvet caressed Nyx's bared arms as she shifted, her insides rioting viciously. A sheen of cold sweat draped her spine and the nape of her neck, and she was aware of the sound of panting. The nightclub distractions were not easing the burn of her gums or her pulsing agony. The incandescent lights, heavy rock music, and abundant scents in the club were not helping her clawing instincts at all. Instead, they seemed to beckon, taunting her to staunch her agony with the irreversible death of an innocent.

Hch-a-hch-a-hch-a. With a start, Nyx realised the panting sounds were coming from her. Her dark irises flared, appraising the crimson club, trailing over dancing guests and looking for a glimpse of Alexander or Tobias. The twins had disappeared into the bustling venue after she'd told them to meet back at the stairs in an hour, forking off in opposite directions. They'd gone to scope out the hallways tucked beside the stage on either side, while she'd wandered toward the crowd, enthralled by the rock band on the stage. That'd been half an hour ago.

Part of her was grateful that neither of them would see the clammy quality of her skin, the tremble of her hands or the permanent grimace twisting her face as cleaving, breath-snatching bolts of pain raked her frame. They wouldn't hear her panting like a … *like a beast,* she thought, fighting an irrational desire to laugh. Her heightened senses collided against her skull like a sledgehammer, thudding continuously before her ears pricked and she turned toward two men who grappled near a marble pillar to her left, the lights of the stage a halo. Glass shattered against the polished floor as one of them slammed the other onto a tabletop.

It took her a moment to note their appearances, an ash-blond pinned to the dark surface of a tabletop by a raven-haired man with silvered irises, the corded muscles of his tattooed arms bunching to keep the man beneath him pressed to the table. In the blink of an eye, the man below twisted, slipping from his captor's grasp before the pair circled each other like lions contending their territory.

Entranced by the brewing violence, Nyx's laboured breathing eased. She leaned over, watching as the brunette strode forward and the blond met him halfway. The *thwack* of a fist colliding with flesh sounded in her eardrums, followed by a soft grunt of pain as the brunette staggered back several paces before righting himself and starting forward once more. She winced in pain, twisting her lips in the same moment the silver-eyed man curled his fist and swung, the bones of his knuckles colliding with the blond's nose. The sickening *crunch* followed by the tangent smell of copper and something sweet burst in her nostrils. Blood gushed from the blond's nose and he scrambled to cup his face.

Nyx bolted from the shadowed seating area, eyes wide as the racing of her heart thrummed in her veins. A desire to quench an insatiable itch dragged its talons across her throat as she forced herself away, through club-goers, in the opposite direction, trying to get away from them, until the light of the sensual hallway beside the stage engulfed her. She felt how her control seemed to wax and wane, her nails sinking harshly into her palms as her mind churned. *End it now, Nyx. They're just cattle awaiting your beck and call,* crooned a darkly timbred voice that faintly resembled her own. Confusion and conflict harried her as she pivoted at the hallway's end, gaze darting between the three forking corridors. *Which way was out?*

With a soft sound tinged with pain, she darted down the empty corridor decorated like the club's entrance to her right. Dark wooden doors dotted the hallway, silvered Roman numerals screwed to their centres as she approached one and grasped the handle, stifling a groan when it ceased to turn. Darting to the next door, she barely registered the three digits above as she twisted and pushed, relief guttering pain as the door swung open. She slipped inside. Her back pressed into the dark wood, head tipped back. *Hch-a-hch-a-hch-a.* Recollection seared her skin and the three digits on the door registered in her mind too late.

A throat cleared with an air of expectancy, snuffing out her short-lived relief as her eyes snapped open. Her head swung toward a lavish seating area, a black table surrounded by black leather couches sprawled on a darkly coloured rug. Soft chandelier lighting illuminated a man occupying one of the settees, one ankle propped on his slack-clad knee. A woman in a tiny black dress trembled beside his leg with a split lip and a trickling gash across her forehead.

Fury seized Nyx, requiring everything in her to contain it. Her hands twitched at her sides before she rolled her shoulders and dragged her gaze from the woman in black to the forest-green of the man's irises. His pristine white dress shirt contrasted starkly with the leather furniture as he swirled amber liquid in a cut crystal glass.

"Hello, Nyx," Leon drawled, a charismatic smile curling his lips. "It's been too long since we last spoke, don't you think?"

Nyx eyed the man disdainfully. "It hasn't been long enough for my liking, *Leon*."

"Don't tell me you're holding a grudge too?" he said in a bored tone, bringing the glass to his lips, and downing the amber in one swallow. "You and Orion seem to have more in common than I thought."

"I'm surprised you're surprised. Isn't it common for people to *want* you dead?"

A muscle twitched in his jaw before he moved, quicker than thought. The glass he'd held clinked on the surface of the table at the same time his hand curled tight around her throat. Something ancient and terrifying swam in his gaze, freezing her as she strained to hold his stare. His fingertips pressed harshly into the soft flesh, making it difficult to breathe.

"*Careful, fledgling.* You're only alive right now because I willed it."

"Are you sure?" she goaded, her voice rasping and odd to her own ears. "From what I remember, *you* wanted me dead. *You* left me for dead after you'd told me I'd die. Like you *thought* I would." She paused as his grasp tightened. "I guess you don't know everything, huh?"

Leon tutted, squeezing until her eyes widened and the little oxygen she'd inhaled was snatched from her. "You're forgetting something, Nyx. Much like my sons keep forgetting who I am and what I've done for them."

"Like keeping them imprisoned?" she choked, straining to get the words out.

Leon glanced at the woman on the floor, trembling with terror. "You haven't completed the transition yet," he said it almost in surprise. "But that's okay, I'm here to ensure you do. Well, *she's* here to ensure it," he corrected, gesturing to the woman behind him.

"I'm not going to kill her," Nyx fought out.

"Aren't you?" Leon prompted, a knowing glint to his gaze. He smiled lazily.

She thought of the glass prison, the invisible dome and lack of control enforced by a simple otherworldly command. She felt sick. "No, I won't."

"Are you sure?"

Nyx's gaze narrowed, determined as she held his stare. "Over my dead body," she spat.

Leon hummed, eyeing her for a moment. "Unfortunately … I don't want you dead. Not anymore, at least. I *need* something from you, and I can't get it if you're … no longer with us." He chuckled at his own joke. "I know now that I should have *personally* ensured you got in through those pearly gates but since you're determined to live. I plan to make your immortal life hell."

Nyx's hands raised against her violation, grasping his as her lungs screamed. "Do your … worst. It won't … do you … any good."

"Maybe not but I'll enjoy watching you fight my commands. You did such a *wonderful* job at fighting them before… and not many can once their will leaves them. My girls certainly can't. It was quite admirable, really. You," he peered closely at her, his eyes seeming to find her very essence, "are stronger than most."

Nyx shrank inside from his gaze. She felt naked and hollow and like he could see right down to everything that made her, *her*. His eyes exposed her very self, like he could see her changing, see what she was becoming … and he understood. The ancient vampire murmured before something shifted across his features and he stooped down so his soulless green eyes filled her sight. She felt the words more than heard them.

"*Feed. Complete the transition.*"

A garbled whine tumbled from her lips, her eyes screwing shut against the glass dome prison her subconsciousness threw up, pounding subconscious fists against the smooth barrier as the pain that'd faded away upon Leon's appearance returned ten-fold and with a vengeance. Agony seared her gums, her fingernails digging into her palms when Leon released her and air rushed into her lungs with a ragged breath. Her insides felt as though they were being stretched and spun, then set on fire. She felt his satisfaction at her pain, his desire to ruin her—to crush her will.

The twisting of the door handle and the clinking of its mechanisms drew Leon's gaze away from Nyx, a disgruntled sniff skittering to her ears before he whirled and disappeared behind a large bookshelf that swung on silent hinges. A resounding thud accompanied the doorway's closure before the door through which she'd come opened to reveal Tobias and Alexander. Their eyes roved over Nyx as she staggered away from the doorway and over to the trembling woman with the split lip. Alexander hurriedly sidestepped her and gently helped the woman to her feet, guiding her past Nyx and out the door as Tobias made for Nyx. His grip was iron on her forearms as she lunged at the bleeding woman, her irises white-gold. A dangerous snarl clawed up from the depths of her chest.

"Nyx, this isn't you," he stated, directing her deeper into the room while she sucked in ragged breaths of air. A shaky hand lifted to cup her neck as she sank to the carpeted floor and Tobias pulled her into his lap. "It's okay, just breathe. You're safe now. We've got you."

She groaned in agony, blistering heat racing through her bloodstream, vision darkening. She was dimly aware of Alexander returning as he deftly closed the door, locking it with a quick twist of his wrist before crouching down beside his brother. His fingers wove through Nyx's as she gasped. She pressed her cheek into Tobias's shoulder, seeking to rid herself of the wave-like pulses of pain consuming her senses.

"Make it stop," she moaned, her silvered voice muffled.

They could do nothing but hold on tightly, whispering soft assurances that did nothing. Time seemed to pass.

She whipped her head to Alexander, the white-gold discoloration of her irises burning like a wildfire. "Please, Alex. Make it stop."

Alexander swallowed thickly. “I can’t do that, Night,” he said.

“You have to … *please,* ” she begged, crying out as a blistering bolt sheared off the edge of her heart. “If you kill me, it’ll go away.”

“We’re not going to kill you,” Tobias stated firmly.

“Please—”

A loud protest of groaning wood startled the trio as the door flung open and a platinum blond loomed on the threshold. Orion strode into the room, slamming the door with a backwards kick before he crossed the room and crouched down in front of Nyx. He glanced at the twins as Alexander and Tobias froze beneath his scrutiny. His eyebrows raised, confidence bleeding into his body as his all-black form rippled, hiding little of the definition of his taut form when he angled his head and the snake curling around a cross earring swung back and forth.

“I was starting to think you wouldn’t come back,” Nyx croaked.

The unearthly blue of Orion’s irises softened, like the tone of his orotund voice as he subtly gestured for the twins to leave. “I made a promise, didn’t I?” he murmured, a fissure of satisfaction in his diamond-shaped features.

Tobias gingerly removed Nyx from his lap and the pair reluctantly left.

“But—” she started, cut off by Orion’s movement.

He waited a moment before he hooked an arm beneath her knees, the other winding under her arms before he rose and moved to the plush cushions of the leather couch, sinking into the fabric with her in his lap. With a gentleness that surprised Nyx, despite the chaos in her head, Orion brushed a strand of hair behind her ear, cupping her cheek within his hand.

“I was *always* coming back … I just had to deal with some pests first,” he assured, his fingers grasped her chin, angling her head while he scrutinised the white-gold of her irises. “It couldn’t wait any longer either. Not with how long you’ve drawn out the transition.”

Her tongue darted out to wet her bottom lip. “I—just … I *need* more time.”

Orion’s lips pursed, a sympathetic glint dappling his eyes. “You don’t *have* more time, little dove.”

“But I can fight it! Just … help me,” her voice wavered, cracking against her wishes.

“I can help you,” Orion assured, concern etched on his face. “If you stop fighting it.”

She opened her mouth to protest, the response perched on the tip of her tongue before Orion sighed and his hands cupped both sides of her face, his glacier gaze cutting a clear path into her chest.

“Nyx, listen to me. If you keep fighting the change, it’ll kill you.” His voice lowered, taking on a soft edge she’d never heard from him before. “Do you want that? Do you want to die?”

“You said you could help me, were you lying about that as well?” she said, her lip curling as pain, pain, so much pain wiped out thought.

Something pleading and foreign crawled across Orion's features, his gaze darting away from her as if the room around them would provide him with answers. A deep frown creased his forehead when his gaze met hers and stuck. "I *need* you to help me. Help me, help *them.*" His thumb caressed her cheek, a desperate edge to his eyes. "I *can't* help them without you."

She swallowed thickly as the promise she made on Elveszett Bluff caught in her mind and his irises pierced her soul. Despite everything he'd done to her, she couldn't condemn Niko, Kotori or Kade—she wouldn't condemn them to a fate Leon controlled. She knew their pain was hers. She'd felt it, felt *them*, and the feeling was living death. It was worse than the pain that gripped her now. She could bear all the pain in the world, as long as it was her own.

"*Yes,*" she murmured, noting the barest angling of Orion's head as she held his gaze with steel-infused determination. "I'll help you, just *please* … make it stop."

XVII

Nyx

Neon lights and a cornucopia of sound jostled Nyx's senses as a heady tide of saline wind buffeted her back, and the buttery whiff of popcorn burped out over the night. The sky above was blotchy and a twinkling of stars peeked out from beneath ragged cloud cover while she rested on a barricade and waited for Orion's return. It'd been several tens of minutes since he had disappeared into the nightlife, sinking into the ever-moving passers-by in search of her meal—the ticket to her immortality and freedom from the pain—and she hadn't glimpsed him once.

She wondered as her stare appraised strangers, if the twins lingered beside the windows of their apartment above the comic store, gazing out across the boardwalk with jittery unease after she'd climbed onto the back of Orion's bike, and they'd left the *Candence* behind those hours earlier.

Delighted screams tinged with wonder boomeranged in her ears, distracting her from her thoughts. The throbbing pain in her temples and abdomen had seemed to retreat to a bearable level since Orion's appearance. A fact she reminded herself to ask him about when he returned from his search for someone worthy—*unfortunate*—enough to garner his interest.

While he searched on her behalf, Nyx mulled over the choice she was about to make, weighing it. Which path should she take? Choosing one would save her life but shunt her head-first back into that world of blood and darkness. Choosing the other would kill her, kill them, let Leon win. It was a balance she couldn't find, knowing in her heart of hearts which path she'd already chosen—because Leon couldn't win, and because the darkness called to her. It was where she belonged.

Nyx had vowed to never let herself turn away from something she wanted, to deny her truth. She knew on an instinctual level that trying to be something she wasn't would never really stick anyway, that it'd be the worst decision she'd ever make. Even if it was the socially acceptable one. So, with irises as dark as deepest onyx and a halo of neon around her, she raised her head and looked at the boardwalk-goers near the Ferris wheel and the steps leading to the shoreline of Celacali. *Was this for the greater good?*

It never failed to surprise her the popularity of the tourist destination, the clusters of children darting past with beguiled grins and carnival bags in their hands, the plastic crinkling as they tore around the rides. *The children*, she thought again, as the idea snagged. Leon and the children. The two were more opposite than night and day, and they were wrong. They shouldn't be in the same sentence together. *More wrong than her?* A plague of questions and unattainable answers whirled like a cyclone.

Then, as though a bolt of electricity raced through her veins, Nyx's stare caught the approaching figure of Orion. He cut a striking image all in black through the lively crowd of tourists and locals. His stride was measured and self-assured, and he seemed to part people to the right and left of him without ever touching them. Like Moses and the Red Sea. He exuded knowledge of the hierarchy he apexed—a predator amongst the prey and somehow … they knew it too. Before Orion caught her staring, Nyx quickly masked her curiosity behind disinterest as he came to her side, hip against the barricade.

With irises as striking and eerily blue as glaciers, Orion peered down at her, waiting for Nyx to turn to him before the clicking of a lighter sounded and the nicotine scent of smoke cloyed in her nostrils. A smug smirk uplifted the edges of his lips when she turned to him, tendrils of white-grey smoke curling around his face like the serpent tattooed on his wrist.

She gestured for him to speak with a curt flick of her wrist and raised eyebrows. *Using your own tricks against you,* she thought.

Orion rolled his eyes with a zealous shake of his head, bringing the cigarette up to his lips to take another drag before he blew out a breath of smoke. "I found your … *meal*."

"And?" she prompted, gaze darting to the passers-by.

"*And*, it's time you learned the thrill of the hunt," he said, angling his head mockingly when Nyx made a low sound of disapproval. "What? Did you think I was going to hand them to you on a silver platter?"

"That would've been nice," she mumbled, toeing the ground with her shoe.

Orion tutted, dropping his cigarette to the floorboards before squashing it under his heel. "That's not how this," he gestured vaguely between the two of them, "works."

She pushed herself off the steel barricade, folding her arms. "How does *hunting* someone help me?"

"How else will you understand your own instincts? You and I aren't the same, therefore, why should our instincts be?"

"Okay …" With a shuddery breath and uneasy rake of her fingers through her curls, Nyx nodded. Her stare clashed with his before she gestured to the nightlife around her, voice hushed and tinged with conviction. "Let's do this."

Orion straightened, eyeing her carefully. "Are you sure?"

"Do I have another choice? You said I didn't *have* any more time so, let's stop wasting it."

"You *always* have a choice, even when it seems like there isn't one. So, I'll ask again. *Are you sure*?"

An image of old-fashioned weighing scales flashed before Nyx's eyes. *The greater good, the bigger bad.* She took a breath and made her choice. "I'm sure."

A moment of silence lingered between them as he seemed to consider her words, his eyes burning blue. Then, the moment passed and he pushed himself off the railing, taking her arm and leading her through passers-by, slipping around the many with slick ease. Watching. Waiting. Stalking. And then striking with a prowess Nyx felt stir in the marrow of her bones. It called to the warped sliver of her being she knew wasn't a fatal flaw. At least, it wasn't to Orion as he led her beside the closed video store.

There, he released her arm and inclined his head to the dankly lit alley beyond.

"Two rights and a left," he murmured, lingering as if he silently passed the reins of control to her.

Nyx paused, fingers twitching at her sides before she sucked in a fortifying breath and started for the shadows. Adrenaline and anticipation curled around her senses. Something eagerly shifted in her chest like a leopard slinking from one tree branch to another, bringing a heady sensation as she rounded the alleyway's corner, trailing her fingers over the chipped bricks. It was like, with every step she took, her body instilled a new strand of her heightened senses into her bones, vibrating through her bloodstream like a live wire or a bomb set to detonate at a moment's notice. Her newfound anticipation—instincts of her vampirism—and the knowledge of Orion's presence faded to nothing. Every fear she'd cradled about her transition rocked away, becoming insignificant as a deeper sensation she'd tucked to the deepest caverns of herself unfurled, creeping to the forefront of her mind.

Soon, they were the only thoughts she possessed.

Nyx blearily wondered why she'd been so scared, energy seemed to ripple throughout her body, she felt alive. Why had she been so adamant about refusing herself this freedom? It suddenly all ceased to matter when she rounded the last corner and paused between several bollards. Her stare trailed over the lamppost-dotted carpark of the lively fairground at her back. A final call of logic battled its way through the Sleeping Beauty thorns of desire that had grown inside her. *What if I can't do this?* she thought, worrying her bottom lip between her teeth as her gaze nestled on a dark-haired man with an ivory-coloured skull tattooed on his bicep. A feature she *shouldn't* have been able to see as clearly as she could from where she stood, several metres away. *What if I just ... can't? What if I choke up at the last moment?*

Suddenly, Orion was behind her, his eyebrows furrowed when she glanced at him, his steely irises ablaze with an inferno she'd seen before. The tell-tale sparks of a pending kill. "You can," he whispered as if sensing her thoughts. "You just have to believe you can."

"But—"

With a soft sigh of fabric, Orion positioned himself in front of her in a way that made Nyx tilt her head back so she could hold his gaze.

He was so close.

"You're capable of *great* things, little dove. Some will be good, and others … will be devastatingly *dark* and *terrible*. It's who you are at heart that matters. Everything else is irrelevant."

Nyx found herself speaking before she could stop herself, "And if I'm a bad person at heart, what then?"

Orion seemed to consider her lips as his curled into a malignant grin. "Then so *fucking be it*. I meant what I said."

She stared, her gaze never faltering. "When?"

"The night you killed Kai," he said, his words almost inaudible, his breath on her.

'You'll never have to be ashamed of those urges with us. Not now. Not ever,' she thought, the words whispered in her head. Somewhere inside her, a spark burst and she … ignited.

He was so close.

Orion gestured pointedly to the dark-haired man who leaned against the hood of his car and Nyx's gaze broke. She looked at the Ivory Skull who lingered alone and knew then why Orion had chosen him. He was one of the men who'd harassed her the night Orion had made his appearance known, the dangerous glint to his eyes revealed the truth to his statement—that he'd never been gone.

"Let it all go, Nyx. *Embrace it.*"

PART TWO

When is a monster not a monster?
When you see its darkness and love it anyway.

XVIII

Nyx

Life is the beginning of all things, the manifestation of a god's will to point out a path to be traversed and followed, the small stirrings of potential. The gift of life was celebrated like the spring solstices on the cusp of a bountiful harvest, the scent of flower pollen permeating a balmy breeze, the condition that distinguishes animals and plants from inorganic matter. But Nyx knew that for there to be one side of a coin, there needed to be another. Life might have been the beginning of all things—a revered occasion wreathed in celebration and delight—but death was the end to all, the other side. At least, that's what the world wanted her to believe.

The soft and defiant crunch of stones accosted Nyx's ears as she stepped toward the dark-haired Ivory Skull, pausing to toss an unsure glance at Orion, who inclined his head toward the man beside his car. It was a little gesture but the push she needed. Nyx knew little about the transition she sought to complete, each crunch of the loose stones eerily in tune with the thudding of her heart, but she understood the actions she needed to take. The first had been the easiest; *ingest the blood of an immortal.* A decision she hadn't made but couldn't loathe. Not in the cloud-covered darkness of the night or with the shadowy presence of Orion behind her. The weight of his steely gaze seared into the middle of her back as the knowledge of his actions drifted across her mind. From there, it'd been like a slow-acting poison, leeching into her bloodstream until she couldn't ignore its presence and agony cleaved a constant path of fire within her body.

Tha ... thump, tha ... thump, tha ... thump.

With the screams of adrenaline-induced zeal and the clattering of rollercoaster wheels on tracks shooting the sky above her, Nyx slipped between two cars with otherworldly ease, eliciting a shiver of surprise. Orion had urged her to look at her intended victim—the start of her immortal life—and Nyx knew he'd decided with a symbolic notion in mind; a silent weight of the truth behind his words.

Tha ... thump, tha ... thump, tha ... thump.

The man's dark curls skirted the underside of his jaw, tousled and dancing in the coastal breeze like the tresses of Nyx's own hair, tumbled down her back. She'd have been able to place the man's involvement with the Ivory Skulls even without the ivory ink etched into his bicep, it was written all over him in other ways; dark-washed denim clung to toned legs as he sprawled over the hood of his car. His heavy hands moved from his belt buckle to his groin, crudely asserting himself, but it was the way he looked at her; he leered, and his eyes were flat and hard with the promise of taking without asking.

Nyx knew the last step of her transition lay in the man she stealthily approached; every ounce of fear she'd once felt, now she shoved aside.

An eerie disconnect clicked into place like the pieces of a puzzle long forgotten, awaiting the return of its creator. Nyx knew she wasn't remarkable-looking but the look in the man's eyes—widening in nasty delight—told her otherwise. He straightened the hemline of his black T-shirt and angled his body toward her with a grin while she feigned disinterest, darting her gaze to her fingernails.

Tha ... thump, tha ... thump, tha ... thump.

"Not interested, huh?" he drawled, referencing their past interaction. A smug cat-who'd-cornered-the-canary look seeping over his face.

Nyx's gaze flicked up beneath her lashes. Her shoulders rose in a nonchalant shrug that drew his attention to her neckline. A betraying glance she caught with dark satisfaction, a preening hum zinging through her bloodstream. She feigned a look of intrigue. *If he wants the naïve and innocent woman, he'll get her ... with a twist,* she thought as the man centred his attention on her.

His gaze became hungry, a look cemented in attainment as his head cocked and his dark brows furrowed. "What happened to the *spitfire* I first met, hm? Or was that just an act?"

As much as Nyx hated the slow step he took toward her, she let him advance with the mistaken assumption that she was interested in him. The weight of Orion's gaze prickled across her skin as the Skull's hands grasped her waist, his fingers splaying over the swell of her hips. When his head dipped beside her ear, Nyx looked up and saw Orion over his shoulder.

"The name's Dries, sweetheart. Remember when I make you scream it," he crooned.

An amused tilt lifted Orion's lips as he breathed out a cloud of white-grey smoke, a mocking widening of his eyes complimenting a delightfully unpleasant zeal.

Nyx fought to stifle a laugh, before she tore her gaze from Orion to Dries, trailing her fingers from the hands at her waist to his broad shoulders with a sliver of, what she hoped, was sensual ease. She wondered if she truly needed to try when Dries' grasp tightened and she pushed herself up onto the tips of her toes, lips brushing against his ear as her stare locked with Orion's.

"Oh, Dries," Nyx crooned, watching Orion as she spoke. "You'll be the one who screams, not me." Orion watched her as excitement burned her like a fever and she wondered what made it better—worse, Orion's eyes or the quickening of Dries' heart.

Tha ... thump, tha ... thump, tha ... thump.

"Wha—"

Before Dries could pull away, Nyx's fingers grasped the collar of his T-shirt, white-knuckling the fabric as the burning, prickling sensation skated over her cheekbones, jawline and eye socket. A faint, cleaving tear rent the upper and lower section of her gums where her canines and incisors elongated to accompany the smooth shift of her features. Like the stinging of her irises as they leeched from brown to white-gold, a sensation she hadn't noticed until—before her mind could register it—she closed her eyes and plunged her fangs into the soft flesh of Dries' throat.

Nyx briefly wondered if she'd regret her actions but it was fleeting. She knew she wouldn't, knew she'd stumbled back into the world she'd thrive in. Like a night-blooming rose unfurls its petals in the darkness, *she knew*. As the coppery quality of Dries' blood coated her lips, filled her mouth, her tastebuds with every euphoric swallow, *she knew* that she'd revel in the bloodshed just like the men who'd dragged her into their world. It wasn't a speculation of her nature, *that* Nyx knew for certain, it was a surety born from the moment she'd met Kade. Nobody had forced her to follow him from the bookstore or to climb onto his motorcycle the following night. She'd gone willingly. *She'd* made that decision. Just like she'd decided to tear into Dries' jugular.

Nobody forced her. This *she knew*.

Tha ... thump, tha ... thump, tha ... thump.

The rustling of fabric startled Nyx from an almost sleep-like reverie as she sensed, more than saw, Orion appear behind Dries, his glacial orbs trained on hers before they snapped open and focused on him.

"Depending on how you want this to go, little dove. It can go two ways," he said.

Nyx's frown prompted him to continue, like the sight of her tearing into Dries' throat was nothing.

"Your bite—*our bite*—is like a class four haemorrhage. We can slow the already ... *painful* process down or quicken the rate of blood loss with a thought. Quickening the process will kill him in under a minute, slowing it could take," his lips pursed as he seemed to consider his words, "it could take *fifteen* minutes of pure agony."

With a ragged breath, Nyx raised her head, crimson dripping down her chin and throat as her white-gold irises held Orion's. Her hands grasped Dries' shoulder tightly, an animalistic aura radiating off her as the dark-haired man struggled, an awful gurgling sound slipping from his lips as they spattered him with his own blood. Nyx's head cocked to the side as she wondered why she didn't feel empathy for him.

Orion tutted mockingly and his hands clamped around Dries' arms, pinning him in place. Stepping forward, Nyx reattached herself to the gushing wound on Dries' neck, pulling mouthfuls of blood into her mouth with desperation derived from months of prolonging her transition.

"Nyx," Orion began, waiting for the low hum that vibrated from her chest before continuing. "Make sure you ruin the flesh of his throat like an animal would."

A grunt of acknowledgement rumbled from her chest as she tightened her grasp and a garbled last groan tumbled from Dries, the man's knees giving out on him while the racing of his heart sought to continue pumping blood through his veins. His lungs rasped with each inhale, the sound mesmerising in her eardrums like the slowing beat of his life-giving organ. It reminded her of the fluttering of a hummingbird's wings and the droning of a jackhammer before silence plunged her senses and she lifted her head, finally. Eyes clamped shut and face tipped to the sky, Dries' corpse was forgotten as she released him and Orion unwrapped his fingers, the Ivory Skull cadaver crumpling to the bitumen with a boneless *thud.*

Nyx swayed as she stood until something wet fell on her cheekbone and she startled, eyes snapping open before another droplet hit her face and Orion's gaze shifted with pride beneath the beginnings of rain. "Why did I have to ruin his … neck?" she murmured, somewhat dazed, raising a hand to wipe the blood.

Orion's lips curled with a dark smirk, delving into the pockets of his jeans before he extended a cobalt handkerchief to her. "It's the beginning of a message."

She accepted the piece of fabric to clean her skin of the remaining stain of blood. "What message?"

With a fluid, dance-like movement, Orion looped an arm around her waist, and steered her away from the cooling body. His eyes locked with hers as he wrapped his arm around her shoulder, leading her away from Dries' corpse with a dark chuckle.

"What message are we sending?" Nyx prompted, not letting the question go.

"That the rulers of Celacali are back and *we* won't kneel to anyone. That Leon can't control us," Orion said, smiling.

Nyx smiled too, her head angled so she could peer up at Orion while he led them past cars to his awaiting motorcycle. "I like that message. It carries the weight of an empire set to fall."

"It's a reminder too."

"Of what?"

Orion glanced down at Nyx, his irises alight with a blue inferno. "That if you mess with one of us. You mess with *all of us*."

XIX

Nyx

"If Dries was our first message," Nyx started as she descended the marble steps of the cave with Orion close behind, "We *need* a course of action for whatever we do next. We can't mindlessly kill Ivory Skulls without a reason."

Her gaze held his as she shrugged her jacket off and draped it over the back of the nearest couch. Moonlight tumbled through the glass-patched ceiling, dappling her shoulders as she dropped and stretched out with a sigh. *It felt good.* It felt like basking in the painless aftermath of completing the transition she'd fought for months. *Why did I fight it?* she wondered, an unnatural buzzing in her bloodstream. It came alongside a sharpness to her senses she couldn't ignore, noticing the bubble-like grooves of the cave's roof and the faint hum of electricity of the hidden light fixtures. *Everything is* ... different. *Like I wasn't really living until I died—*

"Leon," Orion started, interrupting her thoughts, before a grimace twisted his features and his hand pressed against his temple. "Your blood—"

"My blood … what about my blood and Leon?" she said, a frown creasing her forehead as she tried to understand his broken sentences.

"He doesn't want it," Orion gritted out between clenched teeth, like it took everything in him to get the words out.

"You're not making sense, Orion. *Spit it out*," she said, huffing in frustration.

"I *can't*," he snapped, smoothing a hand down his face as he crossed the room and sank into his throne-like chair.

"Why not?" she said as she watched him, the tendons on his neck popping as he gripped his chair.

"Because. Leon. Doesn't *want.* Me. To." Orion's jaw was a hard line as he produced each word like a birth.

She watched in fascinated disbelief as Orion seemed to fight an invisible foe. She saw as his body lost its rigour mortis and he slumped from the exertion. His strained expression replaced by something guarded. Some unacknowledged part of her ached, just a little, at the tremor of distress in his irises—there one minute, gone the next—and then, a thought crept across her mind, whispering suspicions.

"He commanded you, didn't he?" she murmured, unwilling to raise her voice for fear it might wrench Leon's control to the forefront of his mind.

Orion opened his mouth as if he wanted to answer but couldn't, closing it with a flare of disdain. His head shook, condemning him to a prison. One with smooth glass walls that Nyx remembered well.

Her hands balled into fists at her sides to rein in her anger. "Okay," she breathed, nodding as she mulled it over. "What *can* you tell me?"

"That we need to kill four others," he said, a no-nonsense edge to his tone.

"That's … *specific,*" she said, holding his eyes. A huff of laughter, then that unsettling glint she was getting so used to.

"In the months of you playing detective with the twins, what have you learned about Leon?" he said.

"Not much," she admitted, straightening.

"What if I told you what I know?"

A crease cut her brow as she observed the familiar way he now lounged in his chair and pulled a cigarette from an open packet. The stretch of time as he clicked his lighter, lit the cigarette and inhaled, hand upon his knee. This contentment at hiking her desire for answers to an all-time high was displayed in the drawn-out actions of … of nothing! It was maddening and *he knew it!*

"Orion," she pressed, silvered voice laced with her growing frustration as his lips twitched.

"You already know the story of how I met your father, but what you don't know is how the Monroes and Montes' banded together to slay Leon," he said, waiting a moment before he continued. "Azeil was new to his detective career in 2012 and had been put on his first s*erious* case that would lead him to stumble upon the existence of vampires. Do you want to guess whose … *nasty* crimes caught police attention, or should I tell you?"

"Get on with it," she muttered, urging him to continue with a shake of her head.

"Okay, okay," he drawled, lifting his hands in a show of mock surrender. "Leon has a long history in Celacali and none of it is nice. He's notorious for his interest in innocent blood, *children's* blood—"

"*Children,*" she interjected, horror carving a wicked path through her chest. She'd known, *she knew*. The missing children.

"Yes, *children*," he said, wedging the blade of horror deeper into her sternum. "And Azeil was put on a case to find the person responsible for the missing and murdered children that continued to grow on a scale that shocked the city."

"So, you're saying my father *accidentally* stumbled onto Leon's vampirism because he killed children? But what does killing four others after Dries have to do with that? How will that affect Leon?" she said, confusion making itself at home in her head as she waited for Orion to fill in the blanks.

"Because Azeil realised *after* Leon's 'death' that he was the unknown person bailing the Ivory Skulls out of jail."

"Why would he do that?"

"The Skulls are his eyes and ears, little dove. It's how he watched us when we thought he was dead," he explained, providing the first clue.

"Who exactly are we killing and why?"

"Kyree, Viliaris and Mire are Ivory Skulls loyal to Leon. They are favoured by Phaelyn and Qadira enough to be trusted with information from Leon, but Cassia is Leon's … guilty pleasure. He's always adored her—his mortal mayor—and lavished riches upon her over the decades, for *years*," Orion said, scoffing as if the last part left a bitter taste across his tongue.

"Mayor?" Nyx wasn't sure she was getting all of this.

"Yes, mayor," Orion said, lowering his gaze at her. "You know, higher-up official? The face of the city?"

"I can understand the three tied to the Skulls but aside from Leon's … *love* for Cassia—the mayor," Nyx added pointedly, "why are we killing the mayor?" She paused, shaking her head before she hastily rushed to voice her thoughts. "Never mind that, *how* are we getting close to Cassia? The Skulls will be easy enough but her? No way."

"Take it easy, Nyx," Orion cajoled. "Cassia and Mire will be our last kills because they're the highest in Leon's graces and I'd rather dispose of them *with* my pack. Kyree is a confirmation to Leon that we're coming after him and Viliaris dead will tell him that we're coming for Kotori, Niko and Kade, since he has access to Leon's estate and regularly meets with him."

"What about Mire and Cassia?" Nyx asked with dark curiosity.

Orion's lips pursed with consideration as if weighing up whether to tell her. *Or the void of his companions troubled him more than he was willing to let on,* she mused, sensing the tension gathered across his shoulders and neck. *Why else would he wait for their return before disposing of Mire and Cassia?*

"Cassia is my way of saying 'you took something I cared about," Orion finally said. "So now I'll take something of yours. But she's also more than that. Despite her social standing, she doesn't use her sway for good," he stated, watching her watch him. "It's a waste. She has a rare opportunity and she *wastes* it. She could have done something about those kids …"

"I … don't think I follow?" Nyx asked.

“Let’s just say that she’s part of the reason why the disappearances of those children are swept aside. Nobody goes against her,” he said as though the words left a sour taste in his mouth.

Nyx eyed him closely for a long moment, letting his words hang between them before her head dipped and the wrongness of Cassia’s actions settled. Orion wanted to rid the world of Cassia because she stood by—*helped* hide—the crimes Leon committed. Children were taken off the streets of Celacali and slaughtered and people knew they were disappearing but seemed not to know enough to stop it. Although it seemed Cassia’s diligence had faltered if the police knew of Jesse’s disappearance, and it made Nyx wonder why. Why had Jesse slipped through the gap of Cassia’s lies? What was different about him than the others? *How many children had been taken?*

“If Cassia is hiding Leon’s crimes, why do the police know about Jesse?” she asked finally.

“I don’t know,” Orion gave up. “But whatever it is, I only know that her death will go some way to satisfying the debt,” he murmured. “That includes my brothers.” He looked at her and there was no mistaking the longing for his companions haloed in his eyes.

Unsure of how to broach his honesty, she redirected the conversation back to the final name on Orion’s list, “And Mire?”

“Mire is one of Qadira’s favoured mortals and that’s a hard feat to obtain since she rarely finds interest in humans aside from when she kills them,” he said, snuffing out his cigarette. “So, he’s the last piece of these games once I have—” A frustrated curse clanged across the cavernous hideaway as his eyes flashed with ire.

Another sire block, she thought with disdain for the man who puppeteered Orion’s silence. She pushed as much of her determination into her tone, hoping he’d see—*hear*—her silent plea and trust her enough to find a way around the command. To *let* her help him be free of it like they sought to free Kotori, Niko and Kade.

“Whatever you need to find, I’ll help you find it, Orion,” she said, meaning every word. His all-consuming gaze sparked with an emotion she chose to ignore.

“Careful,” he drawled, a lilt to the word that whispered of how much he wanted her not to be. “That sounds like something you *shouldn’t* offer willingly.”

“No?” she murmured, the heady thrumming in her veins prickling like static.

“You don’t offer yourself to monsters, little dove,” he crooned.

A thousand desires filled her and she pushed at them all, shunting them to the depths of her mind, unwilling to acknowledge them or the parts of her soul they whispered to.

“Well, it’s a good thing I joined the club, then,” she breathed, smile fading.

“A good thing indeed,” he drawled, a faint smile ghosting his lips.

Orion’s irises blazed like the centre of a flame, white-hot and entrancing before his orotund voice wrapped around her and she fought to tamp down the pattering of her heart.

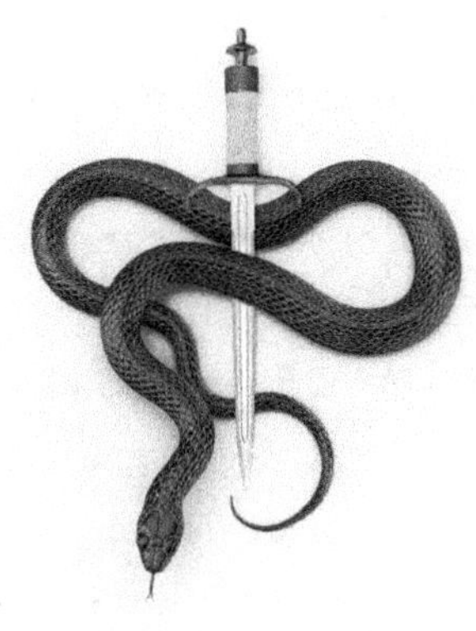

XX

Nyx

"How do you do it?" she asked.

Orion's features were marred by a terse frown when he turned to Nyx, glancing down at her with his shoulder pressed into a shop's front and tendrils of smoke curling around his face. "Do what?"

Nyx breathed out harshly, ringed fingers plucking at the ink-coloured straps of her cargo pants. Her grey-flecked irises darted to Orion in one breath and, in the next, they rested on the passers-by filtering from the car park, through the storefronts, to the fairground portion of the boardwalk.

"How do you decide who lives and dies?" she clarified, these thoughts plaguing her since she'd killed Dries the previous night.

Orion's eyes seemed to gloss over as Nyx turned to him, a tell-tale tremor puncturing the steady beat of his heart. She could hear it, but it was as though he wished to hide his motives behind the reinforced walls of his guard, as his gloved fingers toyed with the silvered bracelet around his wrist.

An unpleasant chill had begun creeping across Celacali and Nyx waited tensely for his answer. Her physical pain had gone, dissipating with the slaking of her thirst. But now a new pain had taken its place—the pain of guilt or discontent or fear … of herself.

Dries' death had thrown up two things, two conundrums since she'd completed the transition. Nyx didn't know whether to be grateful that the pain razoring her insides was gone—gifting her instead with an eerie hum like a temporarily satisfied motor—or disturbed by the sharpness of her senses, the buzz of the neon-lit rides and the scent of a child's scraped knee dragging across her mind. Was she wrong for taking a man's life to save hers? Yes. But Nyx couldn't find it in herself to care, grateful to be given another chance to live a life *she* wanted—to live a life Asher would have wanted for her, and one she hoped her father could be proud of … as disgruntled as his support sometimes was. Then there was the whole greater good, thing. If she'd given up and not transitioned, Leon would have won. For whatever reason, Orion needed her help, and she couldn't just give up when she first had to help them. Kade, Kotori and Niko. They were the catalyst in this whole damn formula. *Them* and *him*. It made her head hurt just trying to unravel it all.

"It's simple," he stated, not realising the effect of his words. He pushed off the store-front and started through the crowd, tossing her a look over his shoulder.

Nyx hurried after him with a frustrated sigh. "How's it *simple*?" she questioned, falling into step. She kept him at arm's length, still so unsure around this man. *Still.*

"Because you don't *have to* pick who lives and dies." He glanced down at her, grasping her elbow before nimbly steering her around a group of rowdy teenagers. "You know those instincts I mentioned earlier? There's a type of … lure we have, it attracts people to us—"

"Like a Venus flytrap attracts flies?"

Orion's unimpressed stare fell on her, his hand releasing her elbow as he sidestepped a small child. "I sometimes wonder why I entertained Kade and Niko's fascination with you. Right now … is one of those times."

Nyx's stride faltered as she brushed several loose curls behind her ears, the half-up, half-down style fastened into a neat braid at the back of her head.

"You are such a self-centred asshole," the words dropped on reflex. "If it wasn't for the others, I would—I would—" *Fuck! I would have, what?* He was so unbelievably … up himself, she could … kill him. But he'd probably enjoy that. Enjoy letting her try. "You're sadistic, petty …" she cast about for a better insult while he watched, seemingly fascinated at the display of struggle on her face.

She knew Orion had saved her life by starting her transition from human to a vampire, but she couldn't forget the events that'd led her to that moment where he'd been forced to help her, or risk her dying. The memories of his fangs tearing into her throat, now that she'd experienced the ease of taking a life by the same means. Why did she feel a smarting of pain at his words? Was it that she'd *willingly* given this lightning storm of a man a piece of herself without her truly knowing?

"Manipulative?" Orion suggested, smirking.

Could it have been the reminders of Niko? Of his cyanic gaze straying to hers before his hands curled around Ares' leash and he too, tucked away a piece of herself she'd gifted him. But, just like she'd given Niko an irreplaceable shard of herself, Nyx had somewhat knowingly given Kade another. Though, she'd handed it to him before she'd known of their natures and with the Avonsano Ocean as her witness. Orion *was* manipulative. He was the king of manipulation and she always played right into his meddling hands.

"Blue-eyed—" Nyx blurted as she scuffed her boot against the wooden planks, she didn't know *why* Orion's words pained her, but they did. He *hurt* her and it always seemed to come as a shock. "Royal pain in my ass," she finally flung the insult at him, not caring.

There was the slightest flick of a widening pupil. Then it was gone.

"That's right," she said, realising too late her unwitting use of the word royal. She ran her tongue along the edge of her canines. "You wanted me *dead* in an unmarked grave for my father to find."

Orion's demeanour visibly cooled. "And yet, here," he gestured toward her and the nightlife around them, "you stand. In one piece. Your heart is *still* beating."

"Not from lack of trying," Nyx bit back acidly.

"I saved your life." He pivoted on the spot, ignoring glances his presence elicited. "Twice."

"Because *you* endangered it, to begin with."

"I did it for them!" Orion's orotund voice carried true and sharp, drawing the attention of passers-by before he strode toward her and grasped her.

Leading her, albeit gently, to an awning-shrouded boutique that sold plants and flowers, the leaves of a monstera brushing her hand as they slipped around the building's corner. Assorted pots of flowers from peonies to daisies brightened the side-street that forked off beside the abandoned hideaway Nyx knew well. He abruptly released her before putting space between them. And when he spoke again, his tone was soft, laced with something she *almost* mistook for anguish and guilt; like whatever he was about to say kept him up at night.

"It's *always* been about them … for as long as I can remember. Even your involvement in our lives was for them."

She held her breath, dread coiling sinister in her stomach.

"And now … look where that has got them."

Nyx's spine straightened beneath the weight of his words, shoulders squaring, chin raising as a prickling crept at her eyes—tears wishing to tumble down her cheeks. "Don't you *dare* blame me. I didn't do anything to them—I couldn't if I tried."

Orion spun, his irises eerily punctuated in the alleyway's darkness. "Didn't you? I go to sleep knowing *I'm* the reason my brothers are tortured," he hissed.

Nyx's eyes widened with his words.

"What? You thought they were free? That Leon *forbade* them from seeing you?" he uttered, surveying her with keen eyes.

"I—"

"I *feel* their pain, hear their screams, smell their blood and I *see* their torment through our shared bond. A bond you're now a part of so, strap in for those sleepless nights, *little dove*."

"You mean days," she muttered, her gaze dropping as her admission slinked across the alleyway and Orion's stare prickled her face.

"What?" he said, "You know?"

"I feel their pain too, Orion," she said quietly, her words twisting her face as she looked up at him. "It's worse than anything I could ever …" She shrank back as he moved towards her.

"You've already felt their pain. *How?*" he asked, seeming to grow larger.

Nyx let confusion guide her as she shook her head. "I—the bond?"

"Only a *vampire* can feel its pack's pain, and you hadn't completed the transition yet," Orion said, filling in the blanks of her knowledge before a sharp curse tumbled from his lips. Ire heated his eyes. "*Leon*. Of course."

"Of course, what? I'm not following," she said.

"A sire can manipulate a pack bond to *force* perceived pain onto whoever they wish. It's frowned upon by vampires—dangerous to someone's will," Orion said, his stare burrowing into her. "Force too much of someone's will onto another and they'll lose themselves … use too many sire-commands too often, and they'll become mindless—*puppets*."

"Why are you just—"

"Telling you now?" Orion interjected, dragging his leather-clad fingers agitatedly through his hair. "Because my decision to save *your life* cost me Kotori, Niko and Kade. And as much as I try to look over that because they'd want me to, I can't. Every time I look at you it's a reminder of what I did. *I* tainted the bloodline."

The golden glow of his lighter flame leapt across his features as he struck it, disappearing in a sharp inhalation of nicotine and an angrily exhaled breath of smoke. His next words cut.

"I should've let you die."

His words were a knife thrown with lethal precision and Nyx stumbled a step backward. Her eyes stung with traitorous tears and when she spoke, her retort was mashed with the hurt he caused her and the agony of the missing trio's presence. "I *hate* you."

Orion scoffed, a malignant smirk uplifting his lips. "You say that so often, I wonder what your basis for comparison is."

* * *

Bold, capitalised letters adorned the police tape fluttering in the buffering wind, dark and unforgiving clouds lingering above the fairground clustered with news channel vans, police, and a coroner's vehicle. Officers darted back and forth across the bitumen, some keeping the growing crowd and reporters back while others blocked boardwalk-goers' view of the body Nyx knew lay behind their makeshift black cloth barricade. The flashes from cameras bathed the blue metal stones with light, followed by the incessant exclamations from news reporters to the officials tasked with the murder she'd committed, Orion at her side—their combined frustration with each other manifesting in the grisly nature of the raven-haired, Ivory Skulls' death.

"Chief Silvia!" called a blonde dressed in a dusty-grey pantsuit, her hair fastened to the middle of her head in a neat bun. "What can you tell us about the death of Kyree Adams, a member of the Ivory Skulls? Was this a gang-related attack?" she paused briefly to allow an answer, and when none came, forged on, "Any leads to suggest the murders committed by Kai Salas, charged with multiple counts of murder three months ago, are linked to these deaths by a copycat?"

Nyx couldn't hear the answer, if there was one. *Kyree Adams*, she mused. From beside the mouth of the alleyway, Orion loomed beside her, his shoulder pressed into the bricked walls, waiting. *Another name for another corpse on our list,* she thought.

"They're like vultures," Orion stated, gesturing to the reporter who continued to toss question after question at the dark-haired chief of police.

Silvia's aquamarine eyes locked on the woman with an air of authority. His entire body language exuded an unwavering edge Nyx respected, immediately understanding why her father spoke so highly of him.

"They're *always* the first on a scene after the police. Like vultures," Orion said.

"And what does that make us? Hyenas?" Nyx questioned, glancing at him, their previous tiff still smarted.

"Hyenas?"

"Don't they wait for the apex predator to leave the carcass before they descend?"

Her eyes trailed over the flashes of red and blue lights atop the police cars scattered around the lot, recalling the savagery of their attack on Kyree. Just as they'd planned the Skulls' death to be since Orion had revealed the ties the gang held to Leon; the sire vampire's eyes and ears who had watched his sons in his 'absence' in exchange for their 'immunity' from the police. Their petty crimes were swept under the rug with a few careful manipulations. *I wonder when Dad learned about Leon's ties to the Ivory Skulls,* she thought, curiosity prickling her mind.

"But we're not waiting to *descend* on him for the scraps of our leftovers."

"Then what are we doing? Because I don't understand why we have to be here."

A disbelieving breath passed from Orion's lips. "So, there's no satisfaction in the aftermath of the kill for you?" he prompted with a knowing hum, smirking when Nyx tossed him a glare.

The metallic tang of Kyree's blood cloyed on Nyx's tastebuds, and she thought of how the man's blood had coated her skin hours before a passer-by found his body and alerted the authorities. Now she was one of two perps lingering on the outskirts of the parking lot, revelling silently in their crime. She thought of Kyree's garbled pleas as they rolled across both their bonded minds lazily. Thick and weighty like his blood. Nyx wondered why, as she had when she'd murdered Dries, she didn't feel ashamed. Was it because of Orion? Some inane sense of righteousness in disposing of the corrupt?

It didn't matter. Whether it was Orion's presence or the taut bond between them after the lingering effects of their argument. Nor did it matter to her if she found comfort in the murder of men who'd harassed her. Hadn't she said men had done far worse for less? She'd always been open about her opinions, voicing them for Niko and Kade to hear with little regard for the consequences of her words—not that they'd ever judged her. But it made her wonder why Orion supported her actions, despite his callous and obvious enjoyment in killing. Did he feel obligated to? Was it for Kotori, Niko and Kade like he'd said? Or was there something else?

"Nyx!" came a distant shout from across the parking lot, breaking her morbid train of thoughts before she glanced at Orion and then to the direction of the voice.

With soft curls cut to the nape of his neck and eyes a shade of Argentine-blue, a big man jogged over from his position beside the veiled area near Kyree's body, away from the crime scene, the white of the forensics logo stark upon his chest. Nyx eyed the blond in black carefully, trailing her gaze over his plain T-shirt, jeans and boots, the silver of his jewellery catching her eyes before she met his. Out of the corner of her eye, she saw Orion survey the forensics scientist frigidly.

"You are …?" he asked.

Nyx fought a sudden urge to grin, watching the unnamed man as he glanced unsurely at the imposing presence of Orion … *so territorial* … before she lightly nudged his shoulder and tipped her head toward the alleyway. Orion's eyes narrowed, relenting.

"Nyx?" the man said softly like he wasn't sure she was who he'd thought now that he was in her presence.

Nyx brushed a hand down the front of her shirt. "Depends on who's asking …"

"Donovan Carter," the man quickly supplied, seeming to stumble over himself in a rush to explain himself. "I worked with your father before he resigned, I'm a forensic scientist who doubles as the city's coroner."

A forensic scientist in the presence of the murderer he's looking for? she thought. *A lamb in the lions' den.* "*Oh,* you're that Donovan," she said instead.

Donovan's eyebrows arched with joking surprise. "*That* Donovan?" He chuckled and a fond glint flared within his eyes. "Good to hear Azeil hasn't changed."

Nyx angled her head, recalling her father's gaping presence and the events that'd led to his step-down from the position in the case that'd brought them to Celacali. A case she'd been a suspect in. The conflict of interest that'd forced her father's hand and the chief's when he'd been forced to *unattach* Azeil from the position in favour of an unbiased verdict.

As if my father would be swayed in his bias because I am his daughter, she thought bitterly. She knew Azeil would do anything within his power, but move that mountain for her? Not if it risked his job and his passion.

"You make it sound like he had a choice when he resigned, but we both know he didn't. Not with me being a suspect to a murder," she said, her voice clear.

"I—"

"I didn't kill those people."

"Nobody said you did."

Nyx's lips curled into a dangerous smile, her eyes flaring with a malignant light. "Didn't they?"

"No—"

"Then tell me, Donovan." Nyx stepped forward, aware of the authoritative gaze upon her. "Why is the chief of police watching us like I killed the man behind that," she gestured to the veiled area, "barricade?"

"Because he wants to know why Azeil, the famous detective of Celacali, vanished without a trace," Donovan said, seriously, earnestly. "We all do."

Nyx shrugged, sizing him up. "I guess you'll have to ask him yourself … *if* he returns."

"Will he come back?"

"I don't know," she admitted softly.

Before Donovan could respond, Nyx turned and strode down the dankly lit alleyway, ignoring his call of her name as she rounded the first bend and found … Orion. He'd been waiting for her. As if he knew something she wouldn't voice. That Chief Issac Silvia still believed *she* was to blame for the various murders even *after* the four of them had pinned the blame on Kai—the only murder she'd committed *then*. Upon his death, the articles she'd seen on the news in the days after her *almost* death had declared Kai as the killer responsible for the murders, shifting the focus away from her, just as Orion, Kotori, Kade and Niko had intended.

"Wipe that grin off your face before I do it for you," she grumbled, wandering past him.

"What's it feel like to be suspected by the chief?" Orion goaded, stalking behind her.

"Shut up, *Orion*."

Nyx halted her stride when Orion appeared in front of her, blocking her path as the cross with a snake curling around its centre swung from his ear. A saccharine smirk paired with, *was that pride?* as his voice lowered several octaves when he stepped forward.

Stooping his head down beside her ear, he whispered provocatively, "*Make me*."

Her gaze darted to his lips when he pulled back. A heady hum seemed to thrum between them before she forced herself to meet his eyes. "I hate you."

"I'm sure you do," he murmured, gaze darting to her lips before returning to her eyes, stepping closer to her like he wished to vanquish the minuscule distance between them, more. "But something tells me that you hate me a little less than you'd like to."

"That doesn't change anything. It won't make me forget," she stated, ignoring the traitorous stutter of her heart when Orion's hand grasped her waist, and he pulled her closer to him until her chest was pressed against his.

"I'm not asking you to forget."

"Then what are you asking me to do?"

"To live without fear or judgement. To be everything *you* want to be, even if the world deems it wrong." The gloved fingers of his opposing hand stroked up her arm to the nape of her neck, curling amongst the tresses of her hair. "I'm asking you to live the life you want to live."

With a stolen glance at his lips, Nyx forced herself to ask the question on the tip of her tongue despite the reminders of their past flickering before her eyes. "How do I do that?"

"By seizing every moment the world offers like it might be your last," Orion drawled, his head angled as he craned his neck so his lips were a hairsbreadth away from hers. "Life is merely the art of dying. It's how you *choose* to die that truly matters."

"What does tha—"

A low sound rumbled from his chest—half-tut, half-hum—before he tightened his hand in her hair, pulling her closer as his lips brushed against hers.

It seemed he waited for her to protest or shove him away. *Like I should,* she tried to think. Instead, the weight of his hand on her hip and the cradling of her head in his palm, felt like dangerous things, things that should be, *must be* wrong. Except, Nyx suddenly didn't want to do what was right anymore and, as her hands grasped the lapels of his jacket and her lips moved in sync with his, she let herself indulge in this moment like it could be her last, it was almost more than she could stand.

XXI

Qadira

Mortals hurried to and from storefronts of the Eastern suburb streets as Qadira surveyed them from an apothecary-turned-café rooftop. She tracked the subtle shift of a woman's grasp on her shopping bags and an impatient child dragging their feet further down when their parents paused to admire something through a windowpane. The smell of freshly brewed coffee danced across the breeze as sunlight warmed her arms, and, as she drummed her chrome nails upon the stone ledge, her black T-shirt, jacket and jeans contrasted her cool-toned features strikingly, capturing many gazes while she waited.

She'd ignored most as she'd slipped through the throngs and into the coffee shop, batting an eye at Noveen as she climbed a staircase leading to the rooftop. *Not that sweet Noveen could stop me,* she thought with a bemused huff as she sensed how the blonde, Noveen Owens, with sharp cheekbones and a delicate dusting of freckles tracked her path from behind the safety of the counter. *Leon paid her parents too well for her to ruin this meeting.*

The Skull, Viliaris, with whom she was now meeting, apparently wished to waste her time. He'd been informed of the plan several days ago by Mire and she'd hurried to ensure Leon's wishes—orders—were fulfilled. *Tiresome,* she thought as she tapped faster. She could have been doing *anything* else of importance to ensure Leon's life in Celacali would be eternal, not to mention ladling out endless pain to those wayward *problems* of his so called sons. Orion, Niko, Kotori and Kade would pay for their disobedience. But it seemed, as Qadira searched the patrons knotting the street below, that Viliaris cared as little for his own life as her 'brothers' cared for theirs. Always thinking there was going to be one more chance. *A fatal mistake,* she thought, and smiled.

The irony of Orion, Kotori, Niko and Kade's refusal to comply embedded itself in her chest alongside Viliaris' tardiness. Neither party liked the other but, without knowing it, they mimicked each other—making their own rules in a game that wasn't theirs to dictate. Qadira hadn't accepted her vampirism at first. Nor had she forgotten the grand promise Leon had lavished her parents with, before they'd passed centuries ago, had failed to come to pass: marriage to Orion. She should have been his bride. He should have been hers, till death did them part. Instead, the sight of him lashed her insides. To be reminded of something she'd never have; a love he refused to give.

He'd given it to her, a fragment of her soul crooned, dragging its razor-taloned truth over her innards as she hurried to hide it and more rushed to replace it. *He could never love you. He* didn't *choose you. You are everything Nyx is not.*

You are everything *Nyx is not.*

Her fingers curled as she straightened and wandered from the ledge, pacing the length of the roof to quell her anger, mind trying to remind her of a weakness she chose to ignore. *It didn't matter, not really,* she abolished, longing to believe herself as stray strands of her hair brushed her cheeks. *Worth wasn't dictated by a man. It was found in oneself.* So, why didn't she believe it? *Why* did she continue to agonise over what-ifs? Orion had every chance in the decades they'd known each other to care for her, but he never had. He'd firmly squashed her interest from the start.

I don't want *another person gifted to me by Leon, and you shouldn't want the lies he promised.* And, almost as if it'd been an afterthought or flicker of his humanity, Orion's voice had softened, urging her to choose her path. *Fight his commands before you lose everything.*

If only she'd known the 'everything' Orion spoke of was her free will—the ability to *choose* her path—before Leon's commands had burrowed their hooks into her mind, chipping away at her consciousness over time and she *willingly* fulfilled his orders. Soon, time would run out for Phaelyn beneath the weight of Leon's commands, one too many pressing on her will, and soon … too soon, she would slip away from her too.

"Should I come back later, or?" Viliaris drawled, gesturing to the staircase with a jut of his thumb, dark jeans covered in a fine dusting of sand.

Qadira whirled, a sneer twisting her lips as she appeared before him in a burst of preternatural speed and gripped the collar of his violet-purple shirt. Her crystalline irises seared into his soul, knuckles leeching white. "Do you think this is *funny*?" she breathed, finding satisfaction in his widened eyes.

"I just—"

With a disdain-filled scoff, she released his shirt and shoved him back. "You're a fool with a death wish, and I didn't come here to *waste* time. I came here for intel on that fledgling," she spat.

“They’ve been following me,” Viliaris said, gaze dropping in shame.

Qadira’s brows quirked with intrigue; stare honed on the mortal whose heart galloped beneath his sternum. “Of what possible interest would you be?”

“I know—”

“You know nothing we don’t *want* you to know, Viliaris,” Qadira cut him off. “It’s what you agreed on when Leon chose you alongside Kyree and Mire … of course, Kyree didn’t fare so *well*.” A vapid grin obscured her features.

Viliaris started toward her with fury and a scathing accusation in his eyes. It always amused Qadira when mortals sought to intimidate her because she wasn’t afraid and never would be. They just never realised how deadly she was. Didn’t know how easily she could render their heads from their shoulders or carve them apart like an artist driven by tragedy. Nor did they know how she’d relish in their bloodshed as she bathed herself in their life-giving elixir or the sweet agony her bite could bundle them in. They didn’t know the *half* of what she was capable of as they clung to their short-sighted beliefs but that was okay, because she never shied away from a challenge … and hearing them plead for their insignificant lives was always sweet. Humanity wasn’t her equal and it would never be; they were food and could be disposed of quicker than a snap of her fingers.

“I know they want me dead,” he said, rough voice raising a few octaves.

“Oh?” Qadira prompted, stalking to the building’s ledge to lean against it. “Why is that?”

Raking his fingers through his brown tresses, Viliaris appraised her as if the answer should be obvious. “Because I’m a Skull,” he said.

“That you are … but that doesn’t mean anything. There are other gangs that want you dead. You’re not an innocent man,” she said, recalling the extensive history of the Skulls in Celacali.

The Ivory Skulls had been a foreign concept in Celacali before Leon moved to the coastal city and swayed several men to his side. He’d promised them riches, power and to remain untouchable by the confines of mortal laws if they would do his bidding under the guise of a gang. His lackeys. They had been Leon’s eyes and ears over the years, bloodline after bloodline joining the Skulls until they became a *true* notorious gang nobody could touch. Nobody *except* Leon.

To some, Qadira recalled from the years she’d spent beside her sire, he’d uttered sweet promises of immortality. They never obtained it, of course, as he’d slaughter them before they could revel in any success. Leon gave but, like the will of a mighty god, he took until there was nothing left to give. The blood in their veins and the flesh on their bones was just penance.

“Reggie saw them following Kyree before he wound up dead and if anyone is ever on a hitlist, it’s someone in power. I’m not dying for that shit,” Viliaris said, starting toward the door.

Qadira moved, blocking his path, a look of devilry on her face. “So, you’re going to run scared?”

Viliaris narrowed his eyes with unveiled suspicion, distrust lurking in the creases of his brow. “Why should I trust you?”

“You shouldn’t,” she said, stepping aside to gesture fluidly at the door. “But if you’d like to go, nothing’s stopping you. See how long you’ll last out there without my advice.”

“What is … your advice?” he asked, relenting.

“I think … Orion cares for Nyx enough to *fear* losing her,” the words bit through her lips as she said them. “Do with that what you like but I suggest you don’t hesitate.” She watched his expression keenly before he dipped his head and strode past her.

Qadira stared at the door for a long moment after Viliaris left, her thoughts churning. She’d told him the truth—Orion did *care* for Nyx. It was suddenly so obvious—she swallowed a sour taste and checked herself. They were siblings, after all. She’d only had to consider Kotori, Niko and Kade’s behaviour. And if their interference in disposing of Emilia was anything to go by, Viliaris was walking dead the minute he’d left the rooftop. Leon wanted to test a theory surrounding Orion and Nyx’s recent movements. Leon had seen the truth of the matter long before her. *This was going to be interesting*, she thought with a satisfied grin.

God had turned his back on Celacali and left Leon to rule in his place; a true god to a realm clutching onto imposters and now there was no turning back from it. Humanity would kneel or it would die, because a forgiving god was a weak god and mercy would not come to those who crossed Leon. Only death.

XXII

Kotori

"How long are you planning on staring at the floor?" Qadira asked, her gaze prickling across Kotori's skin as his hair grazed his jaw.

His teeth clenched as he *tried* to ignore the absence of weight of his shoulder-length tresses as well as the women—his torturers—who waited for acknowledgement. The rhythmic clenching and unclenching of his fists against the metallic armrests did little to calm the brewing storm in his chest, spine aching. Days had passed since Leon's visit. Not that Kotori minded, the quiet of the cell gave him time to simmer, to envision the ways he'd like to ruin—*rip*—Leon, Qadira, and Phaelyn to pieces for the things they'd taken from him. It gave him time to process how he could move forward, weighing his options, determined to attain retribution in the right moment. His dark gaze lingered on the blackened patch of ground beside his chair, untapped rage scalding his insides.

His tribal necklace and hair were nothing but ashes and the cloying stench of something singed. His freedom was in the hands of a man who sought to control him. But it was also guarded by the woman he so longed to see again, her strong will and fight permanently engraved in his soul—her life trickling like grains of sand in an hourglass. He knew something was wrong, could sense it in the blade's edge of Phaelyn's knives.

Leon saw Nyx as a problem, but why didn't he just kill her? He couldn't hide his loathing of her and the *disobedience* she instilled in his sons. *In us*, Kotori thought. That much he knew from Phaelyn and Qadira's goads. They'd found enjoyment in leaving him with pieces of Leon's plans. *But what were those plans, and what did they have to do with Nyx?*

Fingertips skittered over Kotori's shoulders and the muscles in his back tensed beneath Phaelyn's hand as he glimpsed her leather-clad form in his peripherals. He closed his eyes against a swell of anger, irises lightening before he breathed in a steadying breath and reopened them, glaring at her. His blood coated her skin from the pair's efforts to *purge* him of Nyx's influence over Leon's orders. His chest, abdomen and shoulder blades ached. Dark, crusting blood clung to his skin like a second skin, the gleefully given knife wounds that littered his flesh scabbing in some places while others continued to weep, trailing down his body until they soaked into the fabric of his pants. He knew enough about the effects of silver if it was injected into a vampire's bloodstream to know that his wounds *should have* already healed, knowing the untainted and liquified version was responsible for his slowed healing qualities.

Phaelyn grinned up at him. "Lighten up, Kotori," she crooned, knife clutched in her hand. "If you want to be mad at someone. Be mad at *Nyx*, she's the reason we visit you every morning."

Kotori scoffed, rolling his eyes. "This isn't Nyx's fault."

Qadira strode forward, waiting as Kotori's stare lifted to hers. "Oh. Well, she and Orion killed Dries *and* Kyree. You know who they are, right?" she asked.

He nodded, recalling the Ivory Skulls loyal to Leon. "Their deaths … *upset* Leon?" he asked. "Weren't they just disposable pawns?"

"Mortals are always disposable pawns," Qadira replied. "These ones, however, Leon wanted *alive*."

Kotori arched his dark eyebrows, curiosity thinly veiled behind his stony expression. "Why? They were gang members with criminal records longer than the lines for Illusion's rollercoasters."

Qadira paused momentarily before a startling grin split her face and her dark eyes flickered to Phaelyn.

Kotori's instincts rose—they knew something he didn't. Their shared looks and matching grins of delight settled uneasily in his stomach, dragging over his shoulders and chest like an oil-slick. He wondered what brought such grins to their faces, down here in the sublevels of Leon's estate and his singed-hair room. It was something, he realised, he was going to have to work out for himself. The overhead lights cast disconcerting shadows as his mind darted after them in search of answers. He didn't care what brought the pair satisfaction, content in envisioning how he'd kill them once he was free. He'd rip them apart piece by piece until they *begged* him to end it, to free them from the endless agony. But he had to find out what they grinned about so smugly.

Phaelyn continued to stare and an unnatural weariness that Kotori knew was the effects of the silver in his veins, began its weakening work. In time, he knew, it rendered a vampire—regardless of their age—as powerless and susceptible to injuries as a mortal. He might have been fine if they hadn't returned every morning to reopen his wounds, waiting until he blacked out from blood loss, and injecting a fresh vial of silver into his bloodstream. But he didn't black out and he couldn't stop them coming as they descended—he couldn't *fight* them.

Like he hadn't been able to fight off the men who'd left him for the wolves those centuries ago.

Phaelyn's sharp laugh jolted him from his thoughts. "You don't know, do you?"

Kotori levelled her with a desolate expression. "How would I know anything outside of what happens in this room? I've been kept *prisoner* for three months. You've been doting on *every single one* of Leon's commands like the lap dogs you are. It almost seems like you don't have … free will," he spat.

Phaelyn bristled and moved toward him before Qadira placed a placating hand on her shoulder, her gaze locked on Kotori. "Careful, Kotori. It isn't in your best interest to goad when you don't know what we know," she warned.

"And what *do* you know?" he said.

The pair shared a look like the ones before, snide, as Qadira's eyes—so much like Orion's it was unnerving—pinned him in place. Phaelyn toyed with the blade of her knife, twirling it in her hands before she gently pressed her thumb to the tip, splitting her skin as if testing its sharpness.

Her gaze lifted. "You're dearest Nyx is …" she trailed off as if she expected him to finish her sentence, but when he didn't, a spluttered laugh danced across the room. "You really don't know, do you?"

"Know w*hat*?" Kotori snapped, losing his patience with the younger vampires he'd known since before Niko was turned. They'd been turned several decades after him and had vanished into thin air in the late eighties when, he'd assumed, they'd died. *Obviously, not the case*, he thought wryly.

"Nyx completed the transition two days ago," Qadira stated, stealing the breath from Kotori's lungs as he stared up at her. "We'll see if she makes it past the fledgling stage as Leon has plans for her since they last spoke."

Through the dark satisfaction and excitement Kotori felt about Nyx's completed transition, he furrowed his brows. "They've spoken? When?"

"The same night she completed the transition," Phaelyn scoffed. "She would have been *dead* if Orion and those twins hadn't shown up."

Relief flooded Kotori that Orion *had* been there and that he'd seemingly taken Nyx under his wing during her transition. He knew that Orion would have been symbolic about her first kill, picking someone tied to the past, a death he knew would send a message. *Dries*, he thought immediately. *He picked Dries.* Something in Kotori righted like he'd been on the cusp of falling off a cliff and this new information had pulled him back onto solid ground. He knew he'd tried to convince himself when he'd first become aware of Nyx that his interest was just … part of the plan. Then, after he'd met her, that he'd be satisfied with just her friendship. And for a little while, he had been. But he remembered how his thoughts had changed the night she had killed Kai Salas, calling to the darkest parts of himself that longed to bring her into their world—he'd *wanted* Nyx like he'd never wanted anything else in his long life. And like always, he'd fought and denied himself what he wanted, keeping her at a distance … at least, he'd *tried* to.

He realised now that he hadn't been successful, that he'd never stood a chance when all he'd wanted since Niko and Kade returned from Malor—the pair informing Orion and himself of what Nyx had done—was to nurture her dark streak, protect her like he hadn't been, and learn more about the girl who had turned into a curveball, bringing her deeper into their world … and his embrace.

"But somewhere along the way, you grew attached," came Orion's voice through their shared bond.

It was a sobering thought. Kotori knew Leon wasn't part of the bond and so their communication could not be overheard. At least, not what they shared outside of his sire connection, and he was grateful for that. There was comfort in knowing his brothers were there, and that only Orion, Niko and Kade could communicate with him. Throughout the time they'd been kept prisoners, Orion had been nothing if not consistent with his updates, the same way Kotori continued to provide his brother with whatever he heard on his side. Aside *from how it'd slipped Orion's mind to share Nyx's newfound vampirism,* he thought. *Even* if *everything he told Orion was careful lies from Phaelyn and Qadira.* Kotori startled for a moment before he shook his head to clear his mind, a delighted sensation warming his chest. *"I guess you were right all along,"* he said, speaking only to Orion.

"About … what?" came the felt reply. Orion could have been sitting right here next to him.

Kotori took comfort in that. *"That she'd ruin our lives if we let her."*

Silence emanated through the bond for several seconds as Orion seemed to mull over Kotori's words, their mental communication closing the distance that separated them. *"No, Tori. I was* wrong *to assume she was disposable and would ruin anything. She feels your pain—*all *your pain."*

"How?"

"Leon has been manipulating the bond, even before she was a vampire. That suspicion you had about sires decades ago … I think you're right. Leon wants *her to know what he's doing."*

"I know," Kotori admitted, recalling the tearing ache in his temples as Leon had cut his hair. *"He hasn't forced her to feel my pain for days, Orion.* Protect her. *We* need *her."*

A ragged breath ghosted the bond and without seeing him, Kotori knew Orion raked a palm down his face as his response filled his mind, *"I was wrong. So fucking wrong."*

Kotori chuckled despite the women who watched him. "*You were right in a way, Orion.*"

"*How?*"

"*She's forever ruined us for anyone else.*"

"*Truly?*"

"*Truly,*" Kotori confirmed with a surety he couldn't misplace. "*After all these years, she's the calamity and serenity we've been waiting for.*"

XXIII

Nyx

A ghostly, sigh-like breeze drifted throughout the cavernous home where the sun's yellow rays and hidden light fixtures provided warmth to ward off the frigid weather. Not that Nyx minded. Ares' head rested upon her thigh and his body spread heat across the right half of her legs with plush cushions cocooning them cosily, her fingers curling around the cuffs of her cobalt hoodie as she chatted with Alexander and Tobias on the couch.

The once easy flow of conversation quailed the moment Orion stalked into the main cave from the tunnelway that led to his room, a location Nyx wouldn't have been able to name if she hadn't been down there, snooping. The twins' shoulders bunched as their gazes locked on him, distrustful. Orion wandered to his throne with a bemused smirk curling the edges of his lips and a flickering of his gaze to her. Nyx hadn't held his gaze long, dropping her sight to the Malamute's pelt, trying to remain unbothered by his presence. *Trying*, and failing, to pretend their kiss in the alleyway hadn't happened, a sliver of her control she wouldn't let slip again. Not until she was sure of his motives—if they'd ever become clear—and if she could trust him. Otherwise, Nyx was determined to keep him at arm's length because of the many things he'd done to her all in the name of a plan. Flickers of a moonlit chase and the blazing agony of fangs tearing into her throat descended once more. A mould-fused warehouse and a bloodstained dagger, the weighted press of an ethereal command. The blistering torment of phantom flames and clattering chains.

"So?" Tobias prompted.

His tone suggested he'd already repeated something twice when Nyx forced herself from her thoughts and refocused on the room around her. "So …?" she parroted, blinking as she noticed Tobias' hand rubbing his jean-clad thigh and Alexander's subtle shake of his head.

"What's the matter, Night?" Alexander leaned forward, his sooty-grey shirt complimenting the pallor of his skin and the colouring of his amber irises. "Are your thoughts more … enthralling than our riveting conversation?"

Tobias snickered, nudging his brother. "You know, I'd pay to know what she was thinking half the time. She's *always* lost in her thoughts." He turned to Nyx with a mischievous grin, ignoring Orion's gaze as he surveyed the pair with mild interest. "Tell us, Nyx, what *are* you thinking?"

"That I'd like to throw the nearest object at the both of you," she replied with a sickeningly sweet smile.

"Oh, evasion," Tobias drawled, emphasising his words with a taunting edge. "Noted."

"C'mon, Night. Now you *have to* tell us." Alexander pressed, silver bracelet glinting in the light like his assortment of rings.

"I hate you both, *immensely*," she muttered, fighting a grin.

Alexander chuckled, pushing himself up from his chair to wander to hers and drop down beside her, slinging his arm casually over her shoulder as the familiar woodsy scent of his cologne permeated her senses. "We love you too … *immensely.*"

"That's not what I said though."

Tobias' eyes rolled at the familiarity of her words, eyes alight with mirth. "It's what you meant though."

The clicking of a lighter interrupted them and Nyx turned to Orion, brows arched. "What now?"

Orion mirrored puzzlement, exhaling smoke. "I didn't say anything," he said.

"You don't *have to*. Your presence speaks volumes."

"Should I be offended by that?"

"Considering you don't give a damn about what people think of you, no." Nyx paused, trailing her gaze across his dark T-shirt, leather gloves, ripped jeans and boots, lingering on the serpent earring of his left ear before she met his stare. "But something tells me that you want something."

"And if I do?" he prompted, leaning into the backrest of his chair, and draping his forearms regally upon the armrests, wisps of smoke curling like the serpent Nyx often was reminded of.

"Then I'd say it couldn't be good."

Orion tipped his head like he wouldn't argue, faint amusement in his eyes. "I'm not a good person, little dove. So, why would my motives be?"

"And why should she entertain your thoughts? Haven't you bitten her, tormented her, tortured her, held her captive and turned her—to save her life after *you* endangered her?" Tobias interjected, seeming to throw caution to the wind as he narrowed his eyes at Orion.

Orion pinned Tobias with his signature Mr. Freeze. "Don't forget the most important thing I've done," he said.

Alexander released a breath. "What was that? Where you abused your supernatural gifts? Or when you almost killed her after the massacre at Chades Cove?"

Nyx dropped her gaze to Ares' fur, hoping to mask the smile spreading across her face as Orion's eyes narrowed upon the twins and a muscle along the underside of his jaw ticked.

"I'd say it was when she killed Kai Salas," he said, pausing as his gaze nestled upon Nyx, "Wouldn't you say the same, little dove?"

With exaggerated reluctance, Nyx met his gaze. A lightness shone in her grey-flecked irises. "I think you need to get to the point, Orion. We know you wouldn't be here if you didn't have one. So, what do you want?" she said.

"I *want* my brothers back, and if *they*," he gestured with a flick of his wrist to the twins, "can help me achieve that, then we're killing two birds with one stone."

"Why would we help you?" Alexander spluttered, almost headbutting his brother.

"If not for me, then do it for Nyx. She wants my brothers back just as much as I do … but you already knew that." He chuckled darkly.

"*Orion,*" Nyx warned, lowly, elbows digging into the soft material of the couch. "No."

"And why not?" he drawled as he gestured to Alexander and Tobias in a sweeping arc. "Don't you want their help to get Niko, Kade and Kotori back? Or was everything you said last night just for show?"

Alexander and Tobias turned to Nyx and Orion locked in a staring contest. It bothered her on some level, that Orion questioned her determination to free Kade, Niko and Kotori from Leon's grasp when she'd been nothing but honest about her intentions. Something she wasn't sure Orion ever had been, even if she knew he'd do *anything* for his companions. Nyx supposed his caution wasn't misguided, knowing the tiniest piece of his past and the betrayal she suspected had occurred, but she wasn't ready to reveal her carnal motives—the one laced with Leon's demise. Not until the time was right.

"Get to the point, Orion. *Now,*" she snapped.

"All I'm saying, is that we could use their help. Our plan's already in motion and they wouldn't be in any danger," Orion stated, his fingers splaying.

"What do you need from us?" Tobias murmured, eyeing Orion like he already knew what was coming.

"The leatherbound book Asher once possessed," Orion stated. "He compiled everything he knew of Leon and vampires into it while he worked alongside your family."

"Why would they have it?" Nyx was momentarily confused. "It's *my* uncle's book," she murmured.

Orion eyed her closely for a long moment. "What makes you say that?"

"Because if it was valuable," she started, recalling the leatherbound book the twins had shown her a picture of and the suspicion she had of its whereabouts. "Asher wouldn't trust just *anyone* with it."

"Then, who would he trust it with?" Orion asked.

"His family," she murmured as realisation dawned.

Ignoring the press of their gazes and weighted silence, she gnawed her thumbnail as her eyes darted around the room. Hurriedly, she shoved herself off the couch, dislodging Ares from her thigh. Asher's face flashed before her eyes, memories of a leatherbound book traipsing across her mind's eye before her Converse-clad feet carried her to the marble staircase. Climbing the steps two at a time, and disappearing down the opening tunnelway, she hurriedly slipped past the door between the cliff entrance and onto the base of the staircase, up, up, up. She didn't know *why* she felt this frantic or *why* it mattered that Orion sought to find the leatherbound book containing such important knowledge, but Nyx wasn't ready to share a piece—the last remaining pieces—of her uncle with him, even if it could help Kade, Niko and Kotori.

It might have been selfish of her to put her grief first, to clutch the last of Asher as tightly to her heart as possible, but she didn't care as her shoes crunched the rocky ground, carrying her to her beloved motorbike. Nyx swung her leg over the seat and started the engine with a twist of her wrist, fingers curling around the grips before she revved the engine and gently released the clutch, disengaging the kickstand.

"Where are you going, little dove?" crooned Orion's voice within the confines of her mind, her head whirling to peer at the top of the staircase. His silhouette was illuminated by the blueness of the horizon as his head angled eerily to the side, his hands tucked into his jacket's pocket. *"What's the rush?"*

Turning her head away from him, Nyx revved her bike's engine. *"The book you're after, the one vampires* can't *see*," she began softly, thinking her response instead of voicing it. *"I know where it is and who had it last."*

"Where is it?"

"Somewhere safe."

"Nyx—"

Nyx twisted the throttle in answer and took off toward the forest in a mass of sea sand and stones, leaving his words to hang in the sky like the stars above her head.

* * *

Yellowed pages of an age-worn book rustled in the crisp and frigid breeze that blew through the cracked-open windows behind the bed Nyx sat crossed-legged on. Although she was rereading Asher's looping signature at the book's front, she was also waiting for the inevitable moment Orion would stride into the lodge house she hadn't been back to in several days. It was chilly but Nyx paid it no mind, thumbing through the pages smelling of ink and…blood, returning to Asher's signature—the *only* thing she could focus on—with a bittersweet sense of comfort, her hoodie sleeves rucked to her elbows.

Over an hour had passed as Nyx had hurriedly located the house keys tucked beneath a pot plant by the front door. Not the greatest of hiding spots but she didn't think much of the house within the acreage of Celacali's furthest suburbs. Chalking up the probability of a break-in to be as likely as her reclaiming her mortality, the house was in desperate need of repair and definitely not an obvious burglar trap. It seemed to always be filled with silence since Asher's death and the showdown it'd contained seemed pressed into the walls.

Silence had greeted her like an old friend, clinging to her skin as she wandered across the lounge room to a cupboard built into the staircase. Her hands had rummaged, discarding trinkets and old board games until her fingers had brushed a coarse, protective sheet bundled around Asher's journal before she'd hurried up the stairs and to her old room, not sparing the darkened entryway of the dining room a single glance.

A sharp rap on the left wall of windows drew her attention away from the pages of the book in her lap, and out the window. Purple-yellow tendrils of a dawn sky hidden behind a thick cloud cover was unusual for the tropical lowlands at the beginnings of its autumn months. Her fingers twitched anxiously. Where she should have been comforted by the gentleness of nature's touch, she wasn't. Something in her bloodstream warned her that it wasn't nature's doing but something else prompting the eerie silence in the already quiet house. And if it hadn't been for Qadira and Phaelyn's surprise visit to the cave, Nyx might have brushed it off as nothing more than a change of the wind. But the birds outside had ceased their chittering and the disconcerting feeling of eyes on her back persisted.

In a movement smoother and more predatory than Nyx thought she was capable of, she snapped the thick book shut and sidled to the threshold of her doorway without a sound. Her fingers curled around the door frame as she stuck her head into the dimly lit hallway, instincts crawling when she dared a step into the hall and paused. As if whatever—whoever—would jump out of the shadows like a slasher film's killer.

"*Never* check the hallway first, little dove," drawled a voice before Nyx whirled toward her room and the windowsill as Orion stepped over it, his boots avoiding her bed and its side table as he stooped beneath the window frame. "That's a rookie mistake in all horror movies. Just like calling out 'hello' is a death sentence, take it from me."

With a roll of her eyes and a soft huff, Nyx leaned into the door frame, keeping her gaze trained on the man who soundlessly slinked. "And what, pray tell, *should* I have done first?" she said.

"Logically, you should have closed your windows and the door."

"Illogically?"

"That still wouldn't have saved you."

Nyx shook her head with feigned disappointment, changing the subject like the turning of a page. "How are the twins?"

His lips tugged into a taunting grin, a playful glint sparking within his glacier-like irises. "Alive."

"*Orion.*"

"They're fine," he soothed, abolishing her racing thoughts with the disgruntled tone of his voice. "We went over the last of the plan, ensuring someone knew the full details while you came here."

"And?"

"We'll wait two days. It'll give us time for the police presence to die down before the … *bloodier* step."

"Let me guess, Viliaris?" she drawled, unintentionally mimicking him, but knowing the answer before Orion spoke.

"Four's better than one."

She didn't miss the way his gaze flickered between her and the book. A sense of satisfaction and curiosity rippled through her chest as she watched him, wondering what secrets the book held and why he *needed* it so desperately. *What did it possess that sent vampires into a tizzy when they couldn't find it? Why couldn't they take it for themselves?* But, as if sensing her thoughts, Orion wandered toward the opposing wall of windows, resting his shoulder into the frame.

Nyx perched herself back on the edge of her bed, pulling the thick book onto her lap. "Why this book, Orion?" she asked him.

"Like I said, it's filled with information on our kind and if someone who didn't have … *good* intentions got their hands on it … they could control your life just by never giving you the truth …" he trailed off, appearing uncomfortable.

Nyx dropped her gaze to the heavy book, running her fingers over the plain cover. "I can't give it to you," she said, her dark irises met his light ones for a moment. In them, she caught the barest flash of annoyance. "Not when Asher went to great lengths to prevent vampires from seeing its contents. Not when it *smells* of his blood."

She refused to meet his gaze beneath the annoyance she glimpsed in his eyes, angling her body away from him like it would shake her budding hysteria. Her knuckles went white, fingertips aching as she tucked the book closer to her chest and she tried to shake the prickling sensation of tears. *Don't cry, little terror*, she heard the voice of her uncle. Her voice rasped, "You *can't* have it, Orion. Not yet. Not until you give *me* some answers. Like why it's so important."

"Nyx. I don't think you understand," he said.

"Are you serious?" she said, cutting him off.

He was still and something … *tormented* filled his irises as if he *couldn't* tell her, even if he wanted to. "I can't see what you're holding," he said. "I can smell old blood … but I can't see the book."

"What do you mean you can't see it?" she said. The oddness of his words momentarily distracting her. "Tell me, Orion!"

"*Can't*," he said, holding her gaze with a seriousness she couldn't ignore.

"Okay," she breathed, weighing his words. "Then, this might be unfair considering … you look like you *can't* say anything, but if it's as important is you're making it seem, you can't have Asher's book. Not when it's protected *against* vampires learning its contents—" she broke off, realising what she was saying. *What had Alexander said? Silver halide crystals.* The book had been steeped in them. The stuff that was used in photographs and films, preserving prints for hundreds of years. She looked up at Orion, sensing a turning of the tables. He couldn't see it, so he needed her. *But why? I'm a vampire too,* she thought. *A full vampire? Or still a halfling?*

"If you can't see it, why can I?" she asked.

His answer was a noncommittal shrug. "Don't know," he said simply.

Nyx thought furiously. There had been no reluctance in his answer that time. He just really … didn't seem to know. "I'll share with you, Orion," she began slowly, "But not until I know the truth. Not until you're free … *enough* of Leon's control."

Something animalistic flared in his eyes like whatever leash held him now pulled taut. He bared his teeth and Nyx fought the urge to flinch, trying to steady her nerves.

"Do you know how easy it would be to kill you?" he whispered in a new voice, suddenly unrecognisable. "After all, the book's right there and you've … served your purpose. I can find someone *living* to read it's pages," he uttered lowly.

Nyx gasped involuntarily. He was suddenly wholly unnerving, more than he usually was, and the change in him was vast, sending chills down Nyx's spine. *Where was this coming from?* she thought, eyeing him like he was a rattlesnake poised to strike. *What had Leon done to him?* Slowly, she lowered the book.

A dark chuckle spilled unbidden from her mouth, it slithered out, followed by a stinging sensation that had nothing to do with tears. Suddenly, she knew her brown eyes bled white-gold and she pushed herself off the bed, sneaker-clad feet carrying her to the doorway. She ignored him following her as she reached the top of the stairs and he wandered into the hallway.

"You can't keep running from everything you can't control, Nyx," he said, tracking her descent down the stairs as he trailed behind her. "Would Asher want you to be caught in a swell of grief caused by his death? Would he want you to live a half-life because of him?"

At first, she glared up at Orion leaning against the banister but there was something in the way he was looking at her. She realised she recognised regret, like his words had caught up to him. She watched him watch her for a long moment as her mind scrambled.

“Don’t you *dare* use Asher as a way to get what you want.”

“I’m not trying to, but if he’s the only way you’ll see reason. Then, so be it.” He raked his gloved fingers through his hair in agitation, like he didn’t know *how* to express frustration or why he needed her to believe him. “It wasn’t your fault, Nyx. It never was.”

“I don’t—” she started, cutting herself off when Orion shifted, appearing before her in a measure of two pulses of her heart.

“Don’t you?” he prompted, cocking his head.

Suddenly, it was the old Orion who stood before her, glowering. This time, she recognised the chill in his eyes and the stillness in every element of his movement.

“I’m very familiar with grief, with betrayal, anguish, and blame,” he said. “And there are only two reasons why someone runs from death like you have been. The first is guilt or knowing they directly ensured a person’s heart ceased to beat. The second, and which I’m going to assume is what you’re suffering from, is fear.”

“I’m not afraid—”

“I wasn’t finished,” Orion interjected, and Nyx tightened her grasp on the book. “Most assume fear is because they’re guilty, so they spend … months convincing themselves they could’ve done something different, that they could’ve saved so and so. But you’re not afraid because you believe you’re to blame, you’re afraid of what will happen if you stop letting the grief consume you. You’re afraid to let him go.”

Nyx opened her mouth to quip a stifling retort but couldn’t. He spoke the truth, and it was icy cold and unrelenting. Suddenly, every breath was consumed by her months-long back and forth of wanting to let Asher go and seeking to cling onto everything she associated with him. Orion gazed down at her with an air of patience and that same foreign gleam of empathy, waiting for the pieces of her pent-up grief to coalesce. Nyx found herself caught between a crutch and what Asher would want her to do.

Maybe her grief stemmed from a place within that sought to clutch hold of everything horrible she’d done and punish herself for it. Somewhere along the way, she’d found herself at home in the wrongness and frowned-upon notions of the world. She knew Orion’s words were true, that there wasn’t a designated time for how long you were supposed to grieve, that holding onto a loved one after their death sometimes caused more problems than it solved.

The dead remained dead no matter how tightly you clung to their memory, the final press of death was uncaring of the lives it governed. Just like life continued despite loss, bringing warmth and serenity in its wake—if only the path chosen was filled with tranquillity. Though Death was eternally cast as the villain in every story as old as the earth itself, Life was a cruel mistress. Capable of twisting someone’s path so it crossed with her twin’s, leading them down the illusionist elysian until it was too late for them to return.

A sharp knock echoed throughout the silent house, jolting Nyx from her dark thoughts as she slowly turned toward the front door, a final thought spared for Orion’s splintered reaction. She would learn *what* prevented him from telling her the truth, *would* learn why she could see paragraphs of Asher's research. Orion shifted beside her, guarded. This wasn't a part of his plan. He twisted the handle and pulled the door open.

"What are *you* doing here?" questioned a rough, masculine voice.

It was one Nyx had heard her whole life and she didn't have to see Orion's face to know a mocking smirk marred it, his glacier irises burning with a fire so intense, she was surprised it didn't burn the man before him.

"I could ask you the same thing," he said.

"Where is she?"

With a disgruntled sigh and the clenching of his jaw, Orion stepped aside enough for a pair of slate irises to collide with hers. Nyx's breath caught in her throat, fingers clenching the leatherbound book as her gaze greedily drank in the familiar dirt-brown curls, the black T-shirt and the creases in his blue denim jeans like he'd been driving for several hours. Her observations halted on the plaited leather bracelet around his wrist and his Converse as worn and well-loved as she remembered.

Azeil's eyes softened, his smile a doppelgänger to hers as he crossed the threshold, managing the short distance in a hurried stride before his arms wrapped around her and his chin rested atop her head, her arms winding around his waist a moment later.

"Night," Azeil murmured.

"Dad."

XXIV

Nyx

Tension lay like a blanket on the room's inhabitants and Nyx wished she could dispel it—to forget, to mend—so she could appreciate her father's return but the stronger, more cautious side of her brain urged her to keep him at a distance while she determined his intentions. The soft afternoon light trickled through the windows and across his face, lightening the hue of his sooty irises. Everyone seemed to stare at the furniture. The ornate whirls and contours of the black metal chairs were cold beneath her arms, fingertips drumming on the vine design while a tendril of smoke drifted past her line of sight. Nyx felt Orion, eyes trained on her father, waiting to provoke Azeil with more than his presence already did.

Azeil's attention was on his daughter, urging her to fill him in on the events that had followed their phone call of more than a week ago. The *exact* conversation Nyx had hoped to avoid answering—omitting all the … bloodstained things she'd done.

The shrill ring of the home phone split the silence, eliciting a synchronised wince from herself and Orion before he released a groan, striding from the sunroom, through the lounge room, into the kitchen and back to the sunroom with the irritating noise blaring throughout the house.

Nyx knew whoever the caller was, was in for a surprise when Orion answered, his unearthly irises locked on hers. "Hello, Alyvia," he drawled, his gaze darting to Azeil.

Azeil straightened in his chair, knuckles bleeding white and then came the droning sound of an ended call.

Orion's attention recentered upon her as he weighed the phone in his palm. "Aw, she didn't want to talk to me," he said, disappointedly.

"I don't blame her, because if you answered the phone when I wanted to speak to *anyone* else, I'd end the call too," Nyx said.

"I'm *hurt*," Orion whinged, striding to his chair with a feigned look of anguish pulling at his diamond-shaped features. "I've been told that I'm a *very*, likeable person."

"Oh, yeah? It must be your … award-winning personality and recognition of others," Nyx stated dryly.

With a snap of his fingers, his lips upturned in a smile that almost mirrored hers. "That's got to be it. What else could it be?"

If not for the flash of memories her mind conjured up in response, Nyx *almost* allowed herself a moment to enjoy the gentleness of their interaction and the ease of their banter. *Almost* allowing herself to catalogue the fall of a blond lock in his eyes as he smiled. *Almost* letting the stream of images from a dimly lit alleyway, the taste of his lips against hers, the press of his hand on her waist, settle.

Azeil coughed, loudly, drawing their attention, and purging Orion of his grin as the centuries-old vampire turned to Azeil. "Nyx," Azeil urged, his eyes darting between them.

She released a ragged sigh. "Where do I start?" she said, cupping the nape of her neck as she turned and gazed out through the paned windows. "I was … ambushed—"

"*Attacked*," Orion interjected.

Did it still bother him? she wondered, surveying him closely before she restarted, "I was *ambushed* by Leon's creations, Phaelyn and Qadira. It was intended as a warning to me to stop looking for Orion, Niko, Kade and Kotori. It earned me several … knife scars and a lovely bruise around my throat."

Azeil seemed to process her words like an ancient, box-like computer whirring loudly when too many tabs were opened. His dark lashes flickered as he blinked once. Twice. Three times before he opened and closed his mouth, a frown drawing as he raised his hand, appearing pained.

Does bearing the brunt of his absence and the void he left in my life register? she wondered. *Do I remind him of the shared presence we both miss?*

"Nyx," Azeil murmured, almost like he was praying to the goddess from the scrolling text of legends.

Ignoring the press of Orion's stare, Nyx met her father's gaze, anguish sharpening her candour. "Don't say my name like that, not yet. That's just the beginning of the past week or so," she warned.

"Beginning?"

Orion hummed, picking his discarded cigarette up from where he'd carelessly placed it on the tabletop. "It's been an *eventful* past week, Azeil. Full of decisions, blood, and choice revelations," he said.

"Decisions?" Azeil pressed, seemingly unwilling to tear his stare from Nyx. It was as though he implored her to answer his questions, to fill him in on everything he'd missed. To mend the bond he'd broken in the tide of his past.

Nyx wondered what Orion's presence reminded him of. She worried her bottom lip between her teeth, dropping her eyes before she forced herself to continue. "I … I completed the transition a few days ago," she said, lifting her gaze from the tabletop. "I've become the monster you fear."

"You will never *be the monster he fears, little dove,"* Orion assured her in the confines of whatever bond they shared. Nyx's head angled fractionally toward him. *"I can't change the things he said to you or erase your memories of that argument but, for whatever it's worth. I'm … sorry for being the cause of his fear."*

Her gaze strayed from Azeil long enough to glean the honesty in Orion's eyes. *"Would you take it back if you could?"* she asked only him.

"I'm sorry for how my actions determined Azeil's reactions, and for the way his decisions were clouded by Niko, Kade, Kotori and my presence in his youth." Orion tossed a glance toward Azeil, something dark crawling over the lines of his cheekbones while Azeil watched the two of them in obvious confusion. *"I'm only sorry for how they affected you,* not *for the things we did."*

"So, you wouldn't change anything?" she challenged.

Orion turned back to her, his eyes filled with a razor-sharp but gentle conviction that jolted her heart. *"I wouldn't."*

"Why not?" Nyx pressed, clinging to the silence before his answer like she needed whatever response he'd give like she needed oxygen.

"The past cares little about the present, little dove. It's better to live a life with regret than to never live at all. The past cares for no one, the present waits for none, but the future beckons with open arms. Greet it like an old friend. Embrace it," his words crooned.

"You know, if you want to have a private conversation, I can always leave the room," Azeil stated, punctuating their conversation with the gravelled timbre of his voice.

Orion turned to Nyx's father, shaking his head with a low, mocking chuckle. "But that wouldn't annoy you quite like this does, would it? I bet you're just *dying* to know what we are talking about."

"You want to know what I'm *dying* to know, Orion?" Azeil retorted, leaning forward in his chair until his elbows pressed against the table's surface. "I want to know what's been happening in *my daughter's* life since I had to leave three months ago to keep my life. When I had to leave *my daughter* behind with the body of her uncle in this house. Do you know what that's like?" he pressed, lips twisting in anger. "To leave your *only* daughter behind with your *dead* brother's body cooling a few rooms over?" He smacked his hand on the table.

Nyx blinked against the pain in her chest, tearing up the scars of Asher. She wished Orion would cease his goads in favour of her sanity—what little she had left. Because, though Azeil's words were directed at Orion, Nyx couldn't deny her own guilt. She realised she hadn't considered her father's grief or the anguish he felt. That he'd lost his brother the day she'd lost her uncle. That although she'd lost Asher—her lighthouse in the vast churning waves of her mind at sea, Azeil had lost his compass—his sense of direction in his ever-changing and fast-paced world.

"Dad," Nyx called gently. "Don't."

"Why not?" Azeil retorted, raising his eyebrows as he gestured to Orion with a curt wave of his hand. "He deserves to know what he's done," his gaze darted to Orion, voice lowered several menacing octaves. "He should know the life he's taken."

"But he didn't kill Asher, you know that," she said.

"Didn't he? Last time I checked, his presence in our lives ensured it."

Orion straightened, squashing the butt of his cigarette against the glass tabletop. "I *didn't* kill Asher. You have Ryder to thank for that."

Azeil's bitter laugh echoed throughout the room. "He killed Asher because of you, but you already knew that. Like you knew he thought it'd draw Nyx back into the room and away from the front door where Niko waited for Nyx when he'd heard her voice," Azeil said.

Was that why Asher died? Nyx thought, gaze flickering between her father and Orion. *Had Ryder hoped Asher would make a sound and draw me* away *from Niko?*

"It sounds to me like you need to trust people sparingly, *Azeil*," Orion drawled, voice devoid of emotion. "First Ryder attempted to kill Nyx, and then he killed your brother. Sounds like something a detective *should have* noticed."

"Don't you *dare* pretend like this isn't your fault." Azeil seethed, visibly trying to control his waning temper. "Aren't you the reason *your* brothers are being tortured?"

"*Enough*," Nyx ordered, raising her voice in the same moment she moved to push Orion back into his chair and toss a stony glare at her father, noticing the detective badge strapped to his belt for the first time as he leaned back into his chair. "Neither of you are in the right, just like neither of you are wrong. *We* lost Asher and were blind-sided by Ryder and Amir." She turned to Orion with a calmness like a calamity waiting to happen. "*We* both are to blame for Niko, Kade and Kotori's situation."

Azeil's soft laughter pulled Nyx's eyes away from Orion as Azeil spoke. "He needs the book you had when I got here, doesn't he?"

Nyx eyed her father warily. Equal parts wanting to know *how* he knew that and keep him at a distance. "What do you know?"

"The book contains a full, detailed layout of Leon's estate. Think blueprints on steroids. With notes on hidden passageways, entry points, weak foundations, the passcodes to each of Leon's underground cells and anything else you'd need to plan an effective jailbreak," Azeil laughed, pulling a sleek phone from his pocket, glancing down at the screen and skimming over its display before he pushed himself out of his chair and started toward the front door. "He needs it to free the men you've been trying to find, and whom we both know you'll help him rescue. He *needs* a mortal to see its contents too … I'm assuming the twins are involved, right? Unless *you're* willing to help him."

"How can *I* help him?" she said, a frown creasing her brow as she hurried after Azeil.

"You share Asher's blood," Azeil stated simply.

"Okay? I'm not following."

"Your blood—*our* blood is a loophole to vampiric lore. Where, had you not been a descendant of Asher's, you wouldn't be able to see *or* touch it as a vampire, but since you are, Asher's knowledge is yours," Azeil explained, his gaze trailing to Orion where it stuck, seeming to fill with unspoken words.

"What—" Nyx spluttered, staunching her response as she ignored the ghostly press of Orion's presence behind her.

Azeil paused with his hand upon the front door handle, propping it open as he turned back to her with a soft smile that did little to hide his distaste for Orion. "I don't resent you for completing the transition, Night. That was your decision to make. Not mine, not Asher's, not theirs or his. It was yours."

A swell of serotonin wept into Nyx's bloodstream with his words. If not for the gold of Azeil's badge catching the light, she would have basked in his words; the feeling of rightness in the tide of her newfound life. "When did you get your badge back?" she said instead.

Azeil glanced down at the detective badge, a hesitant smile spreading across his face. "When I was entrusted with the current investigation in Celacali."

"When was that?" Nyx pressed, stepping forward when he backed over the door's threshold and onto the front veranda.

"This morning," Azeil said, eyeing Orion distrustfully for a moment. His fingers slowly released the wooden door until it swung closed, and the ghost of his parting words touched her ears. "I'll see you later, Night."

With a huff and the thud of his boots upon the floorboards, Orion bracketed Nyx's shoulder, peering down as she turned to him. "I have a bad feeling about this."

As much as Nyx wanted to pretend, she couldn't deny the uneasy sputtering of her nerves and the jittery pulse of her heart. A sigh full of months-long exhaustion trickled from her lips, the weight of the world seeming to bear down upon her shoulders. The unconscious urge to lean into Orion's shoulder flew at her mind, beating out the stability she found in him—in his unwavering presence and the fierceness of his concern. But she held herself back.

"Me too," she admitted softly, staring after her father's once more retreating form.

* * *

Stars smattered the sky's darkness as the crashing of waves roared against the cliff face and sea spray caught in her tousled curls. Nyx looked out upon the horizon of the Avonsano Ocean, her weight on her forearms, the wooden grooves of the staircase platform digging into her elbows. Orion's dark presence loomed, the scent of nicotine wisped around him as she angled her neck to look at the man beside her. The shading of his snake tattoo was emphasised by the ivory of his skin, its forked tongue extended like it scented the air. Nyx knew he was the furthest thing from a saint but what about the *good* he'd done? Was he flawed? Yes, but she couldn't judge when her soul was as stained as his. They were somehow in this together.

"You're staring," Orion drawled, pulling his cigarette away from his lips without tearing his icy stare from the horizon.

"No, I'm not," she said, hastily swivelling her head.

A doubtful hum ghosted the shell of her ears as the weight of Orion's gaze settled on her, and her heart jolted in her chest like hummingbird wings. She turned to face him.

For a moment she felt as if the air had been stolen from her lungs, like an inferno steals oxygen from a forest it ravages, when her stare locked on his. Memories of the kiss they'd shared in the darkness of an alleyway, his fingers twined in her hair sashayed before her eyes.

"I was just … *thinking* about everything's that happened. How much more my life has changed in three months," she said, refocusing on the present while wondering just how much of herself she wanted to bare to him.

His irises lingered pointedly on her chest—her heart—as his pale brows arched with disbelief. "Anything in particular?"

Nyx's mind urged her to seize the small window of opportunity, to use it to understand the world she'd been thrust into, of the vampirism she barely understood. She understood the transition, now firsthand, but she didn't *understand* the workings of the species she was a part of—what being a vampire *truly* was.

"Aside from the transition, being able to walk in the sunlight, blood consumption and mind manipulation, what else should I know about vampires?" she asked, her mind churning as she tried to tie the folklore to what she thought she knew.

Orion seemed to contemplate her question for a beat, bringing his cigarette back to his mouth before he exhaled and offered it to her with a gentle curl of his lips. "Got a few years?"

Without letting herself shy away from the challenge in his eyes, she plucked it from his fingers and lifted it to her lips, inhaling. Nyx couldn't hide her surprise when she didn't cough or splutter, catching his smile before it vanished.

"We don't have many weaknesses despite what media and folklore suggest. There's starvation but that's more like … a coma if we're starved for more than a month, *pure* silver is a paralytic drug, but smaller doses weaken and wooden stakes to the heart *will* kill," he paused, a teasing smirk across his face. "You already knew about the last part … despite your failed attempt on my life."

"And?" she prompted, eager to know more if he was willing to give it.

He held her stare as a sombre edge laced his tone, a lonely, bitter truth, "Immortality is filled with a thousand sights you'll remember fondly but, it won't *ever* prepare you for seeing the ones you love the most grow old and die while life ceases to touch you," he said.

"Was it hard?" she said, peering up at him before she hurried to explain herself. "Seeing your parents die."

"I wish I could say yes, but I didn't see them die. Leon ensured we left my homeland *before* then," he admitted lowly.

"So, you never …"

"No," he said, turning to peer out over the ocean. "I didn't."

Nyx heeded the shift of mood and redirected the conversation back to answers about vampirism, "What else should I know?" she said.

"I don't need to tell you about what the two types of vampiric bites feel like, since you've already experienced both of those," he said, his gaze flickering pointedly to the bite marks—*their* marks—that scarred her flesh when he turned back toward her. "I *think* that's it for now."

"Ah, yes," Nyx said, the beings of a smirk twisting her lips. "Let's not forget *who* bestowed me with the knowledge of a *painful* bite and *who* taught me what a *pleasurable* one feels like."

"Is that a hint or a challenge?"

Feigning disinterest with a shrug, Nyx forced herself to quell her rioting emotions. "It's nothing. Merely a fact like the sun rises when the moon sets."

Orion cocked his head in that eerily, intimidating manner she'd grown used to—and now found endearing. "Poetic but I don't believe you," he said, his voice a murmur.

"Funny," she mused, pursing her lips as his arm brushed against hers, "because I remember you saying the same thing to me when I was telling the truth."

"Say it," he uttered; his glacier irises sharp with a glint she couldn't ignore as her heart jolted, betraying her beneath his knowing gaze.

"What?"

"You don't trust me, and that's fair … all things considered," he paused. "So, say it."

Confusion etched her brow. "Say what?"

"Tell me what I can do to gain your trust like Kotori, Kade and Niko."

"Why do you want my trust? Aren't you the personification of 'I don't need anyone'?"

A muscle feathered along the underside of Orion's jaw, his gaze straying to the moonlight on the waves before he refocused on her. "Sometimes there's more to a person than meets the eye," he said.

Nyx arched both eyebrows in surprise. “What do you want, Orion?”

“I want a lot of things, it’s just … some of them aren’t paying attention.”

“Aw, is someone mad because he can’t *always* get what he wants?” she taunted, peering up at him deviously.

“I *always* get what I want,” he said, his stare flickering to her mouth for a moment, serpentine tattoo shifting upon his forearm as his palm pressed into the wood beside her hip. “One way or another.”

XXV

Azeil

Sirens echoed through the police station where a row of tinted windows ran along a wall overlooking a crowded reception area, sunlight dappling the tiles as Azeil started down a sequence of desks. He diverted down a corridor to the left that led to a section of board rooms where Issac Silvia—the chief of police—waited for him. Ignoring the press of a dozen eyes that followed him like a dark shadow, his heart galloped beneath his sternum. *You've done nothing wrong,* he reminded himself despite the prickling of unease along his arms. *Silvia cleared you of suspicion when Kai Salas was found dead.*

As hard as Azeil tried, a piece of his soul pressed against his chest, asking him why he didn't believe it despite his own assurances. Was it because he couldn't shake his memories of the night he'd been forced to flee Celacali to stay alive? Leaving his daughter and his career behind with seemingly half-assed explanations? Or maybe it was the way he longed to purge his nightmares of the gargled sound Asher had made as a friend turned foe before their eyes and blood stained a colourfully patterned shirt. Then, Nyx. Despite every other memory, every other shard of rammed glass in his side, it was Nyx and the tide of unspoken words that stuck between them that hurt the worst.

It was all of it, he thought, pausing before the third door along the corridor. *It was enough to drive anyone mad.*

He knew that most would shun their children if they'd done a *quarter* of what Nyx had—knew they'd blame them for everything as long as they didn't have to take the blame themselves, but Azeil knew it was his fault for not telling his daughter the truth in the first place, and it was a bitter pill he'd swallowed as he'd left her covered in blood on their house's front steps. He had known when he'd kicked her out in the heat of an argument. But it was too late to take it all back now … even if he wanted to.

So, instead, he'd made himself—and Nyx—a promise he was determined *not to* break; to stand by his daughter. Even *if* she put him through whatever fresh hell she'd found herself in, he'd stand by her. He could promise her that much without her knowing. *Even if* she kept the company of Orion, Kotori, Niko and Kade … he'd swallow his distaste for them. For her, he'd try to be civil.

I'm going to need a therapist on speed dial, he silently mused as his mind tossed the conversation he'd shared with her to its forefront. With a long-winded breath, he smoothed a hand down the front of his asphalt-grey shirt and willed his unphased mask to cinch into place as his palm met the steel door and he entered the board room. His stare swept over the room in a measured drag, finding Issac Silvia seated at the head of a long table in the room's centre, littered with case files, empty leather chairs tucked beneath its glossy surface beside him, and a whiteboard of suspects and connections engulfing the wall at the chief's back.

"Azeil," Silvia greeted, gesturing to a seat beside him with a jut of his wrist. "Take a seat. We have a few things to discuss regarding your return and re-instated position."

Azeil's gaze narrowed as he crossed the room, keenly noting the burgundy hue of Issac's dress shirt and the gleam of his watch face. His distrust muttered louder than any siren, his fingers drumming the table's grainy surface as he sat and waited, mind revisiting the past.

"You're doing it again," came Asher's voice from the backseat of their mother's car, tearing Azeil's insides.

"Doing what?" he'd said, a phantom breeze ghosting his forearms.

The crystalline memory of Asher's adolescent features twisted into a mock sneer as he pointed to the window by his ghostly shoulder. *"Tapping on the window. Find another way to release your* nerves, *Eil."*

A warbled scoff alongside his younger-self's dismissal. *"I'm not nervous."*

"Sure—"

"Azeil?" Silvia called, wrenching Azeil from his memories. "Are you okay?"

"I'm fine. A little tired but okay," Azeil said, dismissing Silvia's questions like Asher's sky-blue eyes to the depths of his mind.

"If you're sure—"

"I am," Azeil said, cutting off the sympathy-tinged concerns in Silvia's eyes as he dropped his hand into his lap.

"Then, I have one major concern I need to address that I *should* have asked yesterday," Silvia said, his voice laced with an authoritative edge Azeil knew well.

"Sir?"

"I know you left Celacali due to the loss of your brother, my condolences go to you and your family, but I'm afraid I wasn't honest with you," he explained, watching him carefully.

A frown grew on Azeil's face as his instincts prickled, sensing there was more. "What am I missing?" he said, cutting through the silence.

"The board and I share a similar mindset regarding a recent investigation, and we've mutually agreed on one thing: we *need* you on this case," Silvia said, the faintest of grimaces twisting his lips like the words left a sour taste in his mouth.

"Why do you *need* me? There are other detectives," Azeil said curtly.

Silvia leaned forward until his elbows rested atop the table, hand rubbing a path over the knife scars of his forearm. Something troubled settled in the chief's irises as he nudged a case toward Azeil with a grim set to his jaw.

"Because, for whatever reason, *this*," he paused as he flicked the file open and pointed to a photo of a grinning blond-haired boy with dimples and sun-kissed skin, "is Jesse Stone, and he's been missing for *days*. But what's strange enough for myself and the board to put you on a high-profile case after the bad press of the Salas investigation, is the ties it has to this," he pulled a second picture of a copper-haired girl with high cheekbones and a button nose out from beneath Jesse's. "This is Maria Thomas, and she went missing in 2012 before she was found dead in the same year in Celacali's eastern suburbs."

"So, let me get this straight," Azeil countered, "Jesse tying to Maria, a child of thirteen who went missing on an investigation I shadowed as a *training* detective, qualifies me as the best man for the job?" Incredulity echoed in his voice.

"You're the only detective *alive* who was on those scenes, Azeil," Silvia said quietly, a severe weight to his words.

"That doesn't make me the best fit," Azeil objected.

"I know, but we have a potential landslide on our hands. One child missing is too many," Silvia said, levelling him with a determined look.

"And you're sure you want to give the case to me?" Azeil said, grateful for the opportunity but aware of his reputation all the same.

Silvia waved a hand to the whiteboard over his shoulder. "You're good at your job and find your way on the grisliest of cases, but I know there's no one else who can do what you do—who *thinks* like you. There are too many *threads,* and I don't need them unravelling any further. So, I *need* you on this case. We need to find Jesse and stop whoever took him before they do worse," he said.

"I'll take it on one condition," Azeil said, grasping a hold of the first thought that drifted across his mind.

"Name it. The board wants this solved, and I want to bring Jesse's parents news, even if it's not good," Silvia said, sighing as he reached out to return the photos to the case file.

"You keep my name out of the press."

Silvia surveyed Azeil with wary eyes. “Should I be concerned about this request?”

“Probably,” Azeil admitted, rising from his chair, and pushing it beneath the table. “But what other choice to do you have?”

“Consider it done,” Silvia said, nodding. “But be careful. Something tells me that this isn’t going to be like *anything* we’ve seen before.”

Azeil’s roughly timbred voice carried across the room, “Celacali has a way of doing that, but if there’s one thing I know, sometimes you have to join the lesser evil to fight for the greater good.”

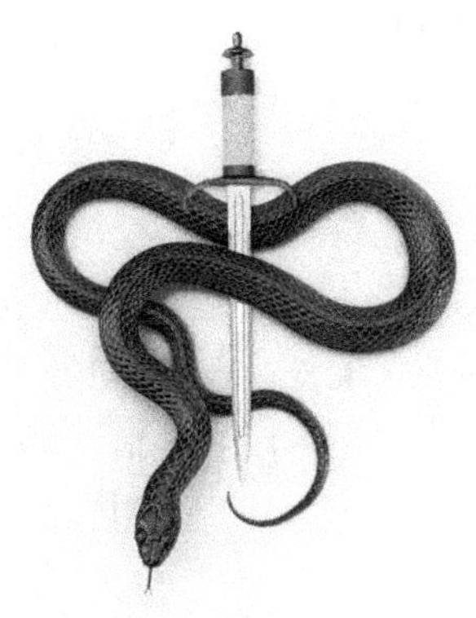

XXVI

Leon

Lavender and teal lights twinkled along the arches of the *Whirl Swinger*—a ninety-two-metre tall variation of a carousel with swings suspended from its rotating top—and its oceanic-themed body and top. Sharks, dolphins and various other sea creatures swam across the metal as Leon lounged on a nearby bench. His stare was fixed on the spinning ride, his ears trained on the delighted squeals.

The ride cast flickering, chain-link shadows across his emerald silk shirt and Leon keenly noted the evolution of the boardwalk and its lively crowds—not for the first time since his return—recalling the wooded stretch as nothing more than a pier locals had fished from or docked their boats to in the centuries before when he'd visited the city. It was strange now, like watching sand trickle to one side of a timer, to see such … *modern* technology. He remembered a time where such things were unfathomable—a far-reaching dream of a desperate man.

So there he sat amongst thudding feet and the chatter of a dozen conversations, the past so far out of his reach it almost seemed surreal. A daydream to comfort him over the years he'd walked the earth. *So much has changed,* he thought as he inhaled life. *Horses are replaced by cars. Fireplaces are retired for central heating, quill and ink discarded for phones and computers, humanity so unafraid of forgotten myths.*

He waited for an Ivory Skull. Darlyn. He'd requested his presence after learning of the man's ploy to create his own gang using the benefits Leon provided them. This was distasteful and the longer he waited, the greater his distaste for Darlyn, the soon-to-be *dead* Skull, grew. He wished he didn't have to remind mortals why it was foolish to cross him whenever they forgot their… frailty, but it couldn't be helped. Humans had a short-term memory. They were greedy and didn't appreciate what they had. *They* always *wanted more,* he mused.

Presently, Darlyn arrived and sat beside him, oblivious.

Leon turned to appraise him, fixing an emotionless mask across his features. It wasn't often he did his dirty work in person but when he did, it was a memorable occasion. He catalogued the over-confident posture the Skull held, man-spreading his worn jeans, vested jacket unbuttoned to reveal a white shirt, ivory skull embedded in his bicep as a permanent reminder of his indiscretions.

"This better be good," Darlyn said, brushing his hand over his buzz-cut, topaz eyes on Leon's, boots scuffing the ground.

"Darlyn, I presume?" Leon drawled as he looked away, sunlight reflecting off his own highly polished shoes.

"Yeah. And … you are?" Darlyn said.

Leon pursed his lips, the man's insolence grating his last nerve as he breathed in a calming breath. Slaughtering the man in plain sight *wasn't* smart and would draw unnecessary attention but his ire quickly gave way to something else as he realised, *He doesn't know*. Satisfaction perforated his mood. Mire had not told Darlyn anything more than the basics and yet, the mortal had met with him, regardless, caring little for his life in his foolish delusion of power.

"Leon McIntyre," Leon said, ages-old irises fixed on Darlyn, whose eyes widened a fraction. He cocked his head to the side, a pleased chuckle rumbling from his chest. "So, you've heard of me then? *Great.*"

"I thought you—Mire said the founder of the Ivory Skulls was dead. That he's been dead for … *years*," Darlyn said, stumbling over his words giddily.

"Here's a tip," Leon began as he turned back to the Whirl Swinger and the people shuffling from the ride, new replacing old. "Don't believe everything you hear."

"You should be dead," Darlyn said, his tone etched with confusion.

"You'd be amazed at how many times I've heard that."

"But …" Darlyn trailed off, "That's not possible."

"For the likes of you it is," Leon drawled.

"*How?*" Darlyn pressed, his eyebrows arching high across his brow.

"For someone whose life rests in my hands, you ask so many *irrelevant* questions," Leon said, enjoying the way Darlyn's heart stuttered at his words.

"My life?" Darlyn parroted, a sombre edge to his voice.

"I'll tell you something that's served me remarkably well in my lifetime, Darlyn," Leon said, waiting until he knew Darlyn's attention was unwavering before he continued, "Mortals are disposable."

The beginnings of a smile played across Leon's lips as Darlyn reared back like he'd been slapped, scrambling to his feet, and clutching the backrest of the bench.

"What—" was all he accomplished.

Darlyn's panicked heartbeat filled Leon's ears amidst the boardwalk's cornucopia of sounds, finally, fear bled into the mortal's eyes.

"*Sit,*" Leon ordered, a familiar ethereal command in his tone.

Darlyn reclaimed his seat with gritted teeth, gaze darting for someone to save him. "What is this?"

"Unimportant."

"But—" Darlyn started, his words gritted through his teeth before Leon cut him off with a scolding hum.

Leon's gaze locked on Darlyn. "*You will find Nyx tonight and inject her with this,*" he paused to retrieve a silver-filled syringe from his pants pocket, sliding it safely into Darlyn's vest. "*You will tell her it's from Phaelyn and say* nothing *more.*"

"But—" Darlyn protested, fear cleaving his irises.

"There's something about Nyx I need you to test. She has so much … *will*, it makes me wonder," Leon paused, his gaze flitting over Darlyn's face. "What is it about her blood-line that makes her so *different* from my children?" A beat of silence before he breathed a contemplative sigh. "She would make quite the addition."

"Then take her. Make her your prized … daughter," Darlyn said, hesitating upon the last word as his eyes brimmed with a pleading undertone. "But let me go."

A displeased sound rumbled from Leon's chest as he considered Darlyn with a sneer, his voice laced with a simple truth. "Tonight, you *will* die."

"*Please*. I don't want to die," Darlyn pleaded, a desperation-tinged tremble to his voice so different from the confidence he'd exuded minutes before.

Shadows of the Whirl Swinger's swing-seats flickered over the Skull's terror-filled features, passers-by with showbags and stuffed animals oblivious to their exchange; a result of a simple manipulation of perception surrounding the chair. They thought they saw an out-of-service stall. Nothing interesting here.

Leon rose from the bench and peered down at Darlyn, lips twisted with disappointment, fingers shooting his shirt cuffs. "You mortals rarely do," he said. He gestured to Darlyn with a flick of his wrist. "But loose ends like you *must* be disposed of. Disloyalty is a sin."

XXVII

Nyx

Joyous and yet haughty calliope music trickled through the gaps in the wooden planks of the boardwalk, muddling with the thudding of footsteps and the bustle of tourists. The moon hung high in the sky and incandescent light dappled the darkened sand. Her leather boots and the pads of Ares' paws sifted the grains as they wove between the pillars along the boardwalk's underside. Her pupils expanded to accommodate the poor lighting, so it appeared as if she wandered a sunlit street rather than the shadowed depths of the night, the clarity of the darkness eliciting a warm feeling in her chest—a deeply woven satisfaction she revelled in.

The tell-tale shift of sand beneath feet ghosted her ears, her head angling to her left to find Orion walking beside her with the grace and silence of a serpent slithering through foliage. He was, as usual, dressed entirely in clothes of the darkest shades, from his pants to his crew-neck T-shirt, black on black. The only exception were his bracelets.

If it were not for a primal sense of the hunt percolating in her blood, Nyx might have worried about the closeness of humans and the potential of being caught, might have worried about her father's involvement in the investigation she and Orion had kickstarted in their pursuit to free Niko, Kade and Kotori from Leon's twisted grasp. Might have, but didn't. As they slipped around wooden pillars and ducked under jutting beams, their focus was intent on the blond-haired Ivory Skull whose adrenaline-filled heartbeat was a soundtrack, his sloppy footfalls rattling above them. She turned to Orion, lips quirked, eyes deepest onyx and, with an incline of his head to the Malamute at her side, Nyx swiftly tapped her linen-clad thigh, drawing Ares' attention. Then she murmured a low command

and he lowered himself onto his belly, almond irises trained on hers while he awaited her next order. He watched her, waiting, as if to prompt her into letting him be more than a guard dog.

"I still don't understand *why* we had to bring him if he has to stay here," Nyx muttered, glancing worriedly over her shoulder at Ares as she followed Orion deeper into the boardwalk's underbelly.

Orion released a huff of breath—part-sigh, part-groan—his frigid irises flickering toward her. "Because you might as well use the mutt's obedience and appearance to your advantage. A lot of people will avoid a dog if it's alone without a leash, especially if their markings seem … aggressive," he said.

Nyx hushed a laugh, straightening the pulling sensation of her maroon-coloured straps against her neck, the ribbed tank top baring her arms to the warmth of the night's air. "You think *Ares* looks aggressive? I think his markings are cute," she said.

"Says every woman ever about *any* animal that could rip them to shreds," he drawled, side-eyeing her with a shake of his head.

"We don't all say that."

Orion paused, swivelling. "No? So, a snarling wolf wouldn't make you say, 'Ooooh, look, isn't it gorgeous?'"

"That's not fair," Nyx protested, a frown creasing her forehead as she peered up at him and the shadows across his face. "It's a *wolf*. They *are* beautiful because of their natural tendencies, but it's about the survival of the fittest. Not appearances."

"But if you saw one in the wild?" he redirected, ignoring her protests.

She pretended not to hear, turning toward the sound of the Ivory Skulls' thudding heart as Orion's amused chuckle slinked across the sand. "What's the next move, Orion?" she murmured, tossing him a look before she took a step and his hand darted out to wrap around her forearm.

"Do you remember what I told you about the boardwalk's design? How it juts into the ocean for several hundred metres or so but will end at the shoreline beneath the underbelly?" he questioned, his hold light upon her arm as his gaze brimmed with steely conviction and determination.

"I do."

Orion dipped his head in a satisfied nod, releasing her arm and taking a step back from her. "This is where we split up—"

"What? That wasn't the plan," Nyx exclaimed, eyes narrowed to a blistering glare.

"Wasn't it?" He cocked his head, feigning a look of confusion while his lips twitched with amusement. "It must've slipped my mind."

"I hate you."

Orion tutted, hands tucked into his pockets as he began walking backwards, grinning.

Groaning with irritation, she asked, "What then? And why do we have to split up?"

"It's the same as it always was except, we have to split up so our *friend* can't slip past us and onto the open stretch of shoreline. We have to split up so we can herd him to where we want him." His eyes seemed to lighten in the darkness. "Survival of the fittest, remember?" Then he pivoted and disappeared into the shadows, one with the darkness.

It was a habit of his, she realised, seeming to enjoy his ability to slink around undetected and without disturbing the night's silence. A faint smile lifted the corners of her mouth before she resumed her path beneath the fairground underbelly, the breeze off the ocean carrying sea salt and the sweet-smelling fragrance of narcissi to her nostrils. An eerie sensation tripped up her spine and across her shoulders, spreading down her arms, chest, and legs until she felt the resounding lull in the tips of her fingers and toes. She thought of the power and ruination she could reap, if she wished. Nyx wove around a pillar, trailing her fingers across the surface as her senses zeroed in upon the Ivory Skull, leading her deeper in, leading her darker down.

Tha ... thump, tha ... thump, tha ... thump.

Nyx wondered if she should have been concerned, about her satisfaction coating her tongue like honey trickled over pancakes, or if somewhere between the night she had met Kai and now had always been her path, if she'd always been destined to delight in the thrill of the hunt or the wet warmth of unsavoury men's blood coating her skin. Had she always been intended for this lifestyle of death and darkness? Somewhere, tucked away in the furthest corners of her mind, something protested the rightness she felt as she ducked beneath a low-hanging beam, bellowing its disagreement like the cries of a rage-driven solider, seeking to claw its way to the forefront of her skull and purge her of the *wrongness* it loathed.

A wrongness Nyx *never* wanted to be free of.

The clattering of a metal can startled her from her thoughts, her head whipping in the direction of the sound. Footsteps thudded above her, screams tangling with the heartbeat her heightened hearing tried to pinpoint. The smashing waves colliding against the shoreline muddled her fractured focus as she strained to control her new senses. Flickering, neon strobe lights irritated Nyx's eyes, a dull throb pulsing in her temples as her fingers twitched nervously. The sense of being watched heightened.

"Not funny, Orion," she half-called into the shadows, gaze darting from pillar to pillar in search of his familiar platinum hair.

Tha ... thump, tha ... thump, tha ... thump.

"Not Orion," came a rough voice with a lilted accent before a sharp, pricking sensation blazed across her throat and she shoved backwards.

Too late. A ragged gasp spilled from her lips as she shakily raised her hand to her throat, eyes wide and trained on the empty syringe the Ivory Skull waved patronisingly at her as she pulled her fingers from her neck.

"What did you do?" she gasped.

"It's just a bit of silver, sweetheart. No need to get so … worked up about it," he jeered, rolling his shoulders, distaste in his eyes. His face portrayed a man whose desperation and warped desires had led him down a path of no return, one ending with his death or someone else's. A man who was easy to be controlled. "Phaelyn told me to say *hello* and that you have her to thank for this."

Nyx's eyes tracked the syringe as he tossed it to the sand with a scoff, confirming her suspicions and plunging her with a sickening sense of dread. *What happened to a vampire with silver* in *their bloodstream?* No good would come of this. Her mind scrambled in search of information about silver and the effects it had on vampires, keeping her stare trained upon the glaring man with dark intent.

"What's the matter? Don't know what silver does to you?" the blond crooned, a perverted grin stretching his lips.

"You're not Viliaris or Mire," she murmured instead, mind latching onto *who* he was.

"Correct."

Her vision distorted and spun like a broken film before she hastily blinked the sensation away and forced herself to refocus, to fight the silver in her veins. "Then who are you?" she said, gaze darting between three figures of the man.

"A nobody," he paused as a low hiss sounded and her vision settled enough to glean the haze clouding his eyes. "But he wants you."

Could it be? she wondered, seeing his pained wince. *Is he* commanded *to be here?* "*Who* are you?" she repeated, a firm edge to her tone despite the swaying of her senses and the dread elicited by his words.

"A *dead* end," he spat through gritted teeth, eyes brimming with disdain.

Swallowing the lump in her throat, she wandered several paces away from him, grappling for the mental bond between herself and Orion before she collided with a blockage that sent her nerves skyrocketing. She stumbled and her legs felt as unsteady as a foal learning to walk. A jittery sensation crawled over her skin and across her mind, hands trembling at her side as she blinked once. Twice. Three times, to try and clear a foggy haze. The Ivory Skull watched her, his stare searing into her skin, branding her flesh. The slow step he took toward her sent her stumbling back several paces. An old fear raised its head and gripped her while she scrambled for footing, desperate to re-establish control. The same fear that'd protected her from Kai's wandering hands or the death she'd caused since she'd turned. A fear she loathed with every pore of her body, with every atom. But she supposed there was always going to be *some* downfall to the pedestal her newfound immortality had placed her on. Everything powerful was bound to have a fatal flaw, and hers just happened to be the short time she'd been a vampire and a silver-filled syringe.

So naïve.

A fully-fledged vampire *could* survive a stake plunged into their body if the odds were in their favour—a fact she'd learned *after* Orion, Niko, Kade and Kotori had disappeared—nor would it paralyse them like it'd done to her upon Elveszett Bluff. Silver, however, would weaken a vampire regardless of its immortal lifespan, ridding them of their immortal strengths and senses until they could barely hold themselves upright. It left them vulnerable to mortal wounds and without the strength to defend themselves from those who wished them harm, like this Ivory Skull who intended to make her death as slow and painful as possible.

Sensing it, her brown irises flickered white-gold, lips curling into a snarl when he dared another step toward her, and she stumbled back. "Don't take another step, or I'll—"

"You'll what? Fight me off?" he snickered, gesturing to her trembling body with a lazy sweep of his arm. "You're struggling to stay standing, girl, but you seem to think you'll be able to win this battle?"

"I lose a battle when *I* say so," Nyx snapped, tripping over the bolted base of a pillar in her retreat, her back colliding harshly with the sand-covered floor, fingers digging into the grainy ground as she pushed herself into an upright position and her arms quivered with the movement. "Not some puppet."

"Puppet?"

"Isn't that what you are?"

"I'm *not* a puppet."

Nyx scoffed, ignoring the narrowed tilt of the man's eyes and the squeezing of his hands beside his legs. "You're just a piece on Phaelyn's chess board."

"I'm trying to stay alive since you and your boyfriend want me dead. Since *they* want me dead," he stated, lilted voice taking on a deeper edge as anger coloured it.

"Not … boyfriend," Nyx protested, it was becoming an effort to speak. She grimaced after each word left her lips. *Orion, where was he?* An eerie grin split her face.

The Ivory Skull frowned, coming closer with a sneer twisting his features. "What're you smiling at?"

She tipped her head back to peer up at the gang member. "Right about one thing … *sweetheart*," she got out.

"And what was that?"

"We want you dead."

Where Nyx had assumed the clinking of metal was Orion's bracelets against his skin, she realised a moment too late that she was wrong. Metal didn't clink against flesh. The metal-on-metal sound was Ares' name tag on his steel collar. The muffled thud of his paws against the sand brushed her skin like the grains they flicked onto her clothes. A deathly growl reverberated from the Malamute's chest when he halted between two pillars, head lowered, lips pulled back from his teeth in a blood-curdling snarl, ears pressed flat against his head, hackles along his spine raised.

There would be no saving the Ivory Skull from his fate in Ares' maw. It was in the toss of Ares' head, the spittle flying, the twitch of his muzzle and the agitated ripple of the corded muscle beneath his pelt. It all signified one thing to Nyx; Ares' willingness to protect her. It was loyalty she knew would end in a bloodshed, that she could stop with a simple command, *if* she willed it.

"You think this mutt will save you?" the man crooned as he dared another step toward her trembling frame.

The silver was muddling her senses in a way that made his voice sound like he was close one minute, and far away in the next. Blinking up at him through heavy-lidded eyes, she struggled to hold herself upright, an unnatural weight pressing upon her shoulders as the man inched closer and something in the air shifted.

His fate was cast with his next step and the shift of muscle along Ares' haunches as the Malamute launched himself at the Ivory Skull. The beast closed the short distance between the two in a few short strides before the white of his teeth flashed and a pain-filled bellow rent the air.

The sharp, biting tang of blood permeated Nyx's nostrils, mixing with the salt scent of the ocean and sweet fairground above when Ares knocked the gloating man to the ground and his canines ripped into skin with a wet tearing noise. Agonised sobs escaped the man's throat, gurgling past his lips in a sound too fluid-logged to be good while Nyx watched emotionlessly, content.

Orion appeared from the shadows and a string of curses slipped from his lips.

Pale irises darted between her and the Malamute before he strode forward and grasped Ares' collar, tugging the bloodstained dog from the Ivory Skull. Orion seemed to consider the man, wet breaths passing his lips as the vampire's gaze trailed over the mauled flesh of the man's chest, arms, and throat. A faint flash of satisfaction appeared in his eyes before he stooped down and grasped opposing sides of the man's head. He twisted with a *crunch* and the Ivory Skull slumped, heart unbeating, gaze unseeing.

Orion threw a glance at the black and white Malamute, who licked the blood from his muzzle with adrenaline-filled eyes, then to Nyx, surprised. Nyx remained where she was, blinking up at him from beneath heavy eyelids.

A beat of silence passed as Nyx watched the shift of Orion's expression before he breathed out a ragged sigh and his fingers raked through his hair. "Well, shit. That's one way to create a helvíti hound."

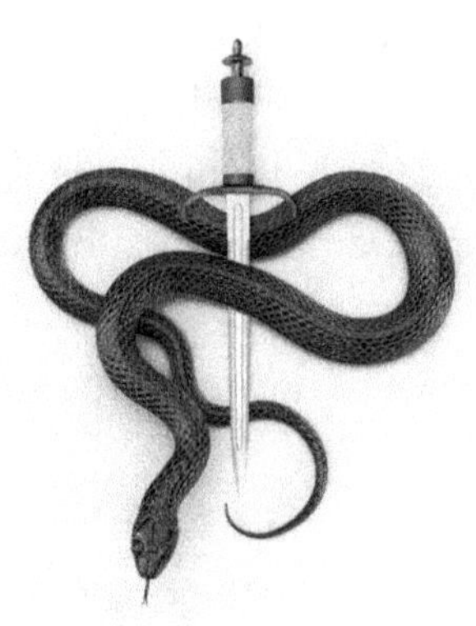

XXVIII

Nyx

"What the hell is a helvíti hound?" Nyx uttered, budding anger and frustration rising. She glared up at Orion, who stood before her, gazing down at her couch-ridden form.

He released a pent-up breath, eyeing Ares beside Nyx on the plush, grey couch with a weighing gaze. "It's a type of vampiric protector. Their genetic makeup compliments ours when they're combined, creating a 'helvíti hound'," he explained.

"But what *is* a helvíti hound?"

"An immortal protector or guard dog for vampires."

"Immortal?" she breathed. "You made my dog *immortal*?"

"Whatever you're thinking, stop," Orion ordered, stooping down so he crouched before her. "That's not how it works."

Nyx's eyes narrowed, forehead creasing as she eyed Orion with poorly reined anger. "How does it work then?"

"Helvíti hounds *have to* be loyal to a vampire *before* they turn. Their sole purpose is to protect an immortal being forever. It's a process that can only begin if the canine kills someone who tried to harm or kill their vampire or halfling counterpart." Orion tutted when Nyx opened her mouth to interject, pushing on with his explanation. "It's like our transition in the sense that it truly begins once a life has been taken except, they continue to age until they hit maturity and then they're true helvíti hounds."

She pushed herself into a sitting position, stare locked on his. "If it's like a vampire's transition, then you somehow gave my *dog* your blood without me noticing."

Orion stilled as his eyes met hers. "I did."

"When?"

"The night you left the cave after I said I needed the leatherbound book," Orion admitted. "Alexander tried to warn me against doing it—"

"And Tobias? Did he warn you?" she pressed, the sense of being shoved and tumbling from a petrifying height clinging to her.

Orion's gaze flickered to the floor. "No, he understood why I did it. Encouraged it."

Something shifted in Nyx, fracturing a piece of her faith in Tobias while simultaneously swelling when she thought of Alexander's protests. It rankled and she hurriedly pressed the heel of her palms into her eyes. She wished she could hide from Orion, a defence mechanism she both loathed and treasured before she pulled her trembling hands from her face and deftly shoved herself up from the couch.

As her boots connected with the stone floor, Nyx staggered, the world tipping on its axis, sending her to the ground as black spots speckled her vision. Orion moved quicker, his cigarettes and sandalwood scent filling her nostrils as his arms caught her, righting her. Pressing lightly upon her shoulder and pushing until the cushions of the couch cocooned her, her eyelids fluttered closed.

"Are you *trying* to kill yourself?" Orion snapped, frustrated. "You were essentially *drugged* less than two hours ago and somehow, you think you're perfectly fine to storm off." A sharp bark of laughter as he paced before her. "Newsflash, sweetheart. Even we're not invincible to the after-effects of liquid silver."

If her eyes had been open, she *might* have caught Orion's frantic gaze, noticed his faltering pace or his agitation. But she didn't. Her eyes stayed closed against the nauseating feeling pushing and pulling her in two different directions while he turned his back to her, staring at the vast empire sprawled on the wall behind them.

Nyx wanted answers, but she began to think instead, of Orion, of the muscles seeming to ripple beneath the fabric of his T-shirt in a way she wished she didn't find so … captivating. She thought about it now behind closed eyes. And, *god*, did she wish the colour of his eyes didn't kickstart her heart the way it did. Or that determined loyalty he held toward his companions and his protectiveness of them, of her.

"Why did you do it?" she murmured, the only important answer to her.

"It seemed appropriate. You've been attacked by Phaelyn and Qadira, cornered by Leon and now, you were drugged by a puppet to them all." Orion cleared his throat. "I thought that, for whatever reason, if I'm unable to be here, then you need backup. Two's better than one."

"You did this … for my protection?" Nyx reiterated, eyes opening.

"Like I said, it's better to have more protection than not enough."

She nodded slowly, glancing toward Ares who slept with his head propped on his paws. The blood that had once covered his muzzle was nowhere to be seen, his white fur purged, but the colour of his coat had changed. Now it was dark, almost like he'd been dunked into a vat of ink.

"Is he supposed to look different? Or am I seeing things?" she asked, voicing her puzzlement.

"His appearance will change more than the darkening of his pelt," Orion confirmed. "His teeth will lengthen a few more inches than they already are, and his overall temperament will be more like a wolf when he's *protecting* you. Oh, and his eyes … well, they'll be more white-gold than brown."

"Oh."

"Everything else about him will stay the same … with all our strengths, of course."

"Of course," she muttered, as she tried to sit up. "What happened to the body?" She frowned, eyes darting to his. "Why can't I remember more than you saying something about helvíti hounds?"

"Because you passed out," he paused, "about a minute after I said that."

She groaned, ignoring Orion's bemused chuckle. "What about the body?"

"The police found it like we intended them to. Except, we didn't have to fake the animal attack this time. Ares did that for us."

"You're not funny."

"I thought it was funny."

Nyx's eyes widened, her hands pressing into the cushions as she hurriedly sat upright. Black spots once again distorted her vision, the after-effects of the silver clinging to her like a vice. "Do you think he knows it's us?"

Orion arched his eyebrows, peering down at her. "Do I think Azeil knows it's us? I'd say the thought has crossed his mind, but unfortunately for him, there's this thing called evidence that he needs first… *and* the whispers of Celacali say he's been entrusted to a different investigation."

Nyx longed for Orion's words to hold more comfort than they did and chase trepidation from her nervous system. A part of her wondered if this would have been easier had Kade, Kotori and Niko been here. She wondered if Azeil's reappearance and assignment to the investigation linked to the head vampire they sought to vanquish was karma's way of laughing in her face. A whirlwind of what-ifs Nyx struggled to formulate into coherent piles. She didn't know what compelled her to voice her thoughts, but some part of her felt the need to share them with Orion. Would he understand how she felt?

"Orion?" she began, unsure of how to phrase her next question. "What's stopping you from telling me *why* you need Asher's journal?"

"Leon," he murmured, so softly she might have missed it if it wasn't for her heightened senses.

The truth etched in that single word clamoured in her mind. It all confirmed his earlier behaviours, and repeated like a mantra feeding her anger toward their vampire sire. The thorn in all their sides. *Why doesn't Leon want me to know what's in Asher's journal? And what did Uncle Asher know that Leon wants hidden—that Asher hid from* all *vampires ... except for those of his bloodline?* "What did he do to you?" she said, breaking the silence and her train of thoughts.

Orion's gaze locked with hers, brimming with silent anguish and she knew—without him needing to say—that Leon had taken something Orion treasured more than any object or memento. It was in the way his fingertips traced the armrests of his chair, in the way he looked at her now.

"You've always been the one who called the shots, right?" she pressed, suspecting she now knew the answer.

"Yes," he admitted.

"And … now you're not?"

"*Trapped*," he managed between gritted teeth as a wince distorted his features—there one breath, gone in the next.

Dread lodged in her chest as the pieces tumbled into place. Leon controlled Orion with a sire command, *trapping* him in a prison she remembered only too well. Bright hate flared in her for him, hate for Leon and … worry for Orion. Or was it anger or fear or … love? Defining was confusing, she just knew she'd do whatever she could to free him from those ties—to free them all. Time was ticking. Too many of Leon's commands frayed wills, Orion had said, and she couldn't—*wouldn't*—let Orion, Kotori, Kade or Niko become lost within the glassed prison of their minds, wouldn't let them become *half* the men they were.

Orion released a soft, chuff. Like he'd been holding his breath and couldn't keep the air trapped any longer. He sat back on his black-iron chair, arms draping regally over the armrests, an ankle propped upon his knee as he seemed to right himself amid the bindings of Leon's control.

"I used to complain about the constant rock music," he began, "the riffs of a guitar solo or Niko's stink of weed. And if it wasn't him leaving his records all over the place, it was Kade and his sketchpads. A walking art supply … all those abstract decorations he handmade." He looked down, fidgeting. "Hell, I complained about Kotori's books. You could follow a trail of everywhere he'd been by his books. He left them stacked beside the couches, in doorways." Orion laughed, but the sound was empty. "And now, all I can see is them, is all of it. The ghosts they left behind." He exhaled and the sound was heavy.

Nyx chose not to say a word, letting him speak. It was the most she'd ever heard him say, seriously, about his brothers. She waited.

"I'm not a good person by any means, but they made *everything* easier. They made life worth living."

Silence.

Nyx wasn't sure how to respond to his candour so, instead of provoking a coiled serpent, she redirected their conversation, "I'm assuming Leon is going to pay the consequences, right?"

A slow smirk trickled across Orion's lips, ethereal irises devoid of emotion and yet, *brimming* with smug satisfaction. His mood lifted. "Yes. Tonight was proof that we're getting under his skin and I'm *sick* of his … *control*."

"So glad I helped confirm that theory," Nyx uttered drily, adjusting her position on the couch. "I'd *hate* for Phaelyn to be disappointed with her findings or for Leon to *lose* his … sons."

"But disappointed they will be," Orion said and this time, when he looked at her, his smile was real.

*   *   *

"Aside from your bouts of *luck*, what other combat skills do you have?" Orion asked, his face shadowed by clouds.

"Luck?" Nyx parroted, rolling the word over her tongue as if she thought she'd heard him wrong. "You think everything I've done was *luck*? I *barely* survived everything that was thrown at me. Didn't I die?"

Orion appraised her silently with an intensity Nyx could *feel*. It disarmed her as she held his gaze, wondering what he was thinking while the breeze of Elveszett Bluff buffeted against her back and the weariness from the final remnants of silver leeched from her bloodstream, drawing away like a fever lifting.

"Your heart stopped about … two hours after I gave you my blood," he said, voice taking on a sombre edge as he dropped his gaze to the ground. "You bled out, despite Kotori's stitching and my blood, *that's* why Niko, Kade and Kotori weren't there when you woke."

Nyx's heart jolted as she blinked once, twice, and then three times as her mind fought to catch up. A feeling akin to having her legs kicked out from underneath her suddenly overwhelming. *I never won, not really*, she thought, worrying her bottom lip between her teeth before she shook her head and squared her shoulders, determined to not let this piece of information send her into a spiral of hysteria.

"They thought I was dead?" she said.

Orion lifted his eyes from the rocky ground, an unspoken apology in his eyes. "Niko and Kade did, but neither of them had witnessed the beginnings of a transition. Kotori was sceptical but the others were too caught up in their emotions to *see* the truth … *that's* why I sent them away, not because they needed to sleep."

"How did you know I wasn't dead?" she asked, her mind felt stuck in a groove.

"I was present when Kotori, Niko and Kade were turned. I've *seen* the transition from start to finish more than once," he said, rubbing his palms together before he straightened and swiftly changed the subject. "Now, back to why we're really out here."

"Yeah, that. Can't we do this tomorrow? During the day," she said, eyeing the moonlit shrubbery with a purse of her lips.

"You're going to show me what you've got. You're going to *stop me* from getting to you, even if it's violent. Right now, I want you to forget that I don't wish to harm you. Now, *I'm* your enemy," he said, stepping toward her like a lion stalked a wildebeest.

Breathing in a fortifying breath, Nyx dipped her head in a show of readiness, her stance widening as she prepared herself for whatever Orion chose to do, recalling every lesson on self-defence and hand-to-hand combat her father had taught her. As her heart collided against her chest, Orion shifted in a burst of preternatural speed and, without missing a beat, she whirled out of his path. Her surprised and delighted laughter echoed across the sky when he pivoted to face her with an irked scowl.

Her hand lifted in a taunting wave. "Missed me," she drawled, tossing him a wink.

"You're awfully cocky," he said, brushing a palm down his shirt.

"What can I say, I have an … *exquisite* teacher. He's very humble."

A low hum emitted before he moved and she nimbly ducked beneath his arm, landing a swift kick to the back of his knee until the soft *crunch* of gritty earth sounded in her ears and he crumbled to his knees. Nyx's head cocked, a bemused grin etched across her face as Orion huffed in annoyance and pushed himself up from the ground, dirt falling from his slacks.

"Watch yourself, little dove. Cockiness *is* an evil in itself and too much will kill you," he warned, circling her.

She spread her arms out in an encouraging gesture, grin sharp as she tracked his movement. "Well, c'mon then, do your worst."

His pale eyebrows arched, his head dipping before his lips stretched with a malignant grin. "Don't say I didn't *warn* you."

"Excuses, excuses," she mocked.

Orion started toward her. Dodging his lunge, she skittered around his shoulder, smiling when she whirled to face him and came face-to-face with nothing. Her heart lurched, grin slipping as she turned, ears straining to hear.

"Nyx."

Her stomach knotted as Orion's eerie drawl ghosted her skull, while she continued to search the tree line and rocky terrain for him. It was like he'd … vanished. There one moment, gone the next, and he'd done it as easily as breathing. *Where the hell did he go?* she thought. How *does he* do *that?*

"Nyx."

"Evasion, really?" she called out to the gaping *nothing* that stared back at her, the sensation of being watched prickling her flesh. "You're *awfully* good at hiding."

A startled scream wrenched itself from her as a leather-clad hand curled around her throat and dragged her backwards, a chest pressed into her back. Orion's chuckle rumbled from him to her, sandalwood and cigarettes washing over her senses. His lips brushed her throat.

"Hiding suggests fear," he murmured, releasing her throat as he spun her around to face him, his hands settling on her waist. "And I don't fear you."

"That's a shame." Feigning disappointment, she held his unearthly gaze.

A current passed between them, zinging through her veins with a ferocity that *almost* made her gasp as her palms settled on his abdomen, fingers twisting the fabric of his shirt. It was like whatever she felt for him—that she *couldn't* let herself acknowledge—didn't want to be shoved aside. It *wanted* to be accepted and heard, not feared and hidden. She knew it like she knew the end of one day brought another; it wanted out and with every day, Nyx found it harder to ignore. *How much longer can you lie to yourself?* the sliver whispered. *You can't run forever.*

"I pity anyone who dares to cross you," he said, almost a whisper.

"What makes you say that?"

"It's the truth."

"Is it?"

"If anyone is foolish enough to cross you … they cross *us*, and we'll revel in reminding them of that," he said, his stare holding her prisoner as his voice oozed a bloody promise. "I *pity* the person whose life will end if they endanger yours."

"How can you say that?"

Orion shrugged, his grasp tightening on her waist. "Because … somewhere along the way it stopped being about revenge."

"But—"

"For you, we'd—*I'd*—tear the world apart until everyone's blood whoso*ever* wronged you, stains my hands. For *you*, we'd do *unspeakable* things … but you already know that, don't you?"

"I do," she murmured, a heady thrum in her veins.

"We'd gift you someone's heart on a silver platter if you wished it," he said slowly as his hand trailed up her side until it settled at the nape of her neck, twining in her curls as he stooped his head a fraction from her lips. "That's how much control you have over us. *That's* how we're yours as much as you're ours."

XXIX

Kade

The stench of rot polluted the room—*cell*—of the grey-toned sublevels Kade was a prisoner in. Kept away from his companions while the metallic stench of his unwashed blood and the decomposing carcass of Aloys continued to rise. Kade winced at both the memory of his hawks' screeches of agony and the pain smarting across much of his bare upper body. His flesh was littered with bruises and savagely drawn cuts, his blood trickled slowly down his chest and collected on the floor, droplets beading and falling from the tips of his elbows as his healing abilities fought—to no avail—against the silver in his bloodstream. *Mind over matter,* he thought bitterly as he tried to will his flesh to stitch together. His mind was obviously elsewhere as a constant drip, one he couldn't stop despite his terror and his anger, continued to *be* the matter.

Will this be what kills me? After everything*?* he thought, a seemingly distant part of him clinging onto hope—of his freedom. *Will I die like a mortal trapped in the body of an immortal?* It irked him how easily Leon and his *puppets* had rendered him so fragile, so mortal, and susceptible to their unforgiving blades whilst he was forced to grit his teeth against the pain, tearing at his wrists with every frantic tug against the metal bindings. Tired, sore and frustrated by the chain secured to the ceiling when all he wanted was to tap into his sadistic fantasies, ruining Phaelyn, Qadira and Leon so *thoroughly* that they'd beg for a simple death. He'd make them regret knowing his name. For trying to stand in his way of what—who—he'd waited *two years* to attain. Waiting … somewhat patiently for Nyx to move to Celacali after they'd sent the ball rolling all those months ago. When all he'd wanted to do was snatch her from the streets of Malor whenever he returned, before she had moved to their city, without Orion's knowledge. There had been plenty of opportunities to pull her into the shadows before she could scream, before anyone would notice she'd disappeared.

Those nights she had walked home from the ancient-looking library she frequented, or when she'd caught a train to a concert venue, or left Xander's condo after their weekly movie nights, the parties and clubs she'd visited for friends' birthdays—the possibilities had been endless. And he wasn't about to let them—or anyone—stop him from reclaiming her. Not even if he'd been the reason for that uncertain edge to her whenever she laid eyes on him. *I'll make it right*, he thought, straightening like it would ease the ache of his legs. *I'll be* better *for her. She deserves that much.*

He knew he should be ashamed of his actions and thoughts, both past and present, but some part of him *wasn't*. It was as if from the moment he and Niko had seen Nyx snap in Malor, *he* had snapped. He was ambiguous by nature; unpredictable one moment, and then predictable the next. An unclear personality he'd cultivated until it suited the image he *wanted* people to see, learning that it was better to be underestimated in a world of people quick to judge, than for them to see him as a challenge.

Kade preferred the friendly, joking and somewhat charming persona over his truer, sadistic and unorthodox nature, where he spared collateral damage little thought. And maybe that's why he didn't really regret what he'd done to Nyx—his deceptions and betrayals were familiar ground—in his warped path of attaining her. As if she were an object rather than a person. But she wasn't an object for him to attain. As much as his thoughts contradicted him, he *knew* she was more than that. That she'd always be more than that. Despite the lengths he barely stopped himself from going to in the two years he had waited for her, like the sun waited to see the moon, desiring to know her and the bloodstained mess of her mind—to know *who she was*. He vowed with every trace of 'good' in his bones to give her the life she deserved … even if he wasn't the person she wanted to be with at the end. *Of her immortal life*, he thought with profound longing. He smiled, remembering Orion's update via their shared bond. Kade would try, for Nyx, for a moment of her attention as long as he could experience her vampirism and the bloodshed with her. He could settle for that.

"Can you settle for a moment of her attention?" came Orion's voice through their bond, startling Kade when he realised, he'd let his mental guards drop. *"Because you're not the kind of man who lets something they've waited for, slip through their fingers."*

"I'd do it for her," Kade replied, ignoring the prickling sensation of his features sharpening and rutting beneath the tide of his fatigue and pent-up anger—he'd been unable to hold his mortal features for several days and often found himself changed with the facial structure of something angelic and demonic combined.

"You'd give her up ... just like that?" Orion pressed, voice laced with doubt. *"After everything you've done, you'd let her go?"*

"It doesn't matter what I want, Orion. If she decides, after everything *that she doesn't want me, I'll let her go like we promised her those months ago. I'd do that for* her.*"*

"Why?"

"Because she deserves someone better, someone less ... obsessed."

"Obsession can pay off," Orion mused playfully.

"I stalked *her, Orion. For years. When will that* ever *be okay?"*

"I bit her, took away her free will and *tortured her but I'm not giving up on her,"* Orion listed his aggrievances in such a matter-of-fact way it was galling. *"So, why are you?"*

So typical Orion, Kade thought. After all these years, and he was still surprised. *"She deserves someone who will worship the ground she walks on, who would burn down the world if it harmed her,"* Kade said, a longing for Nyx's presence deep in his chest.

"And you wouldn't do that for her? You wouldn't fight *for her?"* Orion pressed.

Kade could almost picture the way his brother's eyebrows arched as he dared him to disagree. *"I don't think I can be the man she needs,"* Kade admitted, his golden irises dropping to the bloodstained floor at his admission, grateful Leon hadn't forced his emotions—pain—to be felt by Nyx again.

"You're getting cold feet now?" Orion's mocking laughter seemed to echo through their bond. *"I think it's too late for that."*

"I don't have cold feet,*"* Kade snapped.

"Then what are you trying *to say, Kade? Because the reflection time you've had for three months doesn't seem to be working. Have you* truly *given up so easily?"*

"I'm saying she deserves more *than I'll ever be able to give her!"*

"But how will you know if you don't try to be that person?"

Kade blamed the silver laced in his bloodstream for his lack of control as he abruptly closed the bond between himself and Orion, but he knew there had once been a time in the earliest months of his transition when he'd been unable to control his two masks, like now—one misleading, the other something derived from nightmares. He knew he'd always been impulsive, and he *might have* reasoned that was what had set him on a path destined to lead to Leon. All because he'd turned down his father's offer to become his partner and CEO, of the family business. Kade had cared little for the empire Natanaël Artus had built. A part of him wondered if his father would have ordered a hit on him if he'd accepted the offer—demand—like the obedient son he had raised, but Kade suspected it would've only prolonged the events to a later date.

He couldn't change it now. Couldn't forget the ruination of his art studio and the artworks within, the shattered windows he'd enjoyed painting in front of—day or night—the shards of ceramic sculptures he'd spent *weeks* moulding and carving. Or the shredded canvases stained and decorated with acrylic and oil paints. His creations, his empire. The way he'd felt the moment the studio door closed behind him and his gaze swept across the large, industrial-style room with its open layout, glass walls overlooking a lush forest with rolling hills and a babbling river that connected to a vast lake. All gone. Instead, images of his ravaged oasis were what remained; torn paper covered in charcoal and defaced pencil sketches had littered the floor beside broken furniture, pencils, paintbrushes, and art supplies trashed and scattered everywhere.

Kade remembered the way his boots had crunched upon the broken glass and the blow to his head that had come from behind, sending him to his knees.

His grasp tightened now on the chains secured to his wrists, teeth clenching as he tried to shove the memories to the back of his mind—where he'd let them fester for years—unwilling to relive that moment of his life, his masked attacker—*attackers*—and the brute of a man who had raised his curled fist, striking Kade's face before the c*rack* of his nose breaking sounded and blood gushed down his upper lip and chin.

Kade saw the calamity of his past as if he stood in the wreckage of his art studio now and not in the sublevels of Leon's prison. He *felt* several pairs of roughly calloused palms and the cruel press of fingertips along his arms as he tried to blink the swell of his memories away, the eerie dragging of his feet while he fought to free himself from the men with varying masks of demonic-looking features. *"Let me go! Don't you know who I am?"* he'd screamed. His eyes screwed shut, fingers curling around the chains at his wrists, an agonised bellow of something between rage and anguish spilling from him.

Nothing but laughter in return. "*We know who you are. You have your father to thank for this ... he sends his regards*," a voice he didn't recognise.

The flash of a blade danced behind his eyelids followed by the unforgiving drag of steel across his flesh. Once. Twice. A third time ... a fourth ... fifth ... sixth. Kade harshly tugged at the bindings, ignoring the tear of his flesh as another shout tore from his throat and the slashes bled into each other until he lost count.

He relived the cuts again and again until he knew he'd never deserve Nyx, that he was wrong for her, that he couldn't be what—*who*—she needed him to be. Though he might've believed he was destined for hell, his bloodstained past and monstrous qualities had earned him the title of a denizen of the dark domain. To him, Nyx was the heavens, a being perfectly combined of good and evil. Of light and life. Of hope and serenity. He was a mere demon who had set out with the intent to destroy the life she'd built—the fresh start she'd longed for—until all she knew was him and the darkness he favoured. That had been the plan.

Until he had come to know her.

Kade hadn't known he'd needed her in his life until she'd stumbled unknowingly into it. The phantom scent of books filled his lungs as his mind wrenched his memories to its forefront. *Look! And see!* they seemed to taunt him. He didn't believe in things like 'love at first sight' but somewhere, between the moment she'd almost dropped a copy of *Inkheart* to the floor, to when his eyes had met hers, something had quieted in his soul and obsession had given way to a tenderness he faltered at.

He could promise to *try* to be the person she needed, and he'd spend the rest of his immortal life trying to make up for the mistakes he'd made while knowing her. She was his *angel,* and he was the demon who'd always lurked in the shadows, watching when she didn't know it. Except, an angel like her couldn't fly down to hell with him. The only way to hell from up there couldn't be described as flying, not when his influence—Niko, Kotori and Orion's—had lured her, sending her tumbling, her wings torn from her, piece by piece. He envisioned himself catching her before she hit the ground, his forehead pressed to hers and his grasp tight on her, vowing to protect her from the world and the dangers it possessed. Until his last breath.

Is that what I would do?

XXX

Nyx

Waves lapped at the shoreline of Chades Cove, where people were clustered around a blazing bonfire, seeming to have forgotten the events that'd stained its sand in their pursuit of revelry. Nyx's leather-clad shoulder pressed into the trunk of a towering tree that bracketed the secluded cove from the boardwalk's glow upon the horizon. Flames the brightest shade of tangerine cast long shadows across the sand and the sun-bleached logs spaced around the fire were occupied by various Ivory Skulls—who'd claimed the abandoned cove as theirs—seeking a lull. Rock music played from the speakers of a boombox, while others danced with partners, their hands stretched to the night sky.

The longer she watched from the shadows, mirrored by Orion, the more she longed to blind herself from the tide of her memories. She saw the tree at the top of the sloping hill, bone-white irises tinged yellow from its middle to the crimson-ringed pupil. She hurriedly blinked away what came after, the terror-filled chase through the forest. Memories of wandering hands and an eighties track playing in the background. Of languid grins and patchworked skin, of teasing banter and eternal gazes. Of a deeply timbred chuckle from a towering brunette and the lightness of Orion's eyes as he straddled his bike with regal ease. Nyx wouldn't forget the firelit party or the malty taste of whiskey on her tongue. *I was so naïve,* she thought. As unknowing as she was to the quartet's vampiric natures then, she wouldn't trade the elysian filled night for anything, now.

"Nyx," Orion called softly, his voice almost muffled by rustling leaves overhead.

She caught his subtle shift toward her before the gentle brush of his fingers against hers startled her from her thoughts and she let her hands fall. "Hmm?" she managed, eyes widened a fraction. "I heard you the first time. You don't need to repeat yourself."

A momentary frown at her biting response dappled Orion's features, gaze tracking the uneasy shifting of her hands, senses tuned upon the thudding of her heart. "Repeat what, little dove? I only called your name."

Nyx began to disagree but found she couldn't, her lips pressed tightly together as a sinking sensation entrapped her and she willed herself to forget.

"Nyx?" came the muffled call of her name, drowned out by the roaring in her eardrums as her eyes slid shut.

Trying, and failing, to purge herself of fire-lashed flesh and dark stains soaking sand, of singed hair, and blistering, shredded flesh. She swallowed the echoes of sharp and desperate pleas from an auburn-haired woman and the haunting end of her life in the cove. Nyx's blurred vision blearily registered as she forced her eyes open and sank to her knees.

"Nyx, hey. *Breathe*," came Orion's voice.

A sharp curse when she didn't respond, the jangle of steel bracelets followed by the featherlight caress of fingertips across her cheeks. A blurred figure cradling her face between his hands, thumbs tracing circles into her skin, cigarettes and sandalwood engulfing her senses with every intake of breath.

His voice was tinged with worry—*panic*. "Hell, you can hate me for the rest of eternity, but you have to *breathe*."

"I—*can't*," she forced out, eyes screwing shut as she sucked in sharp, uneven breaths. A feeling akin to iron bands weighed on her chest like bags of sand, seeking to drag her beneath the depths of her past terrors.

"You can, little dove," Orion assured, his orotund voice lowered several octaves in a pleasant, soothing manner. "I need you to open your eyes for me, focus on me and not your thoughts. Can you do that?"

Nyx relaxed her eyelids and blearily opened her eyes, meeting the ethereal, glacier-blue of Orion's, pinning her in reality as the roar in her ears quieted to a dull murmur. She leaned into the palms cupping her face, allowing herself a moment to be comforted, cataloguing the soothing and methodical caress of his thumb and the darting of his eyes to her lips. The heady sandalwood and cigarette scent of him. *Him* and the thrall of his dark soul, the insidious crimes he'd committed. *That's how I'll die,* she mused silently. A bitter sting of traitorous insecurities brought forth by her past terrors. *You'll be brushed aside when he's through with you. Until there's nothing left of you but screams.*

Orion blinked.

Nyx jolted and she *felt* the shift in his persona as his guards—like hers—rose and cinched back into place. She wished she hadn't moved and pushed whatever progress they'd made backwards because as she turned to him, she fought the urge to flinch from the cool distrust in his eyes. His jaw clenched like it was taking every ounce of his strength to mask the tension coiling between them and the yawning divide Nyx had widened in her haste to protect herself from her thoughts.

"Orion …" she trailed off. "I—"

His head shook as his lips pressed together, a scathing ache to his gaze as it flickered to the bonfire and then to her. "Don't apologise."

"But—"

Orion's gaze trapped her, pinned her in place. "I get it. I *deserve it*," he said.

"Orion," she began, grasping the serpent skin of his forearm when he turned to walk away. "I'm … sorry. I panicked. You were there, both now and then. And I—I couldn't separate memory from reality." Her tongue darted out to wet her bottom lip, grasp tightening on him as she noted the tilt of his head in her direction; the only indication that he was listening. "I was terrified that night. One moment I was a part of the most … boundless of lives, and the next, I thought I was going to die." Her voice caught, lowered to a murmur. "I was *terrified* of *you*."

A beat of silence passed as they stood, perched precariously upon the edge of truth. One wrong move would be enough to send them plummeting to the jutting rocks below. Nyx held her breath as Orion turned to face her, her honesty laid bare. An emotion flickered and Nyx *almost* missed it. A fracturing of his mask like a single splinter.

He straightened, squaring his shoulders against whatever else he felt—that he didn't want her to see. "Stay here until you see my signal." He strode toward the flickering bonfire and left her standing in the darkness.

Left with her warring emotions, she tracked his swift retreat, partygoers seemingly at ease with his arrival, Nyx knew her actions had plunged a chasm between them and their combined turmoil of letting someone in and allowing their defences to drop. She also knew there was more to Orion than he let her see, a story she shouldn't have known. Guilt speared her because she knew she shouldn't have been snooping. She *knew* he wouldn't have wanted her to know those pieces of himself unless he *chose* to share them. Guilt clung to her skin like a sheen of oil, slimy and hard to remove, as she followed his purposeful trek through the beachgoers. She recalled her unwillingness to share what she could read in the leatherbound book and how he'd watched her combing through its contents—as blank as parts of it had been to her eyes—in the moonlight tumbling in from the cave's ceiling. Or how he'd dared to return to Leon's estate with the newfound information the twins *had* been able to provide them from the paragraphs she couldn't read—a simple video call allowing them to decipher it and explain whatever they could learn—and he'd learned of Leon's plans, overhearing a conversation between him, Qadira, and Phaelyn as he'd ordered them to *fetch* a loose end from Celacali for its safekeeping.

But that'd been three days ago, three days of Orion following the Ivory Skulls—mortal pawns he'd told her Leon favoured because they could be disposed of easily—and overhearing countless conversations in their pursuit of *who* Leon wanted protected until they'd found the unlucky mortal; Viliaris Cree. This was a man Nyx would enjoy ridding the world of, a stark yet intricately sketched skull the lightest shade of ivory tattooed onto his right bicep, ruddy brown eyes lingering on the dancing groups of women and their friends with a callous smirk uplifting his lips. She knew without confirmation from Orion, that this was the man with past ties to Ryder and Amir they were searching for—a fact Nyx and Orion heeded with wary preparation.

"Do you see him?" Nyx queried, opening the bond she shared with Orion and the trio they sought to free.

A beat of silence passed before she felt his answer, *"I do."*

Her stare flickered to his as she recalled the twins' incessant draw-back to their plan. A condition they'd fixed into place as soon as Orion had stated that they wouldn't be involved, that they were to stay home and lay low. *"Lure him to the clearing, right? Or can we traumatise some Skulls instead?"*

His lips twitched as he fought the urge to grin before he tucked both hands into the pockets of his dark jeans and inclined his head toward the oblivious Ivory Skull. *"I'm going to have to deny that request ... at least,* this time."

A brush of heat from the flames caressed her face almost like it sought to welcome her and she remembered Niko instead.

"You know, we practically kissed just then." A cheeky grin split across his face as he waggled his eyebrows and knocked his shoulder into hers.

"You're an idiot," she said.

Her mind conjured up how she'd rolled her eyes. A painful ache lodged in her chest, filled with a sliver of her longing, of the way she missed his presence and the lifeful nature of his personality, of how he always brought a smile to her face or the way his embrace comforted her in ways she never thought possible. And when she thought of Niko, it brought memories of Kade. The swish of liquid in a bottle, Kade downing a mouthful of whiskey before he'd tapped Niko's shoulder and spoke in a low, taunting jeer, *"I guess we all just kissed then, hey, Niko?"*

As Nyx's feet carried her closer to the partygoers, a doppelgänger ache to the reminders of Niko came with the memories of Kade. The way the light played across his tattoos, his mischievous eyes, of the press of his lips against hers as a rock song played softly in the background, his enigmatic quality.

The Ivory Skull's gaze landed on her, a prickling across her flesh she felt like the raising of goosebumps. Eidolon hands settled upon Nyx's shoulder, waist, and hips, feeling as though they lingered for a moment while her mind centred her within the recollections of her life, and others seemed to ghost over her skin as if it'd all been a part of her imagination. Her lucidity settled in the span of two beats of her heart, enough of a reprieve to weave around a cluster of partygoers and wander past the brown-haired Skull. She tossed him a wicked, salacious glance, and right away, he began to hungrily follow her toward the shadow-blanketed forest with an anxious clenching of his fists.

Orion's amused voice trickled into her mind, so imbued with his delight she could picture the smirk twisting his mouth as she slipped around groups of people and the shadowed tree line reached out to welcome her. *"Would you look at that, little dove? It seems he hasn't heard of a wolf in sheep's clothing."*

"Don't sound so smug", Nyx drawled back in her head, fighting her own smile.

"So, you're not *thrilled by his naivety? Or the ease of our allure and how prey comes to us willingly?"* he prompted with an all-knowing tone.

She could feel his black-clad form slinking into the tree line as he stalked toward her and the clearing they'd settled on leading the Ivory Skull to.

"C'mon, don't be shy," Orion whispered guilefully. *"Admit that you like the darkness of this life, that you like the bloodshed."*

"We'll agree to disagree," she murmured, ignoring the thrum that passed through their bond, almost like Orion's chuckle reverberated down a line.

The rustling of leaves overhead and the soft crunch of foliage beneath her shoes soothed the unease Orion's words elicited—another truth she wasn't willing to accept just yet. A moment later, footsteps sounded from the tree line, following her into the forest's darkness. With several, purposeful zigzags around tree trunks, Nyx tossed a look behind her to the dark-haired man, ducking beneath a low-hanging branch and swiftly side-stepping some jutting rocks and fallen tree limbs. She paused beside a tree, resting her shoulder into the bark before she raised a hand and beckoned him closer with a curling of her finger in a 'come hither' motion and a saccharine smile.

As he eagerly quickened his pace, she whirled and rounded the tree, hiding. The reward of bloodshed lingered on the tip of her tongue, ambrosia she found herself longing to taste despite Tobias and Alexander's insistence that she stayed out of the murders now that Azeil was back in the city. She *craved* the metallic and decadent liquid, coveted the feeling it evoked within her and the crime of taking life, the ruination of her own mortality with each death she caused, desire chipping away at her human instincts in favour of the darkness she'd grown to love.

"You're her? Aren't you?" came the shouted question hurled at her back.

"That depends on *who* you think I am," she replied, continuing her path toward the clearing with her sights set upon the Ivory Skull as she walked backwards.

"You're the mortal Leon's protégés turned without his consent."

Surprise gutted her insides as, for a moment, Nyx forgot the ties he had to Ryder and Amir. She straightened at the clearing's edge, squaring her shoulders, and tilting her chin until she seemed to peer down her nose at him. "Why does he want you alive and under his protection?" she said.

The dark-haired man, *Viliaris,* chuckled, his scuffed sneakers toeing a fallen branch before he crept closer to her unwavering form. "Ah, so you and the blond were the ones who've been snooping the past few days."

"Answer the question, *Viliaris.*"

"Why do you *think* he wants me alive?" Viliaris reiterated, tossing his smug question at her face. "C'mon, indulge me since you and your boyfriend want me dead."

A muscle along her jaw twitched at the familiar quip at her and Orion's association. Her silvered voice lowered several, menacing decibels, "Rumour has it that you know something. Something that was once kept in yours, Ryder's, and Amir's possession but that's now in mine." She waited, head angled as a dark smile settled across her features. "Now, correct me if I'm wrong, but Leon wants the book I have and the information between its pages, and since he can't … *attain* it, he's settling for an interpreter. *You.* A *mortal* who can see its contents since he … *can't.*"

Viliaris opened his mouth to protest but before he could, she took several steps toward him with a *tinge* of her newly garnered speed until she stood mere centimetres away. A feather of breath left his lips.

"So, tell me, Viliaris. What do you think he'll do once he has what he wants and you're no longer any use to him?" she said.

"He's promised me his protection like he promised Ryder and Amir."

She tutted mockingly, gaze darting to Orion over the man's shoulder as he appeared from the shadows. "And look what happened to them."

Viliaris scoffed, gesturing to her with a disgusted sweep of his hand. "Am I supposed to be afraid of you, Nyx?" A low hum emitted from his throat as he dared a step forward, a sneer curling his lips. "I have *nothing* to be afraid of. Not when Leon wants … you, and not because of Orion, who—" he said as he whirled to find the glacier-eyed vampire on his left, "Leon waits to welcome back home," he finished smugly.

"Oh, he can wait," Orion spat.

"Are you sure?" Viliaris goaded, furrowing his brow in mock consideration. "Don't you have something to lose?"

Orion strode forward and he gripped the fabric of Viliaris' shirt, pulling the Ivory Skull harshly to him until their noses almost touched. The timbre of his voice was frigid, *deathly,* when he spoke, "I have *nothing* to lose. *Nothing.*"

"I beg to differ. Because somewhere along your way, you let," Viliaris gestured with his chin toward Nyx, "her in. You and I both know that Leon's going to enjoy taking what *little* you have left."

A snarl broke from Orion as he shifted so swiftly Nyx missed the placement of his hands until a sharp *crack* echoed across the forest and Viliaris crumpled to the floor. Orion's fists clenched and unclenched at his sides, the muscle along the underside of his jaw ticking, an inferno raging in his irises as Nyx watched his control slip. The blue of his eyes flickered white-gold, then blue and back again. She could only stand rooted in place, her gaze darting to the corpse between them and then to the smouldering vampire in front of her. An enraged growl ripped from his chest, startling her before his spine locked and his eyelids slid shut, head tipping up to the night sky for a moment as though he'd find his control in the waxing moon.

With a shuddered exhale, Orion's eyes snapped open and locked upon her, once more devoid of emotion. Where once was rage, now was cool control. "Let's go, little dove."

"But—what—?" Nyx spluttered, gesturing shakily to Viliaris and the unnatural angle of his neck while Orion approached her, gently grasping her forearm as his hardened gaze softened. "This wasn't part of the plan, Orion."

"I know."

"Then … *why?*"

Orion's lips pursed, a warring of emotions flickering through his eyes before a harsh breath passed between his lips. "Does it matter? We were going to kill him anyway."

"Of course, it matters!"

"Does it? What difference does it make?" Orion pointed to Viliaris, eyes ablaze. "He's dead and *this* won't change that. Neither will knowing why."

"But—"

"No, Nyx," Orion breathed, his voice hushed. It was as if his anger had been spent, leaving him with a centuries-old exhaustion. "Dead men don't talk, but their bodies do. Let's go home." He gently led her toward his motorcycle tucked between two trees across the small clearing haloed by the moon.

Home, he'd said. She realised the cavernous house *was* her home. Except, it wasn't the home she longed for, not quite, not yet. Deep in her heart of hearts, she knew that home was not home without the quartet who'd turned her world upside down.

XXXI

Nyx

Silence.

Pure, tension-filled silence slithered through the cracks and crevices of the cavernous walls, clinging to her body until it echoed in her ears and resonated in the marrow of her bones. Nyx's gaze alternated from the book perched upon her thighs to Orion, who sat straight-backed in his dark throne, fingertips drumming on the armrests. She peered at him from her white hanging chair, noting his unrest that hadn't lessened since they'd returned from Chades Cove over an hour ago.

As Nyx's gaze resettled on the classical romance in her lap, Orion shoved himself up from his chair and started pacing like a caged beast. The movement made her think of Ares and the comfort she found in knowing he was still with Alexander and Tobias, safe from the tensions here. Her gaze darted traitorously to the exit. Then back to agitated Orion who reminded her of a time bomb, waiting to go off at any second. The constant rhythm of his stride grated on her nerves, making reading impossible.

She abruptly closed the hardback with a sharp *snap.* "Are you *still* mad about Viliaris?" she questioned, silvered earrings brushing against her jawline. "I thought you said *it didn't matter.*"

Orion's pacing slowed a fraction before he came to a stop beside the black marble statue of Cerberus, the three-headed dog. The tips of its ears reached Orion's hips. "It doesn't," he said.

Her eyebrow arched, unconvinced by the smouldering anger rippling off him like the heat of an inferno. "Well, *something* has been bothering you since Viliaris. He really got to you that much?"

"Like I said, *it's nothing*," he dismissed.

Her eyes lit in a dark challenge. "I don't believe you," she uttered boldly, daring him to disagree with her. "I think Viliaris touched a nerve you've tried to keep hidden. Even though you *say* this is about sending messages to Leon, it's something *more*."

"*Stop*," Orion warned lowly, irises flaring with each word she spoke.

Her head bobbed and reason tumbled from her lips, seeming to condemn him, "I think you're afraid. You're *afraid* of having a weakness—a soft spot—where they can hurt you. *Me*."

"You're wrong."

"Am I?" she prompted, leaning forward in the hanging chair until her hands curled around the woven base and her unbound tresses cascaded around her shoulders. "Leon *does* have something you care about; your brothers."

"Leon does what Leon wants because he can. He doesn't give a shit about what I think or what will affect me," Orion said.

"Are you sure—"

"Would you stop asking me that?" Orion snapped, cutting her off impatiently.

She eyed him carefully as the tension in the room seemed to thicken, hanging between them so intensely a knife could cut it. She untucked her feet and stalked toward him until she glared up at him with centimetres separating them.

It infuriated Nyx that she had to crane her neck to hold his gaze just as the slow creeping smirk that pulled at his lips bothered her. She *shouldn't* find his smile and the mirthful glint in his eyes attractive, *shouldn't* find his self-confidence and blasé demure enthralling. And she really *shouldn't* remember the press of his lips against hers or the way his hands had curled in her hair and gripped her waist.

But she did.

And as if that wasn't bad enough, the memories of her first kill and his presence over Dries' shoulder sent her heart careening in her chest as a salacious thrill shot down her spine. All those bad, bad things.

God, did she hate him more for it.

"Well …" Orion interjected as her eyes narrowed.

"Who asked for your opinion?" Nyx queried. "All I'm saying is that Viliaris got under your skin, and I want to know why because you *don't* change plans unless they're not going to end in your favour."

He shrugged, serpent-embellished hand raising to run through his hair, corded veins rippling, sending a lick of heat curling in her throat.

His glacier gaze flickered to her like he could sense the traitorous tide of her thoughts, his smile widened, tone taking on a heady edge even as the words he uttered weren't intended to be sensual, "And what if I just wanted to end his life quicker? To ruin Leon's chance of attaining the book? What then?" he drawled.

A terse sigh spilled from her lips while her fingers twitched. She wished to wrap them around his neck and choke some sense into him. "I don't *get it,* though."

"What don't you get?" Orion prompted, stepping closer to her until she had to crane her neck further to hold his gaze. "I wanted him dead so, I killed him. It's that simple."

"No," she disagreed, shaking her head.

Orion's gaze seared into her face. "What are you *really* asking me?"

The weight of his question pressed upon her, taking up space between them while she blinked up at him. Trying, and failing, to find the right answer. *Why wasn't he willing to trust me enough to believe my intentions were true?* Orion didn't care for her. He didn't care if she lived or died, he only cared for the sake of his brothers—his *only* loyalty to Nyx. Conflicted, Nyx cautiously broached the subject she thought was bothering him.

"It's not your fault, Orion," she said. "You only stood up to him, to a narcissistic vampire with a warped desire for a family. It's not your fault Leon has them."

Orion's laugh split down her sternum like a dagger. "For once, it's not about *them.*"

"It's not?" she murmured in disbelief.

"It's not. It's about *me*. And what *I* want."

Taken aback, she stammered, she'd gotten it wrong, *again*, "What do you want?"

He looked at her with an intensity that *almost* stole her breath. He leisurely swept his stare across her face down to the tips of her feet and then back to her onyx irises. Something … that invisible weight … pulled taut between them. She backed up a step.

His head shook. "As I said, it doesn't matter. And it won't matter until you're ready for the truth," he said.

Nyx stooped down and plucked a book off the top of a pile tucked beside a couch, hurling it at him in sheer frustration. It was too much, all this … whatever it was. Her sneer became a snarl when Orion stepped aside and easily dodged the flying object.

"You missed," he said with an amused tut.

"And you're a *prick*, so I guess we're even."

"I'm doing you a favour," Orion drawled, a mock frown plastered over his face.

"You're not doing *shit*."

He chuckled. He was so annoying!

"You're not," she repeated, exasperated. "You can't even *trust me* … why can't you trust me?"

"Because trust got me *killed*!" Orion snapped, his face shifting and rutting until the nightmarish mask slipped into place and white-gold irises stared back at her filled with a poorly reined anger.

Nyx's breath locked in her throat as she waited for him to calm down and for the explanation she knew lurked millimetres below his anger.

With a shaky control, his features reverted to normal and Orion's voice rang eerily across the cavernous hideaway, "Blood means *nothing*, little dove. It's a formality thrust upon us the moment we're born, forcing our hand and our beliefs until we're governed by it."

A heartbeat passed as Nyx's mind churned the unspoken story beneath the little information he'd allowed her to glean. Cautiously, she said, "What's … your story, Orion? What aren't you telling me?"

His stare darted to the floor like he wasn't sure how—where—to begin. And then, he simply started talking, "I was born in the city known as Silkgulf in 1618, a city little more than ruins now in history books. I was the second-born heir to the ruling monarchs, the second of three children, and the one entrusted with the birthright to someday claim the title of king."

"*King?* You're a royal?" she asked, even though she already knew. His sudden directness was disarming all the same. Her shock was true.

"Only of a long-forgotten bloodline. Whatever else that came with the royal title disappeared the day I was *almost* assassinated," he said.

Nyx nodded, gesturing for him to continue.

"My twin brother Xensor and older sister Nylora were less than impressed with the birthright I would gain. Both felt as though they'd been dealt a bad hand. Nylora because she was the firstborn and yet wouldn't claim the throne. Back then, it was believed a woman couldn't and wouldn't rule," Orion said, shaking his head with pursed lips. "They were wrong, of course, she was more fit for the throne than I ever was. She was … driven. Razor-sharp and quick-witted. Along with a rather … *violent* love of archery." He smiled sadly and it seemed to convey a hidden world of emotion. "Xensor was younger than me by four minutes, a fact I'd never let him forget until the day I wished I had. He was a warrior at heart. So much so, that our mother worried for him restlessly, pacing the walkways that overlooked the training fields whenever he was amongst the soldiers, learning to fight. He was charming in a devilish way, knowing what to say or what to do to attain whatever he desired. The women of the city flocked to him like moths to a flame." Orion chuckled, a gleam of fond nostalgia in his eyes.

As she listened, Nyx heard a slight, bitter edge to his words. Like he was holding his anger back in favour of portraying his siblings in a better light. As if he could sense the mounting curiosity within her chest, his voice mellowed and as he continued, it seemed tinged with sorrow—for himself or the past he revealed to her, she didn't know.

"I think I was twenty-five when I was crowned king of Silkgulf, it was 1643. It was also the day my siblings orchestrated my death. As soon as our parents had left to attend another court hearing. More of the townsfolk up in arms about their missing children … their plan went into motion. I adored my siblings like I'd adored no one else."

"What did they do to you?" Nyx breathed, unsure if she wanted to hear the answer but dying to know it all the same.

Orion swallowed thickly, striding to the black chair, and lowering himself into its seat with a pained wince. "I'll admit now that it was … something else. The thought, the swiftness of the way they executed their plan. It was *meticulous.*" His fingertips trailed over the intricate detailing of the armrests, gaze flickering to the metalwork. "The first blow came from this chair and not by their direct hand. A careful manipulation to the throne that Xensor's blacksmith friend helped alter, making it so Nylora could control the knife spikes that jutted out from hidden crevices with a simple press of her foot on a floor tile. I hadn't even *seen* it coming before the spikes protruded from the back of the chair and cleaved straight through my shoulders."

"And you still kept the throne?" Nyx blurted in horror, gesturing to the chair he sat in. "You *still* sit in it, even after that?"

"The spikes are only a memory now. Removed several, hundred years ago," Orion stated, shifting in the throne until his ankle propped against his knee. "But this chair is not how I died, little dove. Somehow, I managed to drag myself off it and to the steps of the dais, finding strength, despite the blood loss, to stand before my siblings, the crown they craved still on my head. Not that it mattered, Nylora stepped forward with the dagger I'd gifted her for her twenty-seventh birthday. She plunged it into my chest, its hilt was embellished with a curling serpent poised to strike."

"You're fucking with me right now, right? *That* dagger is the one that killed you?" Nyx shook her head with disbelief, ignoring the flashes of memory tied to the blade.

"I died metres from the throne I'd claimed and lost in the same day. A blade gifted to my sister embedded in my heart, while my brother looked on as he tossed the bracelet I'd given him onto my chest with a sneer." Orion paused, his gaze falling to his lap and the bracelet he tugged around his wrist. "I still remember the last thing he said to me like it was yesterday and not centuries ago."

"Oh God," Nyx said, unable to fathom anything worse than what he'd just told her. His own brother and sister. It explained *so much.*

Orion's gaze darted to hers, pinning her in place and jolting her heart. He said, "'You might have been king but now, you're *nothing*. You were destined to be forgotten and betrayed by those who you care about most. *Maledictus.*'"

"*Maledictus,*" she repeated, rolling the word upon her tongue before the little Latin she knew turned like a key in her mind. "*Cursed.*"

XXXII

Orion

Silkgulf, 1643

A sandalwood breeze permeated the rolling landscape of Silkgulf, a cobblestone castle perched at the valley's top, overlooking the city as dark shadows ghosted the land. Hundreds of candle-lit windows glared orange at Orion as he gazed across the empire of his birthright, the bitter tang of copper on his tongue reminding him of the mortality he'd lost—of his siblings' betrayal. *A king for a day,* he thought with a bitter scoff, toeing the dirt as the blood-slicked fabric of his white tunic clung to his chest. *And I lost it all.*

"It's hard, isn't it?" the man called Leon said.

His voice drew Orion's attention away from *his* kingdom to the man at his side. A man Orion had believed—spent years believing—was his parents' adviser, loyal to the Tyrie dynasty for decades. That was before he'd learned the truth on the altar of his family's tomb and he'd woken to find his siblings, Nylora and Xensor, gloating over their successful assassination. His dear siblings whom he'd slaughtered to complete the transition thrust upon him, their blood now staining his shirt. He surveyed Leon with distrust, wondering *how* no one had suspected his beastly—*vampiric*—nature.

Because that's what Leon was, a beast. He was the monster mothers warned their children about, telling them of a beast who lurked in the shadows. He was the man behind the missing youth of Silkgulf that had plagued his parents' rule for years. He'd been right under their noses. All the while, Leon had stood by their sides and offered guidance, what the king and queen could do to help. He'd offered sympathy to the parents, for their missing children, telling them patience, they may yet be found, and he'd offered compassion, that soon their suffering would end … but it was all lies and he, the orchestrator of their suffering. Everything had been Leon's careful manipulations, all the searches wild goose chases. It had always been him; a monster hidden behind the mask of a man.

Orion's lips curled into a hateful sneer, glacial irises looking Leon up and down. "You don't get to *sympathise* with me. Not when you made me this … *thing*," he spat.

Leon's algae-green eyes widened a fraction before he shook his head, lips twisting, fingers straightening the cuffs of his cream-coloured tunic. "Careful, *boy*. I gave you a gift," he warned.

"You made me a *monster*."

"Monster? I gave you a *gift*," Leon repeated, like he didn't understand Orion's anger.

"I should be dead," Orion murmured, anger guttering in the wake of his admission.

A softness swept Leon's gaze as he hesitantly reached out to grasp Orion's forearm, offering him a reassuring grin that turned Orion's stomach. "But you're not, and that's good," Leon cajoled, his tone sickly sweet.

None of this was good, Orion thought with narrowed eyes as he wrenched his arm from Leon's grasp. His siblings were dead, and he s*hould have* been a corpse himself. Not this creature of myth. Not overlooking *his* home with a rust-eaten shack at his back, a piece of tin clanging a repetitive tune until all Orion could hear was its grating song and the thudding of a heart.

Something inside him reared its monstrous head, the moon hanging high in the sky above like a pendulum of his fate. His newfound senses seemed to hone in on the racing of a heart and, as he strained to pinpoint its location, he realised with a sick plunging in his chest that the sound was coming from *inside* the shack.

Turning back to Leon with an icy glare, his voice cut the night, "Why can I *hear* a heart coming from there?" He gestured to the building with the point of his finger.

"A test," Leon stated, a gaping darkness stretching in his eyes before his tone took on an eerie, sing-song quality. "*Come here,* child."

The *crreak* of the shack's door drew Orion's stare from Leon's, horror making itself a home in his bones as a girl no older than seven with fawn-brown curls and dark eyes wandered across the grass-patched ground to Leon's side, wringing the front of her nightdress in her small hands. She peered up at Orion with wide, red-rimmed eyes as her heartrate spiked, and Leon's hands rested upon her tiny shoulders. The heart jackhammered.

"You're *sick*," Orion said, wedging distance between them.

"What I *am* is your *sire*, and you need my guidance to survive … unless you want your instincts to drive you insane," Leon said, his tawny-blond eyebrows arched expectantly.

"I'd rather be insane than whatever *you* are." But as he said the words, a sharp pain pierced his lungs and he gasped, his breath suddenly shallow. "Uh," he managed as he stumbled back, sudden agony eclipsing all else, ice-cold like the onslaught of a thousand winters.

"Did you know that vampires can control mortals with a simple command? A vampire, however, can only be controlled by their sire," Leon said menacingly as he dropped his gaze to the girl.

She began to cry, upsetting Orion further. *This was madness*. He took another step back, but couldn't leave. He couldn't leave that *thing* with a child, not while he still had a breath left in his body. That was not the man his parents had raised him to be. He was not the monster Leon wanted him to become.

"I couldn't care less about the lies you tell," he said, fighting for air. "I'm *not* being part of your sick game," he coughed, desperation setting in. What *could* he do? He could lunge for the child and take her … where? They wouldn't get far if he only had two gasps left to live.

"Oh, Orion," Leon drawled, mock disappointment in his voice, "I had hoped you wouldn't fight me. That you'd obey me without interference, but your mortality stands in the way."

The pain abated, like a lifting haze and Orion fell to one knee, eyes alight like a blue flame. "My mortality isn't the issue. *You* don't like my *humanity*," he said, sucking in air.

"I don't like your disloyalty. I *saved* your life," Leon bellowed, startling a whimper from the girl.

"And I'd rather be dead," Orion uttered lowly.

"Death is not a fate I offer you," Leon murmured, his softly spoken words as clear as glass. "You will, however, test my sire abilities."

And then, just as the haze of pain had lifted, it returned. But this time, it wasn't his own. It was *hers*. Orion could feel the staggering weight of her torment drowning his own, making it worse, *so* much worse. It was like smothering to death while his every perception, drawn to a pinprick accuracy, immolated. Over and over till his mind felt slack with affliction.

"I will do *no* such thing," Orion said, his chest squeezing as he fought to purge the young girl's terror from his mind. He could feel her heart beating in his head, like the wings of a desperate bird. Terror.

THU-THUD. Terror. *THU-THUD*.

"You won't have a choice."

"There is *always* a choice, and I—promise you," Orion fought to grit out the words, "That if you take mine, I'll make you—nngh." he struggled. The pain was excruciating in his head, his body, all over him. "Live to regret it," Orion vowed.

"Your hate will pass but your loyalty won't." Leon paused as if his thoughts sidetracked him before his gaze sharpened and refocused. "Your efforts are admirable," he said, pleased, "but pointless." A tangible silence stretched between them before he spoke again, "*Kill her.*"

Leon's command hung in the air like a double-edged sword as something *unnatural* curled around Orion's mind, burrowing into his skull as if nails were being driven into the foundations of a great, glassed dome. Each nail stole a shred of his control—free will—as a high-pitched keen echoed in his ears, every piece of his soul battling for release while his teeth gritted against the pain razoring his temples.

One nail, two nails, three, four, five, six, seven—

The girl, the girl. She was so small, so innocent. Her blood on his hands. His scream came first before he forced a single word through his clenched teeth, "*No*!"

"I said, *kill her*," Leon ordered, nudging the girl toward Orion.

"I won't," Orion said, shaking his head doggedly.

A sense of falling from the ravine to Silkgulf's north seeped into his bloodstream like a serpent's venom. As Orion held Leon's stare, he understood the terror a mouse must feel as it tried to uselessly outrun the toxin in its blood and the snake awaiting its meal. He understood it with a bitter tasting clarity as the maw of Leon's command clamped down around his mind, wrenching his control and sending him head-first down a path of no return—the path of *Leon's* choosing.

Somewhere in that chasm was relief, from no longer having to choose, no longer bearing responsibility. To just *do* as one was told.

"That's it," Leon cajoled, a grin spreading across his face. "It's not so bad."

Despite how hard Orion fought Leon's command, he couldn't stop the otherworldly control as his eyes burned and bled white-gold, features rutting and sharpening beneath the planes of his face with a sensation that reminded him of a blade's edge. His boots crunched in the gritty dirt as he took a step. Then two, before his newfound senses lurched him forward in a burst of preternatural speed and he stood peering down at the trembling girl.

Please forgive me, a part of him murmured to whatever gods would listen, as he grabbed her arm, a wail slipping from her lips. Another, deeper part made a promise to Leon. He could take what he wanted from Orion but one day, he'd find his weakness—not pawns or trinkets, no allies or control, no. Orion knew then if he knew his sire at all, *innocence* was his weakness.

He took one last look at the girl and tried to make her understand that he was sorry. Sorry for what he was about to do. His mouth opened. He was sorry he was not strong enough to stop this. Not yet. White fangs shone as his jaw unhinged unnaturally and she began to scream. So sorry, he would make it quick.

One day, Orion vowed, Leon would die with his greatest weakness glaring back at him.

XXXIII

Nyx

Cursed.

What was it like living an immortal life with that as the final word you heard before mortality fled you? Nyx wondered as that one word clamoured in her head. She stood aghast, she'd heard the fondness Orion had held for his siblings in his voice. A brother and sister who'd murdered him in cold blood. He'd died believing Xensor's parting words to be law, an omen he'd carried throughout his immortal life and the centuries that'd passed. She wondered what it'd cost him, if that ice-cold demeanour he nurtured was something he'd *had* to do to protect himself from his past or if somewhere along the way, he'd simply succumbed to the darkness and despair he reaped. Nyx could understand if he had, recalling the moment that'd changed her life irrevocably and the blood that'd stained her hands when she'd freed herself of Kai and his phantom presence in her mind. Did she walk the same path beside Orion? How had he survived?

Her thoughts spilled from her lips as words, "How are you here?" She shook her head, hurriedly correcting herself. "*Alive*. How are you alive?"

A scoff laced with disdain rippled off the walls. Orion's face tipped to the hidden lighting fixtures until the glow seemed to halo him and he returned his attention to her. "Dearest *Leon* saved my life. He'd been parading as a royal adviser and high-ranking official under my parents' rule for decades and was free to roam the castle as he pleased. That day, he heard the commotion, saw the retreating figures of my siblings from the throne room and, of course, the scent of blood was hard to ignore. A beacon of foul play led Leon to me."

"But wouldn't it have been too late?" she questioned, a definitive crease on her brow as she puzzled over the inner mechanisms of vampirism.

"You would think so, wouldn't you?" Orion stated, seeming to understand her thoughts. "But no, it wasn't. There's a … window of time after the heart stops that vampirism can take hold. Beyond it and you've missed your chance. The ingestion of vampiric blood doesn't need a heartbeat to infiltrate your system, but it's strange in the sense of *how* it works. It's a type of decay that riddles the body until there's no way of removing it, and yet, it'll leave you unscathed if immortality isn't something you desire."

"But—"

Orion levelled Nyx with an unimpressed look, head cocked like he knew what she'd say before she spoke. "Even *if* you haven't consciously acknowledged it."

"Isn't that a lack of consent?"

"Isn't *that* why you're alive?" he drawled, throwing a bitter truth back at her.

"Nope," she quipped, ignoring the slow shake of Orion's head. "Some … head-strong vampire started my transition after I'd been staked by wannabe hunters."

Orion hummed, the sound rumbling from his chest before his voice tantalised her like the caress of fingers down bare skin. "You should thank him someday. He did you a favour."

She eyed him carefully, appraising him. "We'll see."

"He'll be waiting *eagerly*," Orion said, straightening in his black metal throne, leaning forward until his forearms draped regally across his thighs. "But anyway, back to *how* I'm able to grace you with my presence and my *delight* in knowing Leon. So, after Leon had slipped me his blood and I'd regained some coherency of my surroundings, he urged me to stay still and allow the servants to find me 'dead', if you will. An uproar was made, tears were shed, and I was moved to the royal altar above my family's tomb."

"Altar? Everyone thought you were dead and your body was moved to an altar? Outside in the elements?"

"It was a tradition of my family and the people of Silkgulf, to be left with the gods for a day before a body was moved to its final resting place," he explained, glacier gaze on the floor. "And I suppose it worked in my favour when Leon's blood, and his return, helped me attain my thirst for vengeance."

His stare darted to hers and the breath in her lungs lodged in her throat as she waited for him to continue, waited for the weight of whatever he was about to say to lift from her shoulders. "I killed them to complete my transition."

"Nylora and Xensor," she breathed as something cinched in her mind. Some part of her recognised Orion's revenge, reminding her of her own satisfaction upon Kai's death.

"Yes," he confirmed, peering up at her from beneath his eyebrows. "I *slaughtered* them when they'd come to gloat over my body and the success of their plan … and if I try, I can remember the *taste* of their blood. I can remember the crimson that stained the white marble altar, can *hear* the patter of blood as it dripped down the steps. I can even *smell* the earthy breeze from the dense forests surrounding Silkgulf, and I can *see* the fear in their eyes as I took their lives."

"And did you …" she trailed off, uncertain, the question perched on the tip of her tongue. Her bottom lip worried between her teeth, gaze surveying him from head to toe. "Do you regret it?"

Orion's gaze darted to her lips. "As much as it might surprise you, little dove. I've always stood by my decisions—I've *always* acknowledged what I want."

A sharp glint flared in Nyx's eyes as their earlier conversation flitted across her mind, her subconsciousness seeking answers. "So, how did getting rid of Viliaris give you what you want?"

Orion's posture straightened. "You're back to this? Again?"

"It doesn't make sense—" she tried.

"There isn't always a motive, *sweetheart*."

"There *must* be. I don't—*why* did you kill him? All he did was taunt you with some bullshit about Leon."

"Bullshit?" Orion repeated, his eyes paling. "How do you *still* not get it? After all this time."

Her hands trembled with nervous energy, unclenching and clenching at her sides. "I know Leon has Kotori, Niko and Kade but—"

"No, Nyx," Orion interjected, staunching her pacing with a simple cautionary tone.

The grey flecks of her eyes lightened with her confusion, eyes darting across the planes of Orion's face, hand raising to rake through her curls. "What?" she said.

He muttered something inaudible, drumming his fingers against the armrests. A low, sigh tumbled from his lips a moment later, his unearthly gaze upon her—seeing the pieces of her she wished he wouldn't, those pieces still vulnerable and unsure. "As much as it's been about *them* … a part of it has *always* been about *you*."

Nyx was rooted to the spot. And he was there. When he raised his hand to cup her cheek—mere centimetres separating them—she didn't move. She was too caught up in the intensity of his gaze, the way it pinned her in place with curiosity and made her long to run away in terror all at once.

"Nyx," he tried, voice pitched lower intended to soothe her racing mind.

"*Orion*," she warned, stepping back to create distance between them and the shifting of her thoughts—of a desire she couldn't grant.

He matched the next step she took back with one forward.

"You don't know what you're suggesting., you *don't* understand," she tried.

His lips quirked with that charismatic grin, mirth rising with each step they both took—one seeking to create distance, one seeking to close it. "Don't I?"

She knew she was back-pedalling in the desperate hope that she could tuck the last of her cards to her chest, to hide them from Orion because she didn't *want* to accept the truth.

She knew that once she did, there would be no going back. She had seconds to think—a breath to decide—before she let herself fall into an unknown abyss. *Would he catch her?*

"This," she gestured curtly between themselves, voice poised like the calm before a storm, "doesn't make sense. *We* aren't compatible."

"Maybe, but we make one *hell* of a team. Don't you think?" he crooned, a salacious undertone in his words as he stepped forward once more and her back collided with the wall.

She glanced side-long at the wall at her back, noting the casual way Orion's arm lifted to bracket her along her right as she trailed her gaze back to his. "What's with guys and pinning me in place?" she muttered.

Orion's eyebrows arched with his amusement. "I'm sorry, did you want me to …" His hand left the wall to tuck nonchalantly in his pants. "Better?"

"Much," she confirmed with a dip of her head, eyes darting across his face and his lips before she could stop herself. "It doesn't change anything though."

"Then tell me to stop. To leave and not come back because, for once, I will. But you have to *say it.*"

And there was the problem, she thought with a fissure of distaste. Because how could she say it when her mind conjured up the perfect memory of his lips against hers? Or the weight of his hand upon her hip and his fingers in her hair. How could she tell him to leave and not return when she couldn't forget the dominating presence of him that she'd grown to … love? In this moment, *he* was what she wanted. Maybe she was insane, had lost her mind those three months earlier, but she didn't care about what was right and what was wrong, because all she wanted was *him.* She wanted the darkness of his soul that seemed to mirror hers like a figured eight. For a moment, she didn't know what to do as her eyes remained locked on his. Her unspoken truth bared for him to see, nestled on the tip of her tongue like the sweetest strawberry.

Her reply came unbidden with the softness of a summer breeze, carrying her admission to his ears in a way that sent a shiver down her spine. "I *can't.*"

Something flared in Orion's eyes, like the spark of a flint igniting kindling before he swiftly closed the sparse distance separating them, one hand grasping her hip. Nyx's heart raced when he paused a hairsbreadth from her lips, pulse thrumming against her throat, lips parted, gaze trained on Orion's. It was like he wanted her to *act*—to *want*—as her fingers tentatively skittered up his chest to settle at the base of his skull. Her fingertips toyed with his platinum hair, gaze darting to his lips for a moment before she met his awaiting stare and something shifted in the air.

"Tell me you hate me, little dove," he whispered against her lips, voice a heady drawl. "Tell me that you *loathe* me, and you don't want this—that you don't want me."

She sighed as she leaned in and tore her gaze from his mouth. "*I can't.*"

As the weight of her admission descended, and before she could convince herself she hadn't meant what she'd said, she closed the final millimetres dividing them. Her lips ghosted his in a kiss, a seedling of doubt inching in before a low sound came from him and his grip tightened upon her, pulling her closer to him, lips moving against hers in a way that snuffed out uncertainty and fed her confidence.

He pulled away a few seconds later—seemingly with exaggerated reluctance—the blue of his irises darkened by desire. "Last chance to back out. Because once I have you, even if it's just once, I'll want *all* of you. It's all or nothing, Nyx. I won't have you hate me for something *you* decided so, are you in or are you out?"

As if to emphasise his point, Orion untangled his fingers from Nyx's hair, trailing them down her chin to the base of her neck, carefully wrapping them around her throat. It was a little scary, lurching her heartbeat as she recalled how easily he could hurt her. But, she trusted him. Whether it was because he'd saved her life on more than one occasion or the way he'd helped orchestrate her descent into the world's darkness, to be with him, she couldn't say. He snatched what little composure she had, every time.

"Whatever *this* is, it's not going to be easy," she cautioned, peering up at him but feeling as though she held his stare head-on without their height difference. "It'll take time and patience to establish … whatever this is. You'll have to learn to *trust* me, and so will I. So, are *you* sure?"

"I'm sure," he replied, a soft smile upturning the corners of his mouth. "We have eternity to get it right."

Nyx hummed in acknowledgement while she waited with bated breath for Orion's next move or hers, if she could pluck up enough courage to make the next move. The hand that wasn't holding her throat slipped downward and wrapped around one of her wrists, unwinding her hands from the back of his neck before his fingers laced with hers and he released her throat, leading her toward the tunnelway before his room. For a moment—a lapse in judgement—she worried that he was taking her to the cavernous room he'd once tormented her in until they passed it and entered the hidden opening of *his* room. Her gaze surveyed the room she'd been in once before, noting the familiar features of the furniture, lingering on the shelf where she knew the Tyrie crown resided before Orion drew her attention back to him with a gentle tug of her waist by one hand, while the other lightly grasped her chin and redirected her gaze to his.

When Orion's lips next met Nyx's, his movements were subtle and tentative. A phantom press against her mouth, like he wasn't sure what her reaction would be now that they were here. But as her hands raised and her fingers gripped the inky fabric of his shirt, his kiss deepened. Filled with pent-up frustration—at her or himself, she didn't know—teeth grazing her lip in a teasing manner, she could feel his need as her lips moved against his in perfect tangent, his serpent-embellished hand trailing up her waist to tangle in the tresses of her hair. She matched the steady pace of his kiss, fingers gripping his T-shirt until her hands balled into fists beside his hips. Her teeth lightly grazed his bottom lip, eliciting a sinful shiver down her spine as she toed his boundaries—restraint—like someone dipping their feet into water. Bit by bit. Her heart raced in her chest as Orion pulled away from her, head dipping as his mouth pressed possessive kisses to her jawline.

The warmth of his breath tickled her cheek, Nyx's eyes fluttering shut at his orotund voice, "Do you kiss everyone you hate like this?" he said.

"Like what?" she murmured, her eyelids snapping open when Orion started to urge her toward the edge of his bed and his lips brushed her ear in the same moment the back of her knees collided with the silk-covered mattress.

"Like you can't get enough of them." His head raised from her jaw until his stare bored into hers, tone laced with sinful desire. "It's almost as if you've … *imagined* this moment once or twice before." His head cocked, eyes flaring gold. "Tell me, little dove. Does this excite you? Do *I* excite you and the needy, ache of your cunt?"

She couldn't deny the pulsing ache of her clit or the urge to press her thighs together and soothe the throbbing between them, because he did excite her. In more ways than she thought were possible and ones that would make even the most righteous of gods blush. She knew it would please Orion immensely if she admitted it, but she also knew he knew *exactly* what he did to her in this moment and all the times before.

So, instead of answering him, she rolled her eyes with mock disappointment, pushing herself up to close the distance between her mouth and his. Kissing him with the fervour of the words she chose not to speak, her tongue traced the seam of his lips before he granted her access. She tasted the raw tang of nicotine. Maybe she would regret being so bold, but for now, she revelled in the thrill kissing him provided. He sank onto the bed's edge and pulled her onto his lap, her legs straddling his waist. And before she knew it, she was lost in the depths of him.

Orion's kisses paused upon the darkened scar of a bite mark on her neck. His teeth nipped at the soft expanse of skin and a startled gasp of pleasure tumbled from her mouth. Then, as if her whirling mind and pounding heart weren't satisfaction enough, his steely gaze darted up to hers. A moment's warning before his grasp tightened and he switched their positions until her back met the silken fabric of his bed and he peered down at her, a sinful smirk on his lips.

As her mind scrambled to catch up to her body's desires, Nyx gazed up at Orion with dark irises and blown pupils, head raising to reconnect their lips as he settled between her thighs and his palm cradled the left side of her face. His thumb idly stroked patterns into her cheek, stare locked on hers as he pulled away and dropped his hand to his side. Her heart jolted in her chest with surprise as he sank to his knees at the bed edge—as he knelt for *her*—palms resting against her jean-clad thighs.

"Last chance, Nyx," he warned, fingertips tracing patterns in the fabric covering her inner thighs as he gazed through his eyelashes at her.

Nyx's lips quirked as she pushed herself up onto her elbows. "You keep saying that but you haven't done anything to warrant a warning. At least, not yet."

"I'll say it once before you're unable to say anything other than my name—"

It was now or never. *I either take the plunge and be damned for trying or ... or what? The fall will kill me.* "Orion, Orion I. Want. You," she said, repeating his name, shifting with him when he moved with a swiftness that did little to hide their supernatural attributes.

He gently knocked her elbow from beneath her, ruining her centre of gravity. He was suddenly there, with her. His fingers skittered up her thighs to the waistband of her pants, serpent-embellished hand nimbly unfastening the button, dragging the zipper down with agonising slowness. She raised his T-shirt up over his head, moving up with him, placing kisses on the lean, hard muscle, tongue darting out to touch his skin. They moved back and forth, each time with less clothing.

"Nyx?" he murmured distractedly, his gaze trained on his fingertips grazing the hemline of her black panties.

"Mmm?" she murmured.

"You are very, very distracting." Orion's palms smoothed over the flesh of her inner thighs, dragging up and then down to her knees before he fluidly parted her legs to his smouldering gaze.

He seemed to ignore the press of her gaze when she pushed to her elbows, resting her weight on her forearms so she could peer down at him. The darkness of his eerily blue irises followed her body and she gasped as he bent his head to lightly trail his tongue up her thigh. She jolted at the sensation, teeth clamping on her bottom lip to suppress a soft whimper bubbling at the back of her throat. Her fingers curled in the silken sheets. Orion licked one last, broad strip along her inner thigh before his lips latched on the skin above the femoral vein and her eyelashes fluttered. She lowered herself back to the mattress until her curls haloed her shoulders and he sucked a tantalising hickey into her skin. Her heart careened in her chest as her clit ached from his ministrations. His hands nestled below the crook of her knees and a mocking tut tumbled from his lips before he descended upon her thigh, despite her subtle squirming, sucking harshly until a darkened hue bloomed on her skin.

The utter *satisfaction* emanating from him was undeniable, a steady trickle like water droplets down a windowpane. "This," he started, trailing off as he readjusted his grasp on her and started sucking another hickey into her skin, teeth nipping at the red-tinged mark, "tastes good."

An aroused hiss tumbled from her parted lips, back arching as he took the soft flesh between his teeth and pressed down ever-so-slightly as she fisted the sheets and her eyes fluttered shut. After a few seconds, where Nyx thought she might combust, he pulled back and ran his fingers over his new mark; darker than the rest with a slight indentation of teeth as his voice caressed her body with sensual ease.

"*This* has been worth the wait—*you* have been worth the wait." Orion stilled, gaze raking over her body before a low hum vibrated from his chest and to her ears, fingers plucking at the waistband of her panties. "These, however, will have to go."

Before she could think to reply, Orion's hands grasped the fabric and tore, tossing the garment to the floor, then he parted her thighs until he rested between them. Nyx's eyes snapped open in the same breath as Orion descended on her bared cunt, attaching his mouth to her throbbing clit and sucking hard before his tongue traced her inner labia. The sudden action caused her back to arch, one of her hands releasing the sheets to grip his hair as a loud, surprised moan left her.

His name fell from her lips in an almost wail as she felt him smirk and he growled against her, sending vibrations through her body as a needy gasp accompanied the slight roll of her hips. Wanting more than he gave with a neediness she both loathed and desired, his grasp tightened on her legs as he doubled his efforts. Now his tongue circled her clit before diving inside the wet heat of her, alternating between tracing her entrance and the nub of pulsing nerves above. His left hand trailed up her leg in a path of featherlight caresses, finger pressing halfway in as his mouth worked her. She groaned, her grasp tightening on his hair as he sank his finger knuckle-deep.

"*Fuck*," she breathed, eyes screwed shut as Orion started to move the digit in tune with the drag of his tongue, curling the tip of his finger until her body jolted with pleasure and her knees sought to close upon his head; a movement stopped by the firm grasp he held her right thigh with.

"Orion," she whispered.

He raised his head as she opened her eyes and lifted her head to peer down at him. There was no denying the male satisfaction brimming in his gaze, a smirk upturning his lips, her wetness smeared over his mouth while he continued to thrust his finger—a second one tracing her entrance, the tip pressing into her—tantalisingly, a feigned look of confusion plastered across his features.

"What's the matter, little dove?" his smirk grew as he plunged his second finger into join the first, thumb circling her clit as a tightening sensation built in her abdomen and a throaty moan erupted from her lips. "Is there something you want?"

"Orion—" she tried as his fingers continued their sinful ministrations and she could feel the traitorous trail of her arousal trickling over his hand. The coil within her stomach seemed to tighten, amping up with each caress of his thumb.

"*Tell me* what you want, so I can give it to you," he crooned, emphasising each word with a steady thrust.

Maybe it was the way he spoke or how he seamlessly reattached his mouth to her cunt, tongue swirling over the throbbing bud of her clit that pushed her mounting orgasm to her very edge. Or maybe it was the pent-up, tension-filled interactions leading to this moment, but something within Nyx coiled so tightly with her arousal that she could do little more than moan his name and twist the sheets in a white-knuckled grasp, her head tipped back as he thrust into her, out of her.

"*You. I want you,*" she confessed through the bond they shared, lips parted by lust-filled pants.

And with the next thrust of his fingers—their tips curled inside her until they pressed against a spot that sent her mind reeling—and the purposeful drag of his tongue, Nyx's orgasm washed over her in a tide of endorphins that did little to disguise the sharp burst of pain upon her inner thigh as Orion suddenly pulled his mouth from her core and embedded his elongated teeth into her skin. Her body flooded with aphrodisiacs as he drew her blood slow, swallowing several mouthfuls before his tongue traced over his bite mark to seal the wound.

Nyx's mind spun, like her body, as Orion pulled away from her, withdrawing his fingers and pushing himself up to come to her side, the mattress dipping with his weight. Fabric rustled as he moved her further up the bed and she was safely nestled against his chest. He covered her with the inky sheets in an easy sweep of his arm before his fingers lightly grasped her chin and tilted her head. His irises were softened by an emotion she couldn't decipher before he dipped his head and his lips met hers in a gentle kiss.

His honeyed voice caressed the depths of her mind. "*Thank you,*" he said.

Her brow furrowed, heavy-lidded eyes blinking up at him. "*For what?*"

"*For trusting me enough to be yourself—enough to accept the parts of yourself you don't want anyone else to see. Thank you for being* you."

"*It's nothing.*"

His head shook, a familiar tut spilling from his lips. "*It's* everything."

XXXIV

Niko

Drip-drop, drip-drop, drip-drop.

The crisp bite of sea salt laced every blood-tainted inhale Niko could manage past the burning of his lungs and the mess of his face, torn flesh oozing crimson from his split eyebrow, lip, and broken nose. The darkened depths of the tank sank a frigid bolt of terror into his sternum, its disturbed surface lapping against the perimeter and sloshing over the edge from his struggle to escape the constant cycle of drowning, falling unconscious, to waking and beginning the vicious torment again.

He released a pent-up bellow of anguish, terror and lust for retribution, his fingertips digging harshly into the armrest of his metallic chair as the door to his prison closed behind one of his tormentors. The chair moved to connect with a steel walkway surrounding the tank. Niko raised his head and saw Qadira, the cyanic-blue of his irises sharpened by his thirst for freedom and desire to see her, Leon and Phaelyn reduced to nothing. *Mere bloodied and ruined hunks of flesh*, he thought. Until their screams faded into memory and disconnected interactions.

Until he was *free*.

Niko hadn't realised how much he'd revelled in his freedom until Leon had taken it, reminding him of a formidable feline as it paced on its short leash—desperate to feel the dirt beneath its paws. As Qadira climbed the grated staircase, he realised he'd taken much of his immortal life for granted. *You don't know what you've got til it's gone*. Now she stood before him with an amused tilt to her lips like the wounds she'd created pleased her. He surveyed the leather that clung to her legs, boots sleek with a slight heel, and a dark-leather knife holster that criss-crossed over her chest and ribcage. Her expression was ugly, the things she did were … ugly. *No wonder Orion always refused her advances*, he mused with the faintest urge to laugh. *No mind of her own.* He found amusement in that thought as the broad planes of his face ached—prickling his skin while his body fought to mend itself despite the silver in his bloodstream.

He recollected Qadira and Orion's past, and Niko wondered if part of her willingness to follow Leon's orders was because of Orion's disinterest in her. He wondered if Orion's firm but respectful rebuffs had created bitter resentment in Qadira. One that, over the years, had turned into hate, into revenge. That maybe, just maybe, she wished to make Orion feel what she'd felt those years ago and the only way she could do it was with a knife.

He knew one thing for certain. She was heartless. Qadira would plunge a knife into a chest and watch terror pool in her victim's eyes before she'd ruthlessly drag the blade through flesh, slicing from sternum to groin, tumbling innards to the floor and wet agony to rent the sky. *That* was what he feared the most as his hands gripped the armrests, and he ignored the burn of his torn flesh around his wrists because he knew who Qadira longed to gut. *Nyx.* He knew the joy she'd find in hearing Nyx scream, of seeing her blood on the floor, of the terror of her death.

"I'll see you soon, Nik. I promise," came a silvered voice that drew a sharp intake of breath from him, a longing to pull Nyx into his arms blazed through his veins as the weight of his unspoken feelings pressed on his shoulders.

"Nyx," he murmured; husky voice taking on a deeper and more reverent edge. *"How are—who taught you how to use the blood bond?"*

"Who do you think?" Orion stated with a smug undertone.

"But—"

"We'll see you sooner than you think, Niko," Orion assured before his presence, and Nyx's, vanished from Niko's mind.

Niko's eyes darted to Qadira as his mind reeled, tracking her path as she wandered the outskirts of his watery prison. He knew she'd only come to see him, to survey her damage. Now, she sought to find something else to perk her interest. She descended the stairs before pausing in the open doorway. A wicked grin curled her lips at the whirring of the chair's mechanisms as the frigid water licked his boot-clad feet. The chair recentered itself above the tank.

"Don't do this, Qadira," Niko pleaded, pulling against the metal cuffs at his wrists. His words whispered of a deeper meaning than the terror he felt with the lowering of the chair, stare locked on hers.

Qadira crossed the room in a burst of speed until she stood, resting her forearms on the slight barrier of the tank. "Oh, Niko. Don't worry," she soothed in a way that sent a cold shiver down his spine. "She'll be here soon enough, and I'll enjoy ripping her to shreds."

"If you touch her—"

A mocking laugh cut him off, echoing off the concrete walls before Qadira sobered. "You'll what? *Kill me?*"

Niko's gaze seemed to drain of emotion, his upper lip curling until it bared the sharpness of his teeth. "*Oh, Qadira.* I wouldn't kill you … at least, not straight away. I'd make you suffer, plead, *scream* for mercy." He leaned as far forward as his bindings would allow. "You can recall the lengths and *art* of our more … *sadistic* kills. Right?"

"How could I forget? They're almost as … *horrific* as Kade's, but no one will top the art he finds in a kill," Qadira said, showing a rare glint of fear.

"When I'm through with you," he said, his cyanic gaze surveying her from head to toe, "those deaths will look like child's play compared to what I'll do to you."

"And … what would you do?"

"That depends."

"On what?"

Niko's grin twisted into something depraved. "On whether I want to see your insides … or rip you apart *piece by piece*."

XXXV

Nyx

Starlight dappled the obsidian-coloured roof tiles, haloing Nyx like a vengeful archangel while she peered over the ceiling's ledge, a hand curled lightly around the tiles, body lowered into a predatory crouch as her blood thrummed with anticipation for the week-long build-up to the ensuing fight. Orion bracketed her shoulder, his stance mirroring hers as they waited for the tell-tale *snitching* of the estate's front gates to unlock—unleashing Pandora's monsters upon the sleeping world.

As the gates to Leon's estate clicked open, confirming its workings and whereabouts from the leatherbound book, and Orion's recent scouting of the building, Nyx looked at him with a dark grin, eyes ablaze. Her gaze wandered to their shadows slinking over the brick-paved courtyard, where wisteria climbed the walls, stone pillars and iron balconies, the front gates at their back as they crept across the roof. As they approached the french doors, Orion paused, gesturing for her to wait while he stepped off the roof and landed gracefully on the beige pavers, surveying the moonlit area before he urged her to follow him. She stepped into the darkness with a short plunge from the roof. Landing with the ease of a panther, her hands adjusted her black ripped jeans, boots thudding once against the ground.

She appraised the two-story stone building, windowpanes bathed in darkness. A dark-wooded veranda hugged the pale stone, illuminated by solar lights secured to its poles and the ceiling beams, outdoor seating and tables placed artfully among potted plants.

Most considered silence a comfort—something to settle pent-up worries and grievances—but Nyx couldn't, not when her instincts bellowed warnings. Urging her to run or stay and fight whatever—*whoever*—lurked inside because she owed Kade, Niko and Kotori that much. She owed herself the chance to fight for the life she wanted. With them.

"Through here," Orion said, holding a door open.

"And then down three hallways, two lefts and a right before there's a dining room. Enter it and head toward the second sliding ladder, the book is inscribed with a crescent moon on its spine. It opens a doorway to the sublevels," Nyx stated, slipping through the doors. "Did I forget anything?"

Orion chuckled, following her into the entry of the building, his palm guiding her toward the first hallway to the left of a lavish and sprawling staircase with wrought iron banisters and balconies. "So, you *were* listening. I thought you were distracted by me," he mused.

"Distracted by you?" Nyx said, huffing a soft laugh. "You're delusional."

His eyebrow arched, a devilish glint in his eyes. "You know, your attraction to me *is* easy to comprehend on a physical level. It's our past that makes it hard to swallow."

"How would *you* move forward?" she asked, following him as he released her hand, and they passed hallways and dark furniture.

"I'd start by changing my perspective," he said, his footfalls padding down the hall.

She thought of a nail driven into a coffin.

"There's no use going into something with the same thought process as before," he said, "that could be your downfall before you even begin. I'd start from the beginning. Remember the past, but don't let it dictate me."

"Like a fresh start?"

"Exactly like a fresh start, little dove." He glanced down at her, soft light contouring his features one moment before it fled in the next, plunging them into shadows. "We have an *eternity* to build *this*," he gestured between them, "from the ground up."

Her onyx eyes appraised his, heart jolting in her chest as she turned back to the overly furnished hall, rounding the corner of the final corridor connecting to a dining room at its end. An intricate archway of marble like the steps that descended into the large room was bathed in spotlights. Nyx paused, boots on the threshold, grasping Orion's forearm. "I don't like this, Orion," she admitted. She eyed a mahogany twelve-seater table, chandeliers that glittered in the moonlight and the floor-to-ceiling bookshelves with sliding ladders warily, unsure why a dining room needed them. "Something isn't right. This is too easy." The room made her feel like it was waiting for them, everything was all laid out.

As Orion's stare seared into hers, she wondered if his mind threw him flashes of a different house and an eerily similar admission she'd made on the back of his motorbike, like hers did. Did he think of the life lost and the ones taken? Maybe.

A moment passed between them before he glanced into the room. "And if you're right? What then?"

"Then we re-evaluate and come back another time," she said.

"I can't do that, Nyx," he said, turning back to her. "If you don't want to do this, I won't make you. But I *can't* leave them behind, not again."

She sucked in a breath, nodding. Her tongue darted out to wet her bottom lip, eyes determined. "Ok. Then that's what we'll do. We'll get them back. Now."

He shook his head. "You don't have to do this. You don't owe us—"

"I *want* to do this," she whispered, her eyes flickering to the sliding ladder across the bookshelf and the crescent moon on the book she could *just* make out along its spine. "Despite everything, *they* don't deserve this. Nobody deserves this." Nyx was grateful when she thought of the way Alexander and Tobias had grumbled upon hearing they wouldn't be included in the rescue mission. Orion had opted out of risking their lives as decoys. She moved swiftly and her fingertips grasped the book's spine.

"Let me. Please," Orion said, resting his hand atop hers.

His eyes were lighter, mottled by desperation as he stepped forward, winding an arm around her waist to pull her behind him. A stark *shh-clink* sounded. Mechanical whirring and clicking rumbled beneath their feet and the dark-stained case towering above them slowly slid aside, its ladder folding into the floor. Dread curled in Nyx's stomach as she peered around Orion's back. Fire-bathed wall sconces mounted on the stone walls of a secret hallway illuminated a shadowed staircase leading to dank-smelling sublevels. The cells lay beyond.

Nyx wasn't afraid of the darkness shrouding the entranceway, nor did she dread walking down the steep flight of stairs to the cells. Her heart collided with her sternum as her eyes locked on the two figures at the base of the staircase, grinning up at them. Their teeth were bared and knives glinted at their waists as Orion's grasp tightened around her. Phaelyn's head cocked eerily and Qadira lifted her hand, waggling her fingers. She noticed the pair's leather and linen attire was strung with knife sheaths crafted from the purest silver.

"Orion," Qadira said, dipping her head in greeting before her eyes locked on Nyx. A dangerous grin uplifted her lips; all teeth, no warmth. "Hello, *Nyx*."

Nyx's spine straightened beneath the pair's gaze, slipping from Orion's grasp to stand by his side, shoulders squared as she peered down her nose at the woman. "Qadira," she said, her eyes darted to the brunette beside her whose fingertips toyed with the hilt of a knife, "Phaelyn."

Qadira's lips twitched, eyes blazing with cold delight. "I'm sorry to be the bearer of bad news … but our *guests* aren't permitted visitors."

Orion laughed, his boots colliding with the stone stair as he stepped forward, and a glint of unease flicked in Qadira's eyes—unnerved by the older vampire. "Well, it's a good thing we weren't *asking* for permission because you're going to *step aside*."

Nyx heard the tell-tale whisper of his compelling command and the pair grimaced.

"Let us pass," he said. "You're also going to let us release them, watching us walk back past you and out of the estate. *Got it?*"

Phaelyn recovered first, appearing to shunt his command from her mind with a deft roll of her shoulders and the retrieval of a terrifying blade, twirling it artfully as she widened her stance. "No, Orion, that's *not* going to happen. *Leon* doesn't want that."

"Ah, that's right," Orion drawled, clicking his fingers and daring several more steps. "You don't have a say because *Leon won't let you.* You're puppets pulled by strings attached to the puppet master—*mindless pawns*."

Qadira's lips curled into a snarl, her eyes bleeding gold as she bared her teeth. Nyx remained behind Orion, unsure of the back-and-forth between them. A slither of distaste wormed its way through Nyx, slick like oil on skin as she wondered *why* these women acted on orders and stood by Leon's side. Was it respect for the tyrant with warped ideologies? Or was it something else? Something darker—more unsavoury—that kept them loyal and willing to carry out tasks handed to them. Nyx supposed she'd never know if they acted from a place of loyalty—soldiers at the disposal of a king—or if the threat of something else kept them dutifully leashed to Leon. If his hold on them was escapable at all, or if his talons had sunk too far in where pulling them out would cause more harm than good. How long had they been under the patriarch's thumb?

Tha ... thump, tha ... thump, tha ... thump.

As something tangible in the air cloyed like thick smoke around Nyx, her eyes darted uneasily to Orion's back as he waited, like she waited, for the dominos to tumble. Beginning at her chest and clattering down the stairs, before racing through Orion's legs and to the women blocking their path in an array of sounds to come. She wasn't sure she'd be ready when the pair struck, and her fingers twitched anxiously at her sides. *"I stand by what I said earlier,"* she stated, pushing her thoughts into the pack bond they shared. *"I don't like this. Not one bit."*

"Trust your instincts, little dove. You're right to be on edge," came his reply.

Nyx's forehead creased for a moment as her eyes darted to the fire-lit corridor over the pair's shoulder, attention homing in upon the steel door metres away and the men kept as prisoners behind it. A split-second distraction. A single pulse of her heart. The final domino clattering at Phaelyn and Qadira's feet as their eyes locked on Nyx and they moved, darting forward before she could react.

Phaelyn's silvered blade tore through her bicep, her back colliding with the frigid steps as she grappled with her attacker and the knife aimed at her throat. Through a tangle of arms, she glimpsed Orion's swift block of Qadira's attack as a hiss escaped clenched teeth and she shoved Phaelyn hard enough for her to stumble back several paces. She scrambled to her feet with her next inhale, onyx gaze livid as her fingers pressed against her arm and came away slick with blood. Nyx's nose screwed up, irritated by her failure to anticipate Phaelyn's first move while Orion fought off Qadira, silver glinting in the corner of her eyes. Phaelyn stared at her with a mocking pout, her fingertips toyed with her blood-stained knife, and her silvered gaze smouldered. Then, she raced forward and Nyx sidestepped her arching swipe, bumping into the corridor's wall as the blade *swished* past her cheek. Whirling to avoid the smooth jab at her ribs when she spun on her heel to land a retreating blow, Nyx's heart leaped as she ducked, a pocket-sized knife *whizzing* over her head to clatter against the stone floor. A steel door loomed at Nyx's back and, as the blade struck the ground, Nyx's eyes locked on Phaelyn's—a calamity awaiting destruction. Nyx's lips quirked before she whirled in a movement imbued with as much unnatural speed as possible, her boots barely touching the gritty stone in her pursuit of the pocket-sized knife while Phaelyn's pursuing steps echoed in time with her heart. A sharp burn raced across her skull when Phaelyn's fingers gripped her hair, yanking her backward until she stumbled. Hurriedly, she righted her centre of gravity, ignoring the burn as she swiped the knife from the floor and whirled, bringing the blade up and across Phaelyn's forearm. The hand fled her hair as a steady trickle of crimson splattered the stone.

Drip-drop, drip-drop, drip-drop.

Orion's shout of pain pulled Nyx's focus from Phaelyn, her default reaction of concern shadowed by the bellow of her instincts and the *swish* of a blade before she felt it pierce the flesh above her hip, sinking hilt deep. *No!* A startled gasp spilled from her lips, grasping the small knife in her hand as she ground her teeth together and retaliated in a cruel, detached strike. Silver flashed in the torchlight, the heavy stench of blood in the air, and her heart pounding as she lifted her arm. Phaelyn's stare was anguished as Nyx dragged the serrated blade from the top of the other woman's spine to its base, shredding Phaelyn's skin.

Nyx saw the agony flare in Phaelyn's eyes and heard her mirrored cry of pain, drawing Orion and Qadira's attention to them in the same moment. Qadira slipped around Orion and raced toward Nyx, eyes blazing with fury, her features sharp and her lips drawn back in a ferocious snarl. Nyx shoved Phaelyn away, dislodging the blade from her hip. Her eyes flickered to Orion, skimming the split of his lip and the trickling blood from his arm as his stare locked with hers. His head dipped in a movement she *almost* missed, as he rushed forward and curled his fingers around Qadira's wrist, tugging her backward.

"Go," Orion urged, gesturing to the steel door with his chin. "Get them out!"

Nyx hesitated, a protest perched on the tip of her tongue despite the phantom of his voice, repeating four numbers to her that she knew would unlock the door. As much as she wanted to free Niko, Kade and Kotori, she didn't want to leave Orion behind with Qadira and Phaelyn.

"Now, Nyx," he called, whirling to avoid Qadira's slicing strike until he stood between Nyx and the wrathful woman.

"But—"

Orion tsked, cutting her off. "Don't worry about me. I can hold them back long enough for you to get through that door, but you need to go *now*."

Phaelyn's laughter echoed down the corridor, trailing unpleasantly across Nyx's skin. "Go on, Nyx. *Save them*," she crooned, the *drip-drop* of her blood replaying in Nyx's ears. "Your life is Leon's now, no matter what you do."

"You're still breathing because Leon *wants you to,*" Qadira drawled, picking up where Phaelyn left off. "His will is the *only* one that matters."

Orion's head angled toward the pair, his eyes bleeding gold for a moment before Qadira's arm raised and a soft *whoosh* ghosted the corridor. A pin-like burst of pain spread across Nyx's collarbone as her gaze dropped to the dart she tugged from her skin, a metallic droplet beaded and mixed with her blood perched on the tip. *Silver*, she thought with dread. *Not again!* Tossing the dart to the ground, she spun on her heel and sprinted for the reinforced door, blocking the scuffle of Orion, Phaelyn and Qadira from her mind. Quickly, she closed the short distance and skidded to a halt, fingertips hovering over the glowing keypad.

Her mind blanked, tripping over itself as she blinked and tried to calm her heart rate—to slow the spread of silver in her bloodstream. *At this rate, my body should be building up a tolerance*, she thought half-hysterically. Pressing the numbers *9-5-2-7* and a green-lit button, she waited for a vial-like icon to fill and empty. Nyx's heart drummed against her chest, blood slicking her skin. The wound on her hip throbbed with a painful vengeance as her senses muddled with the silver and the sounds of Orion fighting to keep Phaelyn and Qadira at bay seemed to fade.

She pressed a steadying hand to the metal doorway as the well-oiled entrance swung open and she gripped her small knife hilt until her knuckles bled white. A curse glided past her ears as she surveyed the harshly-lit hall, her coordination swaying as if she stood on the deck of a mighty sail ship. As she stepped into the sterile-looking area she saw five unlabelled doors. *Which one?*

Squinting in the white light, unsure of which door would lead to the men she sought, the heavy door at her back closed with a *snick*, startling her enough to bypass the first two. Nyx strained to hear the commotion of Orion, Phaelyn and Qadira but found she couldn't hear anything at all now. She had to make a choice *and fast*, she thought feverishly. Riding on the heels of this, she wondered suddenly what she'd find. Would it be the men she remembered? The men who hollered at the night sky, their grins stretched widely over their faces. Or would they be beyond her recognition—her help? She didn't want to consider Niko's lifeful nature snuffed out beneath Leon's vile hands, or Kade's Cheshire-Cat grin permanently erased from his features. Or Kotori's soulful and serene presence wiped from his personality. She could not face the thought of her memories being nothing more than an illusion—a fantasy she created to comfort herself after the trauma Kai had left behind. She wasn't sure how she would survive—*live*—without the unbidden space they had pioneered for themselves in her heart. Her hand brushed the handle of a door at the end of the hall, pushing down and stepping into a room smelling strongly of singed hair and blood. She saw silver restraints secured to a metal chair in its centre. Otherwise, the room was empty.

Her relief was short-lived, instead, replaced by crippling fear. She wasn't sure if she was strong enough to face whatever lay behind the next door she crept toward, something urging her toward it. But she had to. *No more hiding, no matter what.* Nyx's fingers wrapped around the handle as she pushed down and opened it with a gentle nudge, pulse thrumming. The blur of silver was seemingly forgotten for a moment as her eyes flickered between three figures tied to uncomfortable-looking chairs, fraying rope at their wrists. The fluorescent light was garish and the sight confused her, unease slithering around her ribcage as she stepped inside with the caution of a deer in a field during open season.

"Nyx?" came a familiar voice, Kade's fuscous gaze nestled upon her face as he leaned as far forward as his bindings would allow.

Niko and Kotori shifted in theirs as she drew nearer. Kade's skin was coated in crusting blood and pinkish scars as she crossed the room, his clothes dirtied by their stain, sandy curls mussed and tangled. It didn't matter to Nyx as a warmth spread in her chest and the urge to wrap her arms around his neck and kiss him overcame her. There were too many unspoken emotions between them. She hurried, pausing in front of him to slice through the rope at his wrists before she twirled the knife, the blade safely tucked in and her hands sank into his hair. Bending to meet him, her lips met his. Kissing him with every ounce of her relief, concern, happiness, and adoration she could muster—at least, she *thought* it was mere adoration—Kade's hands touched her face, her arms, his fingertips pressing into her hip before she jolted with pain and pulled away.

Kade raised his right hand from her hip, fingers slick with her blood. "You're *bleeding*, angel," he stated, almost like he wasn't sure she knew.

"I know," she admitted, slipping away to approach Niko. Her fingers pressed lightly against her wound and the one on her bicep. "Courtesy of Phaelyn. I've got to hurry."

Kade shook his head as she peered down at Niko and the shuffling of unwoven rope clattered to the floor. "She's dead, I *promise* you that," he said.

Nyx hummed in acknowledgement, attention on Niko and his soft grin, her eyes appraising him and the crimson stains around his wrists. His freckle-like scars that ran diagonally across his face were illuminated by the fluorescents, rockstar hair messier than usual, clothes dripping water on the ground. Nyx knew with an unfaltering certainty that she felt something more for Niko than lust, something sweeter and more tranquil trickling over her skin like decadent honey. She wasn't ready to admit to herself that it was more than the budding flower of love—like she wasn't ready to admit the same flower blossomed whenever she thought of Kade—but it was there. That much she knew as she sliced through the rope at his wrists and he shot up, pulling her unceremoniously into his embrace.

Nyx couldn't stifle the scream that left her as Niko's movement turned her hip. He let go as if burned, but the silver in her blood blurred his face and her voice was high and silvered, "Celacali hasn't been as fun without you, Nik," she said, pain making her words hitch. She loved how his eyes lit up.

"Chica, what's wrong?" Niko asked but his question fell on deaf ears as Nyx turned to the last prisoner.

"It's okay," Kotori said, the low timbre of his voice etched with a playful jest. "I don't mind being tied up … I'll wait."

"Yeah, yeah. We're getting to you," Kade drawled, returning to her side. He'd been busy removing his restraints, so he hadn't seen Nyx's wound.

"At a glacial pace," Kotori quipped.

Nyx felt her heart flutter, Kade's hand extended toward her before she grasped it, turning to Kotori who was watching the reunion with a faint grin and wolfish impatience. Her heart jolted, leaping and stumbling, as she gazed at the ebony-haired man and the jarring change to his appearance. The shoulder-length hair she'd so adored was now short to the nape of his neck, tendrils tousled and framing his pronounced cheekbones. So different—like he was missing a part of himself. She noticed immediately the vacancy of the handmade necklace and its charms around his throat and a bolt of sadness shot through her, knowing on a fractional level what they had meant to him, of the milestones in his life and his past they had represented.

"Kotori," she breathed, stepping towards him. Already comforted by his earthy scent, she touched the crumpled fabric of his jacket and for a moment, she allowed herself to breathe him in. She tried to blink the traitorous black spots and woozy sensation from her body, the silver in her bloodstream gathering strength.

"I'm sorry—" Kotori began, voice rumbling.

"It wasn't your fault," she said. "I don't blame you for the things Leon did. That's not your fault." She glanced at Niko and Kade as her vision guttered. "It's *not your fault,*" she repeated, the room beginning to spin.

Niko and Kade's brows furrowed, seeming to register the oddity of Nyx's body language and the way her fingers gripped Kotori's arms for support rather than affection when suddenly, the steel door swung open to reveal Orion.

Relief flooded Nyx's gut as she swayed and Kotori adjusted his grasp on her, their voices coming and going as spots staccatoed her sight and her blood dampened her clothes. She blearily caught movement, Niko's approach blocking her view of Orion and Kade as a ringing collected in her ears, voices came and went.

"What's wrong with her?" came Kade's worried voice followed by a brush of Niko's fingers against her face.

"It's the silver," Orion stated, sounding close even if Nyx couldn't pinpoint what direction his voice came from. "Qadira hit her with a dart."

“Please tell me you killed those bitches,” Niko said.

Her vision plunged into darkness as Orion chuckled bitterly and there were more sounds, voices, fading. She smelled Kotori as he hoisted her into his arms, her hip pain muddled as he tucked one arm beneath her legs and the other around her back. *Maybe it was head pain, or was it her arm?*

“I tried, but they fled before I got the chance,” Orion said. “Phaelyn gave me a message from Leon.”

“And?” Kotori asked.

“To be grateful for our freedom because soon, he’ll be coming for us,” Orion’s voice dropped several octaves: colder than the glacial tone of his eyes. “And for the life he didn’t permit.”

Their voices echoed in Nyx’s ears before the frigid grip of unconsciousness pulled her greedily into its embrace.

PART THREE

A villain is a villain until they fail to fit your story …

XXXVI

Orion

A tense, almost uncertain silence stretched between Orion and his companions as the soft light of dawn cascaded from the natural skylights, the snap of wood in the fire barrels twining with the crashing waves on the cliff face. The weight of their swift retreat from Leon's estate in the hours that'd passed seemed to press on Orion's shoulders. His gloved fingers drummed against the armrest of his throne, a cigarette perched between the fingers of his opposing hand.

He appraised his brothers for a long moment. Each of them had retreated to different places in the cavernous living space. It was such a small thing—for Kotori, Niko and Kade—to seek space over each other's company—but Orion *hated* it because *never,* in the decades he'd known them, had they sought to be apart. His brothers had always been *in* each other's presence; whether it was sharing a couch, sitting atop furniture in their rooms while the others continued like they hadn't noticed or harassing and hunting the abundant mortals of Celacali. It was why they'd always worked, why they were such a formidable unit. Because of their closeness, because they understood each other.

But now, Orion knew something had changed. Leon had unbalanced their perfectly weighted scales and for that, he vowed to ruin him, dissolve his control over them. Until he was nothing more than blood and ash.

Orion's stare lingered on Niko—whose fingers idly toyed with the tresses of Nyx's hair as her head rested in his lap. She remained unconscious to the world, only the acidic stench Orion associated with silver stung the air. He shifted his attention to Kade and the way the tattooed blond paced restlessly, his glances falling on the occupied couch. Orion could almost taste his turmoil. And where Kade's ended, Kotori's began, like the darkening clouds of a brewing storm, thunder encasing his persona. He lounged beside the makeshift bookshelf —half in shadow, half in the morning light—a waiting wolf. His stare was on Orion. "What do you know about Leon's plans that I don't?" Orion questioned, eyeing each of his companions in turn.

A sharp, disdain-filled scoff tumbled from Kade's lips, his head shaking as his eyes lightened, and he raked his blood-crusted fingers through his mussed curls. "*That's* what you want to know? Are you serious?" his voice wavered, eyes screwing shut while he breathed in a ragged breath. "After everything, we've been through … after everything we've lost, *that's* what you ask?"

Orion nodded, absorbing Kade's anger and hurt before he carefully voiced his next question, "Would you rather talk about your torture?"

Kade's stare flitted to the stone floor, eyes away from Orion. "No. If it was up to me, I *never* want to. I just want to forget but … I *can't*."

Before Orion could formulate a response, Kade turned for the tunnelway leading to his room, passing Kotori before a pair of soft screeches emitted from the forgotten alcove. Kade halted. *Of course! He didn't know*. Orion watched as he parted the gauzy curtains and stepped into the softly illuminated space. Orion had watched Nyx feed and nurture the hawk chicks since the night he'd startled her with his return to the cave, but a sound—part laugh, part broken sob—echoed across the cave, rippling down the labyrinth tunnels. Kade's murmur carried to the others, his voice laced thick with emotion as they heard him coaxing the chicks into his arms.

He re-entered the main living space, and looked at them. "Perdre une partie de soi n'est qu'un chemin vers un autre, oublié. Un chemin qu'il faut recommencer," he said.

"*Losing a part of yourself is just one path to another, forgotten way. One you need to start again*," Orion replied, translating Kade's words.

As Kade's gaze lifted from the hawks, Orion considered the lengths Leon had taken to torture his sons and force their loyalty because, while Leon had allowed *him* to be free, it had only been to keep him closest to the pain. Leon had stolen fragments of Orion's soul by uttering simple commands, stripping Orion of his control and strength that he'd so protected after he'd turned, vowing to *never* let another dictate his fate. He'd forced Orion to suffer each of his brother's tortures as well as his own.

Now, his freedom was the price he paid, something he hadn't known he'd needed until it was well and truly gone. Forced apart from his brothers and to break the promise he'd made—to protect them from harm. He'd been unable to stop it, stop Leon. He'd been trapped like a fly in a glass, powerless. And he knew, looking at his brothers now, that Leon had been meticulous about what would hurt them most. He knew Leon had done something to Aloys, he'd felt the pain of Kade's grief through their bond and Kade's reaction now said it all. Kade *had* lost a part of himself in the wake of his freedom.

Orion's relief at having Kotori, Niko and Kade back seemed to dim, overshadowed by the lingering presence of Leon and the aftermath of his control. He knew pain wasn't simple and all he had wanted was his brothers back—wanted them *free*. But he *wished* he could help them forget, wished he could go back in time and drive a stake through Leon's heart, wished he could erase Leon but … then the four of them would have ceased to be. Maybe their non-existence would have been better than this. *Endless torment. More than anything,* Orion wished he could remove Leon's commands—of silence and deceit—from his mind so he could share the information he possessed, of *why* Leon feared Asher's journal—of *why* Nyx's blood tainted Leon's bloodline.

Orion longed to tell them how they could free themselves from Leon's control, and he would, he'd been trying, he merely had to *test* his theory first. Time was against him. He knew that the more he fought the commands, the more pieces of himself he lost. Little by little, the control he exerted in remembering the rules, not allowing them to take hold, the more Leon's will manifested itself in other, insidious ways. Every foot of ground he gained, he lost in the battle of retaining himself. Soon, he would weaken and then he could no longer think, like a puppet. He knew this but he could do nothing else now, but wait.

Kotori's deeply timbred voice split through the swell of Orion's thoughts, dragging him from his mind as he refocused on the room around him. "We know *something,* but the sources aren't … *credible*," Kotori said, warning in his eyes.

Orion's pale eyebrows arched. "What do you mean? Who's been giving you information?" He turned the weight of his gaze to the rockstar blond. "Niko …"

"Phaelyn and Qadira. They were constantly *dropping crumbs* about what Leon intends to do next, to get a rise from us," Niko said, annoyed.

"Did you give them a rise?" Orion asked, glancing at each of his companions in turn.

"I did," Kade admitted, trailing his fingertips along the back of the black and white hawk. "But you would have as well."

"And what was so *rise-inducing* that you reacted?"

"Nyx."

Half aware of Kade's response, Orion's gaze darted to Nyx before he realised she was still asleep, oblivious to the world around her. His expression drained of emotion.

"It better not be what I'm thinking they said, Kade, otherwise heads *will* roll. I can promise you that," Orion vowed.

Kotori pushed himself off his ledge and crossed the room, his dark presence emphasising the words he uttered, "He wants her gone because she's *corrupting* us."

"I'd let her corrupt me any day," Niko murmured, raising his hands in mock surrender when Orion, Kotori and Kade turned to him. "What? I would."

Orion laughed and immediately, the atmosphere in the cave shifted, thinned. "That no longer checks out."

"What do you mean?" Kotori said, frowning.

"Phaelyn and Qadira seem to be under the impression Leon wants Nyx *alive*," Orion explained, a fissure of disdain darting through his eyes as his voice deepened. "I *won't* let him have her. Over my *dead* body."

"Why would he want Nyx alive if she's a *problem* to him?" Kade said, gaze flitting between his companions.

"I don't know," Orion admitted, a troubled frown embedded across his forehead. "But he's not going to get her. I promise you that. We also need to get rid of Leon before two pieces of our past interfere with the lives we've built."

"Woah, wait a damn minute," Niko interjected, narrowing his eyes as the jesting persona fled and was replaced by clean-cut focus. "What's that supposed to mean? When were there *two* pieces?"

Orion's gaze darted to Nyx. "Azeil is back."

"He's in Celacali?" Kade murmured, leaning forward with the hawks tucked carefully into his lap before he rose and returned them to their makeshift nest. He reappeared in the living space in a blur of movement, baleful delight etched into his signature Cheshire-Cat grin. "Why didn't you say so sooner? I'd *kill* to visit Azeil."

"Kade!" Niko scolded. "You can't do that to her. Not to Nyx. Not after Asher."

"What difference does it make, Nik?" Kade said. "We were going to kill Asher anyway; Ryder just beat us to it."

Niko's upper lip twitched as Orion spoke, "That's enough, Kade."

Kade chuckled; a sound laced with a taunting undertone Orion knew well. "Oh, I'm sorry. When did *you* give a damn about Nyx? After everything you've done to her, and I'd *kill* for a distraction."

"We're no saints but you can't kill Azeil," Orion's voice remained calm.

"I never said I was. I just want to *forget*," Kade snapped.

Orion knew Kade had been through hell in whatever handcrafted torment Leon had made for him, he knew Niko and Kotori hadn't escaped their torment either, and so they stood, unflinching in the tide of Kade's anger as he lashed out—at them.

"Careful, Kade," Kotori said. "She's one of us now, and we protect our own."

"One of us?" Kade repeated, scoffing with a shake of his head. "When has she *ever* been one of us? Wasn't she a means to an end?"

A laugh laced with hurt and surprise echoed across the cave, the shift of fabric drawing Orion's attention as Kade's anger vanished and his gaze locked on Nyx. Her irises blazed like a million suns, chin angled up, tongue tracing her teeth as she rose from the couch. He watched as she batted Niko's hands away from her when he moved to steady her, pride filling his chest as she approached Kade.

Nyx came to a stop mere centimetres from him, peering up at him. She leaned in, warning and understanding becoming one. "Say it again, Kade. To my face."

"Nyx—" Kade tried.

"No," Nyx said. "If you *truly* mean it, say it to my face. Not behind my back because it's easier for you to stomach. I haven't spent the past *months* looking for you to hear this. So, make your decision now or I'll make it for you."

"*Nyx*," Orion warned, coming to her side.

She scoffed, turning to him while Kade's gaze tracked the movement as if he wanted to remember it in the aftermath of her fury. "No, Orion. He's a grown man, he can do his own talking. Now, sit your ass back on your *throne* and smoulder."

Orion couldn't hide the amusement he felt or the way he loved her bite as he raised his leather-clad hands and stalked to his black metal throne, leaving Kade to the she-wolf in their midst. A wolf whistle split across the cave before Niko's husky laughter filled his ears, Kotori's lips quirked with a grin as the pair watched Nyx like Orion.

"Now," Nyx began, trailing her gaze over Kade. "I know you've been through hell. I also know that I'll never be able to understand it, not all of it …" she faltered, remembering the blinding agony of Kade's torment. "But this," she gestured to him, "isn't going to get you far. Take the time you need to process what you've been through because there's more pain coming, and hopefully there'll be a final end to it but you can't fight it like this." She looked around at them all. "We have to do this together. Come find me when you're ready, are we clear?"

Kade shifted the weight of his body from one foot to the other, lifting a hand to anxiously toy with his earrings. "I didn't mean what I said."

Orion noted the way Nyx surveyed Kade—cautious and hopeful. He noticed how she seemed to restrain herself, forcing herself not to concede to the first whisper of regret and hastily uttered apology. He waited for whatever she prepared herself to say.

"I deserve more than that," Nyx said, a profound weight to her voice as she reached out and gently laced their fingers together, squeezing his hand. "Anger is a formidable motivator but it's also a bringer of great ruin. I know."

Not for the first time that Orion had known Nyx, he was enthralled by the inner workings of her mind. She was right, in every sense. Anger *was* a dangerous motivator but ruin is not what they needed. At least, not their own. It would bring bloodshed and anguish into someone's life.

Like they'd brought bloodshed and anguish into hers.

XXXVII

Nyx

White lights dotted the driveway of a lavish and abstractly designed house, its grey-toned walls shaped like two books stacked atop each other, the top half appearing to jut out while the bottom half flowed into a set of stone steps. Topiary hedges decorated the front yard, bordering the driveway and some of the house's side, flowers of various hues were tucked between the hedges or climbing a cream-coloured fountain in the centre of the paved driveway. Upbeat music underscored the star-flecked sky, the moon full and waxing, casting incandescent light over the house party. Nyx was reminded of Malor, the fancy house she approached was almost as extravagant as those there. The side effects of the silver had finally worn off and her hip had healed. It had been three nights of fever dreams, an IV drip and questionable home-cooked meals of varying content including copious amounts of sulphur-rich ingredients. A little OJ, a lot of water and a lot of sleep. Thankfully, she hadn't had to do it alone.

She knew the northern suburbs of Celacali were considered the 'rich' part with its over-the-top and maximalist architecture of the houses—mansions or borderline *castles*—earning their inhabitants style status and as Nyx observed the gated and guarded community, she recalled how security had ordered any vehicles without a permit to park on the verge when one of the rich locals was throwing a party. She wondered how effective this could be if they only checked cars. *It's not like there aren't* other *ways to get in and harm someone,* she thought, her heeled boots echoing off the steps as she side-stepped partygoers. She tucked a forged permit into her pocket before her ring-clad fingers laced with Niko's. *It was always good to be prepared, after all.* And, as much as she tried to ignore the prick of pain in her chest, she couldn't stop herself from looking for Kade over her shoulder. It felt almost instinctual for him to be there, even after what he'd said two days ago. A small part of her faltered when she didn't spot him. The things he said always hurt her, even when she knew he didn't mean them.

Now, he sought to wedge a divide between them because he believed it was the only way to protect himself after his torment. Nyx wished he wouldn't, that he'd trust her to not run away if he talked to her but he didn't, and she couldn't blame him. It wasn't like he could forget. She wanted to let him have his space—to find peace with his demons—but she wouldn't let him hurt her any more. This was not the past.

She deserved better than that.

The quartet deserved better than that.

And this was what Nyx wanted … to live *this* life even *if* it cost the lives of everyone at this party. Truthfully, Nyx knew she'd commit heinous crimes for them and where it should have disgusted her—terrified her—she couldn't find it within herself to maintain the emotion. It was as though her immorality had embraced that warped and twisted shard into her being, and it had saved her from herself. Or they had saved her, and she hadn't realised until she no longer felt as though she was just … *existing.*

* * *

Blood coated the walls of the once … *lively* house party, staining the carpet and furniture a sickening red, the metallic scent like the sweetest ambrosia when Nyx lifted her head from the throat of a partygoer. Her gaze surveyed the room as she extracted her fangs from the man's jugular. In the same moment, Niko pulled away from the man's wrist and released his grasp on their shared victim, watching with unmoved eyes as the body hit the ground. Niko's mesh shirt clung to his chest, the black material hiding little of his defined pectorals or the sheen of blood that covered his skin like it covered hers.

Logically, Nyx knew she shouldn't have grinned as widely as she did. *Shouldn't have* let the delighted laugh that tumbled from her lips escape, but she did and it did. The sound bounced as a garbled scream came from the living room doorway. Her golden-hued irises landed upon a middle-aged couple with wide, terrified eyes that darted over the carnage in their home. *The owners*, Nyx reminded herself before she stalked toward them, uncaring of their fear. Orion, Kotori and Kade barred all escape routes, all as covered in blood as she. She *should have* been sickened by her lack of empathy—of humanity—but she wasn't.

Somewhere in her descent into the shadows of the night, she'd latched hold of the bloodshed that came with it, seeking to purge herself of the world's *rightness* with a multitude of callous and *wrong* actions until it bathed her skin in the blood of those unlucky enough to snare her gaze. She huffed at the thought that reminded her of Orion and the way he—Niko, Kade and Kotori—killed without remorse because they enjoyed it and for the simple reason that humanity *was* their food. It was all one giant pyramid; they were the apex predators at the top of the food chain and the reason behind the coastal city's nickname; Celacali, the City of the Dead.

Nyx noted the flutter of the auburn-haired woman's heart, her pristine blue irises alight with terror, freckled hands trembling at her sides, bunching, and twisting the fabric of her emerald cocktail dress. Her husband's brow was beaded with sweat and his brown eyes darted around the room erratically. His crisp suit was creased above his shoulders. Nyx's gaze trailed to Kade, his stained skin reminding her of his part of the plan as the ruined fabric of his white shirt sent familiarity cascading through her veins. Kade's part had been simple—dispose of the security guard. Just like the part of the plan Nyx and Niko were tasked with; to discard the stragglers of the party as fluidly as possible, and admittedly, they *may* have gotten carried away.

Kade and Kotori watched her approach with dark interest, matching curiosity in their eyes while Orion's presence slithered across the room like a black-scaled serpent. Nyx understood why the couple's stares remained locked on her, knowing her skin was covered in the same shade of red as her leather halter top, smoky eyeshadow smudged like the lipstick Niko had insisted she apply, Kade at his side. Even now, Nyx could feel wet spots of blood decorating the inky fabric of her trench coat, heavy like a soul.

Orion rounded on the terrified couple, winding his arm around Nyx's waist as he came to her side—*always* seeking an opportunity to spotlight his beloved theatrics with whatever power move he could think of. Nyx fought the urge to roll her eyes, amused as Niko sidled up on her other side, the bodies of the party's stragglers forgotten.

Orion's gloved fingers brushed her curls over her shoulder while his glacial gaze remained locked on the trembling pair. "Don't look so … *terrified*. We're not going to hurt you," Orion crooned, glancing at Niko as he chortled. "Not *yet* anyway."

Nyx's irises returned to their onyx brown as she furrowed her brow and pushed feigned confusion into her tone. "Not yet? I thought that was why we were here?"

Kotori's lips twitched with amusement, eyes trained on her as he seemed to drink in the sight of her and Orion working together to taunt the couple.

As Nyx played, she caught the angling of Kade's head, his hazel-toned gaze on her. *He wants to keep his distance, but he doesn't want to be too far away*, she realised. She suddenly felt a maddening urge to squash the distance between them.

"No, my little dove, you're right," Orion stated, layering his voice with a tone set to soothe. "We did come here to *visit* the Dawsons but we're mainly here for Mrs. … *Cassia* Dawson, not her husband, Seena."

Nyx held Orion's stare, as she directed her words to Kade. "Kade, why don't you and Kotori *remove* Seena? We won't be needing him," she said.

Kade's eyes widened in surprise before he dipped his head, lips tugging into the Cheshire-Cat grin she adored, eyes alight for the first time since he'd returned from Leon. "We'll get onto that right away for you, angel," he murmured, the smile in his voice.

The deep tone of Kotori's voice filled her mind as the man called Seena's pleas rippled in her eardrums. His voice, even in her head, reminded her of the pouring rain, the tranquillity of a forest and the mournful howl of a wolf; *Levenloos.* His voice seemed to travel down her spine and settle like a warm fire in her stomach. She fought the urge to close her eyes and bask in the sensation.

"You've only got to say the word, kleintje, and we'll do anything *for you. As depraved as you want, we'll give it to you."* His dark stare lingered on her as Kade dragged Seena from the room and Kotori followed.

With a soft laugh, Nyx refocused her attention on Cassia. "Now, where were we?"

As the woman moved to flee, Nyx darted forward with supernatural prowess, blocking Cassia's exit. Niko appeared at her side to pin the woman's arms behind her back as she lunged at Nyx, eyes ablaze with anger instead of fear.

Lithely avoiding the wild-eyed fury, Nyx stepped a safe distance away. "Cassia, it's nice to finally meet you," she said. "Though I'm sure we can agree that you didn't want to be *found*. Not that it matters because Orion and Kade are quite … *effective* at finding those who wish to remain hidden." Nyx breathed out a short laugh, shaking her head as Orion flanked her. "Do you know how long it took us to find you?"

Cassia's eyes flashed with resentment, a cruel laugh emitting from the depths of her chest. "Here's a tip, *Nyx*. If you don't want your victims to hide or run for their lives, don't make your intentions obvious."

"Oh, what are my intentions?" Nyx said sweetly.

"You're trying to send a message, like a fool," Cassia spat, unheeding of the darkness in Niko's eyes or the bloodlust that rippled off Orion in waves.

"Trying to?" Nyx pressed, glancing at Orion with an amused quirk to her lips. "Oh, darling, come first light tomorrow … *you'll* be the message."

Cassia blanched as she tugged against Niko's grasp. Her sky-blue eyes widened, darting between Orion and Nyx. "*What?*"

"Leon is quite … *taken* with you. He has been for decades now. You're his pretty little mayor who helps cover his *nasty* habits. So, now you're going to be *our* muse and you'll make *headlines*," Nyx explained.

She stepped closer to Cassia until mere inches separated them, raising her hand to trail her fingertips along the woman's jawline, down the soft column of her throat until they rested upon the pulsing vein in the crook. She understood, as she held Cassia's gaze, why Niko, Kade, Kotori and Orion had always seemed enthralled by the racing of her heart or the heady ambrosia of her blood before they'd bitten her. It clamoured in her own ears now like the roar of a waterfall as her eyes fell shut. That saccharine allure of blood and the scents that clung to Cassia's skin was like a personal imprint no one else possessed. Each individual had a different, *fresh* bottle of wine smell she just had to sample.

Cassia smelled of roses and the sweetness of a spring-harvested strawberry. Something smoky tangled in a tart burst of citrus. Almost a doppelgänger to the colouration of her hair, like a compliment to the freckles over her pale skin. It reminded Nyx of a fruity wine she'd drunk at a winery in Malor with her mother and Xander. The thought sprang pleasant memories of their laughter, the love she felt for them and how much she missed them to the forefront of her mind.

The brush of Orion's lips against her ear dragged Nyx from her thoughts, eyes opening as she forced herself to refocus, and his orotund voice filled her senses.

"She smells good, doesn't she? Give into your instincts, little dove. Embrace them," he murmured.

Niko's cyanic irises sparked, and Nyx couldn't fight the responding bolt of attraction she felt for him, an attraction she thought she'd understood. That she'd once thought was curiosity, not something … more.

"It's like a personally curated meal for you and you alone, isn't it? Take a bite, chica," he urged.

A choked sound emitted from Cassia, but it barely registered as the bloodlust curled around her mind despite the man she'd fed from earlier. Her dark irises trained upon the place her fingers rested, the panicked beat of Cassia's heart drawing a soft sound from Nyx's lips. And, before Cassia could react or try and fight her off, Niko's grasp tightened on her. The fingers on her neck moved to tangle in the tresses of Cassia's hair, tipping her head back to bear her throat.

Nyx's unnatural canines sank into the flesh of Cassia's throat and her screams of agony spiked the marrow of Nyx's bones. One morbid thought rose to the surface of her blood-addled mind, *You can scream until your lungs give out … it still won't save you.*

XXXVIII

Azeil

Red and blue lights danced over the rocky ground as sea spray ghosted Azeil's arms. The thunderous rumble of waves against Elveszett Bluff's cliff face filled his ears in the early hours of dawn as his stare swept across the grim scene before him. A cordoned section of the Bluff was illuminated by portable light fixtures, their white glare making his eyes ache as he peered down at a sheet-covered body, horrified that his investigation had swerved down this path.

He was too young, he thought as he lifted his hand to scrub over his jaw. *He should have had ...* years *to grow up.* "Donovan," he called to the other man conversing with members of the forensics team, a case report secured to a clipboard in his hand.

Donovan excused himself with a gentle smile before he wandered to Azeil's side, eyeing him closely like he wasn't sure what to make of the older man or the grim set to his jaw. But Azeil knew Donovan could sympathise with what such a death meant and with the terror of finding out your child wasn't coming home.

"Azeil," Donovan replied, grey T-shirt dusted in a thin coating of sand like his jeans and shoe-sock-covered boots. "What's the suspected COD?" he said, cutting straight to the point, the boy beneath the sheet between them.

Wheaten-blond curls. Glassy brown eyes. Neck contorted at a wrong *angle.*

Donovan's lips pursed as he glanced down at his on-scene notes, a saddened edge to his tone, "From the initial report, Jesse Stone died of a broken neck. It's too early to confirm the extent of trauma to the body but there's also severe bruising along his arms and ... *bite* marks across his throat."

"Bite marks?" Azeil repeated, focus homing in on the note.

"They *appear* human, but … they're not," Donovan said, wearing a troubled frown.

Vampire, a fragment of Azeil's mind murmured with a certainty he felt like a zap of static. He remembered the case in 2012 where he'd shadowed as a training detective, and he understood why the chief had placed him on this one as he held Donovan's Argentine-blue gaze. That case—like this one—had been centred around missing and murdered children. Except now, Azeil *knew* who had been behind those deaths and couldn't forget the grisly discovery of vampires and learning of that thing, Leon and his *twisted* habits. A part of him wished he'd never heard of Leon. *What if* he'd never learned of Leon, would he have crossed paths with Orion, Kotori, Niko and Kade? Or would he have lived an oblivious life to the monsters who walked the earth? *What if* he'd never met that quartet, would it have drawn Asher's interest in vampirism to a different field of research? Or would Asher have found his own way to the work he'd spent *years* of his life dedicated to? And *if* Leon had died, would Nyx have been forced to navigate the beginnings of her vampirism alone?

Though logic assured him that it wasn't a mistake, that he should use his knowledge to ensure Leon's reign of terror came to a swift end like it *should have* decades ago, Azeil wondered *how* he could dispose of a vampire as old as Leon, and if Asher's research would hold the answers he suspected it did. Why else would Asher spend years compiling everything he knew into one book? Why else would he ask him to remove a fragment containing information on *sire* vampires and the bonds they held to a pack? Why else had he gone to the trouble of soaking its pages in silver after writing it in his blood, so vampires could not read it unless they were from his bloodline? *What did he know?* Azeil wondered, shoving his thoughts to the back of his mind to refocus on Donovan, gesturing to Donovan's notes with guarded irises. "How would you describe them?" he said, careful about his wording.

"Well … everything *apart from* the incisors and canines are human-like, but the other teeth *are* the cause of the extensive damage. The bruising and dried blood around the canines and incisors are too definite to not have played some part in the death," Donovan explained, a disbelieving quality to his voice as if he didn't believe himself.

"So, from your standpoint, what do you think happened?" Azeil said, pulling out a small notepad and a pen from his inner jacket pocket.

"I think *whatever* created those marks on Jesse's throat and the bruising on his arms was the main factor of his death. If his own blood loss was not replenished for days—*repeatedly,* it would've made him less able to fight back. But honestly? I think whoever did this to Jesse … got bored," Donovan said, watching as the coroner approached the boy's body with a gurney, an empty body bag resting on its surface.

"Explain?" Azeil pressed, jotting down the theories alongside his own notes and the ties he couldn't share.

The coroner and his team of officials carefully deposited the small body into the body bag, their gloved hands ensuring the sheet remained in place before they stepped aside and the coroner pulled the zipper closed, sealing Jesse's body from the elements and any prying eyes the surrounding officers might have missed.

It's not like anyone's around, Azeil silently mused. *Nobody visited the Bluff before dawn on a Saturday.*

"Like the killer didn't get whatever they'd hoped they would. Almost as if he was an afterthought, not the real prize," Donovan explained, disturbed.

"You think this was a boredom kill? Why?" Azeil breathed, doubt sharp in his tone as he tracked the coroner to his vehicle. He watched as the gurney was slid into the back and the doors closed with a solid *thud.*

"I don't know what to think, Azeil," Donovan admitted, refusing to tear his gaze from the coroner van until it started toward the Bluff's makeshift road. "*Or* if I didn't know better, I'd say our killer's control lapsed and … *snap*."

Azeil's head dipped in a slow nod, following Donovan's train of thought. "You think the death wasn't planned?" he asked, his eyes wintry.

"Why else would you snap someone's neck after… bleeding them out for days? You've got the control, why stop suddenly?" Donovan said, drumming his fingers atop his clipboard. "I can't confirm anything *precise* yet, not without an autopsy, but I know one thing for sure." Donovan tore his gaze from the retreating vehicle, paying the surrounding officials little mind as they milled about gathering possible evidence.

A weight settled on his features, darkening his irises. His face faltering as if caved by events and Azeil knew, without confirmation, that they were thinking the same thing.

"Jesse didn't deserve to die," Donovan breathed.

The rumble of waves against the cliffside haloed his admission like the soundtrack of a dark tragedy. The tragedy of a stolen life even Death watched with disapproval, knowing his sister—*Life—would not* approve of Leon's actions. So, it seemed only fair he ensure the vampire's stay in Celacali was … shorter and deeper.

By six feet or so …

XXXIX

Nyx

This is the stupidest idea you've had, Nyx thought as she folded her arms across her chest, trapping her body heat in her leather jacket. A rebellious curl wisped around her face from the confines of her ponytail. Her booted feet carried her down the stretch of storefronts lining the boardwalk as she wove between passersby, a piece of information her father had given her swimming in her mind. She was determined to find her own answers despite the danger she knew she was putting herself in. *Why am I looking for a man who's tried to kill me on more than one occasion? Am I suicidal or stupid?*

Whatever the reason to find Leon, it had to do with Orion, Kotori, Niko and Kade as much as it had to do with her wanting to know the truth. How she could protect her future by ridding herself, and the world, of Leon's *poisoned* presence was, she supposed, worth the danger. A sea breeze ravaged the shoreline and knotted her hair as the darkening clouds stole the afternoon light and her thoughts piled atop each other. She navigated a path to the *Pendulum*—a newer ride, like the *Whirl Swinger*, that sheered in a full circle, one arm fitted with seats for passengers, the other, a gondola on an axle, painted a dark red like the rest of the ride.

Azeil had assured her that she'd find Leon on the boardwalk when she'd paid him a visit earlier. He'd explained Leon was intent on reestablishing his ties with the Skulls, meeting with the gang members several times a week in ever-changing locations. How her father had pin pointed Leon's movements to the fairground today with such surety, she didn't know, but she was grateful for the information, alongside a firm reminder to be careful, and she wouldn't squander it. She *needed* answers.

She was tired of the unknowing and upper hand Leon held over her life, mainly because of the control he held over others. The ghostly echoes of Niko, Kade and Kotori's pain—forced through their bond by Leon—the pressing weight of a sire's command—of too many commands and erosion of free will. She was sick of being sheltered and naïve, determination settling in her bones as the thought of Orion, Kotori, Niko or Kade without their wills drove her forward. No one should have the power to tell her how to live her life, make her decisions for her, except her. And didn't free will begin in all of us as children? She *wouldn't* let Leon steal another child or another mind, not if she could help it. She was done with losing people she cared about.

And so she looked for Leon, her onyx stare cutting across the locals and tourists alike until she found him beside an abandoned storefront-turned-haunted-house attraction, his blond hair wind-tousled, inky slacks a constant Nyx was familiar with. As her gaze appraised the man she hated, unease and horror clutched at her heart. A copper-haired girl with snowy skin and brown eyes gazed up at him with naked fear, her sapphire-blue overall strap was crumpled in his grasp, passers-by seemingly oblivious to her distress.

Nyx noted the way people walked in a wide berth around them as she slipped past a stall selling cinnamon donuts, swiftly closing the distance in a burst of speed. "Why is it that every time we've met since your return, you have a *female* in your grasp?" she said, the girl's heartbeat clamouring in her eardrums.

"Hello Nyx, I was wondering if you'd show up," Leon said, ignoring her question with a lazy smile.

A disconcerting whirl started in Nyx's chest as she stepped closer and the passers-by trickled blindly around her. *Can they not see us!*? she thought. Her soul murmured the wrongness of the sensation. She folded her arms over her chest, surveying Leon keenly. "Why would you be waiting for me?" she said.

"I *wanted* Azeil to know where I was," Leon said, gesturing to Nyx with a sweep of his hand. "I've been careful to make sure he knows my whereabouts for days now, and I knew he'd tell you everything if you asked. It was just a matter of when you'd come."

"Well, here I am," she drawled, dark with distaste.

"Here you are," Leon said, his eyes foreign.

"Let the girl go," she said, gaze darting to the small girl who trembled, her bottom lip wobbling. She couldn't have been more than seven years old.

"Why would I do that?"

"Because you already have one child to keep you sated."

Leon's head angled as her words hung in the air between them, his mossy gaze dragging over her features, grasp tightening on the girl's shirt.

As Nyx watched him watch her, she wondered if he feared his *habits* coming to light or if his reaction was a carefully curated ploy. Like he believed playing on her moral compass would make her drop the subject—somehow forget the countless children he'd slaughtered throughout his lifetime. *Yeah, right.*

"How—"

"Why children?" she had no time for chit chat and time was precious.

Leon looked at the small girl next to him for a moment, seeming to come to a decision. Then, suddenly, he let his hands drop, releasing her. She scrambled, leaping for the people around them like a life line, until she disappeared among the throng of the boardwalk, gone.

"They *taste* better," he said plainly, looking after the child with regret.

"I think that's … unhealthy," Nyx said, more to steady herself than anything else.

Leon stepped closer as his mask cinched back into place, giving way to something unsettling. Like a child's feared monster stepping from the shadows to drag them beneath their bed. His stare darted to the people wandering past before his eyebrows arched with an air of satisfaction and he refocused on her, the face of a beast staring back at her, irises leeched of emotion. "As interesting as that is, that's not why you came looking for me. I think you want answers," he said, stepping closer. "I can give you whatever you want, Nyx, but I need something from you first."

Fighting the instincts bellowing at her to step back, Nyx held her ground as Leon drew closer. "You want the book, don't you?" she said.

A brilliantly malicious grin stretched across Leon's face as he raised his hand to cup her jaw, gripping her chin and forcing her eyes to his. It took everything in Nyx to bite her tongue and not shove him away as her skin crawled and she reminded herself of *why* she'd come searching for him. *I want answers too, s*he thought as his mossy stare bored into her, razoring her insides like the bite of winter. *And he can give them to you …* if *you reign in your anger.*

"I do," he crooned, his opposing hand tucking strands of her hair behind her ear.

"Why?" she said, gritting the words through her teeth. Unease flooded her and she thought of the passersby oblivious to them.

"A sire's secrets should remain as such, and your uncle's research endangers this," he said, a frigidity trickling into his tone. "We could help each other."

Nyx ignored his last comment. She wanted help from Leon like a third life. "Secrets you want protected so your *sons* don't learn the truth of your lies? Or to keep us tied to you because we don't know *half* of what we are?" she said, lancing each of her questions like a blade through flesh.

"You are a part of my bloodline … whether I wanted it or not, and that means you'll obey me. You won't ask questions, you won't fight back, and you *won't* mislead my sons any further," he said, fingertips digging into her jaw.

"What would I get in return?" she said, internally cringing as the words left her mouth, feeling like she was betraying Orion, Kotori, Niko and Kade.

"The truth."

"And all I have to do is give you the book?"

"Exactly," he said, gazing down at her with a look she couldn't decipher.

It was *almost* like he was seeing her in a new light. "How would I—" she started.

"Meet me at Chades Cove in four days. *Alone*. Then, you can have everything you want, answered." He thumbed her cheek with an unsettling affection.

"That's all?"

"That's all," he confirmed.

"Okay," she breathed, bobbing her head in a placating nod. "I'll bring you the book."

"That's my girl," he crooned, a pleased grin crawling across his face before his head angled and he released her, starting backward with a waggle of his fingers. "I'll see you soon, daughter."

She watched him vanish with an unnatural ease, blending into the boardwalk-goers like ink in water. The phantom press of his fingers against her chin lingered as she turned and began toward the carpark.

A startled yelp tumbled from her lips when she came face-to-face with Kotori, his darkly clothed form stark in the bright hues of the fairground. "Did you follow me?" she gasped, sucking in a steadying breath to calm the racing of her heart.

"I'm glad I did," Kotori said, gesturing in the direction Leon had disappeared, waiting for her to come to his side before he looped his arm around her waist. "Because he could have killed you and none of us would have known."

"He wasn't going to hurt me," she said, glancing up at him before she focused on the boardwalk around her. *Does he know what I promised Leon?* "I confronted him about the children."

"How do you know? He told you he'd see you soon. *After* you'd called out his habits. For all I know, he could have been threatening you before I showed up," Kotori said, thumb tracing a comforting path atop her hip.

With a soft sigh tinged with gratitude, Nyx grasped Kotori's arm and paused, peering up at him with a soft smile, instilling as much assurance into her voice as possible. "I'm okay."

"You don't need to cross his path alone, kleintje. I'm here—*we're* always here for you." He stooped to press a kiss to her forehead before they resumed their path.

If only he knew, she thought, guilt ravaging her insides until she was sure he'd see her transgressions as plain as day. *If only he knew.*

XL

Nyx

Lush blades of grass dipped beneath Nyx's sneaker-clad feet and sunlight warmed her skin as she wove a familiar path through tombstones with a bunch of irises clutched in one hand and a Green Lantern comic in the other. It had become a habit of hers in the past months to visit Uncle Asher around midday every Thursday, bringing a bouquet of the darkest purple irises with her every time and she couldn't shake the longing she felt, anguish quick to follow, when she remembered he couldn't comfort her now.

She missed him like breath; his hugs filled with warmth and adoration, the way his eyes had lit up when asked what his favourite comic was. He'd blurted, 'Green Lantern' without hesitation. Most of all, she missed his colourful shirts with obscene patterns. She'd even gone so far as to wear one as a makeshift jacket over her white V-neck tee, its aquamarine, purple and pink patterned sleeves rolled up to her elbows.

Now, her fingers trailed across the smooth marble of Asher's tombstone as she rounded it and sat down, gazing up at the carved writing etched into the surface before she leaned forward and placed the bouquet along a ledge at its base. Her fingertips lingered on the stone for a moment longer while the Green Lantern comic rested in her lap. She swallowed the lump in her throat. "Hi, Ash," she murmured, lifting the comic like he'd be able to see it. "I brought your favourite … Green Lantern, right? It's *Green Lantern, Green Arrow*, Number 89. Alexander helped me find it." Nyx wished more than anything to hear his response, but only distant crashing waves answered.

Losing Asher had been like she imagined dying. Or maybe that had been Death forcibly prying her soul from Asher's, rendering the bond they shared through blood, void.

Nothing. She would have traded anything for a moment to speak to him one last time. Even if it was just to hear him call her his little terror. Her eyes lingered on the comic artwork, gnawing her bottom lip before she dragged her gaze to Asher's tombstone.

"I found them a few days ago in the sublevels of Leon's estate." The words sounded hollow and heavy as lead. "He'd been torturing them. The fact that they're his *sons* means nothing. Niko and Kotori seem to understand their freedom and want to get closer to me. Kade on the other hand … wants space. Either it's a divide between us or the space to sort through his torment alone." A ragged breath shuddered past her lips, fingers raking through her curls before she continued. "I—just … how do you give someone space when you've spent months trying to find them? I mean, I know *how* but what if the distance becomes permanent? What then?"

Her fingers toyed with the fabric of Asher's shirt, gaze dropping to her lap and she let the wind answer in his place.

"I don't think I'd survive losing anyone else, Ash. Even if they're not gone. I think the memories of what used to be will kill me."

"Then don't *lose* him, Night. Let him go," came Alexander's voice from over her shoulder, startling as she whipped around to face him. "Set him *free*."

"What? Alex?" Her shock was momentary as the sight of Ares calmed her immediately. She beckoned him with a click of her fingers as Tobias released his grasp on the Malamute's leash. Nyx wasn't sure she *could* let Kade go. At least, not right now she couldn't. Not when she'd just gotten him back.

Alexander shrugged, the inky fabric of his shirt shifting. "I can't tell you how but when the time's right, you'll know."

"Why does that remind me of every movie with a character who gives advice but it's cryptic as fuck?" Tobias said, wandering past his twin to sit down beside her, placing a single purple iris beside the bouquet she'd brought.

"Because it *is* cryptic," Nyx stated, running her fingers through Ares' pelt. She noticed his black fur had grown darker, almost as dark as the night sky while his almond eyes seemed lighter, tinged with an otherworldly gold.

Silence descended on the trio as they all sat together. Her beloved Malamute appeared to have grown several inches and then some since she'd last seen him, a feat she knew wasn't natural but tied to the transition of a helvíti hound. Pulling back his lips to reveal his teeth, she arched her eyebrows at the lengthened expanse of every tooth before she released him with a gentle ruffle atop his head. *He seems more ... wolfish now,* she silently mused, chuckling as Ares' tail *thumped* against the ground and he excitedly licked the underside of her chin.

"Nyx?" Tobias said, drawing her attention.

"Yeah?"

"Be careful. *Please*."

"I always am."

He arched his dark brows, long-sleeved shoulder bumping hers before he straightened. "*Right*. This says otherwise, Night."

A wave of déjà vu descended as he retrieved a folded news article from the pocket of his slacks, unfurling the paper until the headline glared at her. Despite knowing the twins watched her, a soft grin spread across her face as the words: *Mayor Found Savagely Murdered in Northern Celacali Hours After Movie Premiere* screamed across the top. A picture of Cassia Dawson was plastered across the page, taken at an unveiling of a statue in Celacali's central park. Her blue eyes were alight, red-painted lips stretched into a grin and the black fabric of her dress hugged her figure. *Try to ignore that message, Leon,* she thought snidely.

"What are you doing, Nyx? This is dangerous," Alexander stated, peering down at her with the same level of protectiveness her brother Xander conveyed.

"Of course it's dangerous but nothing good ever came without sacrifice. Nothing changes in this world unless you change it." Nyx tipped her head back to the sky, closing her eyes to soak in the warmth of the sun.

"And she was the sacrifice?" Tobias uttered lowly, his tone bathed in distaste.

"She was the message."

"You can't use innocents as chess pieces, Nyx. That's not right," he said.

Nyx opened her eyes as she turned to him, a livid flush spreading up her throat. "Like letting Orion begin the helvíti transition with Ares was okay? And Cassia was *not* innocent."

"Nyx—"

"No," she interjected, shaking her head. "You don't get to lecture me about what's right and wrong when you stood by and didn't try to stop Orion. Alexander did because he knew what Ares meant to me. What did you do?"

Tobias sucked in a deep breath, his stare holding hers. "I did what I thought was right. What I thought would be best for you and I don't regret it."

Before Nyx could retort, Alexander cut in, "Isn't it better to have an extra form of protection as lethal as a helvíti hound? Think about it. He's your immortal protector, *forever*."

"It doesn't change the fact that he should have said *something*. Even if it was a warning. I just … I *needed* someone to remind Orion that Ares was more than a protector," Nyx said, her words trailing off. After all, a protector was a pretty big deal. Her gaze strayed to Asher's tombstone. "Something untouched by them in my life."

"You still have Azeil," Tobias said, reminding her of her father and his return.

"I guess I *should* lay off creating news articles," she murmured, imagining Azeil's disgruntled sigh if he learned of her connection to the deaths.

"Look at it this way, Night. It's not like he'll snitch on you," Tobias stated bluntly, lips quirked.

Before Nyx could utter the dry response perched on the tip of her tongue, a familiar orotund voice beat her to it. Laced with everything bloodstained and corrupt, the scent of cigarettes, sandalwood, and leather drifted to her nose.

"Azeil is many things but you're right to assume he won't *snitch* on her. He loves her too much for that," Orion drawled as the trio turned to face him. Kotori, Niko and Kade flanked him, appearing at home among the tombstones. "But I'm afraid it won't protect him from Leon or the lengths he'll go to, to exact his revenge on us."

"Don't say it," Nyx warned, handing Alexander the *Green Lantern* comic before she stood and faced the men responsible for the city's nickname.

Orion's glacier eyes burned with blue fire, blistering as a blizzard and as punishing as an inferno. "In retaliation to Cassia's death, Leon has set his sights on Azeil," he said.

"How do you know?" she asked.

"Because the missing boy, Jesse Stone, was dumped at Elveszett Bluff with a note the police don't know about, on his body. Leon is playing an eye for an eye."

XLI

Nyx

Nyx held Orion's stare as his words echoed inside her head, 'An eye for an eye …' but that meant … who would be next? She didn't want to even think it but she couldn't help herself all the same. There was only really one other person left, still here, that Leon could possibly use against her. No amount of mental acrobatics could keep his name from her thoughts, *Azeil*. Nyx prayed it wouldn't be her father. Where before she'd been so afraid of what she'd become—of *who* she'd become, now her fear was for him and for them both. If she lost him like she'd lost Asher, she knew she wouldn't survive it, not again. Not when she'd just gotten him back.

Fear gnawed at her chest and her ears seemed filled with the jarring toll of a bell as she wondered which of the gods controlled her fate and why they seemed so intent on endangering her family for the sake of their entertainment. *No, no, no.*

"Nyx," Niko said, appearing in a blur and snapping her out of her thoughts.

She peered at him and saw the beginning of the forest that sheltered the cemetery. Her gaze darted to Orion, then to Kade and Kotori, who appeared to sense her turmoil. Kotori offered her a soft smile and Kade drew closer, tentatively wrapping an arm around her shoulders and pulling her into his side with the same care he bestowed on Aloys' chicks, both now had French names, Beau and Desirae. For a moment, Nyx didn't know what to make of the simple action, her mind snagged on his words in the cave and how she'd urged him to have all the space he needed to sort through his emotions. *Was this his way of saying he no longer needed space?* she wondered, stare lingering on his high cheekbones and the slight crookedness of his nose as he guided her.

Orion led the way, and the twins watched them all.

“Bye then,” Alexander called to their retreating forms.

“Stay safe, Night,” Tobias exclaimed.

She shook her head at the twins distractedly, focusing on the path they now trekked through the lush forest. *Not her father.* Instead, she looked at the wild narcissi blooming beneath the canopy in groups, or as lone plants at the base of trees until their sweet fragrance twined with the ocean air and she silently fought with herself. She released Niko’s hand in her next inhale so she could slip from beneath Kade’s arm, needing to quash the jitter in her veins. She wandered away and sank to the forest floor, leaning her back against the trunk of a tree, head hanging between her knees while she tried to focus on her breathing. In … and out. In … and out. In … and out.

Orion appeared beside her in her next breath, his fingers gently raising her head, as Kade and Niko shared worried glances behind him, inching closer to where she sat. “It’s okay, little dove. *Breathe,*” he murmured.

“I … can’t,” she gasped.

“Yes, you can. I know you can. Breathe in, for me,” Orion cajoled, glacier gaze locked on hers.

She concentrated, gulping, feeling anchored by his calmness, that ultimate sense of *still* that he possessed.

“That’s it … and then exhale.”

“Nyx,” came Niko’s worried voice, booted feet moving to approach her, her eyes darting to him as Kotori’s ring-clad hand settled upon his shoulder.

“Go. We’ll meet you there,” Kotori urged, holding Niko and Kade’s stare. “*Go,*” he repeated, directing it now to Orion.

As Nyx looked to Kotori, she found herself nodding before her mind caught up to her, barely noticing Ares at Niko’s side. “Yes, I’ll be all right. Go with Niko and Kade to…” She furrowed her brows. “Wherever we were going.”

She wanted to scream until her lungs gave out as her focus shifted to the chaos in her head. Wanting to scream until her voice was shredded and raw. What was an immortal life if all it was, was living pain? Her heart couldn’t take the beating. Asher, Kade, Niko, Kotori … Orion. This was why she shouldn’t have grown attached because she was destined to be shoved away the moment things got hard. But things had been hard before, back before they knew Leon still breathed. At least, to her it had been. *Had it ever been hard for them?* she wondered, *like this?* Her eyes dropped from the retreating figures to Kotori, who watched her with the darkest, all-knowing gaze she’d ever seen.

“Whatever you’re thinking, kleintje. Stop thinking it,” he cautioned. His voice was a sound that reminded her of thunder but with the comfort of a sun-bathed forest, the canopy a tranquil shade of green. “Those thoughts *aren’t* your reality.”

“What if they are?” she pressed, daring him to disagree.

"They're not. If they were, you'd know. Don't spend your time plagued by what-ifs and forget to live in the here and now. The past doesn't need you, the future does." He shifted her until he'd situated himself behind her with his chest pressed against her back.

Nyx's heart jolted at the closer proximity to him, the scent of something woodsy like the forest after a rainy day filling her lungs, mind focusing on the soft circles he traced into her waist. "I'm in capable hands aren't I," she mused, tipping her head back until it rested against his chest, and she could glimpse the sky through the tree's foliage.

Kotori's soft laugh vibrated through his chest and into her back, his breath warming the crook of her throat as he leaned down until his lips brushed her ear, "You are."

"Except, it's never been your hands that have been *capable*," she stated, turning her head until there was a hairsbreadth of space between their lips.

Silence descended, a sense of headiness in the air like a live wire crackled and hummed. Kotori's dark stare seared her skin, alight with longing and lust as his eyes darted between her mouth and eyes. *Almost* like he was torn between taking what he wanted and hiding behind the barricades he'd made for himself because … something in Nyx told her he had, that he'd spent his immortality denying himself of what he wanted to keep the target of his want safe, to keep them alive.

His voice was low and gravelly when he grasped her right thigh, pulling her gently until she turned and her legs straddled his waist, "Kleintje."

It was one single word, the only name he used for her. She gazed up at him, his height pipping hers as easily as it did when he was standing. His ring-clad fingers kneaded the flesh of her thighs. "S*trijder*?" she replied, a question in her own.

"*Strijder?*" he repeated somewhat breathlessly as his grip tightened and he pulled her flush to his chest, lips brushing hers. "Am I your *warrior,* kleintje?"

"Haven't you always been?"

A low hum emitted from his chest, one of his hands traversed her waist, past her ribcage before it tangled in the curls at the base of her skull and he cradled her head. "That wasn't the question nor the appropriate response to what you just started," he said, stare blazing across her flesh.

Lust and budding anticipation gripped her. "*What* did I just start?" she whispered.

"Something you shouldn't have. Not after you just had a panic attack."

"I can handle this," she stated, gesturing between their bodies with a carefree flick of her wrist.

Kotori peered down at her, lips quirking into a genuine smile. "I never said you couldn't. I just … don't want this to be something you're doing to forget … Kade."

Nyx's forehead creased at his words because it hadn't crossed her mind, not for a second, that she wanted to kiss Kotori to forget about Kade. She could admit to herself that she'd slept with Niko after she'd killed Kai to forget the blood on her skin, but he hadn't protested or tried to dissuade her. Instead, he'd seemed more than happy to help her in the tide of his lust. Kade had been another moment altogether, filled with anger and unspoken emotion, then there was her argument with Azeil. Had every moment she'd ever kissed one of them or revelled in their touch been her way of forgetting? Of escaping? Had it ever been about them or what she felt? Or was she just as bad as so many others who used people to bury something they didn't want to face?

She pushed herself up and off Kotori's lap, emotions warring. Guilt ate her as the mood shifted and he released her. She couldn't remember what part of the past months had been something she *wanted* to remember. With shaky hands, she turned away from him as a ragged breath tumbled from her mouth and she blinked back traitorous tears.

"Nyx?" he asked, rising from the forest floor.

She shook her head, teeth sinking into her bottom lip. Her silvered voice wavered when she spoke, laced with anguish she wished Kotori hadn't heard. "Has *any* of this been real, Kotori? Or was it all just a lie that I convinced myself was real?"

"Of course, it was real. Every moment," he assured her earnestly. "I can't speak for the others, but I *know* what I feel just as well as you do," his hand gently wrapped around her bicep before he coaxed her to turn around and face him. "*I* care about you, Nyx, and right now, that's all that matters to me."

"But—"

"Before you start blaming yourself for using them to forget, *ask them*," Kotori said, lightly tapping his pointer finger against her temple. "You already know the quickest way to get your answers if in doubt. So, *ask*."

Nyx gingerly lowered whatever guard she kept in place to separate her thoughts from the connection she shared with them, holding Kotori's stare as the familiar sensation of the bond opened, engulfing her in a tide of warmth.

Before she could voice her question in the silent hum of their bond, their responses came quicker, imbued with unwavering surety, "*Not once did you use me, little dove. You're mine—and* ours*—just as much as I'm, we, are yours,*" Orion said.

Niko's husky voice came next, filled with a teasing but no less serious edge, "*I may have been* mildly *joking about letting you corrupt me, chica but there hasn't been a single moment we shared that I regretted. I care about you on a level some would say is love ...*"

Orion, Niko, and Kotori's presence disappeared from the bond in her next breath, leaving Nyx with the weight of Kade's response. The phantom sound of a heavy exhale trickled down the bond and Nyx could almost picture him raking his fingers through his hair, shifting the weight of his body to his opposite foot. *"I know I haven't been the best to you lately and I'm sorry about that. There's no excuse. If you'll let me, I'd try to make it up to you ... in any way that I can. You never* once *used me and if you did, I don't care."*

"But—" Nyx started.

"It's always *been you, angel,"* he assured, voice heavy with emotion. *"From the moment I saw you in Malor covered in Kai's blood, it's been* you.*"*

XLII

Phaelyn

Crimson stained Phaelyn's fingers as they drummed atop the mahogany surface of a twelve-seater table, silvered gaze fixed on Leon at its head, Qadira by his opposing side. She was impatiently patient in the silence stretching across the dining room of Leon's estate, a Georgian mansion made of stone with paned windows and white finishings. Manicured acres of land dotted by maple and pine trees, and a reinforced perimeter of electrical fences ensconced the sprawling building in elaborate privacy. She waited, eagerly, for his orders.

Please let them be bloody, she thought, the beginnings of a wistful smile playing at the edges of her lips. Phaelyn knew her excitement for bloodshed irked Qadira, as her stare lingered on the blonde and the expressionless planes of her face, but she also knew the immortal indifference in Qadira's eyes was anything *but* unwavering. Where Phaelyn was plentiful energy, bold colours and filled with endless conversations, Qadira was sombre, favouring neutral colours and enjoying the silence of her mind. This last was a fatal flaw that had caused more clashes in their earliest days of vampirism than Phaelyn cared to admit.

Yet time, like all things, had smoothed their differences until she understood that Qadira spoke with discreet gestures and pointed looks, learning to rein in her ever-shifting personality, to welcome the silence. *If only for a moment,* she mused, recalling rocky months of a bitter Qadira when Leon had brought her into their family as nothing more than an unwanted orphan. *A child taken from their father because he couldn't pay a debt.* Her immortality had taught her many things about her sire—her *father*—as Leon had laid the truths of vampirism bare for her to see, explaining the gift she'd been given and how to prevent their bond from being severed or *tainted* as he referred to it. And it was so … simple to keep his bloodline pure. So, she wondered *why* Orion, Kotori, Niko and Kade had ruined everything. Even after Leon's warnings that mortal and vampiric relationships were impure, that they had to disregard affection for lesser beings … unless they *wanted* to ruin the family. Family was what Orion, Kotori, Niko and Kade had *willingly* ruined to bring Nyx into their lives. Her chest smarted with anger, disappointment, and something unknown; an itch that begged to be scratched, it whispered in the caverns of her mind with a voice so distorted it was unintelligible—lost to the depths of her errant soul.

"Phaelyn," Leon called, a gentle quality to his voice.

The spruce green of his long sleeves complimented the light tones of his features.

"Why can't we kill her?" she said suddenly, dropping her hands to her lap. As she did, she smeared blood on her slack-clad legs, a remnant of her fascination with slicing open her fingertips with her own blade.

"Because we *need* Asher's journal and only a vampire from his bloodline can handle it," he said, lounging in a high-backed chair with his elbows propped against the table's surface, fingers steepled as his ancient gaze burrowed into her flesh.

"But we can't *see* its contents. What good is a book we can't read?" she said, a whine making her sound churlish.

"I don't need to read it, I *need* to destroy it. Mortals shouldn't possess such knowledge," Leon said, a scathing bite to his tone.

"Killing Nyx is the best option," Qadira said, manicured nails catching what little sunlight the dark tiles didn't swallow as she shifted in her chair.

Phaelyn watched, her eyes flickering between the two before they settled on Leon once more. "She's no good to us dead," she said.

"What?" Qadira uttered, nose screwed with disbelief as she glanced at Leon and he gazed back with something unreadable in his eyes.

"I find myself … torn," he admitted, a puzzled frown crawling across his brow as he adjusted his shirtsleeves, pulling the fine cotton to his elbows.

"By what? Nyx is a *stain* on our bloodline," Qadira spat, irises alight with anger.

A sigh tumbled from Leon's lips, his eyes brimming with a glint of parental disappointment. "She holds a place with the boys unlike anything I ever had, and she showed … *bravery* when I encountered her on the boardwalk," he breathed.

If Phaelyn hadn't known better, it almost sounded like Leon was … proud. "If you don't want her killed," she asked slowly, "what do you want?" she murmured.

She felt suddenly cold, unsure of the tide his thoughts had taken. She tossed a worried glance at Qadira, who shrugged it off with a flare of her eyes that screamed, '*Don't question him. Trust his decision.*' But she couldn't *not* wonder. Not when it bordered on a reality she didn't want to entertain—didn't want to *see*. *He couldn't* want *her to be a part of their family ... could he?* she thought, horror drenching her insides at the idea, as if Nyx was a contagious disease she didn't want to catch.

Nyx was something she wanted no part of, longing to purge her sire's mind of whatever thoughts he entertained—to keep their family as it was. *Without* Nyx in it. But a tiny shard reminded her that it was her *mortal* fear of abandonment that evoked such a reaction, forcing her to relive the anguish she'd felt as a child when she'd been torn from her father's side and dumped. In an orphanage. So small, yet left with a gaping void a parent had once occupied and the bitter knowledge that she'd *never* see him again. *Was this why she clutched so tightly to the family Leon had given her?* Because she was terrified of being left alone?

"She could be of use to us," Leon mused, glancing between her and Qadira.

"She's better dead though," Qadira said, pale eyebrows arched in a way that suggested she wasn't budging.

"A dead girl can't be a pawn," he said lowly, finality in his tone.

"You want to use her?" Phaelyn asked hopefully. Nyx; a parasite on her family.

Leon shrugged, leaning back, and propping his ankle atop his knee. "Oh, my sweet girls. I believe in being smarter than your foes so, I think it's *logical* to use her as leverage because, think about it. With her, if we *twist* just right … the boys will fall in line *and* we'll obtain Asher's journal," he said.

"She's never alone," Qadira pointed out, the navy fabric of her shirt clinging to her body as she rose in a fluid movement. "And *Orion* won't let her out of his sights after we left that boy on the Bluff."

"I wouldn't be too concerned about that, my viper," Leon drawled.

"What aren't you telling us?" Phaelyn pressed, keenly noting the smug shift of Leon's body language with narrowed eyes.

"When our paths collided on the boardwalk … Nyx and I, before she scared away my meal, we made a … deal. Asher's journal and live *free* of my presence, or no journal and forfeit her life," he said.

"She'll bring you Asher's journal?" Phaelyn pressed, rising from her chair like the perfect shadow to Qadira until Leon was forced to peer up at her.

"She'll meet me at Chades Cove in four days," Leon said, smiling.

"Will she?" Qadira quipped, rounding the back of Leon's chair to flank her side.

"Nyx is rash and driven by anger, of course she'll meet me *without* her protectors," he said, unfazed. "I've decided I quite enjoy our time together. She's refreshingly … different."

"And if they find out she's meeting you? What if they fight back?" Phaelyn prompted knowingly, recalling the venom in Orion, Niko, Kotori and Kade's tones whenever Nyx's wellbeing was threatened.

Leon's mossy irises held hers, brimming with depravity she knew so well—*felt* in the marrow of her bones. "Then, we *cut* flesh from Nyx until they're swayed to *think* before they act. I w*ill not* have my boys corrupted by her," he said.

Phaelyn's rapt attention was disrupted by Qadira holding her hand. She jerked away, annoyed. Her sister was always watching her, constantly watching like there was something wrong. Her head resumed its tilted position as she resumed listening to their father. It was always nice to listen, his voice made her feel … so … light.

"And I *can* make a life I didn't grant *yield*. She'll fall in line … one way or another," he said, rising to his full height and dwarfing them both before he gestured to the room's doorway. "But for now, find me another child … I grow weary without sustenance."

Like so many times before, Phaelyn dipped her head with the faintest grin curling her lips—silenced were any thoughts of protesting—and followed Qadira from the room without a backward glance, eager to provide for their sire in a show of their gratitude for their immortality. Why would they want their mortal lives back when the world was theirs to reap?

"What are we taking this time?" Qadira murmured as they climbed the marble steps and strode down the lavishly decorated hallway, glancing side-long at her sister with a wicked grin. "Another boy or a girl?"

Phaelyn considered Qadira's question as her fingertips ghosted the hilts of her knives strapped across her chest, giddy anticipation in her heart. "I find myself feeling sentimental, Qadira," she drawled, a feigned tinge of longing in her tone.

"Whatever for?" Qadira replied, matching her voice with fake bewilderment.

"Do you remember the brown-eyed, raven-haired beauty he gifted each of us for our first kills?" she said, remembering how Qadira had mentioned her first kill description and how it had matched Phaelyn's perfectly.

"What of it?"

"I say we gift Father a girl like that."

A pleased chuckle echoed down the desolate hallway as Qadira's stony features brightened, her hand skittering affectionately over Phaelyn's shoulder. "What a *splendid* idea, Sister. I can already see her little eyes filled with terror," Qadira said.

Phaelyn's lips stretched with delight, an unsavoury hue leeching her eyes. "Oh, how she'll scream." A faraway knocking of a thought swam through her memory like a deep sea diver. *This was wrong, there had been others.* She caught a whisp of it, "Yes," she said, distracted and frowning as she struggled to thread the thoughts together, "Like all … the children before her."

XLIII

Nyx

Sunlight dappled the forest floor, spilling through the gaps of the tree line as Kotori parted a towering hedge, urging her through with a jut of his chin before he followed behind her as the shrubbery sprang back into place. Nyx's gaze nestled upon an ancient-looking mill, her eyes wide with wonder as Kotori grasped her hand and led her toward the motley stone worked building with an industrial-styled front door and a refurbished fengshui wheel. A black wrought iron balcony stretched out from the third floor, arched windows decorated with multicoloured, stained glass gazed outward, and a limestone path cut its way through abundant narcissi. White, variegated ivy climbed the walls and hung from the balcony, tendrils brushing Nyx's shoulder as they passed.

Her breath caught in her throat as Kotori pushed the rolling door open because, if Nyx had thought their cave at Elveszett Bluff was a hidden oasis, it didn't compare to the ivy-covered mill. Niko and Kade's heads lifted in unison, gazes locked on her as she marvelled at the interior and Kotori slid the wooden door closed. As her eyes swept across the room, drinking in the cream, beige, and soft white tones, she assumed the building had been abandoned long before they had found it. Still, she couldn't shake her wonder. "What is this place?" she murmured, refusing to tear her gaze from the heavy wooden beams criss-crossing the ceiling, vaulted like an Escher painting.

"Kotori found the mill several years ago and decided to make a home-away-from-home but, for now, we'll lay low here and figure out what our next move is," Orion said, his voice carrying across the room.

"Lay low?" she repeated, smiling at Orion. "Is that in *any* of your vocabs?"

"Not particularly," Niko admitted, grinning.

As she turned to follow the intricate carvings in the beams with amusement in her eyes, she couldn't stop the soft gasp as her eyes found the ceiling and its gold-bathed highlights, alternating pieces of the stonework painted in metallic hues. There was something otherworldly about the mill and she was rendered speechless by the sprawling artwork on the domed ceiling.

It was like a Renaissance painting, fluffy clouds and the first smattering of stars were effortlessly depicted across the stone's dusk sky. Her gaze found Kade, who watched her admire his work appreciatively, secretively.

"Did you …?" she trailed off, gesturing to the ceiling as if the beauty of it had stolen her ability to formulate sentences.

Kade's grin grew, a soft laugh tumbling from his lips as he crossed the floor and rounded an oak coffee table placed in the centre of the room beneath a gold-wrought chandelier. "I did," he confirmed, glancing up with pride. "Down to the very last star."

Nyx's intuition whispered that every detail was hand-painted with practiced ease. "How long did it take?"

"A little over a month," he admitted, eyes adoring as she marvelled at his work.

"It's … *beautiful*," she murmured, gaze locked on the ceiling.

"It is," Kade agreed.

The weight of his gaze pressed on her shoulders, pent-up emotion between them palpable. He looked right at her as he said, "It's absolutely *stunning*."

Nyx wasn't sure when he had moved, but in the span of her next breath, he stood inches away from her and it took everything in her to hold his stare. His intensity stole her breath even as her mind reminded her of the space he needed. She knew Kotori, Niko and Orion watched, but her focus was Kade and the way his tattooed hand easily grasped her waist, pulling her closer while the other cupped the base of her skull, fingers tangling in her curls.

"*Kade*," she warned, everything unsaid frozen between them even as her eyes darted to his lips.

"Yes?" he murmured, a stray curl tumbling in front of his face in a way that kickstarted her heart.

"You need space not … *this*."

"That's where you're wrong, angel," he said, leaning down until his lips skirted hers. "Space is a safety net for those afraid of their emotions, of those too afraid to admit what they should have said a long time ago. And I'm not afraid of what I feel. I'm afraid of losing you because I let you slip through my fingers, once."

His grasp tightened on her waist and her tongue darted out to wet her lips. His eyes followed the movement before they returned to hers.

"I *won't* let Leon take *you* from me or anything else."

Nyx blinked up at him, unbelieving as his lips pressed against hers. Tentative at first before her palms rested on his shoulders and her fingers crumpled the fabric of his shirt. She returned his kiss with fervour. She'd missed him so terribly. Though his reaction to seeing her again had been everything to her, his words in the cave had hurt. They had filled her with turmoil, a rug being pulled out from beneath her feet. Now, as their lips moved in unison, she wondered if what they felt for each other was enough to mend it all. If—together—they could rebuild something for themselves that they both took comfort in, righting wrongs and becoming who they *wanted* to be, with each other.

Nyx pulled away and peered up at Kade, his bruised lips twisted into a grin she recognised, before he rested his forehead against hers. She knew in that moment, that they would; that for each other, they'd do *unspeakable* things to ensure it. So, before she could talk herself out of saying what she wanted to, Nyx opened the bond they shared and uttered a truth she had held to her chest for too long.

"*Kade?*" she started unsurely, watching as his head angled and his eyebrows arched.

"*Yes, angel?*"

She swallowed the lump in her throat, gazing up at him with conviction in her eyes. "*Maybe ... it's too soon to say what I want to say but if it's true, what if not saying it is a one-way ticket to ruin?*"

"*Does what you want to say feel ...* right? *Can you feel it in the marrow of your bones?*"

"*Yes.*"

The Cheshire-Cat grin she loved stretched across his face at her response, fingertips gently squeezing her waist. "*Then set the truth free.*"

"*Kade Artus, fellow browser of bookstores,*" she started, grinning. His soft chuckle filled her ears and dimples appeared in his cheeks, a new lightness to his eyes as she recalled the night they'd met on the boardwalk in the aisle of a bookstore. "*You've turned my world upside down since we met ... you're the moon to my sun. You're a piece of my soul I didn't know I'd lost until I found you.*"

"*Nyx Monroe, new girl of Celacali,*" he started, memory in his words. "*I may have started this journey with an obsession, eyes on you even when you thought they were imagined, but in the hell of Leon's prison, I realised something important.*"

Her gaze darted to his before she kissed him, seeking to engrain her feelings into the embrace Kade eagerly returned. He pulled her impossibly close as if holding on.

His voice filled the caverns of her mind, both a reverent promise and a confession, "*You are the sun to my moon, angel. For the rest of our eternity. You are my* everything, *and I promise to be the man you deserve from today until forever. If you'll let me, I'd like to start to make amends for everything I've put you through. Tomorrow?*"

"*What would tomorrow look like?*"

He smiled as he peered down at her. "*Are surprises off the table?*"

"It depends on what you have planned."

"I can't make any promises," he said, laughter splashing the caverns of her head.

Nyx eyed him for a long moment before she dipped her head in an approving nod, a faint smile obscuring her features. *"We'll see,"* she murmured, leaning up to press a kiss to the underside of his jaw.

"You know, when I told him to 'kiss and make up', I didn't think it was going to get so *literal*," Niko drawled, his husky voice breaking the moment.

Nyx glanced at where Niko sat lounging across a beige three-seater couch. Orion's glacier gaze was trained on her when she looked at him, regally situated in a plush armchair shadowed by stacks of books.

"Of course, it was going to be literal, Nik. There's something … eternal about their bond. Even the gods are on their side," Orion said.

"The *gods*?" Niko repeated, a feigned look of outrage as Kotori rolled his eyes from his position by a large arched window. "Are you saying that what Nyx and *I* have *isn't*?" he bleated.

"You're so dramatic, Nik," Kotori said, spluttering.

"Nuh-ah," Niko protested, cyanic eyes lighting up when Nyx was within reaching distance and he grasped her free hand to get her to sit beside him, slinging a strong arm across her shoulders and pulling her into his side as Kade sank down on her opposite side, resting a tattooed hand upon her thigh. "You're doubting us." He glanced down at her as she smiled up at him. "Kotori and Orion seem to doubt us, chica. They believe what we have is not written about in love songs. Like we *aren't* the contents of a rock ballad."

"What's that saying again? 'Haters gonna hate'?" Nyx said, laughing.

"*Haters?"* Orion repeated, rolling the word over his tongue with a dark glint of devilry in his eyes. "I'm full of love."

"*Right*," Kotori drawled. "Let's not ask any of your enemies, oh wait, we can't … they're dead."

Orion shrugged, pulling out a cigarette. "I can't argue with that."

"Pushing up the daisies with some *serious* mutilations," Kade muttered, turning his head to the ceiling.

And, just like that, her turmoil was forgotten. In their presence, nothing mattered. "Of course, *your* artistic qualities don't shine through in your kills, right?" Nyx jested, waiting for Kade to turn back to her with his Cheshire-Cat grin.

He lifted his palms in mock surrender before his fingers toyed with his denim pants. "Guilty as charged. So, tell me, what's *your* dark little habit at any stage of the hunt?"

Three pairs of eyes branded her skin as she held Kade's stare.

"I guess you could say I let them believe they're in control … while I play the part of the prey. Easy. Meek. *Pliable*," she said sweetly.

"Like that time on the boardwalk," Niko stated, voice husky as he thought back to the Ivory Skulls who'd harassed Nyx before she'd punched one of them and he had shown up. "I should've seen that coming."

Kotori's dark brows furrowed. "What are you talking about?"

Niko's head whipped toward him, glancing between Nyx and Kade, puzzlement in his eyes. "Didn't I tell you?"

"Tell us what?" Orion interjected, sharing a look with Kotori, who shrugged his leather-clad shoulders.

"Back when we first 'stumbled' upon Nyx, Ty and some of his mates thought it would be a good idea to mess with her. Well, she perfectly portrayed the victim. Batting their wandering hands away, *trying* to walk away but coming up short when they stopped her."

Nyx shrugged, this violent tendency of hers was revealed and they seemed proud of her. She knew, almost as keenly as she had suspected Ty's death to be of their doing, that they would do *anything* to ensure she thrived in their world, and so she basked in the glow of their pride now, her cheeks heating. "What? There's an art to it," she said, looking at each of them in turn.

Niko glanced down at her with a brilliant grin, dipping his head so his lips were inches from hers. "It was … something else to see you do it," he said.

"Before you start making out," Kotori interrupted, wolfishly grinning as Niko released an annoyed groan. "I think we need to talk about Leon and what you need to expect from our sire. You can kiss wannabe rockstar later."

"Kotori's right, little dove," Orion said, interrupting as he tossed a pointed look at Niko, who raised his hands in mock surrender. Kotori seemed to visibly relax. "Leon is our current priority and from what I've learned of Phaelyn and Qadira's movements, we need to be on guard," he said.

Kade frowned, fingertips tracing idle circles on Nyx's thigh. "We already know they want Nyx dead because she's *ruined* Leon's little idea of family. What else is there?"

Nyx recalled Qadira and Phaelyn sombrely, lips pursed in thought. Leon *did* want her dead for ruining the makeshift family he had constructed … except, Phaelyn and Qadira's words ghosted her mind, whispering of something she refused to entertain. *He wants me alive, but why? So I can decipher Asher's book as a descendant of his bloodline?* She also knew Leon wouldn't let her die before he got Asher's journal. *Family.* Leon had called her his daughter because of her blood ties to Orion, his son. The thought was sickening but he already had two loyal *daughters*. She knew the lengths Qadira and Phaelyn would go to, to please their sire and, somewhere along the way—in the twins' tide of digging through various historical city and church archives to find information on the elusive duo—Nyx realised family was … something they'd never had either.

Qadira was born in 1912 to a large family of Norwegian immigrants who'd moved to Regoa—the continent home to the cities Nyx grew up in—and the small city of Imfe to Celacali's north. Once farmland, now a place famous for its cathedral and mechanical advances. The eldest of Leon's adopted daughters had stumbled into his path by mistake when Leon had lived in Imfe intermittently, returning in the winter months throughout his immortal life. The details of *when* Qadira had been turned grew fuzzy the further the twins had searched but ultimately, all paths led to a lavish proposal—to Orion.

On the other hand, Nyx had learned that Phaelyn, born in the 1990s in a small town east of Faycairn, was stolen from her parents at the age of five as punishment for a debt her father couldn't repay, struggling to provide for his only child when his wife, Phaelyn's mother, had passed a year after her birth. The youngest of Leon's daughters hadn't come from much, but it hadn't surprised Nyx that Leon had found her in the foster system a year *before* her eighteenth birthday, after learning her history, taking her in and raising her as his own. But the details of her turning all pointed to Qadira. It was, Nyx mused, as if the vampire girl had refused to live without her chosen sibling.

Apart they were dangerous, but together they were a death sentence. A pair of Grim Reapers searching for souls, clean-cut and lethal in their precision to carry out Leon's—their father's—orders without question. *Why* would you sever the hand that fed you?

As Nyx's thoughts churned and the weight of her recent interaction with Leon on the boardwalk pressed on her, her thoughts seized on a single moment filled with resolute clarity when she realised her next step was simple; for her to survive, she needed to fight like she always had. To end a bloodline or lose her own. To stand by and watch life pass her by, or make sacrifices and save the ones she loved the most.

He asked me to meet him at Chades Cove in four days, she thought with a fissure of guilt as she remembered Leon's assessing gaze and the way he'd hesitated before allowing the little auburn-haired girl free from his side. Like he hadn't wanted to release her and lose his meal but he had—to keep his dirty secrets from prying eyes.

"He didn't spare us, you know," Kade said, something dark dappling his eyes as Nyx turned to him and then back to Kotori, new dread plunging her chest.

"His idea of family is iron control, solid hierarchy, never to be tested," Kotori said.

Nyx listened with rapt interest as he began to talk.

"My tribe believed our hair and its length, was something akin to prestige. A universal respect that passed between the men, women and children. At the threshold of adulthood and until the day we died, we cut a single lock of our hair every full moon as a token to the Levenloos wolf." His ring-clad fingers found the strand of hair he spoke of, a dark strap of leather twined around the ebony lock with tiny handcrafted charms and three small feathers pinned at various sections. "It is bad luck for a Levenloos man or woman to have their hair the same length as the piece reserved for the Levenloos wolf. It is usually a profound omen of death," Kotori explained. "The elders of my tribe said it was a summoning of our animalistic God of Death and, if one didn't respect our God … they were shunned from the tribe to ensure its safety. With my hair at this length, I would be shunned. I would be *nothing* to my people," he said.

"But … you didn't *choose* to cut your hair, Leon did," Nyx protested, scrambling for ways to reassure him. "I don't know the beliefs of your tribe, strijder, but if someone else committed the act, it *wasn't* what they—what you—wanted. That punishment would be for *them*."

"I don't think—" Kotori started before she cut him off.

A dangerous glint obscured her eyes as she considered what Leon had put the group through. It made her see red, a colour she longed to see stain her hands as the life drained from Leon's eyes and every atrocity he'd committed was brought to light. She hoped he would be haunted by her in whatever afterlife beckoned him and that he wouldn't know a moment of peace. Her gaze held Kotori's as she rose from the couch and crossed the room, claiming the space beside him. "I hope whatever god he evoked will tear him apart … *limb by limb.* And if I can nudge that fate along, so fucking be it."

"Kleintje …"

"I *promise* that Leon will regret doing that to you, I promise. On the Levenloos wolf."

An impressed whistle split the room from Niko, Kade's responding holler and Orion's slow clap filling her ears as Kotori's hand nestled at the nape of her neck and his lips met hers in a searing kiss filled with everything he couldn't say. Her hands reached out to steady herself on his chest, the corded muscles rippling beneath her palms as the hand at the base of her skull angled her head to deepen their kiss. Every sensual movement of his lips against hers was a conveyance of his gratitude, every lust-inducing drag of his tongue against hers traced his respect for her, his adoration. Every moment they'd spent together built like a storm until she found herself at its centre—at *Kotori's* centre—safe within the arms of death and despair reincarnate.

She was safe with the monsters in the shadows of the night.

The chiming tone of her phone drew her away from the tantalising taste of Kotori's lips. She unlocked her phone with irritation and opened a message thread from an unknown number. A picture of a familiar warehouse glared back at her from the phone's screen, a jarring chord blaring in her ears as she straightened. Her eyes darted over the bloodied message scrawled across the concrete floor with a picture of her and Azeil lying in a puddle of blood.

'Keep an eye on the mortal parts of your life, Nyx, because you never know when they'll … disappear.*'*

A sharp curse tumbled from Kotori's lips as Niko, Kade and Orion appeared at her side, peering at the picture.

Nyx's knuckles bled white as she gripped her phone. "And just like that," she said through clenched teeth, "Leon makes his first move." Orion made a displeased sound as Nyx turned to face him, "The games begin."

XLIV

Nyx

A kaleidoscope of colour cascaded from the stained glass windowpanes of the millhouse, bathing Nyx's bared back in hues of pink, yellow and blue as she lay across a tattoo bed, her chin on its leather headrest and her arms wrapped around its underside. The hum of the tattoo gun was a comforting a sound, despite the scratching sensation of the needle piercing her skin. As Kade worked, she recalled his request for their time alone and the way his *surprise* had been revealed, a warmth making itself known in the caverns of her chest.

When they'd returned from a restaurant well-known for its burgers, her gaze had swept the millhouse, finding Orion, Niko and Kotori situating a tattoo bed, trolley with ink, gloves and tattoo gun, she'd turned to Kade in delight. Only then had he revealed the artwork he'd created for her; a piece he'd spent hours on, perfecting it until it was ready to be turned into a stencil. She'd seen the hope in his eyes, that she'd like it. And she did, she *loved* it.

As the black ink was tattooed into her skin and Kade's rhythmic movements, shading and wiping, occupied her senses, she pictured the artwork he'd shown her. Its crescent moon with shadowy divots that reminded her of a wolf's paws entwined with a serpent, scales spotted like a cheetah. Feathers were artfully placed in the background of the snake and moon. A moon for her, a serpent for Orion, paw prints for Kotori, the cheetah was Niko, and the red hawk feathers, all Kade. It meant the world to her that he'd designed her such a thing. A silent message that spoke volumes; that she was a part of their pack, a part of them and now she wore it on her skin. "I never knew you could tattoo," she said, bemused.

Kade paused to wipe the excess ink from her skin, the buzz of the tattoo gun twinning with his laugh. "You're only thinking that now? When I'm almost finished?"

"No," she said, a smile stretching her lips even though she knew he couldn't see it. "I thought of it earlier, but the meaning of your art is occupying most of my thoughts."

"And what do you think it's meaning is?"

"I have my own suspicions, but I'd like to know yours. After all, you drew it," she said, gaze fixed on the scuffed floorboards.

"Honestly?" Kade prompted, his tone hesitant.

"Honestly," she confirmed, wishing she could turn around to face him but longing for the tattoo to be finished at the same time.

"I said things I shouldn't have after you got us out of Leon's estate. I lashed out at you when it wasn't your fault. I pushed you away when I needed you the most. None of this," he paused, wiping the ink from her skin before the familiar itching sensation of the needle scratched across her flesh, "will ever make that right but I *needed* to create something that voiced everything I *should have* said to you. You *are* a part of us, angel, and I wouldn't change it. You are everything we—*I* need in this immortal life."

"So, it represents my… belonging in this pack?" she asked, cinching his explanation alongside her suspicions.

"It's more than that," Kade admitted, the tattoo gun's hum vanishing as he situated it on the portable workstation by his hip, tearing a piece of paper towel and dousing it in an antibiotic solution. "It's my way of saying you're a part of me—of all of us—like a twin soul."

Adoration swelled in Nyx's chest as the cool of the tissue kissed her skin and he applied a layer of tattoo film to her back. The design sprawled between her shoulder blades downward along her spine, where it could be seen if she wore a singlet or a shirt with a low-cut back. Kade gestured to her to look and Nyx rolled carefully off the table. A silver, full length mirror stood waiting for her and she approached it with badly contained excitement. *Mirror, mirror on the wall* … she thought, gasping.

Nyx didn't know much about the deeper meanings tied to animals, but she knew enough to appreciate the specific way Kade had incorporated them into artwork. She knew a cheetah was often used to symbolise focus; chasing ambitions that drove her through life and a journey of self-discovery. A wolf or its paw prints were obviously about strength and so, she guessed, showed the potential of the wearer. She pondered the snake … could it represent her transformation from mortal to immortal? *Rebirth.* She pictured Orion's eyes, so cold, yet always burning. A snake had been in the Garden of Eden and opened the way to sin … *or to freedom*, she thought. Shedding one skin for another. And the hawk feathers … she considered Kade, then thought of Aloys, of the hawk chicks, surviving without their parent … protection and determination.

"Nyx," Kade began, waiting until she turned to face him, and he handed her a shirt that wouldn't rub against her skin before he continued. "If … after everything, you *want* me to let you go, to just be … friends, I'll do that. Whatever you want."

"Kade—" she began.

"I won't be the person who uses you as a punching bag or that you feel like you're walking on eggshells around. I love you too much to do that so, if you need me to let you go … tell me," he said, swallowing. He almost sounded desperate.

If there had been any doubt clouding Nyx's mind as to the depths of her feelings for Kade, or those he shared for her, they vanished in the face of this new selflessness. His gesture of walking away from her, from someone he loved on the slightest chance that it would be in her best interest. If he could choose to put his love for her below her needs, then every crime he'd ever committed couldn't make him the bad guy.

"I don't need you to do that," she said, turning from the mirror.

"But I—"

"Kade," she began, reaching up to cup his face between her hands. "You are human … *ish,* and if there's anything I know about mortality, it's that mistakes are *meant* to be made because without them, we learn nothing about the good and the bad. We learn *nothing* about who we are."

"I don't deserve you."

She drew him closer to herself, looping her arms over his shoulders until her lips brushed his. " I appreciate the gesture, more than I could ever say, but … I want you *in* my life. Immortality would be wasted without you."

XLV

Kotori

Kotori had spent little time in West Celacali in his years in the city, but he admired the beauty of the rural properties and land, their sprawling paddocks of flowing grass dotted with occasional narcissi, the valleys with pristine lakes and babbling rivers, gravel stones crunching beneath the soles of Kotori and Nyx's boots, the chitter of birds filling their ears as they wandered up the driveway leading to the Monroe house. Their bikes left tucked in dense shrubbery at its entrance in case Azeil was home as Kotori's dark gaze lingered on the horses grazing in the paddock that lined the driveway.

"Since when did Azeil have horses?" he said, turning to Nyx with a frown as the lodge house loomed a hundred metres away.

Nyx's ochre gaze followed Ares' bounding stride as he darted from post to post at the fence, sniffing the paint-chipped beams before returning to nudge Nyx's hand with his muzzle. "They're not his," she said. "They're wild and roam West Celacali. The bustle of the city scares them enough to keep the herd safely away from danger."

Kotori's stare lingered on Nyx when she turned back toward Ares, keeping the Malamute in sight. He soaked in the simplicity of their time together without his companions. As much as he cared about his chosen brothers, he was naturally possessive and solitary, enjoying his moments of peace as much as he enjoyed spilling blood or herding prey. His gaze trailed across the planes of Nyx's face, uncaring of the house they approached in pursuit of Asher's leatherbound book as he greedily drank in the sight of her happiness, and the soft laugh that tumbled from her lips whenever Ares rushed to her side. He appreciated their time alone.

"There are wild horses in Celacali?" he said, almost to himself as he tried to recall someone mentioning them in his lifetime.

A soft hum traversed his ears when Nyx tossed him a glance, curls dancing around her shoulders. "They've been here for as long as I can remember. The black one," she said, pointing to a beast of a horse with a sleek coat and a white marking down its face as she rested her elbows atop the fence, "he's the stallion of the herd."

"He looks terrifying," Kotori mused, bracketing her shoulder.

He gazed at her, enthralled by the way she extended her hand and clicked her fingers until the stallion's head turned in their direction, watching her in the same way she gazed upon the horse. So much innocence, so much good in one person. How did she stay so uncorrupted? He'd seen Nyx in her darkest moments, seen her embracing their life of crimson tides, now *her* life too. Yet she did not descend into madness or depravation, did not lose the mortal threads of herself and become decrepit and bitter like … like Qadira and Phaelyn. She was like a split locket, alternating glassy light and opaque shadow, depending on which way you held it. She was a contradiction and he marvelled at her.

"He's not," she assured and, like the stallion sought to confirm her words, its nose brushed her palm and it gently nibbled her fingers. "He's a softie until you endanger his herd. That's when you see the true stallion shine through."

"Speaking from experience?" Kotori asked, leaning a black denim hip into the fence.

"No," Nyx said, a soft smile ghosting at her lips, stroking the stallion's face before she pushed herself off the fence and started anew toward her family's house. "When it's breeding season and all the mares have foals, he's *extremely* protective. I've seen him chase down a cougar that got too daring … let's just say, it didn't return the following year."

With a huff of a chuckle, Kotori followed her, minding Ares who paid Nyx and him little attention as he bounded up the remaining metres of driveway to the veranda-wrapped house. A part of him was relieved Azeil's car was missing from the front yard while another wished he was here, fuelled, he supposed, by his decades-long anger, but now that Asher had passed and they'd slaughtered Amir and Ryder, it seemed he'd sated his vengeance. It might not have gone the way he'd wanted it to go but, in the end, they'd all been swept into Death's embrace. Thinking of Death, he thought of Phaelyn and Qadira. Their taunts loomed large. Kotori could see how they bothered Nyx, her fingertips brushing her pocket like she awaited their next message at any moment, shoulders tensed, gaze always straying to the shadows.

"They're not going to harm you, kleintje," Kotori cajoled when she startled at Ares' sudden, gruff barking.

The Malamute's hackles raised, and his attention locked on the tree line to the left of the large house before Kotori stooped down, grasping his collar, and redirected him toward the house with a little tap to his spine. A sharp sound fell from Nyx's lips at his words, surprising him.

She stared down at him from the top of the veranda's stone stairs; her irises alight with a rage he'd grown to *adore* seeing. "If it wasn't for vampiric healing," she said tightly, "I'd say that I have the scars to prove otherwise. But I don't, so all I'm left with is the memory of their knives in my skin," she snapped.

Kotori shook his head, closing the space between them until he towered over her, and Nyx was forced to tip her head back to hold his gaze. The tone of his voice was like the rumbling call of thunder and left no room for argument. He hoped his words conveyed his sincerity, "They're *not* going to harm you *ever* again."

"You can't promise that," she murmured, stepping back from him and starting toward the front door, riffling through her pockets to retrieve the house key.

It took everything in him to not release a frustrated groan, raking his ring-clad fingers through his hair. Not for the first time, he was reminded of his shortened tresses. He wished Nyx would believe him, that she'd *see* he meant every word. That he wouldn't let anything happen to her now that he was by her side, that he'd *never* let anything happen to her again. Not even by their hands. Not again. He wished to eradicate Leon, Phaelyn and Qadira. He wanted them gone yet, he supposed he understood. A promise was based on the future of things to come and predictions belonged to fortune tellers.

He sighed heavily as he followed Nyx into the house, unchanged in the months he'd been held captive. The comforting fragrance of book pages filled his lungs and the scent of *her* was impossible to miss. He stifled the urge to grasp her waist and pull her to him. He imagined the little sound she'd make in response; would she gasp or would a soft laugh tumble from her lips? He forced himself to ignore his desires, following her down the hallway and into her room where he was hit with the intensity of a freight train by her scent.

This is *my punishment for the part I played in her hurt*, he thought with finality, dipping his head like he was confirming his suspicions as his gaze traversed her room. *However, it isn't* all *bad, all things considered.*

"Kotori?" Nyx called, perched on the edge of her bed.

"Yes?" he said. "Did you ask me something?"

She smiled and it almost undid him. He marvelled that something as simple as a smile could render him so … *captivated* but he couldn't deny the way his heart lurched in his chest or the way he wished to kiss her until her lips were bruised. Every ounce of longing he'd ever felt for her paid off in the simplest of gestures.

"I asked why Asher's book is so important," she said, her eyes alight with delight. "I know *why* on some level but why does Orion want it kept out of Phaelyn and Qadira's hands? What danger is a book no vampire can read? How dangerous can it be if only someone, vampire or not, from Asher's bloodline can hold it—can see it?"

Kotori sobered at her question. "I'm assuming you already know that it contains all the blueprints, entrances and codes to Leon's estate, right?"

Nyx dipped her head. "Right."

"That book," he gestured to where he thought the leatherbound tome resided on her bed, "apparently contains the most … detailed information on vampirism possibly ever written. I don't know *how* Asher managed to get it all, but he was revered in his field. I also don't know why Leon never told us the truth or why he thought knowing would make us question our loyalty but … there's stuff in there that could *ruin* him. At least, that's what Orion heard Leon saying. It could be our chance to rid ourselves of him, once and for all."

"You're saying that I've had a *guide* on how to kill Leon for months? That he could have been dead already?" she said, glancing at it in frustration.

Kotori's lips curled into a tantalising, wolfish grin as he approached her, and she peered up at him. "As much as I know you're capable of handling yourself, kleintje. *That* can't be done alone."

"Why not? He's only one man," she said.

His lips pursed in silent disagreement. "That might be true, but he's *one man* who has lived thousands of your lifetimes. He can't be brought to his knees so easily."

Nyx dropped her gaze to the floorboards. "I *can't* lose anyone else, strijder. I *can't* feel that way again, that loss. I *can't* do it again," she whispered.

Without thinking, Kotori sat down and swiftly scooped Nyx onto his lap, her legs straddling his waist as he trapped her with his gaze. "I *won't* let that happen. *Ever*."

Her hands trailed to his shoulders, resting palms down to steady herself. "You can't promise me that," she said, repeating her earlier words.

He leaned closer, holding her gaze as his voice seemed to lower and *darken* several octaves, "I can."

"You can't."

"Kleintje, if I want to promise you the world, I will. If you want me to kill someone for you, I will." A dark eyebrow arched as he dared her to argue. "If you want me to burn the world until it's nothing but ash, *I will*."

"*Kotori*," she said, shaking her head. "I don't expect that from—"

"I wasn't asking, I was *telling* you what I'd do for you. *Willingly*, even if you don't ask."

"But—*why?*"

"Because … there is no obstacle great enough to hide how much I care for you."

"*Care?*"

A deep chuckle emanated from his chest, lips twisted in a genuine grin. "So, Niko, Kade and Orion telling you that they care for you is a no-brainer, but when *I* do, it is?"

Nyx shrugged. "I just … don't understand *why*. I was just a mortal, I'm not that important."

"You've never been *just a mortal*. We started off with … a bad beginning, we had plans that didn't involve you as a person, and you were hidden behind revenge. But … you being you, changed everything. You're like an inextinguishable light … and a dark, like us. You are someone we never were permitted to, could never, … have. What and who you are didn't exist, kleintje." Kotori stooped his head, lips brushing hers.

His lips met hers with the same searing passion and conveyance of emotions, instilling everything he couldn't say into her flesh with every brush of his lips. A be-ringed hand skittered up the silken fabric of her tank top along her spine to cup the nape of her neck, the other remaining firm on her hip as he kissed her slowly. Taking his time, *savouring her*. She clamoured in his mind, filling every thought he had. She was a paradox he revelled in because he had waited for her, staying away until the moment had been right. He couldn't shake the notion that she was the lightning to his storm. A phenomenon that couldn't happen without each component, an ominous beauty with a promise of great ruin.

Calamity and serenity.

Dark and light.

Life and death.

A cough emitted from the window above Nyx's bed and Orion stood there, holding the window open with an amused smirk. He avoided stepping on Nyx's bed and side tables as he ducked through the window, adjusting his trench coat. "Sorry to interrupt," Orion drawled, his tone suggesting that he wasn't. "I come bearing news."

Nyx's gaze sharpened, head angling as her brows furrowed. "Oh no, what?"

The lightness to Orion's manner fled as he sobered. His gaze darted to Kotori over Nyx's shoulder and dread curled in Kotori's stomach then, sensing Orion's response before it came.

"Azeil," he said.

XLVI

Nyx

She wished she'd heard him wrong. Not for the first time…nor the last *Please let Azeil be ok.* Her thoughts rose up as lies when she saw the piece of paper in Orion's hand and slipped from Kotori's lap, crossing the room and snatching it from his grasp.

An eerie quiet settled in her skull, a slight tremble to her hand as her gaze traversed the picture she held in her hand of her father while her mind begged to be spared from this gut-wrenching fear. A fear that bound her whenever she thought about losing the ones she loved the most. She forced herself to swallow the lump in her throat, focusing on the smile across Azeil's face as he conversed with Donovan.

A biting stench of blood permeated her nose, her brows furrowing in the same moment Orion stepped toward her and she turned the picture over to reveal the message scrawled across its back. Four words stared at her, written in an elegant blood scrawl:

Bye-bye, Daddy Dearest.

She crinkled the photo as she lifted her gaze ever-so-slowly and met Orion's. "They've got to go," she murmured; it wasn't optional. Phaelyn and Qadira *would* die if it was the last thing she ever did.

Kotori rose from her bed and strode to her side, grasping her hand in his. "They will. I promise you, kleintje."

"When?" she pressed, her gaze purposefully between the two men. "*Soon*? Soon is my father's name beside Asher's, and I'm *not* losing him too."

Before either of them could react, she started for the door with Ares quick to follow. Niko's broad, cheetah-embellished shoulder pressed into the doorframe as he folded his arms across his Mötley Crüe singlet.

Kade's frame blocked the slight gap behind him. "Where're you hurrying off to, angel?" he said, head angling like a fox when it caught shuffling mice in the grass.

"Looks like you're about to do something foolish," Niko stated, sombrely.

"Protecting the last member of my family that resides in Celacali is *foolish*?" she said, fury rising. "What do you want me to do? *Nothing*?"

Niko shook his head, pushing off the doorway. "Be *smarter* than Phaelyn and Qadira. They *want* you to do this, to act rashly and favour them."

"They're waiting for a reaction, Nyx," Kade said, coming to her side and winding his arm around her waist. "Are you going to give them that satisfaction so easily?"

Nyx bristled at the implication, invisible hackles rising at his words. She knew he saw the glint in her eyes, his lips tugging into their catty grin as she clenched her jaw. Her answer was no and he knew it. No, she wouldn't give Phaelyn and Qadira the satisfaction they craved, wouldn't feed into their wants. Instead, she *would* wait for the perfect moment to strike, luring them into her domain so she could ensure they *never* threatened her loved ones again. That much she could do.

Gradually nodding, she sucked in a calm breath and turned to Orion, who watched her with frigid irises. "What's our next move?"

Orion's lips curled in approval. "We wait for the storm to brew. Phaelyn and Qadira have always loved their games. It's when Leon gets involved that you know there's something more to their stakes," he said.

Nyx tried to remind herself of what Orion had taught her. *You* are *the predator, little dove, and the predator* must *remain in control or the prey will slip through its claws,* she thought, replaying the mantra inside her head. It took a long, protracted moment to instil calm before she eyed Kotori at Orion's shoulder and turned toward Niko and Kade. If anyone knew Phaelyn and Qadira, it was them. So why did she feel so on edge? Like at any moment, something would go wrong if she didn't act first.

No god or greater entity answered her. If they were content to watch her turmoil unfold while the men she'd grown to care for tried to convince her everything would be okay, then … then she raised a mental third finger to those powers that *might* be. They had to wait for the right moment otherwise everything they'd done—and everyone they'd lost—would be for nothing … yes, okay.

As she looked at each of the men in turn, she thought she understood Orion. The stakes. How would she sleep at night knowing that she'd screwed up the one chance to avenge Asher? Sleep would evade her for the rest of her eternity and that would be the kindest evil. Act fast and die young or play the long game, for Leon. "What stakes?" she asked lowly, eyeing Orion impatiently.

Despite everything she felt for him and what she knew he felt for her, she couldn't ignore the way his words sent a jolt of rage through her bloodstream. Just as she knew he couldn't forget what Azeil had done to him and his companions.

"What Orion was *trying* to say was that we'll get to them before they get to Azeil," Niko spoke up. "We promise you that."

"But what if you don't? What then?" she said, meeting his stare, a familiar grip of panic around her throat as her question remained unanswered.

"We won't let that happen, angel," Kade assured.

"You all keep saying that but you don't know that, Kade."

"We don't but it *won't* happen."

Asher's face darted across her vision. His glassy, unseeing eyes as crystalline as the ocean and bright as the stars. His lacerated throat and the crimson staining his skin, flesh ashen as Death came to collect, all replayed before her eyes. A terror-driven chase through the house she lived in—a place she had always felt safe in—before the biting press of a phantom knife to her throat played through her head. Through the flashes of memory came that unending sense of terror and hysteria, reality slipping through her fingers as short, clipped breaths passed her lips, hands trembling as she grasped Kade's shirt to *try* and centre herself.

"Nyx?" came his worried voice through the resounding roar in her eardrums.

"I'm fine," she rasped, palms splaying over his chest even as she refused to lift her head from his chest—to leave his safety.

Orion's voice sounded far off, fragmented shards of his words in her mind as she fought to find footing in the maelstrom of her mind and body. The 'lizard' half of her brain determined to keep her away from everything that terrified her or evoked memories of Asher's death as Niko and Kotori's scents washed over her, soothing her. She was vaguely aware of Kade shifting her weight to Kotori.

"How long has she been having panic attacks?" Kade asked, voice worried.

"A while now," Orion admitted.

"*Orion*!" came Niko's frustrated exclamation, his fingers tracing patterns into her arms as the roaring in her ears started to fade.

"Kleintje," Kotori murmured as she blearily tilted her head toward his face. "Try to match your breaths with mine. Can you do that for me?"

She nodded and focused on the steady rise and fall of Kotori's chest, breathing in several shaky breaths. The steadying pulse of her heart and every inhale gradually matched every one of his. The faint whirring in her eardrums faded to nothing as she focused on mechanical movement. The blurred edge to her vision inched softly back as she opened her eyes and blinked, her sight sharpening, the tightness of her chest lingering. She pressed a grateful kiss to the underside of Kotori's jaw. Then, Niko's calloused palm smoothed over her waist before it settled on her thigh, thumb tracing circles into her jean-clad leg. She turned to press a doppelgänger kiss to Niko's jaw; a silent thank you. "*How* are we going to do this?" she asked.

Orion and Kade shared a look, twin grins brimming with devilry.

"We reclaim *our* city with the might of a storm," Orion drawled.

Kade seamlessly finished his companion's sentence, "And we'll stain it in their blood and their screams." He grinned.

"They'll remember who brought them to their knees," Niko added, his irises burning with a dark promise of bloodshed.

Kotori was the last to speak, "We'll make them regret *ever* knowing our names."

XLVII

Nyx

Waves broke along the shoreline of Chades Cove as Nyx killed her bike engine and gazed across the trees separating her from Leon. The afternoon chill pressed upon her like an omen sent from the gods, warning her against the path she was taking.

She could feel Asher's leatherbound book as if it burned a hole through the satchel slung over her shoulder. Dread and guilt warred in her chest as she dismounted, knocking the kickstand into place and sucking in a ragged breath. *Am I doing the right thing?* she wondered as she started down a well-trodden path, oceanic shrubbery clawing at her dark-washed jeans. *Is Leon's promise of freedom worth giving away Asher's research?* She couldn't shake the guilt burrowing into her chest. *What would Asher think of me?*

Nyx knew she *should have* told Orion, Kotori, Niko or Kade the truth of where she was going before she'd left the Bluff with an easily constructed lie, assuring them instead, that she was going to see the twins. But now, as she navigated the trees surrounding Chades Cove, she wondered if she should open the mental bond she shared with them and explain her real whereabouts.

Would that save Azeil or endanger him if Leon learned of his sons' presence? she thought, because she knew there was no way Orion, Kotori, Niko or Kade would remain at the Bluff if they learned the truth. She made a decision. She knew what she had to do—what *could* ruin everything she'd built with the men she'd grown to love—but she wouldn't fail, not this time. Not with the stakes at risk—of the life at risk. She looked up abruptly as a twig snapped beneath her shoes and her stare clashed with Leon's, her distaste for him crawling across her flesh like maggots in a rotted carcass. *I* won't *lose anyone else. Not this time or ever again*, she vowed silently.

"It's good to see you, Nyx," Leon said, mossy stare flitting casually to her back before a pleased hum carried to her ears and he tucked his hands into the pockets of his grey slacks. "And you came alone … like I asked."

Nyx gritted her teeth against a scathing retort, one of her hands moving to grip her bag strap and bring it closer to her chest. "I can follow *orders*," she breathed, anger masterfully hidden.

"I can see that," Leon murmured.

A glint she couldn't place sparked in his eyes. His appearance, not a crease to be seen on his white dress shirt nor the unbuttoned suit jacket that matched his slacks, was impeccable as ever. His slightly mussed blond hair seemed to be the only element of him that didn't conform. She didn't believe it, it was as styled as the rest of him; shoes as scuff free and polished as she remembered them. It irritated her on a bone-deep level as she squared her shoulders beneath his stare, because she wanted everyone to *see* the true monster of Celacali. She *wanted* it to be unquestionable to all, a permanent stain he couldn't remove, a mark like a brand.

"Did you bring what I requested?" he said, breaking the silence between them as his eyes flicked to the bag over her shoulder.

"I can't confirm that right now," she said as she eyed him warily.

A frown carved Leon's brow before he appeared to catch himself. He pulled a hand from his pocket and gestured for her to continue.

"If I'm going to give this to you," she said, tapping the satchel with her free hand. "Then you give me the answers you promised."

"How will having answers help you?" he said, surveying her like he was trying to understand the inner mechanisms of her mind.

But he promised me, she thought, hearing herself so like a child. "Do you want the book or not?" she snapped, shunting the unnerved sensation she felt in his presence away.

With a drawn-out sigh and irked twitch of his upper lip, Leon straightened as if bored, but the words, "What do you want to know?" came out strained, like he was fighting to control his frustration.

"What knowledge did Asher possess that you want so *desperately*?" she said, watching him closely.

Leon's voice carried across the cove, the distant cry of seagulls nothing but white noise, "Your uncle discovered a coven secret about … *sire* vampires unknown to mortals," he said, simply.

Steeling her spine against the lilt of his tone, she asked the question she—and Orion, Kotori, Niko and Kade—wanted answered. That her, Tobias, and Alexander had spent *weeks* trying to understand when they'd learned of Asher's journal. The answer that had eluded everyone as they'd scrambled to get the upper hand. She needed it now before she gave him the book. If *he learned the truth,* she reminded herself. "*What* was the secret?" she said, pointedly pressing on a suspected nerve.

"I can't tell you that."

"No. You *won't* tell me," she corrected, refusing to waver. Something was not quite right, but she couldn't put her finger on it. *What was it?*

"The knowledge of a sire isn't to be shared with *lesser* vampires," Leon murmured, a dangerous undertone to his voice that rose the hairs along her arms.

"Well, this *lesser* vampire has something you want, and I don't feel like giving it away without answers," she drawled, feigning disinterest. "So, *start talking.*" As soon as the words left her lips, Nyx was hit with sudden, terrifying clarity. *What was all this for?* she wondered, starting. *He could just take it from me. Couldn't he? Why all the banter, all the endless back-and-forth? Why doesn't he just take it? Kill me and be done with this? Was Asher's blood*—her *bloodline—preventing him from taking it?* She raised her black eyes slowly to his green. Hot on the heels of the barrage of questions yapping at her like a chattering Pandora's box came an oddly laconic reply: *He can't. The Monroe bloodline and silver ... could it be a loophole vampires hadn't anticipated? Am* I *a loophole unseen by vampires?*

An indignant scoff tumbled from Leon's lips as he shook his head, looking at her incredulously. "You dare to order *me* around?" he breathed.

She held his stare without flinching, willing her fear of him to remain hidden, as something else, something new percolated. He *couldn't* take the book from her. She didn't know why and she didn't know how it was possible, but she *did* know, with ever-tightening surety, that she was right. "I dare," she said.

"Do you have the book or not?" he snapped, taking a single step toward her.

Without tearing her gaze from him, she nimbly unlatched the satchel with a soft *click* and pulled Asher's leatherbound tome from its confines, holding it up to his eyes and the cloud-flecked sky above. Leon's eyebrows arched with surprise as he looked at her hands, sunlight refracting off his watch face when he paused, halting his advance at the sound of the warning *tut* she emitted.

"Now, *tell*," she ordered, looping the fingers of her opposing hand under the satchel straps, and discarding it to the creamy sand.

He watched her hands with greedy, riveted eyes. It did not escape her notice that he made no move to advance. He kept his distance, albeit small.

"The secret of the sire bond and how you could ... destroy one," he murmured, so low she would have missed it if it wasn't for her heightened senses.

"Was that so hard?" she quipped, storing away what he'd told her for later.

Leon's lips pursed as he extended a hand, palm-up, to her. "Give me the book, please," he said as if strangling, the frustration he felt evident in his biting tone.

He still didn't move, still didn't reach out and take it. It suddenly made Nyx think of that age-old vampire trick about invitations. You had to invite them in before they could step into your home. Was this … like that? A tremor of fear shot through her as she inched forward, reaching out to press the book's spine into Leon's palm. He'd asked and now she was giving. It wasn't by force … exactly, she thought. She held it out but he didn't move. *What now?*

She stood there, arms outstretched. What was she supposed to do now? "Here," she said, waving the book. "Take it."

Leon sniffed the air. Once, twice … He looked at her evenly and as he drew in a third snort, the lines of his face shifted with satisfaction as her heart pitter-pattered.

She forced herself to bite back fear as she hurried to create space between them, her fingers numb on the book. Terror found itself a home in her heart as his gaze lifted slowly, a deadly expression in place of the constipated one moments before.

"Do you think this is *funny*?" he spat as his mask fell and the monster she feared—had *almost* been killed by more than once—rose before her.

He took a sudden lunge forward and Nyx dropped the book. She couldn't help herself, she screamed, "You tell me!" Her breath came out in a rush as she eyed the book on the ground. "Is it?"

Leon took another step and kicked the book—its cover a duplicate of Asher's research tome catching and opening— on pages as blank as a new canvas. A scathing laugh that lacked humour echoed across the cove as the green of his irises flickered to gold.

"*Where* is the book?" he snapped.

"Safe," she murmured.

As if her response snapped the short leash he'd held on his anger, Leon reacted in a burst of supernatural speed and fluidity she lacked, unbridled fury staining his features. A startled gasp was all she had time for as she hurried to maintain their distance and his hand shot forward, gripping her forearm in an iron-clad grip. Gold bled through his irises a moment before a crunching *crack* resounded in her eardrums and pain splintered through her nervous system from her arm. The scream perched on the tip of her tongue died as Leon's other hand gripped her shoulder. Futilely, she tried to one-handedly push him away. Horror razored her insides as she struggled to slip from his grasp, cursing herself and her independence when his free hand punched through her chest with a wet *squelch.*

Nyx had time to wonder if Orion, Kotori, Niko and Kade could feel her agony through their bond as Leon's fingers curled around her racing heart. As she peered into his desolate eyes, she recalled what Orion had told her about experiencing his companions' torment. *I'm sorry,* she thought as pained tears fled her eyes and her left hand gripped Leon's forearm, right arm hanging brokenly by her side. Her mind shot to the men she'd lied to in her desire to protect them, the ruin of her chest a furnace of unforgiveable fire. *I'm sorry I couldn't free you.*

"Do you know how *easy* it is to rip out a heart?" Leon said, lips curled in a sneer. "Nobody would be able to save you. Not my sons or your *brothers*. Not even Daddy Dearest could save you."

Blood slicked her lips which dripped down her chin and onto her chest, where she could see his fist buried in her sternum. The pain was indescribable, a white hot agony of a million scalpels driving through her flesh as soft and weak as an overripe peach. She could feel pieces of herself dislodging, sliding, coagulating.

She felt her soul flutter like a small bird as she glared up at him, a croakiness she loathed carved into her voice, "Then do it. *Nobody* can stop you," she said.

Leon's tongue traced the seam of his lips as his hand flexed around her heart, and for a moment, Nyx went blind. He appeared to consider her words, like they were two chatting neighbours discussing the weather over the garden fence, all the time in the world. "I *need* Asher's journal," he murmured.

She dropped a wet chuckle from her bloody lips before a desert of pain whipped through her and stole bitter laughter. "No. You want the lies you told your *sons* to stay hidden. You want them to be bound to you for eternity, and you're afraid they'll leave if they learn *how* to kill you," she said. She had all the time in the world, too, she supposed. It was just that her world was shrinking to a tiny glass ball as they stood here, and the idea of time just did not seem to fit inside it any longer.

"Oh, little Nyx. I can find other, " he paused, his hand clenching punishingly around her heart, white spots bathing her vision, "ways to control my sons … and *you* would make quite the leverage."

"She," came Kotori's deeply timbred voice from the tree line as she turned to her left and he stepped from the shadows like a vengeful angel in leather, "is *ours*."

"So, get your hands *off her*," Kade uttered from her right, haloed by the sun's rays.

She heard a low whimpering sound as Leon pulled his hand, inch-by-inch from her chest, his eyes never leaving hers until his red-stained fist released with a nasty sucking noise. Dully, as if from a great distance, she realised the whimpering was her.

He surveyed his fingers with sick satisfaction.

Breathing was a bane as her body moved, hastening to mend the wound oozing blood like it tried to mend her broken bones.

Leon's gaze flickered to her pain-filled eyes as he released his grip, ignoring his sons' warning growls when she crumpled to her knees and a sharp hiss echoed across the cove. He seemed alive in their fury as Nyx's vision bleached and he crouched to hold her eyes, settling on his haunches.

"It doesn't have to be like this, Nyx," he murmured, reaching out to tuck a curl behind her ear in a gesture she immediately hated.

"Then kill us and be over with it," she snapped, knives razoring her pain receptors.

She tried to cradle her broken arm to her chest as Kade's scent swept over her and his tattooed hands gripped her, pulling her from the sandy ground and into his arms.

Kotori appeared at Kade's side, a stony look on his face before he angled his head toward his sire. "Leave," Kotori warned simply.

"*Now,*" Kade uttered, irises flaring white-gold.

Leon's head shook with something like sympathy as he rose and Kotori's back filled her vision, blocking her sight, anguish pulling her into the arms of unconsciousness where it could mend her wounds undisturbed.

"I know when to pick and choose my battles," Leon said, disapproval in his tone.

"That's a shame," Kade quipped, the cotton of his shirt brushing against Nyx's cheek. "Because I would've *loved* to remove your head from its shoulders."

"With something you hold so dear in killable distance? I don't think so. Even you know going against me would be suicide," Leon said.

"That may be so … but your time is running out," Kotori said, the rumble of his voice soothing her soul as her eyes slid shut.

"My time will be up when *I* decide it," Leon crooned, the sneer in his words.

Darkness wreathed her senses as her body begged her to fall into its embrace. She needed the promised elysian to mend the injuries she'd sustained, ones she knew a mortal *would have* died from. Kade's grasp tightened on her, the brush of his thumb against her back soothing her, cradling her in warmth.

Kotori's voice trickled into her waning consciousness, "Your time *is* up, Leon," he said, unwavering. "The Levenloos waits to claim your soul."

XLVIII

Nyx

A dull throb smarted in the valley between Nyx's breasts as her brow furrowed and she gingerly opened her eyes against the lighting of Kotori's millhouse. Her arm shifted to drape over her face with a groan that elicited the weight of four gazes. She didn't have to *see* them to know they waited for her acknowledgement, a part of her dreading having to face them after Leon. *Having to face how I lied to them, went behind their backs, and endangered my life for a chance at their freedom*, she mused, listing every mistake she'd made in the hours prior until she couldn't ignore it—was forced to face it.

She cleared her throat. "Before any of you say … *anything*. Just know that I did it for you and, even though it didn't work how I hoped it would, I don't regret trying." She removed her arm from her face to sit up on the couch as she eyed Orion, Niko, Kade and Kotori in turn.

"Truthfully, I don't know what to say," Orion said, blankly. "I can't decide if I want to strangle you for putting yourself in danger or kiss you for caring so damn much," he finished, dragging a gloved hand across his stubbled jaw.

A soft smile quirked the edge of her mouth as she held his stare with affection. "I do favour the latter," she said.

"No," Kade interjected as he rose from the couch and crossed the room, perching atop the coffee table with his arms rested on his jean-clad thighs. "I want to know why you didn't tell us because if it wasn't for Kotori mentioning he'd seen you with Leon on the boardwalk a few days ago *and* Niko dropping by the twins' place to leave pizzas with you, we wouldn't have known anything was wrong."

"I'm sorry," she breathed, reaching out to lace her fingers with his.

"I'm glad you are, but you scared the shit out of me. I thought—angel, I thought I'd lost you," Kade said, his ever-present grin vanquished in the wake of his emotions.

Guilt smashed a wicked path across her aching chest as the weight of her actions pressed on her shoulders and she realised—not for the first time—how much Kade cared despite the rockiness in their relationship. But now, she couldn't ignore the worry in his eyes or the way his thumb traced patterns into the back of her hand.

Niko's scent of sea salt and weed trailed over her senses as he rounded the back of the couch and claimed the empty place beside her, cyanic irises filled with a worry that matched Kade's. She revelled in the comfort of him as he draped his arm over her shoulder and pulled her into his side, pressing a kiss to her temple.

"Kade's right, Nyx," he said. "We had no idea where you were, and I'll admit I freaked out when Alexander told me you hadn't come to their place. With Leon so ... *present* I figured Phaelyn and Qadira's quips had come true." He whispered the words into her skin like he was afraid to create too much distance between them and she'd disappear.

Contempt flared as she pressed a kiss to his jaw, still holding on to Kade's hand as the arm Leon broke twinged sharply. She rested her hand gingerly on his chest, bunching his band singlet in her fist. She was surprised by the healing capabilities of vampirism when she tossed a disbelieving glance to the torn hole in her shirt. "I'm sorry," she repeated for the second time, knowing it wouldn't be the last.

"I know, but please, don't do that again. I can't stand the thought of losing you," Niko said, voice husky with emotion.

"I won't. I promise," she said, pulling away to meet Kotori's dark gaze from across the room. Then she willed every ounce of her gratitude for him—for them all—to seep into her voice, her eyes, and her self. "Thank you."

"For what?" Kotori said, voice a low rumble.

"For trusting your instincts," she said before she shook her head, correcting herself. "For protecting me."

* * *

Illusion Boardwalk was neon, the showbag stalls and the parents who watched their children meandering among the carnival rides. Her dark gaze trailed the bustling nightlife in search of Qadira's favoured Ivory Skull, Mire—an auburn-haired, stocky man with a formidable reputation. *Almost* as formidable as Niko, Kade, Kotori and Orion's reputation. She knew the reason they waited, watching Mire as he conversed with another Ivory Skull beside the carousel, a small white sign pointing in the direction of the ramp that led to the fairground's underbelly hanging overhead.

A warm, salt-laced breeze ruffled Nyx's curls, brushing against her bare arms as Kade's tattooed fingers toyed with the hem of her maroon halter top. Niko leaned into the barricade beside the Ferris wheel, one arm draped over her shoulders while his opposite hand balanced the cigarette he shared with Kotori and Orion between his fingers. Her gaze lingered on Mire for a moment longer before she dragged her attention toward Kotori and Orion—lounging astride their bikes, haloed in the lights.

"Hey, chica?" Niko drawled, a salacious tilt to his lips.

"Nik?" she said, parroting his tone.

"Promise me something?"

Kade chuckled lowly, fingertips teasing the sliver of skin peeking out from between her shirt and jeans. Nyx paid him no attention as knowing darted through her, suspecting what he wanted to ask before the words left his mouth. Her tone was light and silvered in the days that had passed since she'd almost had her heart ripped from her chest. "I'll refrain from saying *anything* just this once …"

"Aw c'mon, don't be like that," Niko said, passing the cigarette to Kotori without tearing his stare from hers. "*Indulge* me."

She rolled her eyes playfully, ignoring the weight of Kade, Kotori and Orion's gazes. "What do you want, rockstar?"

"Promise me you'll come back covered in blood," Niko said, grasping her waist as he turned and pulled her closer.

A mirthful laugh tumbled from Kade's mouth before he rounded Nyx's shoulder and wandered to Orion's side. Niko's devilish grin captured her full attention.

"Do that for me, please. You know how much I fucking *love* seeing you covered in blood, beautiful. I mean, someone else's," he said, specifying.

"What would you do for that?" she murmured, gaze darting to his lips.

"I could think of a few things …" Niko said, his head lowering beside her face until his lips brushed the shell of her ear. "Like my lips on your breasts, leaving marks across your flesh. Or my fingers buried inside you, circles on your clit as your insides clench around my fingers. Maybe even your legs wrapped around my waist as I'm balls deep in you, your hands pinned above your head while your pretty moans tumble from your lips—"

"Don't tempt me, Nik," she said, her lips brushing his.

"It's not a *temptation*, chica," he dipped his head and connected their lips, grinning into the kiss. "If you come back covered in blood, I'll make it worth your while. That's a *promise*."

Nyx hummed in acknowledgement as she stepped out of his grasp and started toward Mire, accepting her role as the unofficial lure for their chosen victim. To lure Mire beneath the boardwalk so they could dispose of … or potentially glean information from the Ivory Skull on Qadira's motives.

"Or I could make it worth yours," she murmured, tossing him a playful wink.

"Be careful, little dove," Orion said, his frigid irises boring into Nyx's skin. His leather-clad thumb smoothed across the flesh of her forearm, her thigh grazing his slack-clad knee as his voice took on a warning edge, "Kotori won't be too far behind you while we stay here." He gestured lazily to himself, Niko and Kade. "If you need him for anything, even if it seems insignificant, you know how to reach him."

"What makes you think I'll need Kotori's help? Mire is Qadira's puppet but he's not invincible. He's also *not* Leon," she said, pulling her hand from Orion's grasp before she stepped closer to him, the pinkish hue of her still-healing chest wound a reminder of what Leon was capable of. "Let's not forget about Viliaris, Darlyn and Dries now."

Orion's lips quirked with a grin, forearms settling upon his handlebars. "Darlyn was Ares," he stated.

A soft laugh fell from her lips, head dipping at the truth of his words before she inched closer to Orion and pressed a firm, reassuring kiss to the underside of his jaw. Turning and slipping from his grasp as he made to pull her closer, a glint of mischief in her eyes as she side-stepped and slipped between the patrons. They were eager to see the night's firework show, she was eager to dance the dance of shadows. Her feet moved seemingly without her and she smiled, finding comfort in the strengthened bonds she shared with her men.

It didn't take long for Nyx to garner Mire's attention, his sapphire-blue gaze nestling upon the side of her face and then back as she passed him and followed the soft, white lights down the ramp to the boardwalk's underbelly, feigning obliviousness when he waited several moments before starting after her. With a carefree smile plastered across her face, Nyx paused beside a stall selling handmade jewellery, fingers trailing over the beaded, leather-plated and metallic accessories as she caught Mire in her peripherals—lurking beside a stall of second-hand vinyls—and Kotori over his shoulder. She pretended to consider a rose-quartz bracelet and then a pair of dagger-shaped earrings before she offered the dark-haired woman running the stall a smile and started anew on her trek toward the shadowed underbelly.

As Nyx's mind drifted to the Ivory Skull following several metres behind, her stare fell on Ares at her side and the ease with which he kept up to her, intent on staying by her side. Even when Niko sought to commandeer his attention and keep the Malamute by *his* side—reasoning that it was safer and less conspicuous if Ares stayed with him. It was a notion she had quickly shut down with a pointed look to Ares and the way he clung to her side as she recalled their earlier conversation at Elveszett Bluff; it wouldn't be believable for her to be without her trusted helvíti hound.

The darkness of the boardwalk's underbelly shrouded her senses for several seconds before her sight sharpened and illuminated the dark space with a clarity fit for midday and not the hours after twilight. She playfully urged Ares to run ahead as Mire's footfalls echoed from the top of the ramp, growing closer the further she wandered and weaved around the pillars. Somewhere in the back of her mind, Nyx registered Kotori's wolfish presence in the shadows. The Levenloos man had slipped over the barricades above and landed upon the sand with unnatural grace, blending into the darkness as Mire's boots met the sand.

His leering voice carried through the pillars and beams, "Qadira sends her regards, *fledgling*," he called, winding around a pillar.

Nyx's stride slowed until she stopped—half shrouded in shadow, half dappled by the neon light trickling from above—and met his gaze head-on, stance widened and imbued with predatory ease. Her eyes were dark ebony in the light of the underbelly, chin angled up against the biting edge to Mire's pronunciation of 'fledgling.' Ares brushed against her side, positioning himself before her with his hackles raised and his head lowered, upper lip curled and twitching with a dangerous snarl.

"*Mire*," she said, acknowledging him with a purposeful dip of her chin. "Qadira's *favoured* mortal … funny, she seems to have *few* of those."

The broad man scoffed, kicking up sand before he took several steps forward and his gaze locked on Ares. A low whistle spilled across the underbelly as Mire's pale-skinned hand gestured to Ares. "A helvíti hound in the flesh … well, I'll be damned. You're not as dumb as I thought," he said.

Her eyebrows twitched with confusion, glancing at Ares as Mire seemed to marvel at him with eerie irises. "How do *you* know about helvíti hounds? You're a mortal."

Mire dipped his head in a nod, pursing his lips before his gravelly voice filled with an air of smug pride, "I'm a *favoured* mortal, Nyx. It has its perks to learning vampiric lore. Just as Asher learned the lore and entombed it in a book … a book *you* have, apparently."

"Asher?" she murmured, surprised as her mind short-circuited before anger rose in its place. "What do *you* know about my uncle, *puppet*."

Mire drew closer and Ares released a low growl in response. The Ivory Skull heeded the helvíti hounds' warning as he halted mere metres away from her. "What? Don't tell me you believed Darlyn—the Skull you killed beneath the boardwalk—died by your will?" he said.

"*No*," she said, warning in her tone as a chilling sound tumbled from Ares' muzzle, mirroring her exclamation as the shadows seemed to shift in her peripherals.

A humourless laugh rang out across the darkness before Mire quieted and refocused on her. "He knew he was going to die, Nyx. Just like Leon intended him to."

"You're *lying*," she said, stepping around Ares even as her mind recalled the Ivory Skull's words. *'Since* they *want me dead. A* dead *end … But he wants* you.*'*

"Am I?" Mire drawled, matching her step forward with two of his own. "Because I think you *know* he'd do something like this … that he'll let you believe you were safe. I think you're smarter than that. I think you know you're not … safe." A dark grin tugged at his lips as he let the last word drag out. He pulled a photo from his jeans pocket, showing her a picture of Azeil sitting beside Asher's headstone. "And neither is he. Not after your … *meeting* with Leon."

"If you touch him—"

"You'll kill me?" Mire said, shaking his head with a low chuckle as he gestured to Kotori, who stepped from the shadows and flanked Nyx's side. "That was on my cards the moment I followed you down here. *I'm* not foolish enough to convince myself otherwise."

Nyx turned to Kotori—her temper finely reined in—before the Levenloos man dipped his head and the brunette duo moved in sync, standing mere *inches* in front of Mire as a dark, depraved smile traipsed across Nyx's features. Mire blanched before quickly masking his unease, focusing instead on Ares who paced restlessly behind them.

Kotori's head cocked, peering down his nose at Mire before he looked to Nyx and his dark gaze softened. "The decision's yours, kleintje."

"Can you smell that?" she said, pointedly glancing at the photograph and the metallic stench originating from it.

Kotori didn't respond. Instead, he moved with wolfish ease and snatched the picture from Mire's grasp, returning to Nyx's side as the Ivory Skull spluttered his annoyance. Kotori handed her the glossy paper. As her gaze traversed the familiar scrawl, Nyx saw red. Fighting the urge to crumple the photo—an urge she found herself constantly fighting whenever Phaelyn or Qadira left her notes—and its bloodied note.

With some effort, she tore her gaze from the picture and pinned her eyes on Mire, Qadira's voice echoing inside her skull like a mantra: '*Soon he'll be six feet under with Uncle Ashy.*'

Soon he'll be six feet under.

With Uncle Ashy.

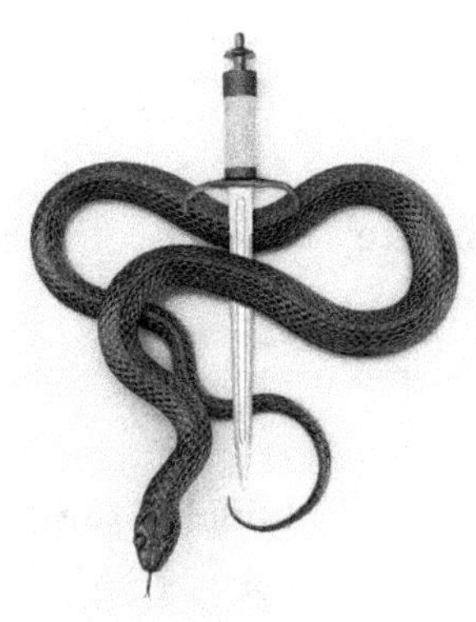

XLIX

Nyx

The wild thunder in Kotori's eyes matched the building storm in Nyx's chest as something in Nyx shifted, the glossy photo crinkling in her grasp. Mire glanced between them, a nervous sweat beading across his brow despite his earlier bravado. No man was fearless of his own death. The racing of his heart skittered past the shell of her ear as an eerie silence stretched between them. He kept quiet, the moment poised. They were more brutal and bloodier than he knew.

She cared little for the fear slashed across Mire's face when she dragged her stare from Kotori, stepping forward with the grace of a leopard, stalking Mire when he scrambled back several paces and his mouth twisted into a grimace. She didn't care as he opened his mouth and then shut it when her irises lightened, his pale skin draining of colour as Kotori flanked her, matching her stride with ease. Something dangerous had settled in the depths of her chest, snatching the little mortality—*humanity*—she possessed until all she felt was the red-tinged flames of her anger and anguish. All she felt was hunger.

Asher had deserved better. Had deserved to see her grow up and chase her dreams. Had deserved to spend hours searching for his favourite comics or telling her stories of mythical creatures. He'd deserved better than a slit throat by Ryder's hand; a man he'd believed was his friend.

He'd *deserved* the world.

Not death. *Never* death.

But no amount of wishing would bring her beloved uncle back. Maybe that was why Nyx's gaze lightened to match the eerie discoloration of her vampiric features, and her hands dragged a terrified Mire closer while he struggled against her grip. Ares' snarl rippled in the shadows, Mire's eyes were wide and imploring, to let him go, despite everything he'd said. She knew he didn't want to die … but neither had Asher, and that hadn't saved him. So why should it save Mire?

"Nyx," Mire began, his sapphire eyes bright with desperation. "Please, let me go. I … I don't want to die."

"I know," she murmured, holding his gaze as he tried to slip from her grasp.

"Then, *please*. Let me go."

She shook her head, adrenaline drenching her senses as her teeth sank into her bottom lip. Despite her better judgement, she felt sorry for him. "I can't."

"She's right, Mire. She *can't* do that," Kotori said, shifting in her peripherals, his shoulder pressed into a wooden pillar, the photo glaring like a blot in the sand.

"Why *can't* she?" Mire said, an irked edge to his tone.

Nyx saw the men, *her* men scattered between the pillars like wrathful angels sent to reap punishment upon mortals as half of their faces were bathed in shadows while the other was haloed by the neon light from the rides above. Niko's fingers grazed Ares' spine, his cyanic irises devoid of their usual playfulness before he raised his opposing hand and waggled his fingers in a mocking wave. Kade's arms were folded over his chest, the tattoos across his forearms clenching and unclenching as she saw how he tried to rein in his bloodlust. Orion's diamond features were framed by tendrils of smoke, cigarette pinched between his gloved fingers as he watched Mire with an eerie tilt to his head.

"If she doesn't kill you … we will," Kade said, lips lifted in his old Cheshire-Cat grin.

It was true. If she failed to end Mire's life, one of them would. Except, as her gaze slid back to Mire, an idea swam in her mind, a twisted game of cat and mouse playing before her eyes. Of Mire fleeing her grasp and darting between the wooden pillars, heart racing as he ran for his life, hope blossoming in his chest. Then, dragging him back into the darkness as he begged her to let him go. As he begged her for a mercy that wouldn't come, not when Nyx—and Orion, Kotori, Niko and Kade—had set their sights on killing him.

Nyx's hold on Mire loosened until she released him, watching as the Ivory Skull's eyes darted across her face with disbelief. "Go," Nyx said, inclining her head in the direction he'd come. "Go before I change my mind."

"But—" Mire started before he cut himself off, shaking his head and darting past her in a fear-induced hurry.

"What are you doing, little dove?" Orion drawled, wandering to her side with his Icelandic gaze snared upon hers.

She angled her head back to hold his gaze, his height no match for Kotori's but enough for her to feel much smaller than him. "Fancy a game of 'cat and mouse', Rion?" she said with a playful grin.

A pleased sound rumbled from the depths of Kade's chest as Orion smiled, drawing her attention to Kade.

"Kade, Kotori," she drawled, fighting the grin that begged to tear her face as Kade eagerly perked up. "Cut Mire off before he reaches the ramp, and herd him back into the centre of the underbelly where Orion and I will wait." Her gaze nestled upon Niko and Ares as she continued, "Niko, Ares stays with you. Wherever you go, he goes."

Niko's cyanic stare sparked with adoration—and lust—as Kade playfully knocked his shoulder into Niko's on his way past, tossing a wink at his companion before Kotori and Kade disappeared into the shadows.

Niko waited several moments before his husky voice carried to her; a trail of goose-bumps left in their wake, "Aw, chica. You should know by now that I'm your willing slave. Anything you want, I'll do everything in my power to obtain."

She blew a mirthful kiss in his direction before she turned and started after Kade and Kotori in her pursuit of a hopeful—and albeit, foolish—Mire with Orion by her side, Niko trailing several paces behind. Something dark shifted in the night, a shard of her soul that felt at ease here, among her pack and the blood they spilled. It smoothed across her flesh pleasantly, cocooning her in a blanket of warmth as her keen senses homed in on a tell-tale scream followed by the sharp tang of blood that carried to her on a crisp breeze, winding around the wooden pillars like black-scaled serpents.

"Rationally," Orion began, peering down at her, "this is twisted."

Nyx's brows furrowed as a bemused laugh tumbled from her lips, a familiar chase through the forest of Chades Cove playing across her mind. "When has anything you've done *not* been twisted?" she said playfully.

"I like this side of you," Orion said.

"This side of me?"

"He's always loved people who know what they want," Niko said matter-of-factly.

Another agonised scream rent the boardwalk's underbelly, drawing her attention away from Niko and Orion to the shadowed figure of Mire, who stood clutching his bloodied side. Kotori and Kade circled him, reminding Nyx of two wolves as the Ivory Skull's gaze darted in every direction, searching for a way out that wouldn't come. She couldn't fight the satisfaction that trickled into her gut, couldn't tamp down her warped pride at the two men who'd kept Mire away from the boardwalk ramp for her, and she couldn't deny the thrill she felt when Mire swivelled around and met her gaze.

He could pray to as many gods as he believed in but none would save him. Not in Celacali, the city ruled by the men at her sides.

Celacali was *their* city of death, despair and carnage.

"Nyx, *please*," Mire said, desperation thick in his gravelled voice.

Her eyes were ebony in the shadows as she squared her shoulders and cocked her head without a fissure of emotion across her oblong features. "I told you to run, Mire … not that I'd spare you," she murmured.

"But, you said—" Mire spluttered, trembling in fear as she stepped toward him and he scrambled back, colliding with Kotori's chest in his haste.

"Don't believe *everything* a vampire tells you, tut, tut, silly boy," Nyx drawled, closing the distance between them.

"Nyx," Mire pleaded, terror poisoning his tone.

Kotori shunted Mire toward her as her words hung eerily in the darkness, Kade swiftly stepping forward and clasping Mire's shoulders in a punishing hold intended to keep the man in place. Mire thrashed against Kade's grasp, flicking up damp sand as his shouts for help were drowned out by the whirring sounds above and the beginnings of the firework show. The loud boom and flashes of greens, blues, pinks, purples and reds smattered the underbelly with unsettling light, bathing Nyx's features as they shifted to her monstrous mask and Mire released a bellowing shout.

She paid Mire's fear no heed, closing the remaining space between them and trailing her fingers tauntingly up his chest as her gaze darted to Kade. She briefly noted the blend of pride and lust in his eyes before her attention slid back to Mire, his body racked with panic. Nyx's fingers curled around his collar. Orion's malignant presence registered beside her in her next breath, his scent of cigarettes and sandalwood filling her lungs as he stooped his head until his lips brushed her ears—almost doppelgänger to the way her lips hovered above Mire's skin, elongated fangs pushing against her lips.

"Now this, little dove, is where it gets fun," Orion said, dangerous satisfaction audible in his voice. "You can either make this quick and painless or torturous and slow. It depends on how you manipulate his blood."

Nyx's brows furrowed with confusion—not for the first time since Orion had taken her under his wing—inclining her head a faction toward him. "What do you mean by *manipulate*?" she said.

"Bite him like you usually would and when your fangs are embedded in his throat, it's all about your intentions. If you want him to die quickly, you'll be able to *thin* his blood to the same degree as a third-class haemorrhage. Or, if you want him to die slowly, you can manipulate his blood, so it thickens and clots," Orion explained, straightening beside her as she slowly nodded in understanding.

Without waiting, she sank her fangs into the column of Mire's throat in the same moment Kade's grasp tightened and Mire's blood traversed her tastebuds. The flavour sent Nyx's mind to sprawling vineyards, the fresh bite of snow, and undertones of cinnamon and blueberry laced with the earthy tone of a forest after a storm. She wondered *how* she associated his blood with scenery and flavours, wondered if it was a skill she'd picked up upon her transition from human to vampire.

Whichever it was, Nyx didn't pay too much attention as her senses zeroed in on the slowed and sluggish pulse of Mire's heart. The eerie, *tha ... ump, tha ... ump, tha ... ump* echoed in her eardrums as she recalled Orion's previous and reiterated words, her intentions clamouring in her mind. She waited, pulling mouthfuls of Mire's blood into her mouth and swallowing the heady ambrosia when his heart seemed to lurch, skipping a beat … then two. Three. Until a deafening silence disturbed by the bustling tourist attraction above filled her ears, Mire's struggle eternally ripped from his grasp as if to mirror the brutal manner Nyx had torn into his throat. She pulled away and his glassy eyes stared at her without seeing.

The phantom presence of Death brushed against her arm, a frigid chill she'd grown as accustomed to as the blood trickling down her chin to her throat where it stained her collarbones crimson. Kade stared at her ravenously as she tore her eyes from Mire's body. He released the cadaver with little regard and stepped over it, tattooed hands clasping her waist before his lips met hers. A surprised gasp tumbled from her mouth, granting Kade access to the cavern of her mouth. She pulled him impossibly close as she returned his kiss with as much intensity as Kade, teeth nipping his bottom lip, then, pulling away with a soft laugh before his tongue lathed a stripe from her jaw to the centre of her throat and he lifted his head, eyes soft.

"Let's get you back to the cave, angel," Kade murmured against her skin as Nyx's gaze drifted to Niko and the lustful fire within his irises. "Niko has a promise to fulfil."

L

Niko

Moonlight trickled into the cavernous living space hidden within Elveszett Bluff from the glass-patched ceiling, the hidden light fixtures tucked among the crevices of the ceiling illuminating the room and chasing away the night as Kotori wandered to each fire barrel and lit them, dredging warmth into the room. Niko's mind was focused on Nyx and her bloody skin. Flashes of salacious imagery stung his head. She was all he cared about.

His stare darted to Kade as his companion—past and present lover—led Nyx toward the tunnelway to his room with a devilish wink. Niko *almost* released a pent-up groan, his long-fingered hands drumming against his thighs as his mind tossed a vivid flash of Nyx beneath him, her lips parted, panting, her curls stuck to the fine sheen of sweat across her skin. Her legs woven around his waist as he plunged into her, alternating kisses to her jaw and whispering *filthy* praises into her ear.

Orion strode past him, amusement etched in every facet of his face as he crossed the room and dropped onto his throne. "What are you waiting for, Nik?" he said.

Kotori loomed large in the scattered dark. "Go *worship* our girl," he said.

Orion smiled, his demeanour taunting. The atmosphere seemed heavy with the weight of lust, of all their desires. Niko started toward his room, walking backwards with a brilliant grin as Orion waved him on. "If we can't *hear* her satisfaction, Kotori or I will do it for you."

"Yeah, yeah," Niko drawled, flipping the pair off as he pivoted and continued to his room, Orion's chuckle echoing down the tunnelways.

As he opened his door, he surveyed the space that was his. Black metal light fixtures bathed his room in a sensual light, artful shadows emphasised framed rock posters, each signed by their respective band members, and his favourite guitar was backlit in its stand, adding to the theatrical atmosphere. Stacked upon a dark, mahogany chest of draws were CDs and cassette tapes. Shelves of the same wood jutting out from the walls contained his vinyl, all his favourite rock bands from Def Leppard and Mötley Crüe to Guns N' Roses and Metallica. Placed on the shelves or upon his bedside table were various beautiful art pieces Kade had crafted for him, each symbolising a time in their lives or a milestone in their decades-long relationship.

Niko could still remember the day Leon had brought Kade to them, the desperation he'd felt when Leon had suggested letting him die despite bringing the tattooed blond back to Celacali, despite saving Kade from bleeding out alone in the shambles of his art studio. Something had raged in Niko, and he recalled the way he'd begged Leon to save Kade, to turn him so the resounding roar in his chest would quiet. Niko would have pledged his entire allegiance to Leon for that single act because he'd spent *years* with Kade, and had shared the darkest parts of himself with him, his dreams and motives in life. Not to mention the years he'd grown to know Kade in a way he'd never known anyone else, learning what drove Kade, what pleased him and what haunted him. Hell, Niko knew what would make Kade moan nothing but *his* name, and he delighted in the sounds whenever he had the pleasure. He loved Kade—and would spend the rest of his life doing so. The same way he intended to show Nyx, from the moment the sun rose to the minute it sank beneath the waves of the Avonsano Ocean, how he loved her. He'd promised himself to be nothing but the man Nyx deserved since she'd freed them from Leon with Orion by her side. He knew he could love them both—love them all—as they deserved. Small-minded slurs thrown against them over the years for their sexualities—Kade's bisexuality and his own pansexuality—fell by the wayside. They were unimportant, they did not endure.

Kade and Nyx sat on the end of his bed, Nyx straddling Kade's waist, his tattooed hands on her waist, her fingers tangled in the tresses of his hair. Niko approached them, trailing his fingertips across Nyx's spine and stooped down to press kisses to her throat.

His heart swelled with adoration for Nyx when she broke the kiss with Kade and turned to him, pressing her lips to his mouth as a low sound threatened to tumble from his throat. "Fuck, *Nyx,*" he said, his voice a husky rasp and his cyanic irises ablaze.

"Nik?" she said against him, driving him insane as she consumed his every thought.

With some effort, he pulled back, trailing his thumb along her bottom lip. Somehow, he managed to put voice to his thoughts, his tone *reverent* and laced with unwavering conviction, "Nyx," he started, pausing at a flash of uncertainty. His gaze flitted to Kade, seeking reassurance from his partner.

Kade's head dipped, urging him to share his feelings for Nyx.

"I know this might be too soon but … *fuck* does it feel right," Niko said. "I—" his gaze darted again to Kade, struggling to find the right words to formulate his emotions.

"I think … I'm not good with metaphors, but you're a piece of my soul I need more than oxygen. You *are* my everything."

Kade grinned into the flesh of her throat. "Go on, little minx. Tell Nik how you feel," he leaned closer, lips brushing Nyx's ear, "I promise he'll make it worth your while."

Niko stepped impossibly close, chest pressing against Nyx's shoulder and cupped Kade's chin in his guitar string-calloused hand, angling the blond's head up as he pressed his lips to Kade's, the familiar taste of him exploding on his tastebuds.

He hadn't realised how much he'd missed this—missed Kade—in the months they'd been held captive, hadn't realised how much he'd taken for granted with Kade until he'd *almost* convinced himself he'd never see Kade again, that he'd die in that watery torment. Niko dared another step closer, allowing himself and Kade a moment to catch their breaths while his free hand settled on Nyx's waist. When Niko was sure Kade was ready, he reconnected their lips and deepened the kiss, Kade readily welcoming Niko's ministrations with a playful nip to his bottom lip and a hum of contentment.

"Fuck, this is hot. If I didn't have feelings for you before, I do now," Nyx said, her lust-filled voice breaking through the haze shrouding Niko's mind.

Her gaze held his when he pulled away from Kade. A slow smile crawled across his broad features as he angled his body in a way that made it easy to connect their lips, kissing Nyx with singular adoration and love. Like Kade, Nyx eagerly accepted his kiss, parting her lips when he deepened it, their mouths moving together.

"Aw, chica, Kade was right when he said I'd make it worth your while because I'll *always* make it worthy of you," he said.

"You've never *not* made it worth my while … it might be one of the reasons I love you," she admitted.

Niko's gaze locked on her, mind reeling. "You … *love* me?"

"Isn't that what you meant?" she started as if she'd just said something foolish.

Niko longed to rid her of the uncertainty she felt. "It was," he assured, pressing a kiss to her lips. "I love you too, chica. You're the spots to my cheetah."

"I think that's my cue to leave you … *alone*. *Enjoy* yourselves," Kade said, slipping out from beneath them and disappearing back through the room's doorway with a Cheshire-Cat grin splayed across his face.

Niko silently claimed the space Kade left behind and reconnected their lips, deepening their kiss with ease. He revelled in the sweet taste of her and the lingering undertones of blood before he pulled away and his hands grasped her top, pulling it over her head and discarding it over his shoulder. A sensual glint shrouded Nyx's eyes as she posed coquettishly.

"What—?" Niko said, puzzlement in his eyes.

"I'd like to try something, Nik. To make you feel something *close* to what I feel for you," she said, curls tumbling over her shoulders like a dark waterfall.

Her palms splayed across his jean-clad thighs before she parted his legs and sank to her knees. A strained sound—part groan, part whine—escaped him as Nyx peered up at him from between his thighs.

"So, will you let me?" she breathed, waiting for his consent like he'd always waited for hers.

Swallowing the lump of arousal in his throat, Niko tried to collect his thoughts. As much as he *loved* the thought of her lips wrapped around his cock, he didn't want her to do anything if her heart wasn't in it. He wouldn't be *that* person who expected things from their partner if they weren't ready to go to that next step. Not now. Not then. Not ever. Nyx's fingers trailed up his thighs to the waistband of his pants, toying with the fabric as her eyes flared with desire. It was becoming difficult to think. "Nyx, I love you, but you don't need to do this to prove anything," he said.

"I *want* to do this for you, Nik. As long as you're happy for me," she gestured to herself with an airy sweep of her hand, "a complete *novice* in the art of giving head, to … try."

There was an uncertain edge to her words that stole Niko's breath, adoration weeping like blood of a wound from his heart. A low curse tumbled from his mouth as Nyx unfastened the button of his jeans and dragged the zipper down with her gaze locked on his.

He watched her kiss-bruised lips. "I don't think you realise how much of a hold you have over me, chica, I'd let you do anything to me, and I'd enjoy every second of it. I'm honoured to be the first person you want to *give* pleasure to."

"Can you promise me something?" Nyx murmured, capturing Niko's attention as he clung to her every word.

"Name it and it's yours. *Forever,*" he said.

Nyx's eyebrow arched doubtfully. "You're being serious, aren't you?"

"Deathly," Niko said.

"Okay…" Nyx trailed off. "Promise me that you'll tell me what feels good or *show me*. Just … help me out a little."

"Ok," Niko rasped, the corded muscles in his arms rippling as he clenched the sheets at his sides. He couldn't tear his gaze from Nyx if he tried, trapped in onyx as she tugged at his jeans and he helped her remove them. He cursed as his cock pressed uncomfortably against his boxers, *begging* to be released. And, despite her previous words, he couldn't stop himself from double-checking she was okay. Wildest dreams or not, he wouldn't let his judgement be clouded by his lust—*love* for her. "Are you sure?" he said.

"I wouldn't be sitting here if I wasn't sure, Nik. Let me do this. If not for you, then let me do it for myself," she said.

A ragged breath slipped past his lips as one of Nyx's hands settled on his thigh and the other wrapped around his cock, stroking the length of him with a firmness that dredged a guttural sound from his throat, head tipping back.

"*Fuck*, if this is your hand job game. I won't last long at all," he said, peering down at her as she continued her smooth strokes, seeming to grow confident with his reactions before she dragged her thumb across his tip. He cursed as Nyx dipped her head and dragged her tongue tentatively across his tip. "Nyx, *please* wrap those pretty lips around my cock," Niko pleaded, bunching the sheets in his fists.

And, before he could teeter any longer, Nyx's gaze locked on his and her head dipped, lips wrapping around the first few inches of his cock. His lips parted in pleasure as she took more of him into her mouth, her tongue trailing across the underside of his cock and the vein that started at its base, following it to his tip where she uncertainly circled the head. Some part of him wondered why she had been uncertain.

If she traces the vein of my cock one more time, I might *combust,* he thought.

His cyanic irises darkened, hips shifting. A moan fell from his mouth; a symphony of praise for Nyx as her teeth grazed his cock and he swore he saw stars, one of his hands darting out to tangle in the tresses of her curls, keeping her hair out of her face as her grey-flecked irises held his.

Nyx bobbed her head, his hand in her hair gently urging her to take more of him. His orgasm crept forward with every graze of her teeth against his shaft or her tongue circling the sensitive flesh of his tip, dragging it closer until he couldn't shake the euphoric undertone from his body. Like a mass of electricity confined within a cloud before an ensuing storm struck and brilliant bolts of purple-white light split the sky.

"Just like that, chica. Just like that," he said, gritting the words out between his teeth.

"What's the matter, rockstar? Are you close?" Nyx taunted, pulling away.

"So fucking close," he rasped, his gaze locked on Nyx and her lips wrapped around him once more. "Chica, do me a favour?"

Nyx hummed and Niko swore, the vibration wrenching his orgasm closer.

"Before I cum, I need you to pull away … because there's something else I want you to do for me," he said, watching as Nyx's eyebrows arched before he continued, "Bite me. On my thigh, on my wrist. It doesn't matter where, just bite me *with* the intention to please." He watched as her frown deepened, before the sensation of her hot mouth around him stole his breath … and his thoughts, rendering him mute.

His mounting orgasm climbed with a vengeance as Nyx's tongue circled the head of his cock before following the aching vein at the underside to the base, teeth grazing his member while his orgasm drew closer.

"I'm close. Fuck, *Nyx*," he said.

She pulled away and wrapped her hand around his member, continuing her firm pace without faltering. He watched as her lips pressed together, grasping his wrist before her head dipped and her lips brushed his skin. A beat of silence punctuated by the sloppy sounds of Nyx's hand gliding up and down on his cock filled the room. Her hold tightened as her thumb smoothed over his tip and a low sound rumbled from his chest. His head dipped when he caught the way she pressed her lips together, trying to stifle her soft pants as her ragged exhale fanned across his forearm.

Through the heady swell of his orgasm and the precipice it balanced him on, Niko forced himself to speak, "Now."

Her fangs pierced the flesh of his forearm and a soft sigh escaped his lips. He waited a moment, relishing in the aphrodisiacs flooding his bloodstream as his head tipped back and he soaked in the heightened sensation—explosion—before he refocused, lust-blown pupils locked on Nyx. As she extracted her fangs from his wrist, trailing her tongue over her marks until they stitched closed, Niko knew he would bear them with pride, ensuring none of his bracelets covered them.

"You know," he began, pressing possessive kisses to the underside of Nyx's jaw before she gripped his chin and her lips met his in a sweet, loving kiss. "*Nothing* in my life has ever been as good without you in it."

Nyx rolled her eyes. "That's not fair to the others, Nik."

"Why not?" he asked.

"Because I haven't been with *all* of you yet. I haven't been with Kotori like I've been with you all," she said.

"And … Orion?" he said, feigning confusion with a pointed smirk. Her eyes narrowed and Niko laughed, already knowing the answer.

"Why do I feel like you already know my answer?"

"Because we share everything … most of the time," Niko said, laughing. "When we said you were ours, we meant it. Everything we do is for you. Anything you want is yours. We might be the kings of Celacali but, we're nothing without our queen."

"*Queen*?" Nyx repeated with disbelief.

"That's what you are," Niko said, adoration in his eyes.

"But—" Nyx started.

Niko's cyanic eyes locked on hers, keeping her entrapped as he pushed every ounce of emotion she evoked within him into his tone—*needing* her to understand their sincerity. "You *are* our queen, chica. A king bows to no one *but* his queen … and we'll *always* bow to you. For the rest of our eternity."

LI

Orion

How much chaos could they reap to keep Phaelyn and Qadira away from Azeil? Orion wondered, drumming his fingers on the armrests of his chair as his mind turned over a slowly forming plan. *Would it keep the duo's attention away from Asher's journal? Protect Nyx from Leon's newfound interest?* He thought of the considering gleam in Leon's eyes and the condemning words Phaelyn and Qadira had uttered. *He wanted Nyx ... for some reason,* Orion recalled, hearing Phaelyn and Qadira's voices as if they were beside him. *Leon wanted Nyx* alive.

Heavy footfalls carried to his ears and he watched Kotori with a hardbacked book clutched in his hands, next to Kade, who strode from the direction of Niko's room. A bemused smirk played on his lips. "I guess *that* answers my question," Orion said, snuffing out cigarette smoke in twin streams from his nostrils.

"And yet, we have nothing but unanswered questions when it comes to Phaelyn and Qadira," Kotori said sombrely.

Orion straightened and his mind returned to his previous thoughts—they had to find Azeil and protect him, they had to find Phaelyn and Qadira and stop them, and he had to ensure *his* pack obtained that missing … information … before Leon did. His mind suddenly felt hazy and he returned to the thought about … the missing … thing. His thoughts felt sluggish. It was easier to think about something else. Nyx. *Was she braver than we'd ever been? Willing to meet Leon alone for* us. He went back to the thought from before, to the … thing. A vision of a locked box turned on its axis in his mind's eye. The box was a foreign object, his brow creased, concentrating … but he couldn't touch it. He wanted to open it, see what was inside. He knew inside was the thing, its shape shifted, causing him to look away, to forget. *No!* In his mind, he turned his head back. To the box. What was inside the box?

He knew. It. Was. A secret.

His breath felt suddenly laboured and he looked at Kotori, pleadingly. "Kotori," he said, drawing Kotori and Kade's attention.

"Orion?" Kotori parroted, dark eyebrows knitted into a soft frown.

"*Why* does Leon want Nyx alive?" he said, capturing Kade's attention as he scrubbed a hand down his face, hoping it would rid him of the ache in his temples.

"Because she has Asher's book," Kade said as if the answer was obvious.

Orion scrutinised Kade for a long moment as something prickled the back of his mind like the truth was at the tips of his fingers but he couldn't grasp it, tumbling away before he could learn its secrets. *There was something else,* he thought with a frustrated sigh. *Leon wanted something* in *Asher's book, but he couldn't* ... why *couldn't he just take it for himself? What was stopping him?* "That's not it," Orion said, rising from his chair with an agitated roll of his shoulders. "That's too easy."

"What are you thinking?" Kotori said, eyeing his companion with dark interest, the book in his lap forgotten.

Orion's gaze flickered between Kade and Kotori, something in his chest murmuring how close he was to the answers he sought. "Azeil said something about Asher's book when Nyx and I saw him upon his return to Celacali," he said.

"*And*?" Kade prompted, urging him to continue with a flick of his wrist, impatient.

"Asher's book is steeped in silver—" Orion started.

"We know that already, Orion," Kade said, his eyebrows arching with an unimpressed frown.

Orion's gaze sparked with ire as he sucked in a ragged breath to quell his frustration, to rid himself of the lingering talons of Leon's commands. "If you'd let me finish, I *would have* said … it's also written in Asher's blood," he said.

"So? How does that make it a book no vampire can read—or handle?" Kotori asked.

Unlike the pain that razored Orion's insides whenever he tried to share information tied to Leon, the knowledge at the forefront of his mind swelled like the sea, *wanting* to be shared. *Wanting* to purge him of Leon's commands and the fraying chips of time—of his mind. And he realised, a moment laced with satisfaction and relief, that he'd stumbled upon a flaw in Leon's commands. He *could* share this knowledge because it hadn't originated from Leon. How could it when Orion hadn't known it himself until Azeil had shared it? A malignant grin stretched across Orion's face as he met Kade and Kotori's stares, satisfaction oozing off him. "Asher's blood is a loophole to vampiric lore *none* of us saw coming," he said.

Kotori's dark gaze sparked with something fierce. "How?"

"Did you know that if you soak a book's pages in silver *and* the blood of its writer, that anyone, human or *vampire*," Orion paused, ensuring his companions were following before he continued, "can read its contents *if* they're of that bloodline."

"Which is why only Nyx ..." Kade began, the first glimpse of hope shining in his eyes, "can read Asher's book?"

"*If* Azeil spoke the truth, yes. Leon *needs* Nyx alive because she is the *only* vampire who can see and handle Asher's book," Orion said, tossing a thank you to whatever gods had granted him this escape route through whatever *thing* he couldn't remember.

A deeply, timbred chuckle emanated from Kotori's chest as he rubbed the underside of his jaw, eyes alight with bewilderment. "She's the *tainted* bloodline—the key to everything."

"Nyx is Leon's greatest weakness," Kade breathed, his fuscous gaze alight.

Orion's gaze held theirs, something fury-laced cutting through his tone. "Oh, she's *much* more than that. She's his downfall."

LII

Nyx

A gruff, baying bark echoed off the cavernous walls, startling Nyx from her slumber as she jolted upright in Niko's bed. Her curls were a tousled mess as her gaze settled on Kotori, Kade and Orion in the doorway, Ares at their side. Niko's groan of displeasure filled her ears as he begrudgingly raised his head from the pillows, her answering chuckle earning her a frigid glare imbued with a thousand daggers. Nyx tried to hide her amusement as she straightened his Def Leppard shirt. The memory of her drifting off to sleep after spending the rest of the night talking to him about everything and nothing in between filled her mind. It was a night she would hold close for the rest of her life. "Is that necessary?" she said, disorientated by the sudden wake-up call.

"Not entirely," Orion admitted, a soft grin uplifting the corners of his mouth in a way Nyx suddenly realised she liked seeing.

Almost as much as she loved his leather gloves and the way his shirts—like the black dress shirt he wore now—emphasised the definition of his back or the veins of his forearms. Though, she suspected he already knew this; a look passed between them. Her attention shifted to Kotori as he ran his fingers through Ares' fur, the black metal of his lip ring caught between his teeth.

"Sorry to disturb you ..." Kotori said, the wolfish grin that grew across his face contradicting his words. "But we have pressing things to *discuss*."

The mattress to the left of Nyx dipped as Niko propped himself up, the sprawling ink of his cheetah tattoo rippling. He leaned toward her and pressed a sweet kiss to her lips, his fingers brushing a stray curl behind her ear. "Morning, chica," he said, his voice deeper by a few octaves. "I don't know, Tori. I think our *discussion* was important, it might've been life-changing," Niko said.

"So, we heard," Kade drawled, his irises lightened by his amusement.

"We have to talk about Azeil and what we need to do next," Orion stated bluntly, stealing the happiness from the room.

"Not even a moment of peace? Really, Orion?" Niko sighed ruefully as he eyed Nyx's frozen face.

Nyx's guards raised as she shook a preternatural stillness from her body. "Okay … what about him and our next step?" she said, freeing herself from the bedsheets before moving to the end of the bed.

"We need to pay him a visit," Orion said, playfulness gone.

"You mean, we'll be doing some troublemaking *and then,* we'll see Azeil," Kade supplied with a cheeky wink, cutting Orion off.

"We need to prevent Azeil's death *and* figure out why Leon abducted Jesse Stone," she said, recalling the missing boy Leon delivered—dead—to Elveszett Bluff.

"Oh, we know why he had Jesse," Niko said, displeasure twisting his upper lip.

Nyx's brow creased as she glanced between the men, trepidation prickling her insides. "Because of his … *habits*?"

"He has a sick addiction," Niko said.

"Children's blood," she said, a heavy sick feeling in the pit of her stomach. Nyx searched his face for a lie—like she'd searched Orion's when he'd first told her—but found none. Instead, horror latched onto her like a fishing hook while her mind wrenched a timeline to its forefront. "Jesse was missing for two weeks," she breathed, more horror mounting. "Leon kept him alive for *two weeks* to what … to *feed* on him?" She looked up for the terrible confirmation.

"For as long as I've known Leon, he couldn't shake that itch, the high he found in *untainted* blood," Orion said coldly. "Innocence is really his … only weakness." A new grimness lit his eyes like he'd remembered something he didn't want to.

"Children? What does that have to do with a weakness?" Nyx prompted. The wrongness of Leon's actions opened phantom wounds in her chest.

"He takes a child, or more, whenever he feels his control slipping," Orion said. "It's like a crutch, an addiction. He's like a junkie who needs his fix."

"*Children* are his *coping* mechanism? That's *sick*," she spat.

"Leon will use Azeil to lure you out, he will. Leon's unravelling because he can't control our paths and he will do horrible things to re-establish his control. Ripping out your heart *would have* been one solution, but then he would lose any bartering control with us, and it seems …" He leaned down as he spoke, so she couldn't miss a single word. "You impress him, little dove. He is interested in you."

"Interested in me how?" she breathed, she could only stare at Orion in horror. Her father was the *priority,* not her. Leon wanted her dead, that was simple. Now this? What had changed? All too suddenly, she remembered what he'd called her on the boardwalk: *daughter.* She looked at Orion, eyes wide. "No," she whispered. "Never."

"Family is all Leon's ever really wanted," Orion said. "At least, his *idea* of a family. A steel-bound host of pets on leashes." His words were bitter and old.

Nyx looked at Orion. She thought of her own dysfunctional family, of her estranged mother and half-brother, of her father, the twins. Family was something she, too, strove for. She thought of Orion, Kade, Kotori and Niko. The way they were, the way they loved. Then she thought of Leon and the notion made her sick. "I will never be a part of his *family*, and neither will you. Ever again." Saying it made her resolute. She had a father she loved, Leon would never, could never replace him.

What does my father know? What did Asher entrust him with? she thought, worrying her bottom lip between her teeth as silence descended and she pondered her thoughts alongside the new information. What were they missing? Had Asher prepared a plan for his research in the event of his death? Was that why the sensation of looking for a needle in a haystack crept into her bones? *Give me a sign, Ash,* she thought, tossing her plea to the heavens in hopes of him hearing her.

"Do you remember what Azeil said when he returned to Celacali?" Orion said, breaking her from her thoughts, a sharpness to his gaze that snared her attention.

A frown crept across Nyx's face as she surveyed Orion. "That he was reinstated as a detective?" she offered lamely.

"Before that," Orion said, "I … can't—" he looked at her, imploring, as if he willed her to see the answers in his eyes.

"He said something about Asher's book," she paused as her eyes widened and realisation slammed into her like a freight train, a soft gasp tumbling from her lips. "Asher's blood. *My* bloodline." Her gaze darted between Niko, Kade, Kotori and Orion. "I can read his book because I'm from his bloodline. *I'm* the flaw."

"That you are," Orion said, a proud grin curling the edges of his lips. "A beautiful, *tainted* flaw."

LIII

Nyx

The distant crashing of waves against the Bluff's cliff face lulled Nyx in the silence of Niko's room as she stared up at the ceiling. Time passed like grains of sand in a timer. Seconds had bled into minutes—ones Orion, Kotori, Kade and Niko had left her alone to ponder—before minutes trickled into an hour, wondering about this newfound information and what it meant for her—what it meant for Azeil's safety. Would it be enough to protect Azeil? Could she use this loophole as an advantage? And, almost like it was an unbidden thought dredged from the depths of her chest. Would she be able to end Leon once and for all?

The scuff of footsteps drew her from her thoughts and her gaze from the grooves of the ceiling, a dark brow arching when she registered Kotori, Niko, Kade and Orion's presence. Niko stalked to his bed and dropped unceremoniously onto the mattress.

Orion's gaze held hers as he strode to the bed's edge and wrapped a hand around her ankle, dragging her closer to him while Kotori and Kade lingered in the doorway.

"*Orion*," Nyx warned, ignoring Niko's presence as he sidled up behind her, muscular thighs bracketing her sides before he pressed a languid kiss to the crook of her throat.

"*Nyx,*" Orion said, parroting her tone as he pulled her closer to himself, the fly of his pants pressing sinfully against her lace-covered core beneath, distracting her from her thoughts.

"Let me go. *Now*."

"Now, why would I do that?" he said, his head angled, Icelandic gaze darting to Niko and the way his companion rested his chin upon her shoulder. "I like this position. *A lot,*" his stare trailed across her flesh and the fabric of Niko's T-shirt, lingering over the valley where it obscured his vision. "But … do you know what would make it better?"

Her lips parted to respond to him but, in the same breath, Orion's chin dipped and Kade darted forward, gently bolstering her balance as he pulled one of her hands away from where she pressed it into the mattress and she fell into Niko's chest. His calloused hands trapped her wrists by her side. Her groan of annoyance filled the room and she tried to push herself out from between his legs, pulling against his hold.

"Old habits die hard," she quipped, trying to pull from Niko's hands. "Let me go. We've got things to do."

"We definitely do," Orion said, a possessive edge to his voice. "And it's definitely hard."

She rolled her eyes and laughed despite herself. "Man-child."

A soft glint bled into Orion's irises, his grasp relaxing a fraction. "You're still covered in Mire's blood, and you didn't even realise. We left you alone, like you wanted, but you can only be alone with your thoughts for so long before they turn dark. *We* just went through some pretty heavy shit and I think *we* need to relieve stress, consider your needs."

Nyx blinked up at Orion with puzzlement before her gaze drifted to the blood crusted to the skin of her arms and chest. "My needs …?" she murmured.

Kade brushed her curls out of her face, a tender action. Paired with Niko's firm grasp pinning her wrists to the mattress, a twisted bolt of arousal shot through her veins.

"Sometimes, the only person who matters *is* yourself, angel," Kade said, "and there's no shame in that."

"But—" she started as Kotori pushed off the cavernous entryway.

He uttered a low command to Ares that sent the Malamute in the direction of the main living space as Orion released her thighs and stepped aside to grant Kotori a clear path. Her gaze remained locked on Kotori as he stalked toward her, and her insides sparked with dark, salacious warmth. The rustling of fabric ghosted her ears as Kade moved in her peripherals in the same moment Niko let go of her wrists and slipped from behind her.

Nyx's gaze darted from Kotori to his companions, marvelling at the well-oiled unit they were as Niko stooped down and pressed a kiss to her forehead before following Kade. He playfully swatted Orion's shoulder as he passed.

Orion lingered, eyeing Nyx and Kotori before a slow smirk crawled across his face and he started down the tunnelway, calling back over his shoulder to them, "I'll leave you to it then."

Now Kotori commandeered the spot between Nyx's legs where Orion had been. "Smooth," she drawled.

He shrugged, the wolfish grin she was familiar with stretched across his face as a strand of his ebony hair fell in front of his face. "It did the job and," he glanced over his shoulder, "it got me a moment with you … where I don't need to share."

Her churning thoughts were momentarily put on standby—a feat she suspected Orion intentionally planned, giving her a reprieve from her thoughts until she had a moment to consider them—as she realised Kade was right. She hadn't been putting herself first. That she'd grown so lost in her pursuit of finding Niko, Kade, Kotori and Orion, she'd forgotten about herself. The anguish Asher's death had caused her—as grateful as she was for the distraction and chance to move on, she knew it wasn't healthy to hold onto such grief and anguish—and the life she'd had *before* he died. Leon's hand around her heart and the terror that her immortal life would end so grotesquely darted across her mind. She thought of everything that mattered; of the bond she'd had with her father before it was tested, her friendship with Alexander and Tobias. She could admit that she missed a simpler life but she also knew she adored her newfound one—blood-stained and unpredictable as it was.

She couldn't see herself without Orion, Kotori, Niko or Kade anymore. The monsters she'd once feared, were now the men she loved. Her home, which hadn't been a place, was found with them.

Nyx's lips twitched as she refocused on Kotori and her mind swerved. His dark locks cut to the nape of his neck framed his face in a way that filled her mind with a multitude of *filthy* thoughts. Of what his lip ring would feel like against her clit or the way his large hands would grasp her thighs, pinning her in place as he forced her to take every ounce of pleasure he gave. How his fangs would feel embedded in her flesh as he fucked her, her wrists bound above her head …

Her gaze locked with his, amusement at his words playing across her face before she spoke, "Aw, strijder. Don't you like to share?"

"I share as well as Orion, Niko and Kade share, but right now … that's the last thing on my mind," Kotori said.

His deep voice caressed her skin like phantom fingers trailing over her arms as he stooped down until his lips hovered inches away from hers.

"And … what is on your mind?" she asked, eyes darting to his lips, his lip ring, and then to his dark, dark eyes.

Instead of answering her, Kotori extended his hand and waited for her to take it, leading her from Niko's room, down the tunnelway and into another she'd never seen before until it opened out into the familiar cavernous bathroom. Chipped white marble basins and an antique floor-length mirror were glazed in a sheen of moisture from a hot spring softly bubbling in the cave's furthest corner. Several towels hung from a scuffed coatrack and a set of mismatched lamps stood at opposing ends of the room, casting warm light into the shadowy space.

How anything works ... beats me, she thought fondly as she saw Kotori staring at her. As if nothing mattered to him but *her.* "Kotori," she prompted, ignoring the way his intense gaze trailed over her flesh. "Why'd you bring me here?"

"Because there's one thing immortality will teach you, kleintje," he said, kicking off his boots. His lips twitched with an almost-grin when her eyes flickered to his hands and the fluid manner he unfastened his dark jeans.

Ensnared by the drag of the zipper, she cursed silently as her gaze snapped to his, revealing nothing but veiled satisfaction. Warmth settled in her blood, igniting a flame.

"That to walk this path, you must *always* take care of yourself, despite everything life throws at you," he said.

The low timbre of his voice corralled her senses before he pulled his shirt over his head, tossing it toward the basins. Words died on her tongue in the same breath as he turned to the bubbling spring and discarded his remaining clothes, baring his broad shoulders, muscular thighs, and browned skin. He waded to its centre until the water lapped at the base of his spine and the defined 'V' of his waistline. She wasn't sure whether to thank the gods for creating Kotori, or curse them. "I don't—" she began, mind whirling with a thousand illogical thoughts. "How does this help me?"

Kotori's dark gaze held hers as his fingertips skimmed the water and she reminded herself that the sensation—a serene sense of *rightness* like a forest with a sunlit canopy—budding in her chest was *more* than something as primal as lust. With Kotori, it was an all-consuming tide paired with the simplicity of understanding, of knowing he would always be the rock in her life. He was her Elysium, beautiful like a dark horse and yet, peaceful like rain skittering down a windowpane. So, it was without inhibition that she slipped Niko's shirt over her head and wandered to the spring's edge when he offered her his hand, dragging her underwear down her legs and stepping into the water. A soft sigh escaped her lips as the warm water lapped at her skin and she peered up at Kotori. His beringed hands settled on her waist, drawing her closer to his chest, his woodsy scent wrapping around her senses.

"I know you like this bloodstained life," he said, drawing her to the pool edge and claiming a seat on the ledge beneath its surface. "But I think you'll *love* the moments where you're not covered in a Skulls' blood, more."

Her lips quirked as Kotori reached for a washcloth tucked among the rocky crevices and she settled on the smooth, stone ledge of the rising and falling cavernous pool beside him. He shifted to face her and cupped her chin with his free hand, dampening the cloth with the other. A shuddery breath left her as the fabric dragged over her collarbones, purging her of Mire's blood in an action so tender it stole Nyx's breath.

In what lifetime will I deserve him? she thought as she appraised his features and the way dark tresses of hair brushed his jaw. She seemed, suddenly, utterly lost in the quiet storm of him. *In this lifetime, he is a part of you. And in the others, he is the piece of yourself you are missing.* "Kotori," she murmured, drawing his attention away from the crusted blood under her throat, to her face.

"Nyx?" he parroted, an undertone of confusion marring his voice.

Nyx wasn't sure what drove her as she shifted and resituated herself on his lap, knees bracketing his hips, her hand grasping the back of his neck to steady herself but when his arm banded around her waist, she found the words came of their own accord,

"I should have said something else after Leon tried to kill me because *thank you* wasn't all I *wanted* to say," she said as she willed everything she'd fail to vocalise into her eyes.

"What did you want to say?" he prompted, discarding the washcloth on the nearby rocks before he pulled her closer to his chest.

"I wanted to tell you that I loved you," she said, a prickle of nervousness crawling over her skin, afraid of how he would react.

"You *loved* me?" he drawled, dark brows arched as his irises sparked and he grinned wolfishly. "Or you *love* me?"

"I *love* you," she said, peering down at him with a softness to her eyes that couldn't be purged. "*Present* tense."

"I could *tell* you I feel the same," he murmured, craning his head until his lips brushed against hers. "But I'd rather *show* you. Will you let me show you, kleintje?"

For a moment, Nyx was lost in the haze of his lust-filled and ... *desperate* tone, almost like he was begging her as she forced herself to focus. "*Yes*. Please ... *show me*."

Kotori's stare entrapped hers before he connected their lips in a slow, sensual kiss and she basked in his presence. One of his hands remained settled on her waist while the other cupped her jaw, angling her head so he could deepen the kiss in a way that made her toes curl. The familiar paradox of his kisses engulfed her as her fingers gripped his shoulders and her hair, cascaded down her back, dipping the water's surface.

Her mind stumbled over itself as Kotori broke away, gazing down at her with a dark look that reminded her of a ravenous wolf—a thought that sent a jolt of lust through her. As his hand left her face and joined the one at her waist, his fingertips trailed down to her thighs before his large palms grasped the soft flesh and he swiftly switched their position, lifting her onto the ledge of the pool as he parted her legs to make more room for himself between them, sinking to his knees while the breath caught in Nyx's throat.

It was one thing to imagine the towering brunette between her thighs, gazing up at her, it was another to experience it. His hands kneaded the flesh of her inner thighs, slowly hiking the tension and anticipation until it took everything in her to not beg him to caress her aching clit. And, like he could sense the tide of her thoughts, he waited.

"Kotori," she began, her tongue darting out to wet her bottom lip as his low hum filled her ears. "Please touch me."

His gaze held hers, his voice as deep and rumbling as thunder, "Show me where."

She leaned forward and grasped one of his hands, bold in her wants as she pressed his fingers against her centre, her eyes never leaving his. Purposefully, she dragged his fingertips over her throbbing clit and down as she rasped out her response, "Here. Please, strijder. *Touch me*."

Kotori's irises sparked, the hold on her thigh tightening as he drew an idle circle over her clit and his lips tugged into a wolfish grin. A soft gasp escaped Nyx's throat as he dipped his head and his tongue lathed a stripe up the slick of her core, circling her clit as she reclined into the rockface, head tipped upward. He readjusted his hold on her as he draped one of her legs over his shoulder. If Nyx had thought his lip ring on her mouth felt tantalising, nothing could compare to the pleasurable brush of metal against her clit, eliciting a hum from her that spurred Kotori to repeat his actions, dragging his lip over the sensitive nerve ending with a firmness that wrenched a needy whine from her chest.

"Kotori—" she started, a ragged moan escaping her as he pressed a single finger into her cunt and started a maddening pace in the same breath his tongue circled her clit. This was followed by the soft graze of his teeth against the bundle of nerves and the slosh of water with his movement. "*Fuck*."

His head lifted from her, dark gaze flitting to where his finger thrust in and out of her before his lips curled and he added another, stretching her with lithe ease as his thumb pressed firm circles into her clit.

A needy whine echoed off the cavernous walls, wrenched from the depths of Nyx's chest as her hands gripped the pool's edge in a tight grasp, relishing his touch with every steady thrust and the attention he paid. Her mind was so lost in the haze of pleasure, she didn't notice when he rose from the ground, supporting her, before sliding a third finger into her in a movement so slick she could only moan in response.

"That's it, kleintje. Let me hear those pretty sounds you make for me," he crooned, every bit the wolfish brunette Nyx saw him as.

Through the desire clouding her mind and the tell-tale stirring of her orgasm, Nyx's silvered voice met Kotori's ears; filled with a wanton plea, "Please …"

The muscles of his abdomen rippled beneath his skin as he pulled his fingers from her, the loss of contact doing little to discourage her lustful gaze. It followed the shift of his muscle, capturing her attention as he gently grasped her waist and resettled on the pool's ledge. She saw his toned legs in a sinful show of flesh—a ravenous and adoration-filled gaze in his eyes. She watched with heavy-lidded eyes as he stood before her—all corded muscle and almond-toned skin, scars and ink—between her thighs. Nyx's eyes filled with sudden curiosity as her attention lingered on a piercing in his skin. "Is that …?"

His stare darted to the barbell in his cock, the black metal filling her mind with a dozen salacious scenarios. "A Prince Albert piercing? Yes," he said.

"Have you always had that?"

"I've had it for over … *four* centuries now."

Her eyebrows arched, equally turned on by the piercing and worried about this first in her sex life. "What—and nobody thought to warn me?"

A chuckle reverberated from Kotori's chest, head shaking in mirth. "Oh, kleintje. I'll take *good* care of you … with or without the piercing."

His umber gaze snared her in their dark depths, holding her captive as he wrapped his hand around his cock and stroked himself, teasingly dragging his tip across her folds while one of his hands grasped her hip. Drawing the head of his cock in maddening circles over her clit, her eyelashes fluttered as he pressed against her entrance.

"What do you want, my *Godin?* Tell me," he murmured.

"I want *you,* strijder," she said, sinful wants ravaging her mind. An easy confession uttered before she pushed herself onto her elbows and connected their lips, kissing him as one of her hands skittered over the corded muscles of his arm and tangled in his dark hair.

His voice lowered several, heady octaves, "Where?" he ground out through clenched teeth, the action sharpening his jawline.

Her eyebrows knitted together. "What?"

"*Where* do you want me, my *Godin*? *Where* do you want my cock?" he rasped, pressing a sensual kiss to her jaw before he nipped at the soft skin of her throat.

"Inside me," she said, gasping as the first few inches of him entered her.

His girth stretched her as her fingertips pressed into his bicep, black-metal piercing flicking her insides, creating waves of euphoria-like sensation. His lips met hers for a moment, kissing her, ravaging her before she pulled away and she looked to where they were connected, processing the inches he still needed to enter her—every *glorious* inch of him that sent her mind stumbling over itself.

Slowly, he eased more of his cock into her.

"Kotori," she murmured, her forehead resting against his, hand trailing up to settle on his shoulder. "You're so … *big.*"

He hummed in response, shifting to press firm, adoration-filled kisses to her throat. "You say that, *Godin*, but look how well you're taking me."

His words doused her in a lust-filled haze as he slowly drew back and plunged the rest of his turgid member into her. A breathy sound—part curse, part garbled moan—fell from her lips, her body seeming to sink into the ledge as he quickened his pace. The head of his cock and the Prince Albert ball brushed a spot inside that made her squirm.

He grasped her hips to cease her writhing. "Not so fast. You wanted me inside you. So now, you're going to ride me out like a good girl." His thrusts deepened as he peered down at her, watching her lips as she panted. "Are you my good girl?"

"Yes," she breathed, gasping as his cock pressed against her G-spot and the budding tide of her orgasm returned in full force as if he'd never stopped toying with her clit. "Fuck, Kotori. I'm so good."

He groaned deeply, head tipping to the ceiling as he thrust his hips to collide with her G-spot. His thumb pressed to her clit, mounting her orgasm as she clenched around his cock, water sloshing against the pool's edge as they moved. "That's it, ride it," he praised, eyes burning into hers.

He watched as his cock thrust steadily into her beneath the water, his teeth sinking into his bottom lip before he refocused on her naked body. His large, ring-clad hand cupped her breast, rolling one taut nipple between his fingers while his head dipped, mouth capturing the other. He circled it with his tongue, sucking hickeys into her skin.

"Kotori," she moaned, breathless and filled with desire.

He seemed to know what she wanted as he pulled away from her breasts, and the hand at her hip tightened. He rolled his hips again, drawing another moan from her as she clenched his girth.

"Yes, my sweet girl?" His lips brushed against hers, her breath on his face as he peered down at her with wolfish delight.

She finally managed to form a coherent sentence through her lust-filled haze, "I'm going to cum. Fuck, let me cum … please."

"With manners like that? Who am I to deny you? Cum for me," he commanded, hand grasping the nape of her neck.

Supporting her head, he drew her closer and his teeth elongated into fangs. He sank them into her throat as his cock brushed against her G-spot. A pleasure-riddled moan echoed across the room and down the darkened tunnelways, no doubt reaching Kade, Orion and Niko's ears as she came, and he swallowed languid mouthfuls of her blood. The euphoric high of his bite filled her bloodstream with a million aphrodisiacs she'd grown to adore experiencing. He pulled away in the next pulse of her heart, his head tipping back as he came with a guttural moan, fingertips sinking into her hips.

Nyx could only stare up at the man before her, awed by the dark-haired vampire, coated in her blood. She watched, hypnotized, as crimson droplets dripped from his throat to the chiselled plains of his stomach. *A god indeed,* she silently mused as he refocused on the room and nimbly hooked her legs around his waist.

She hummed contentedly as he grasped her chin, baring his marks before lathing his tongue over the weeping indents. She felt lighter, better, freer. She nestled her face in the crook of his throat, breathing in his comforting scent of freshly fallen rain and the woodsy fragrance of a forest wrapped around her. "I think your animalistic god brought me to you," she whispered contentedly.

"I believe it did, too … and I'll spend the rest of my life thanking him for bringing you to me," he said. "A strijder is *nothing* without his *Godin*."

LIV

Nyx

The alkaline breeze skittered across her skin, bringing a welcome chill from the warmth of the afternoon heat—the beginnings of summer were unfurling. As Nyx climbed the front steps of her family's home and approached the front door, the shadows of the wrap-around veranda were a welcome reprieve from the sun. She hesitated, her hand hovering before the stained-glass pane of the door. Orion, Kotori, Niko and Kade all lingered behind her and their presence was an endless comfort but still, her thoughts were on Phaelyn and Qadira. A chill that was not the weather scampered up her spine.

As if sensing this, Niko sidled up beside her. A long-fingered hand settled on her waist as she glanced up at him, his tank top revealing glimpses of his tattoo. His legs were covered in obsidian-black leather that made Nyx question *all* of their sanities—they all wore long pants and their signature boots like it was the middle of winter and not the warmest day of the month. A habit from the countless years they'd spent riding their stripped-down motorcycles, now parked haphazardly across the front yard.

She knocked.

And then her father was pulling the door open and looking at Niko, Kotori, Orion and Kade with untapped disdain. A moment of silence stretched between them as she surveyed his dress pants, shoes and the creased fabric of his T-shirt, familiar leather plaited bracelet around his wrist, his dark curls tousled and unruly, like her own. There was a softness to his eyes when he looked at Nyx before he ushered them inside with a curt nod. In the lounge, Azeil turned to face them, eyeing each in turn with his arms folded across his chest—every bit the disgruntled father in the face of her partners. Yet, she knew his distaste for them went further than any relationship.

"To what do I owe the pleasure?" Azeil drawled, his voice gravelled.

"We came to check up on you—" she started before Orion's orotund voice split the room and her brows furrowed with confusion.

"To retrieve the piece of Asher's journal that you stole," Orion said, his words final.

Nyx glanced at Orion, frowning before she rolled her eyes and turned back to her father. "Well, I *thought* we were here to ensure you were safe, since two of Leon's lackeys have been following you around … but, apparently that's not why we're here." She looked to Orion, annoyed.

Kotori—the constant calm of a brewing storm—leaned against the staircase. "We're still here for that reason, kleintje, but Orion's right. We're also here for the information Asher had. Orion learned last night Azeil removed it so that you can read it," he said.

An irked chuckle spilled from Azeil's lips, his head shaking in disappointment as he spoke, "Asher spent years learning the ins and outs of vampirism, compiling it into the leatherbound book you have. *But* the information Orion wants … I removed from the book several years ago upon Asher's request since no vampire discovered the loophole he found."

"Why? What is it?" she said, eyeing her father as her interaction with Leon whispered through her mind.

"The part of his research he had me remove explained how a pack bond can be broken or …" Azeil trailed off, his lips curled as his gaze locked on Orion, "I'm assuming the second half is the part you're after?"

"It is," Orion confirmed while Nyx glanced between the two men.

Azeil looked at Nyx levelly. "Orion wants the piece of Asher's research that explains *how* you can kill a sire or head vampire and since he *isn't* of Asher's bloodline, he can't see or handle it."

"Wouldn't you just … stake Leon?" she asked, her silvered voice uncertain.

Kade's mirthful chuckle sounded as he lounged in one of the chairs, boots propped atop the coffee table. "That would work for any *other* vampire but once a vampire sires someone, they move up in the vampiric hierarchy. It's extremely hard to kill a sire because of their connections to a pack member or members," he explained, carefully.

"So … he's *stronger* than us? Than you?" she asked.

"Unfortunately," Kade said.

"So," Nyx looked to her father, knowing he'd answer whatever questions she had. "Because I'm from Asher's bloodline, I *can* read and … touch his research?"

"Exactly. You're the *only* vampire that can see and touch it *without* being mortal," Azeil said, a proud and yet satisfied glint to his eyes.

"I guess a tainted bloodline does come with its perks," Nyx said, a bemused smirk playing across her lips.

"Let's not forget about Leon and his vampiric upper hand as a sire before you get too excited," Orion drawled, his orotund voice cutting across the room.

"We don't stand a chance without Asher's research," Niko said, a grim set to his jaw.

A drawn-out sigh escaped Nyx's mouth, her hand raising to pinch the bridge of her nose. The memory of Leon's hand fist-deep in her chest sent bitter realisation through her and she half-heartedly prayed for patience. "*Wonderful* … just *wonderful*."

"Communication seems pretty good regarding this plan, I see," Azeil said, ignoring the way Orion, Kotori, Niko and Kade's eyes narrowed at his taunting tone.

Nyx dropped her hand from her face in favour of tossing a tight-lipped smile at her father. "It's a work in progress."

"Nothing wrong with our comms," Niko stated confidently from beside Kotori.

"Whatever you say, knock off *Paul*, but your ass is sleeping *alone*," Nyx said, irritation flaring bright.

Niko's eyes widened, broad features twisting into a mildly horrified expression as his head whipped towards Kade. "*Kade*!" he exclaimed.

Azeil only looked at Nyx, rolling his shoulders before his stare settled on Orion. "You'll need to cut the shit and *communicate* with your pack—*every* member—before you even think about facing Leon. Because if your stupidity or male pride risks my daughter's life … I'll kill you *before* Leon has the chance." His gaze strayed to Niko, Kotori and Kade to confirm and then he turned back to Orion. "Got it?"

"Does it count if she meets up with Leon *behind* our backs and almost has her heart ripped out?" Orion said, brows furrowing with feigned puzzlement.

"*What*?" Azeil breathed lowly, eyes widening as he glanced between Orion and Nyx.

"It's a *long* story," Orion mused, offering Azeil a mocking grimace.

"You're dead*er*," Azeil said, starting toward Orion whose face was twisted with a pleased grin.

"*Orion. Dad*," Nyx warned, stepping toward him as the muscle along the underside of Orion's jaw twitched. "Cut it out."

Orion responded with a sickly-sweet smile, "My death is noted."

"Is it? Because if she's hurt by association with you, you're *all* dead men. *Do you understand?*" Azeil pressed, ignoring Nyx's sigh of disappointment as Orion's gaze narrowed and the blond stepped toward her father.

"You're trying my patience, *Azeil*," Orion said, his honeyed voice laced with a finality Nyx knew was law.

"You're a monster," Azeil spat, features marred by his distaste.

Orion shrugged as he sobered—his companions satisfied to watch the scene play out while Nyx held her breath. Orion wound an arm around her waist, pulling her to him. "Where is it?" he said coldly.

Azeil's eyes lingered on Nyx for a moment before he met Orion's stare. "It's been with you this whole time," he murmured.

"*Where*, Azeil?"

"The cave … hidden among the books," Azeil said. Her father's stare met hers and stuck, brimming with a look she couldn't comprehend. "It's a family favourite."

All eyes were on her, searching her for the clues she didn't know she had. Confused, she dropped her stare to the wooden floorboards as she scrambled to make sense of her father's words. *What the hell did that mean?*

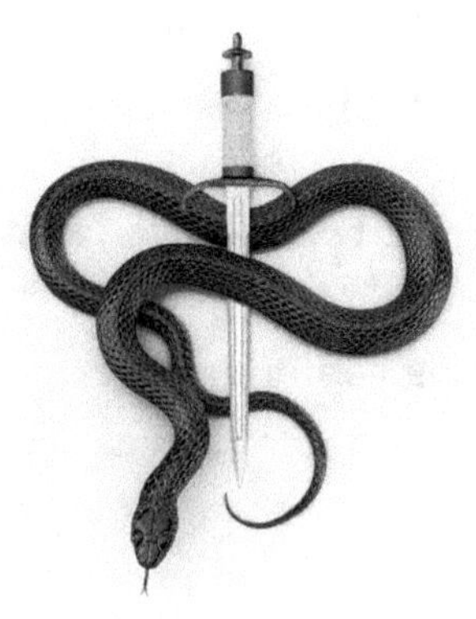

LV

Nyx

Books scattered the stone floor of the living space within the cave, the neat stacks beside the couches knocked over while others lay face-down on empty chairs. The afternoon light illuminated the room and Orion's search for Asher's research was at the forefront of *everyone's* mind since their arrival back at Elveszett Bluff.

Nyx grimaced at the rough treatment of the books, lingering beside the black-marble Cerberus statue, her gaze flitting to Kotori. Silent agony wrestled in his dark eyes as he watched Orion uproot his vast collection in a desperate and dishevelled tide. She tried not to focus on the books that had fallen open, their pages creased and covered in sand—the minuscule grains ever-present no matter how often she saw Kade sweep the floor. She winced at the sound the hardbacks made as their spines collided with the ground, the harsh thumps echoing down the tunnelways when Kotori glanced at her and gestured to Orion with raised brows. As if she could convince Orion to cease his relentless search in favour of their sanity … or hers and Kotori's.

Nyx turned to Niko and Kade where they lounged on one of the couches, seemingly content to watch the chaos unfold. She watched, dumbfounded as the pair passed a joint back and forth while Ares' head rested upon Niko's lap. Her Malamute was happy, basking in the attention. Orion's gloves had been discarded upon his black metal chair, exasperated sighs sounding as he flicked through the pages of a book before tossing it carelessly over his shoulder. "Orion!" she called as her gaze surveyed the dishevelled space. "Don't you think you're being a little … *excessive?*"

A bitter laugh answered her. "*Excessive?*" he repeated, rolling the word over his tongue. "That information is *our* freedom. It's our ticket out of Leon's grasp." He stalked toward her, irises aflame with a century-old resentment. "Don't you want that?"

She held his stare, thinking of Leon and the power he held. Her voice carried, silvered and tinged with steely determination, "I want our freedom as much as you do—as much as we *all* do—but there has to be a better way to find what Azeil hid."

Orion knocked his fist on his head. "Not unless you can get in here, little dove. We tried that, remember?"

"Azeil mentioned something about it being a family favourite but what does that mean, kleintje?" Kotori said.

"I don't know ..." she trailed off as her brows knitted and her gaze drifted across the room, lingering on the books strewn over the floor and furniture. *It's a family favourite*, she silently mused, recalling her father's words. Silence descended throughout the cave as she mulled. A family favourite. Nyx wondered how Azeil had hidden Asher's journal in the cavernous home without Orion, Kotori, Niko or Kade noticing. Or *when* he'd hidden it. Had it been before she'd arrived in Celacali? Or had Azeil hidden it on the day her loved ones had come to 'rescue' her? She appraised the books from Kotori's collection, turning in a slow circle as the weight of stares pressed upon her shoulders.

Her gaze surveyed each book for a long moment, waiting for something to capture her interest or jog her memory before her eyes snared on a glint of golden writing, *The Wizard of Oz* etched across the spine and front cover in an elegant, looping font. She crossed the room and picked the pearl-white hardback up off the floor, brushing the sand off the limited-edition cover.

"I don't think *The Wizard of Oz* is going to help us, chica," Niko said, a playful jest to his husky voice as he snuffed the joint in the ashtray beside the couch.

"Stranger things have happened, Nik ..." she murmured, fingertips skittering over the gold-embellished cover. Flashes of her childhood darted before her eyes as she recalled the nights her father, mother, Asher and Xander had spent with her, reading her the story until she fell asleep. The land of Oz had become a personal favourite in Nyx's life and in the years she'd grown up in Malor. She remembered hearing that story almost every night. Her lips quirked with the memories of Toto and Dorothy, their adventures through the fictional world of Oz as they travelled to the Emerald City. She lifted her gaze from the book to each of the men who watched her with open curiosity.

"Nyx?" Kade called, a slash of silent prompting in his eyes.

"Growing up, this used to be my favourite book," she said. She laughed as she continued, "I used to get *everyone* to read it to me before bed. It was ... it *became* a family favourite because of the memories we associated with it. Asher used to read it to me whenever he was in town, even if it was every night. Even after Dad had told him to lay off before I started reciting it," she smiled sadly at the memory. "It was our *family favourite.*" She opened the book, her gaze roving over Asher's familiar handwriting and the journal hidden beneath the illusionist cover like something from a movie. Seeing it now rolled back the years, taking her to a childhood place. At first, she marvelled at the rows of writing and small sketches, the scent of blood, silver and ink filling her senses. Her grey-flecked irises darted to Orion, holding the book open with her thumb wedged between its pages as she extended a piece of Asher to him. Willing her outstretched hands to save herself and them because she *wanted* to. "You'll find this edition to be … insightful but you'll only see its cover and Asher's signature. Not being from his bloodline and all," she said, watching Orion's frown morph into a grin as he thumbed the page with Asher's signature, dark ink on cream paper.

"Can you read it? Like Azeil said," Kotori said, drawing her gaze from Orion.

"I can," she confirmed, recalling the intricate sketches and information she'd glimpsed.

A soft look filled Kotori's eyes as his reassurance-tinged voice brushed aside her worries. "You're something else."

Dipping her head, Nyx refocused on Orion and the journal in his grasp as she levelled him with a firm look. "I'll share what Asher learned and how we can be free of Leon *but* as soon as we learn what we need … that book will cease to exist," she said.

"You'll destroy it?" Kade said, his face wreathed with shock.

"Some things are best left a mystery," she said, turning back to Orion.

He appeared to survey her for a long moment before his head dipped, in agreement.

"Asher was a clever mortal and if you wish to destroy his journal after we're free, so be it," Orion said, snapping the book shut, and holding it up with a grin. "For now, it seems the land of Oz *is* our ticket to freedom."

"Did Leon bind you all?" Nyx asked, the thought trickling across her mind. "I mean, every single related thought?"

"Well, no. He couldn't bind everything," Kotori said. "He just made certain associations seem uninteresting. You had to work at it." He dipped his head. "I have a memory of something he said in my second year of vampirism that didn't match the picture he'd painted," Kotori said. "It was a simple offhand comment about a sire's weakness if there was a *tainted* link in their bloodline." His gaze darted across his vast collection.

"So, that's why you started collecting vampiric books?" Nyx breathed, finally starting to understand why he had so many books on the one subject.

"Exactly, and ever since, he's been very careful about what he says," Kotori said, gesturing to his companions with a sweep of his hand, "We had our suspicions, but …"

Nyx thought hurriedly about how they'd tried to navigate the labyrinth of Orion's mind … bound in Leon's commands. There was no way anyone could do that alone. There was no way around it … *unless* the information had been unknown to all vampires and a mortal had discovered it—had confined it within a silver book coated in his blood so no vampire could see or handle it *unless* they were from his bloodline.

"We couldn't really focus for too long," Niko began, looking to Orion as if waiting for him to fill the gap.

"Because of the commands," Nyx finished, understanding. "Every time you tried, you'd forget, because that's what he wanted. So he was always safe, would always *be* safe, as long as you don't remember."

Orion's gaze was filled with a warning of the truth he'd been waiting to share. "Leon's control is all-consuming and yet, Asher found a way around a sire command and recorded it in his journal. Asher discovered a vampiric lore he shouldn't and by writing his book, he ensured *you*, a vampire from his bloodline, could possess it."

"Asher knew all along," she breathed, wonder in her tone. "But why?"

"Because Leon once commanded us to turn Azeil, back when he'd wanted another son, and Asher would've done *anything* for Azeil," Niko said, reminding Nyx of a conversation they'd had in Illusion's carpark months ago. "Hell, he almost killed me."

"If it wasn't for Azeil's will to stay mortal, he would've been as vampiric as you and me," Orion said, his glacier gaze filled with a thousand memories.

"And Asher would have lost him … I would've lost him." Nyx said.

"Blood is the essence of all life," Kade said, his irises bright. "Whether you give it or you take it away."

Orion's orotund voice carried across the space, "And in Leon's world where bloodlines are prestigious and *pure,* maybe you could give a gift that takes it all."

LVI

Kade

As the sun sank below the Avonsano Ocean, shadows fought to bathe the cavernous living space in darkness and twilight dappled the stone floor alongside the hidden light fixtures brightening the stone's crevices, successfully chasing away the night's darkness.. Kade's lips twitched, amused by the neatness of the room after the disarray of Orion's search for Asher's journal and the cleanup Nyx had ensured Orion carried out. All the books had been returned to Kotori's shelf while the stacks beside the couches had been resituated under her watchful eye, hours earlier.

Kade admired the woman he'd grown to love, that they all did. He knew that Orion, who hid behind his iron-clad control had, for Nyx, given his control to her *willingly*. This was something Kade knew he shared with his brothers as his gaze strayed to where they sat. Dark adoration blossomed in his chest. They were content in their paths of ruination and bloodshed if it made Nyx happy.

If it made their *queen* happy.

Nyx's head rested on Kotori's shoulder, her legs draped over Niko's thighs as his fingertips traced circles across her legs and Kotori toyed with the ends of her hair. Happy as cats. She was oblivious to their gazes as she read her uncle's journal—with gloves on—a notepad by her side for whenever something to free themselves from Leon arose. From his standpoint across the room, the pages looked worn and yellowed but every other page was glossy and … blank. These pages had to be handled with kid gloves—literally. Although Nyx's blood relation to her uncle meant she could read it, she'd had enough silver poisoning to last a fourth lifetime and so, was wearing the gloves. She'd learned this the hard way. No gloves, after prolonged reading, would send her pink fingertips into blackened beef. Even if she could read its contents and heal her wounds, it was painful and frustrating and … she was soon going to be put off barbecued ribs for life.

Kade watched her, accepting the rightness of Nyx's place with them as he looked to Orion and found the blond's stare locked on Nyx. *He can't shake the knowledge about Nyx's blood and the hunch he has,* Kade thought, recalling the conversation he'd shared with his brothers without Nyx's knowledge. *He believes it'll free us from the sire line because she wasn't turned by Leon. That she is of Asher's bloodline. Because she is the* tainted *link.*

He looked at Orion and his mind churned. Their souls were marked as surely as their bodies from the bite marks they'd left upon each other and the bond they'd forged—eternal as the night sky. Vampirism was a constant selection of *choices*—either subconscious or not. In their world, something as eternal as a bond couldn't be decided by a first glimpse, nor could it be a thing someone built their life around. At least, not to Kade or the majority of their species, who believed that something as eternal deserved the profound respect of both partners and their *choice* to bind themselves to each other in such a way. So, for as long as Kade could recall, vampires made *blood-bonds.*

A blood-bond was an eternal oath, fortified by an exchange of blood and sex that promised protection and loyalty, and was rarely used as a declaration of love. The pale, silvery-white scarring the process left behind in the shape of a vampire's teeth was a symbol of an unspoken vampiric law—if you broke it, you forfeited your life. Kade knew this was rare due to the severe repercussions—being outcast—just as he knew vampires had turned on pack members who'd severed another's bond. It was a vampiric crime punishable by death.

From the lore Kotori had spent decades poring over and which Asher's journal had confirmed— their blood-bond tied them to each other before Leon. Although his blood ran in their veins and tied them individually to him, their sire, they were still bonded to each other. But … what if they could form a new blood-bond with someone outside Leon's sired family? Someone who had tainted his pure bloodline? A *tainted* blood-bond could overpower a sire bond, rendering its control weak and susceptible to *severing.* This was what Orion, what *all of them* couldn't stop thinking about, itching to confirm the truth *and* sever their ties to Leon—from his control—forever. Is this what it was? Could this be the answer?

Nyx's blood could break the sire bond.

Kade's gaze ghosted Niko's neck, Kotori's shoulders, and Orion's forearms as flashes of their past darted before his eyes, lingering on each of the places where he knew a mark resided from each of them, their flesh was marked by each other—Orion's on his left wrist, Niko's in the junction of his neck and Kotori's upon his right shoulder. They kept the marks shrouded by a simple manipulation of mortal perception. There were never questions. His focus remained on Orion as his thoughts spiked. *Would she want that?* he wondered, looking to Nyx as he plucked anxiously at his jeans. The thought of her joining them—*vowing* to be with them made his chest swell. *Would she want to be a permanent fixture in their pack? Would she want to be ... theirs? Would she join us and sever our bond to Leon?* He didn't know. Were the two choices the same?

So, careful to exclude Nyx from the link of communication between himself and his companions, he opened his bond with his brothers.

"*What do we think of making Nyx a* permanent *member of the pack? Regardless of whether her blood is the key to our freedom,"* he said.

Niko's head whipped toward him, the cyanic blue of his irises alight with profound longing. "*Say the word, Kade. Say the word."*

"She's been a part of this pack the moment you brought her here ... at least, to me she has been," Kotori said, his dark stare trained upon Nyx as he peered down at her like she was his entire world—all the while, she remained oblivious to their silent conversation.

Nodding in acknowledgement, Kade turned to Orion, who met his stare from across the room, reclining into his black-metal throne with regal ease. "*Orion?*" Kade prompted.

"*And if she doesn't want to?"* Orion questioned, his orotund voice frigid and calm. "*What then? Will you be content to stay under Leon's control? To risk him taking her from us because he can."*

"He won't *take her from us. We won't let him,"* Kotori said.

"If he still controls us? How will you stop him?" Orion drawled bitterly.

"What makes you think she won't *agree? She* wants *him dead,"* Niko said.

"What makes you *think she will agree?*" Orion countered. *"She might want him dead but she fought the transition for* months.*"*

Niko's features drained of emotion, darkness shrouding his eyes as his husky voice carried through the bond, *"She* loves *us.*"

"Mortal love isn't the same as immortal. Her perception of forever isn't the same as ours, not when she hasn't grasped the scope of her immortality. Are you prepared to let her go if she doesn't want this?" Orion said.

"Ask her," Kotori said, disrupting further response.

LVII

Nyx

Nyx lifted her stare from Asher's journal, a dark eyebrow arching when she realised Orion, Kotori, Niko and Kade's eyes were trained upon her. She waited as confusion nestled in her chest, holding each of their gazes while her mind turned with a thousand thoughts. Slowly, she closed the journal, removing her legs from Niko's lap and folding her hands in her lap. A beat of silence passed and Nyx's intrigue and confusion made her restless. "What's … the matter?" she said, her silvered voice carried across the room.

Kade shifted, his chin propped on his steepled fingers, fuscous gaze swirling with longing. "What would you say about becoming a permanent fixture in our pack?"

Her brows knitted, eyeing them all before returning her focus to Kade. "Aren't I already *permanent*? Or does immortality mean something else to you?"

"That's not what Kade means, kleintje," Kotori said from where he sat beside her.

"Then what *does* he mean?" she said, glancing at Niko and then Kade.

Niko's husky voice was laced with a restrained edge, "He's asking if you'll make a blood-bond with us."

"What's a … *blood-bond?*"

"It's a vampiric oath of eternal loyalty and protection, fortified by an exchange of blood; you drink ours, we drink yours," Orion drawled, picking up the half-explanations to provide her with coherent information.

"Like … an extreme pinkie promise?" she murmured, eyeing him shrewdly.

Orion stared at her for a long moment, blinking. "In the sense of a promise, yes. But it's *more*. It's a sacred law among vampires that isn't broken."

Nyx's eyebrows arched, curiosity piqued as he continued, "If you break a blood-bond … you forfeit your life," he said, the ominous words sending a sinful shiver down her spine.

"*And* we believe it's our first step toward freedom," Kotori said, throwing Orion a pointed look.

"How will it help free you—us from Leon?" she said, brow creased.

Kade coughed. "I'm going out on a hunch that Asher's journal confirms that a sire's weakness is matched by a tainted bloodline... whether you've tied all the pieces together yet or not, your blood isn't from *Leon's* bloodline, Nyx. You're from *Orion's* and *Asher's* bloodline, which means, *if* Asher's research is true—"

"*You're* the tainted link," Orion said, watching her closely. "And *if* that information is correct, your blood *is* our freedom. We've all ingested it once before but, with a blood-bond, it's in our veins *forever.*"

"So, what'd you say, chica?" Niko crooned. "Will you make a deal with the Devil? Will you *taint* our souls?"

"What do I get from this aside from Leon's demise and freedom?" Nyx said.

Her stare locked with Niko's as he spoke, "Every shard of our souls," he murmured, his lips brushing hers with every word, "with our eternal devotion to you … and you alone. All you have to do is say yes, and we are yours. *Forever.*"

A weighted silence descended as they awaited her response, as if they held their breaths. *Did she want to be tied to them for eternity more than she already was*? Was she prepared to promise so much—*all*—of herself to them? Was there any other answer to the question but yes? She knew she was prepared to bind herself to them for eternity, knew she was prepared to spend the rest of her life by their sides. Nyx knew she'd been ready for months, since the moment she'd stepped forward to face Leon and the risk of losing her life. She'd been ready to die for them, and she almost had. So, was their question one for her eternal loyalty, protection and freedom? Or, was it a question of how deeply she loved them? Of whether she was ready to hand them the last tether to her mortality.This time, all the answers were easy.

Her voice carried the weight of her certainty—levelled and final—just as her grey-flecked irises reflected her decision, "Consider my soul sold, and yours tainted."

Niko's grin grew. A searing kiss pressed to her lips before he pulled away and peered down at her. "Do you mean that?"

"Yes," she said, emphasising the word as she draped an arm over his broad shoulder, kissing him with every ounce of certainty she possessed.

A low sound reverberated from his chest as he pulled away and his gaze roved over her, fingers toying with her shirt before he dragged the material up and over her head, tossing it aside. His lips met hers in the next moment, hands grasping her waist as she parted her lips and his tongue dove into her mouth, dragging salaciously against hers.

Fingertips trailed across her bared spine before Niko moved with preternatural swiftness and her back pressed into the soft cushions of the couch. A gasp tumbled from her kiss-bruised lips as she peered up at him and his own hovered millimetres away from hers. He glanced to Kade beside his right shoulder, easily making room for his shirtless companion as Kade leaned toward her, grasping her chin between his fingers and connecting their lips with blistering desire. Nyx registered the fragrance of freshly fallen rain and the earthy tones of a forest, knowing the brunette whose scent twinned around her senses was nearby as Niko discarded his shirt and unbuckled his belt while his hips pinned her in place and Kade greedily took everything she offered him.

His teeth nipped at her bottom lip as he pulled away and his signature Cheshire-Cat grin uplifted his lips, her gaze locked on his while her hand clutched the waistband of his jeans, anchoring herself to him through the tide of her desire. Her insides churned with a need she tried to tamp down by pressing her thighs together, impossible with Niko between her parted legs.

A knowing grin lightened his broad features, his calloused palm smoothing over her jean-clad thigh until his fingertips ghosted her fly. "Aw, chica. You're squirming already and we haven't even started yet," he said.

The deep timbre of Kotori's chuckle rumbled across the room like thunder, ominous and yet comforting all in one before the chilled press of his rings seeped into her skin. His large hand wrapped around her throat, tipping her head until it rested on the backing of the couch. "Nik's barely even touched you and you're already so … *needy* for us. Do you want us that much, my Godin?" he crooned.

His umber gaze was almost black, lips tugged into a wolfish grin and Nyx's heart leaped at the sight, scrambling for something to say in response but coming up blank. Niko nimbly unfastened her jeans and Kade's hand sank into the cushion beside her head, leaning toward her to mark her throat with his teeth.

"I want you to stop teasing me and get on with it," Nyx said, goading him.

A ragged breath passed between her teeth—part gasp, part restrained hiss—as Kotori's grasp on her throat tightened, and Niko pressed a firm circle over her clothed clit, seamlessly in sync with Kade's ministrations upon her throat. The synchronised movements wrenched her arousal to new heights as Niko dragged her pants off her, sparing Kade a glance. The tattooed blond shifted out of his way as his fingers toyed with the strap of her bra and he eyed Kotori with a mischievous grin, before discarding it with the same energy as he'd discarded her shirt.

"Careful, angel," Kade warned, his voice filled with devilry, daring her to continue provoking Kotori. "If you want something, use that pretty voice of yours."

"And if I don't?" she half-whispered.

Kade inched closer, trailing a salacious path from her throat, down her collarbone to the swell of her breasts. Raising his head so his breath warmed her neck, his fingers dragged the strap of her bra down her shoulder. "Then moan for us."

Kotori's lips brushed hers—a purposeful taunt imbued in his actions; close enough for their lips to connect but far enough away that it drove her mad. Niko's hands parted her legs beneath his lust-filled gaze before he sank to his knees between them. Kotori closed the space between their lips in the next moment before she could respond to Kade, kissing her with an all-consuming passion and possessive edge—*claiming* her with Niko, Kade and Orion as his witnesses. When the tattooed blond's mouth descended on her breast in perfect coordination with Niko, whose face was buried in her folds, she acquiesced.

Kotori pulled away, trapping her wrists above her head and she saw the mischief shrouding Kade's eyes. "Kade—" she started, shifting against Kotori's hold.

The *smack* of leather on metal drew her attention to Orion and his discarded glove. His glacier irises sparked with a *starved* longing as he peeled his other glove off with his teeth, stalking to her with a malignant grace that sent a heady bolt of pleasure through her. His gaze dragged over her bared body as if he wished to engrain the sight of her on his retina. Then Niko spread her legs further, dragging a calloused fingertip over her clit in a way that seized all distraction.

For a moment, Nyx lost sight of the room around her, her eyelashes fluttering closed as she basked in the sensation of Niko's fingers toying with her clit and the warmth of his breath as he licked a tantalising stripe up her cunt. She bit her lip, pushing her head back into the couch cushion as she was eaten alive by kisses. Niko's strokes of his tongue against her labia filled her with a smouldering tide of arousal. As if to compete with his lover, Kade's lips found her breast, teeth grazing her nipple before his tongue lathed over the slight burn and she shifted against Kotori's grasp—needing more or wanting to escape the multitude of sensations, she didn't know.

Their hands kept Nyx firmly in place so she was forced to take all the pleasure they bestowed upon her until she felt she could take no more. She barely registered the couch dip beside her until she forced her eyes open, her gaze finding Orion's.

He lounged beside her, his lips twisted with a smug smirk. "Look at you, little dove. All spread out for us. At our *utter* mercy," his dark chuckle caressed her cheek as he leaned toward. "You're so fucking *stunning*."

"Fuck," she rasped as Niko's teeth grazed her clit and Kade alternated to her opposite breast.

Niko's husky voice was tinged with lust as he lifted his head and slid a finger inside her, arresting her breath with his deepening thrusts. "She's our girl, all right," he drawled, curling the tips of his fingers. "She's so fucking *wet*. She's clenching around my fingers even when she's trying to escape by squirming."

Kade trailed his thumb across her lips. "Squirm all you want, angel … you're not going anywhere," he taunted.

Orion's fingers grasped her chin, turning her head toward him as she scrambled to focus on the serpentine blond through the swells of pleasure and the multitude of touch.

"Kade's right, *little regina.* You're not going anywhere until we're satisfied by your pleasure, and you share a blood-bond with us," Orion vowed.

"Ours in every way," Niko finished as she pulled against Kotori's hold, a wavering moan echoing across the cavernous room.

Nyx's mind simply whirled. She was lost in her men, Niko's steady thrusts quickening as her orgasm drew to a precipice and her fingertips pressed into Kotori's hand. A fine sheen of sweat covered her skin as she squirmed against their holds, aware of Orion and Kade's gazes. Every inch of her body was being consumed, all at once. Orion pressed kisses to her jawline and the corner of her mouth, purposefully moving away whenever she tried to connect their lips like he was waiting for something. Whatever he was waiting for, he seemed content to tease her as the others dragged her to orgasm with every entry and suck.

It took everything in her *not* to beg for more, even if she suspected that's what they wanted. "*Please,*" Nyx wailed, succumbing to everything—more pleasure, more of them, more of everything they offered her.

Orion's teeth grazed the shell of her ear, sending an unorthodox shiver down her spine. "Tell us what you want and it's yours."

"More," she rasped, brows furrowing as she heard herself. "I … want more."

Orion's lips twitched. "More … *what,* little dove? Do you want Niko to make you cum on his fingers?"

Nyx's eyes screwed shut at the imagery Orion's words dragged forward, a soft moan escaping her before she licked her lips and tried to right her lust-riddled mind enough to respond. Niko added a third finger, thumbing her clit with a guitar-string calloused thumb and sending her intentions all to delicious hell. "*Shit,* Niko … *please,*" she begged.

Niko's lips pressed an adoring kiss to her thigh as she opened her eyes and peered down at him. "What do you want, chica? Tell me," he said.

She tugged uselessly at Kotori's grasp trapping her wrists as Niko continued to thrust his fingers, never faltering as she clenched around them and her orgasm tiptoed on the cusp. As if sensing her unwillingness to utter her wants, Kade and Niko's ministrations ceased, wrenching a groan of annoyance from her as her eyes narrowed in displeasure, her orgasm inching backward, clit throbbing with desire.

"You don't get to cum until you *use your words*, and that's as simple as it is," he said.

"But—" Nyx spluttered, brow creased with confusion.

"We know you can beg, angel, but we want you to *tell* us what you want. We *always* want you to tell us what you want," Kade said before he slipped from her side and Orion's hand replaced Kotori's, twining his fingers with hers as he kept her pinned in place between them.

The clinking of a belt buckle, followed by the sound of a zipper, captured Nyx's interest when Kotori pulled away, his thumb tracing her lips. Her stare fell on Kade, who now knelt before Kotori, his tattooed fingers nimbly unfastening the brunette's pants. A bolt of lust bloomed in her at the sight, Kade's gaze darting to hers before he tossed her a cheeky wink and Kotori half-helped him remove his pants. Her mouth went as dry as the desert when Kade palmed Kotori through his boxers, her tongue darting out to wet her bottom lip as she tried—and failed—to press her thighs together. Tried to soothe the ache of her clit, her mind overcome by her desire.

"What's got you squirming, little dove?" Orion drawled, knowingly. "They're a sight, aren't they?"

"I thought …" she trailed off, groaning as Niko's fingers brushed a spot inside her that stole her thoughts and he dipped his head, tongue dragging over her drenched slit.

A bemused chuckle of his mirth emitted from Orion, his thumb caressing her throat. "At some stage in our lifetimes, we've all been together."

Anything Nyx was going to say in response fled her mind the moment Kade's head dipped, and he took Kotori's cock into his mouth, his tattooed hand fisting whatever didn't fit as he stroked Kotori in sync with the bobbing of his head. She reminded herself to breathe as Niko's fingers curled inside her and his thumb pressed again into her clit, drawing a guttural moan from her. Ragged breath passed Kotori's lips and his thumb traced her lips, Orion's hand trailing from her throat to her breast where he toyed with her taut nipple. She knew it wouldn't take long for her orgasm to return, their combined ministrations and the sight of Kade on his knees for Kotori wrenched her closer as she clenched. "Fuck," she said, squirming against the tightness building in her abdomen. "*Please.*"

"Please what?" Orion said, his lips hovering over hers.

Her breath hitched at the sensation, gaze fixated on Kade and Kotori as Niko's pace quickened. Orion's displeased tut ghosted her ear, his hand leaving her breast to free her lip from her teeth. She shifted in their grasp as her pleasure crept closer. "Orion, please," she murmured, tearing her gaze to meet his glacier irises.

Orion quirked his brow, waiting with a smirk across his face.

"Let me cum," she finished, resisting the urge to roll her eyes at his smugness.

"See, was that really so hard?" he murmured as Niko's ministrations shifted with a new intent—to make her cum rather than tease her.

His chuckle vibrated into her clit and she turned her head to Kade, a blissed-out sigh leaving her lips at the sight of Kade sucking Kotori's cock. Kotori's grasp on her wrist tightened as he brought her arm closer to himself and Nyx's teeth suddenly ached, her incisors and canines elongating until they brushed her bottom lip.

"That's it, kleintje. Cum for us," Kotori said, his voice laced with a ravenous, almost starved edge as the veins in his arms jumped and he peered down at her.

Niko altered the angle of his fingers and she gasped, squirming against their grasps in the same moment Kotori's fangs elongated and his teeth sank into her wrist. Her mind short-circuited, lost in the collision of aphrodisiac and endorphin that flooded her senses, pushing her finally over the edge. Her orgasm washed over her as her lips parted for a silent scream, an instinctual urge to sink her fangs into Kotori's wrist dancing across her mind. And as if Orion knew, he brought Kotori's arm closer to her and the brunette released a low, dangerous sound.

Without wasting another breath, Nyx sank her fangs into Kotori's wrist and pulled languid mouthfuls of his woodsy-toned blood in her mouth, swallowing the refreshing ambrosia greedily. Kotori's deeply timbred groan ricocheted in her eardrums and he came. Niko's mouth left her cunt as he fingered her through her orgasm, and Kade continued to bob his head through Kotori's. The tell-tale brush of Niko's fangs against her thigh faintly registered as they pierced her skin, dousing her into a headier tide. She felt it as Niko swallowed several mouthfuls of her blood before he pulled away and lathed his tongue over the weeping wounds, an action Kotori and Nyx mirrored when they retracted their fangs a moment later, soft pants tumbling from her parted lips.

Niko lithely pushed himself up from the ground, stooping down to press a feverish kiss to Nyx's lips before he sauntered over to a couch on the other side of the room and dropped onto the soft cushions, wiping his arm across his face. Kade followed his blond counterpart after he rose and pressed a kiss to the underside of Kotori's jaw. Kotori wandered around the side of the couch to sit beside her. His be-ringed fingers grasped her chin, tenderly cradling her face as he kissed her, and a newfound connection cinched into place beside them from the completion of the blood-bond.

She quietly marvelled at the ethereal and all-consuming quality, stretching between them like the rolling planes of the world. She hadn't realised until the bond cinched into place, but she recognised this feeling. When Kade had been the first to bite her *with* her consent, *she had known* she was tied to him forever—to them all.

Orion's gaze locked on hers. A gaze immortal like the heady thrum before a band traipsed on stage, or the calm before a storm. She watched as he unfastened his belt and the button of his slacks, dragging the zipper of his fly down in a salacious tease.

"Keep your eyes on me, little dove," Orion crooned.

"Why?" she breathed, her mind addled by desire.

"Because I want you to know who fucks you until all you know is *my* name," he said, lips grazing hers. "My name is the only one that'll pass those pretty lips."

"Hmm," she murmured. "I think I'll be the judge of what passes my pretty lips." She watched, delighted as a slight flicker passed his normally jaded eyes. She took the moment of imbalance to rise up from her position, pushing herself into him, spinning him round, pushing him backwards. His gaze remained locked on hers as Nyx pressed him into the couch's backing, one hand fisting the material while her other hand slapped his away. "No, no touching. I'm using my words, Orion."

His grin was massive, almost slack as she began to kiss his skin. Starting high on his cheekbone, then his jawbone, then his collarbone. In-between, she'd almost touch his lips, letting him lean forward for a kiss that never came. When he tried to touch her, she'd move away, evading his hands or pressing them down. One by one, she opened the buttons on his shirt, exposing his chest, freeing him from the fabric. Lazily, slowly, she circled his nipple with her tongue, biting the flesh, scraping her fangs across the taut skin, teasing him. Now it was his breath that began to quicken, his eyes that lightened. With a self-satisfied smile, Nyx kissed his collarbone and went lower. She kissed his stomach, then his hip bone and his abdominal V, before she got to his final bone.

She waited, breathing hotly.

Orion moaned as she got closer, breathing on him. "Unhh, fuck."

"Use your words, Orion," Nyx smiled.

Before she could finish the movement, he was on her in a blur. Twisting up from the couch, he slammed into her, his arms like an octopus, all over her, pinning her. His mouth hot and wet and swearing about all the filthy things he was going to do to her. She raised her leg, hooking it into the back of his hip, first one, then the other, her mouth locking on his, so no one could speak. The kiss was hard and deep and frustrated, each of them trying to gain momentum over the other.

Nyx pulled her head back, her right hand slipping between Orion's legs as he shuddered. "I'm going to fuck *you*, Orion until you scream *my* name."

Then, before he could answer her, she lowered herself onto him, his opposing hand settling on her waist as he pressed further into her wet cunt, his hips raising slowly, almost pulling out before he plunged every inch of his cock into her. He muffled her throaty moan with his lips, tongue delving into the caverns of her mouth as if he wanted to consume every inch of her. His grasp on her waist tightened with his deep and self-assured pace.

As they began to pick up speed, his hips slapping against her inner thighs and her fingertips digging into his ivory skin, Kotori grabbed her left leg and spread her wider for Orion. The movement drew a muffled gasp from her. "Shit," she cursed, squirming between Orion and Kotori as her second orgasm for the night crept to the forefront, waiting to shower her in a wealth of pleasure. Her thighs twitched, fighting the urge to close against the pleasure he so easily drew from her, plunging it into her bloodstream as regally as he thrust his hips until his cock brushed a spot inside her. She felt her muscles clench around him.

"That's it. *Just like that*," Orion praised, a curse falling from his lips as her cunt squeezed his cock and he hissed. "Fuck, you're so … fucking perfect."

A sound—part moan, part whine—broke from her lips as her fingers bruised Orion's shoulder and Kotori smattered her throat with kisses. "Fuck, I'm close … so *fucking* close," she said.

"I know, little regina. I know," Orion assured, his lips colliding with hers as he kissed her with a passion that stole her breath. He grasped her hand on his shoulder and traced the crook of his throat with her fingers. "*This* is where you're going to bite me, okay?"

“Are you sure?” she asked, a sliver of uncertainty as she held his gaze.

His mouth pulled into a gentle smile, eyes alight with adoration—*love*—for her. “I am. You’re my *little regina*. You *are* my *little queen*.”

Nyx’s fangs elongated, grazing his throat. Orion’s hand left her waist and cradled the back of her head. Her eyes darted to his for a moment, long enough for her to gauge his expression before her fangs pierced his skin and a throaty groan reverberated through his chest, his taste of sandalwood and a crisp … minty flavour coating her tongue.

Orion waited, seeming to bask in the high of her bite before she retracted her fangs and lathed her tongue over the bite, sealing it as her stare collided with his. He brushed her curls away from his original mark and traced her skin with a reverent sort of longing before he ducked his head and his fangs sank into the pre-existing scar. His thrusts never faltered as Nyx’s orgasm washed over her in a blissful haze. Orion came with an animalistic sound, pulling away from her throat and dragging his tongue over the marks as he continued to plunge into her through both their orgasms until his pace slowed.

She looked at him, her eyelids weighted with fatigue and a stretching sensation in her chest. The weight of four blood-bonds interconnecting leeched her of whatever energy she possessed and she sighed, content. Time ceased to exist and, with her next inhale, the golden-yellow light of a dozen candles bathed the walls in a warm, comforting hue. She lay there, Kotori beside Niko—who pulled her into his chest—Orion, situating himself at her back while Kade settled happily between her legs, his head resting on her stomach. Nyx felt the weight of a world fall away. Physically, mentally, and spiritually; she was whole. She was home —with the monsters of Celacali—in their bloodshed, ruination, and darkness, with their eternal protection, loyalty and love.

They were *hers* as much as she was theirs.

LVIII

Qadira

Qadira drummed the car's armrests, silver-chrome nails filed to sharp points glinting in the shadowed light. Her crystalline gaze was fixed on a doorway along the side-alleyway of the front stores where she knew Nyx's beloved twins—Alexander and Tobias—resided, in the apartment above the comic bookstore.

She looked at her other half sitting next to her. Phaelyn's braided hair and forest-green, long-sleeved shirt, the leather knife holsters webbing over her chest. Her brunette sister always needed managing. Despite the decades of living together, Qadira was still impatient, still hadn't mastered the levelheadedness most older siblings seemed to possess. Instead, she'd always lashed out at Phaelyn and taken the control. Maybe it was her childhood and being raised in the noble house of Imfe, having her every want catered to. Maybe it was Leon's lavish proposal to her parents about tying his bloodline to hers.

A bitter scoff fell from her lips as she left the vehicle and crossed to the side-door of the twins' apartment, shoulders knotting with a decades-old anger and the memories of her *almost* marriage to Orion. *But he hadn't* wanted *me,* she thought, recalling the day Leon introduced them and Orion had stormed from the dining room of her family estate, eyes—like hers, now—blazing as if Leon's words sparked his fire-like fury. *Not like he* wants *Nyx.*

"You're acting on anger, Ira," Phaelyn said, rushing up behind her. "Leon doesn't like when we act on emotion."

"I don't care," Qadira said, eyeing her younger sister as she gripped the handle of the side door and twisted until a *crunch* filled her ears. "We're here for one reason, Phaelyn, and we've wasted enough time *waiting*."

"But—"

"Have you lost all will to think for yourself?" Qadira snapped, whirling on her sister as the weeks of watching Leon's hooks burrow into Phaelyn caught up.

"Leon doesn't want—"

"What do *you* want, Phae?" Qadira said, cutting her off as her gaze softened, imploring her sister to *think* for herself.

It was a quiet torment for Qadira as she watched Phaelyn struggle against Leon's commands, one weeping from her bone's marrow until every thought was filled with worry—*fear*—for Phaelyn and the will slipping from her sister's grasp like hands on a clockface, announcing the minutes someone had left to live. *How much more could she take before nothing remained? How much further would Leon test her?*

Qadira loved Leon like a father, that much she could accept, but she loved her sister and she hated what Leon was doing to Phaelyn, to her. She wished everything would go back to the day she'd first met Phaelyn and Leon had been nothing but a doting father, lavishing them with gifts and granting them their every wish. She wished now, that Leon would give up his pursuit of his family with his sons—that he'd settle for the one he had—with daughters.

It was so much simpler without them, she thought, scrutinising Phaelyn and the glassy, trapped look of her irises. *They just* had *to mess everything up.* "Phaelyn," she tried again, stepping toward her sister and threading their fingers together. "Find a will—*your* will and hold onto it. You can be Leon's daughter without a fight, without losing yourself. *Please.* Come back to me."

"I am with you," Phaelyn said despite the way her eyes seemed to stare *through* Qadira as if even the suggestion of fighting against Leon's commands rendered her thoughtless.

Something dragged down in Qadira's chest as Phaelyn's words echoed in her eardrums, a condemning sound she wished she could purge from her brain. *Was this is it?* she thought, eyes darting across Phaelyn's face in search of *something—someone*—she recognised. *Is this when I lose her? It couldn't be,* and yet, the longer she held Phaelyn's hand and looked for her sister, the clearer it became. She wasn't just going, she was already gone. It was almost impossible to breathe. "No," Qadira breathed as she released Phaelyn's hand and shook her head.

"We have orders," Phaelyn murmured, starting toward the door that led to the twins disconnectedly.

Fury wove through Qadira's bones as she slipped past Phaelyn's shoulder and shoved the door open, a short hallway greeting them. If she was going to lose, she was going to do it taking something Nyx cared about. *A sibling for a sibling.* "It's time to get the twins and leave," Qadira breathed, falling back onto familiar grounds—familiar orders.

"Time, time, time," Phaelyn said, sighing dramatically. "What's with you and the hands of the clock? We're immortal! We own time." Phaelyn laughed, but the sound was distracted and her gaze was splintered—two pieces at war with the other.

A primal thrum trickled into her bloodstream with every step Qadira took until the wooded door of the twins' front door stared back at her and Phaelyn bracketed her shoulder. The chatter of a movie could be heard dully, from inside. She wondered how quickly their hearts would beat when she kicked down their door and a fragment of her being longed to *see* the fear in their eyes. She could almost taste it as she ushered Phaelyn aside and adjusted her stance, the promise of decadent flavours coating her tongue looming large.

Fear was a powerful motivator but Qadira had learned, in the decades of her immortal existence, that it was a dopamine hit if she drank the blood of her prey while they struggled, pleaded, and screamed. Such terror permeated the bloodstream and gave it an ethereal quality, flavouring the blood like a hop aroma in beer. Cortisol and adrenaline spilled into their platelets—it was intoxicating and thrilling. As she drove her foot into the door and it swung open, she grinned a twisted grin that brightened her features and jolted the twins' heartrates. Folding her arms over her chest, Qadira settled her foot on the floor and angled her head, eyes darkly vapid as the twins scrambled from their seats.

Phaelyn laughed again, tossing her head as she stood in the doorway, the whisper of Leon's commands in her eyes, barring the exit. "Hello, boys," she crooned, the silver hilt of one of her knives glinting in the holster around her thigh.

Qadira waggled her fingers in a taunting wave, enjoying the look Alexander and Tobias shared. *Would they beg for their lives? Sisters, brothers, fathers*, Qadira thought morosely. Death comes for us all eventually. But for now, pain would be inescapable as they fought futilely for the other. Blood was, after all, thicker than water.

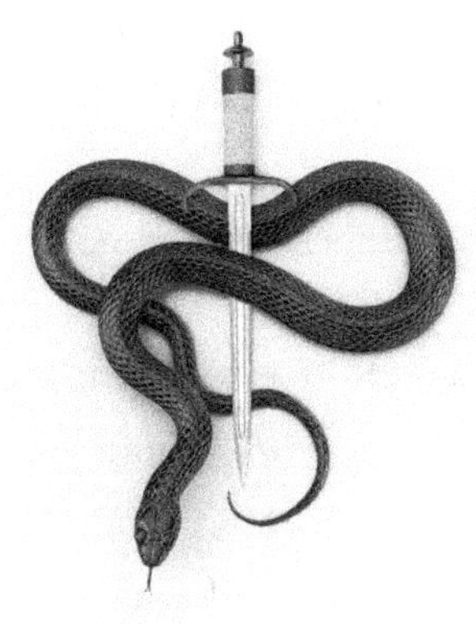

LIX

Nyx

A temporary sort of serenity had taken hold. A brief respite Nyx almost couldn't comprehend, so at odds with the situation, it was as if they were intoxicated. She lay on one of the couches, her legs draped over Niko's leather-clad thighs and her head rested in Kade's lap, her mind filled with a thousand thoughts. *Surely whatever god decided fate had forged hers wrong?* she thought, as she looked around her. *Fate couldn't be this kind, after everything ... could it?* She knew her answer as her gaze drifted to Orion in his black-metal throne, the notepad with all her notes from Asher's journal in his gloved hands a permanent reminder of why she knew fate wasn't kind. How could it be when it'd taken Asher from her? When she'd spent three months grieving over his death and the hole he'd left in her life. Or how could it be kind when she'd been forced to watch her father leave Celacali? Or that Leon existed? Every blessing came with a curse. There was no such thing as fate. It was an illusion of hopes.

Her eyes lingered on Kotori and the leather-decorated strand of his hair, the past he'd allowed her to know staring back at her. She felt a surge of rage at the things Leon had done to him—done to them all. The Levenloos man with a heart of pure gold, who put her needs before his own, protected her life with his, and killed for her happiness. He was *everything* to her: the calm and serenity of a storm, the paradox she craved, her strijder.

If Kotori was the calm to a storm, then Orion *was* the storm. The malignant blond with eyes like glaciers, who commanded a room with his presence, confidence engrained in his every atom, *royalty* in his blood. Where she'd been terrified of him and his blue eyes before, she now only felt a swell of protection, adoration and belonging. She felt at home with him, understood and seen, heard and valued. She felt *safe* in his dark and blood-stained presence—in all their presences—within the shadows of the night. And she realised that was all that mattered.

Nyx straightened as her gaze lingered on the notepad Orion held, fragments of what she'd read, and noted down, not making sense to her. "How *exactly* is our blood-bond going to help us get rid of Leon? And how is he any different from us," she cut Kade off as he opened his mouth to respond, "*Aside* from him being *the sire*?"

Orion's lips twitched. "Myths tend to get muddled and fragments get … lost. Your uncle spent months searching for the truths of vampirism and everything he learned," he gestured to the journal, "is in there."

"Everything I thought was important is on that notepad, but *what* is in there that you want?"

"The truth."

Nyx sighed, rolling her eyes at the vague nature of Orion's responses. "No shit."

Kotori chuckled, plucking her notepad from Orion's grasp before he turned to her with a wolfish grin and crossed the room, crouching in front of her. "We've been looking for this," he said, his thumb tapping against a note of hers that read like a badly curated poem.

Her gaze trailed over her notes, puzzled. "And? It's coded jumbo," she said.

"It's our freedom, chica," Niko drawled, tearing his gaze from the ceiling to peer down at her. "It's *how* we can get rid of Leon."

"*What was created from one can be* undone *by blood. Condemned by the bloodline they created, vanquishable by their bloodline. A blade of tainted blood to kill the sire of immortality,*" Kade recited as if he knew her notes by heart.

"A blade of tainted blood?" Nyx murmured, glancing between them. "Like …"

"If we *obtain* a blade of blood, we'll be able to kill him with it," Orion said, confirming her racing thoughts.

"Just like that?"

"A shot *through* the heart, little dove."

Her lips quirked. "And you're to blame."

Orion's eyebrows arched, a playful glint in his eyes. "Bon Jovi? Really?"

She opened her mouth to respond, the words dying on her tongue as the chiming tone of her phone echoed through the room. Dread curled in her chest, her hand moving slowly to retrieve the device from atop a pile of books. Silence descended as she opened the message thread, foolishly hoping it was Alexander or Tobias saying they'd found a lead tying to one of her notes. Niko, Kade, Kotori and Orion's stares seared her skin. Watching. Waiting.

A ragged breath slipped out from beneath her clenched teeth, her knuckles bone-white as the muscles along her shoulders and spine tensed, stare locked on the message across the screen:

Tick-tock.

Nyx read the words and could *hear* Qadira taunting her. Niko's chest pressed into her shoulder as she forced herself to open the photo attached, wincing when a scalding sense of familiarity rushed through her bloodstream at the warehouse in the picture.

Flashes of a blood-stained dagger and beetle-black eyes flashed before her eyes, *Kai's* terrified expression before she killed him and his desperate pleas rang in her ears. A memory she didn't hate but when her eyes studied the picture on the screen, she wished the similarity of Azeil's bound body in the centre of the room didn't send déjà vu punching through her gut. Her stare locked on Kotori's as she drew measured breaths into her lungs—willing herself to be calm, to think rationally, to be unaffected—and when she was satisfied with her composure, she lifted her gaze to Orion.

"The decision is yours, little dove. Just say the word," he said with heavy promise.

Nyx's eyes darkened with malice. "So … if I wanted them dead?"

Orion's lips curled into a dangerous grin, eyes alight with bloodlust. "Then tonight will be the last time their hearts beat."

"Just like that?" she said, her stare darting to Niko, Kade and Kotori in search of confirmation—each dipping their heads in silent agreement, baleful grins twisting Kade and Niko's features while a ravenous gleam obscured Kotori's iris.

Orion approached her, his voice lowered. "I've never knelt for *anyone* in my life. Not once. But I'd kneel for you if you asked me to."

Nyx's gaze darted to each of them in turn. "Why? Why would you do this for me?"

"Obsession," Kade mused, chuckling lowly at his own words.

"Lust," Niko murmured, pressing a kiss to the crook of her throat.

"Longing," Kotori said, his dark eyes filled with a wolfish glint.

"*Revenge*," Orion drawled, gesturing off-handily to his companions. "We all started on one path, with one intention before you came to Celacali … it's funny how things—*emotions*—change, isn't it?"

"You all wanted me dead," she stated in a 'duh' tone.

"Not *all* of us," Niko said, pointing between himself, Kade and Kotori. "Orion did."

Orion rolled his eyes, tossing a searing glare to the rockstar-blond. "The point is our paths changed. At least, mine did. I grew … *attached* after centuries of convincing myself to not care, that letting myself care for anyone was a weakness but then you came along. And you changed *everything*," Orion said.

Nyx knew what Orion felt for her, could remember the night he'd reappeared and his frustration when she hadn't understood him. The tone of his voice when he'd told her how he felt about her. She remembered the way his lips had pressed against hers and how she'd allowed herself … to try. Still, she waited with bated breath as his thumb smoothed over the apple of her cheek, eyes filled with the same memories as hers.

"I kneel for no one but you," he said. "A king kneels for no one *but* his queen, and you *are* my queen."

The breath caught in Nyx's throat as he dropped his hand from her face, lowering himself to his knee with his gaze locked on hers. *Kneeling* before her, waiting.

"You're *our* queen and we'll stand by your side for eternity," he said. "We are *your* kings to this city, but first … we need to retrieve Azeil and then we can reclaim what's ours."

LX

Nyx

Gravel stones crunched beneath the tyres of Nyx's motorcycle as she came to a stop, cutting the rumble of their engines like a flame snuffed between two fingers. The distant hoot of an owl punctured the night and a swell of déjà vu hit her. The forest clearing opened out and her gaze locked on a familiar worn-down warehouse, forearms braced on her handlebars, vaguely aware of Orion, Kotori, Niko and Kade's presence on both her sides.

Memories darted through her mind as she dismounted and tucked her key into her pants pocket, vivid flashes of imagery filled with the phantom scent of blood. She thought of the pleas of a dying man, a man she hadn't regretted killing. Kai's wide-eyed and panicked final moments were etched into her skull with perfect clarity. Just as the flash of a silver dagger and Orion's malignantly proud grin flitted before her eyes—the beginning of her dark descent into serenity. She revelled in it—in the memories of fraying humanity.

His life ... or hers.

Aside from her moment of uncertainty in the face of Orion's ultimatum, the decision had been easy. Made and engraved in her soul just as the serpentine dagger that had cut Kai's throat, his blood staining the concrete. It had been a full moon then, like the one now hanging above her head. Witnessed and encouraged by the men she loved in all their monstrous glory, as bloodstained as they were. She didn't care—because they were the same, marred by a darkness the world shunned but they'd embraced. Tired of pretending they were something else, something *better*, when they were as corrupt as the pits of Hell. *Hellish indeed,* she mused with a soft smirk as Orion and Kotori wandered to her side, Niko and Kade at her back.

She thought of the hierarchy between them, Orion as the leader, Kotori as his right-hand man, and Niko and Kade's playful personalities earning them the sway of seconds-in-command. *What are we walking into?* She wondered, eyeing the men with a fissure of dread. *How many lines had Phaelyn and Qadira crossed? Was there an end to this* ... hysteria *in my chest?*

"You're really not messing around, are you?" she said, gesturing to their formation with an airy wave of her hand.

"No," Orion confirmed. "Not where Phaelyn and Qadira are concerned."

Nyx's steps faltered for a moment. "That bad?" she said.

Orion's gaze was steely and devoid of emotion as his tone took on a foreboding edge. "*Worse*. They don't know *what* the danger is to Leon but if they learn the truth … they'll be *much* worse."

She wondered then, worried for her father because, were *they* any different—*better*—than the sisters? Or were they all the same? Was *she* any different from Phaelyn and Qadira? Or was she as much a monster as them?

"Whatever you're thinking, angel. *Stop*," Kade said, his shoulder leaned into the open doorway of the warehouse while she was lost in her thoughts. "You *are not* the same as them."

"I think you have too much faith in me," she said, starting toward the darkness of the warehouse.

Niko scoffed, "They don't care about anything. They haven't cared for a *long* time."

Orion's leather-clad hand grasped her forearm before she could respond, drawing her gaze to him and Kotori at his side. "Remember *why* we're here, little dove," he warned.

"Azeil. I know," she supplied, rolling her eyes when Orion released her arm.

"Just *try* and keep a level head in there," Kotori said. "No matter what happens. Can you do that?"

"Why wouldn't I keep a level head?" Nyx asked, not really needing an answer. She was angry at herself that perhaps … she wouldn't.

Kotori's gaze held hers for a long moment as if he *wanted* her to know he saw her—that he understood why she wouldn't react rationally… if the situation arose. That if he were in her place, he'd forget *every* warning to get to the ones he loved.

"Niko, Kade," Orion said, capturing the group's attention as his voice took on a commanding, no-nonsense tone. "You know what to do."

The pair dipped their heads, their eyes alight with baleful excitement. Niko tossed her a cheeky wink while Kade waggled his fingers before they pivoted and disappeared into the warehouse shadows without a sound, darkness welcoming them like an old friend. A moment passed where Orion seemed to be counting—his steely irises trained on the empty doorway as Nyx glanced between him and the warehouse—before his attention shifted to

Kotori, the pair so in tune with each other's thoughts that words weren't needed. A dark smile lifted the corners of Kotori's lips and he strode to the doorway, pausing for a moment before he vanished with wolfish ease.

Orion turned to Nyx after a beat of silence, moonlight playing across his features like the grin that crawled over his lips, amusement and adoration etched into his eyes. "You ready, little regina?" he said.

"As ready as I'll ever be," she said, glancing at the dark doorway before starting toward the silent warehouse with Orion at her side.

The same dank, mould-fused scent from her memories filled her nostrils as she slipped through the door, crumbling concrete and decaying crates littering the floor. Where her mortal senses had hidden the true ruination of the building from her, now she could see every rust-bitten pole and shattered windowpane. She could *smell* every dead rodent. Orion laced his leather-clad fingers in hers.

She marvelled for a quiet moment at the brightness and clarity of her vision, her gaze darting across the room as her footfalls echoed. Her observation was cut to a jarring halt when her stare locked on the gaping hole of the ceiling. Dread wound in her stomach as she followed the halo of moonlight to a man with dirt-brown curls bound to a chair beneath it. And, like she'd done all those months ago, she paused several paces from the silvery spotlight, her instincts tripping over themselves as her eyes flitted to Niko, Kade and Kotori who stood staggered around the man.

It's not him, she reminded herself as the memory of Kai's bound body flashed before her. *It's your* father. *It's not Kai.* She started toward Azeil with a sick feeling in her stomach, hating his silvered halo and the bruises on his skin. The rope around his wrists cut into his skin in a way that made Nyx see red, uncaring of the promise she'd made Kotori as her gaze raked over Azeil's features and she approached him.

His head was tipped up to the sky through the gaping ceiling, a crusted trail of blood from his split eyebrow feeding her anger. *Almost* as much as Orion's grasp tightening on her hand and his arm banding across her waist.

Her stare remained locked on Azeil as her head cocked eerily to the side. "Orion," she warned lowly, upper lip twitching with the urge to snarl. "Let … me … *go*."

"I can't do that, Nyx. Not until you start thinking rationally. Not with your *fledgling* instincts. They won't do you any good, not here. Not in the future," Orion stated, a conviction to his tone that Nyx loathed but knew to be the truth. "*Breathe*."

"How am I supposed to *breathe* when I don't know if he's okay?" she snapped.

Orion heaved a sigh. "If you were calmer, you'd have noticed his heart, but because you let the fledgling instincts kick in … they might be survival instincts but they're dangerous if you don't know how to be *level-headed*. They'll cloud your judgement and get you killed, got it?"

With a twitch, she shoved Orion's arm away and turned to face him. "Is that what you think will happen? That I'll be *childish* and get myself killed? Because—newsflash—if you were so worried about my interference in your life, maybe you should've stayed out of mine," she said.

Orion's gaze darkened, filling with a familiar look Nyx hadn't seen since she'd first met him. His orotund voice dropped several dangerous octaves, laced with a thousand knives. "What are you saying?"

"What you were thinking when you met me." She gestured to Azeil, remembering when Kai had once sat in his place and the turmoil that had filled her chest then, forgetting about Niko, Kade, Kotori and Orion's stares as she grew lost in the sensation she recognised—thought she'd torn from her chest.

They were still there, she realised. Her fears. A naïve sort of inner turmoil carved from her fear of eternally being an outcast. Of never being accepted for who she was, instead, being what the world wanted her to be. And in the wake of her fear, she sought to distance herself from the men she loved before they could do it for her, hoping to save herself from her self-crafted pain.

"I'm an impulsive liability," she breathed out, refusing to meet the four stares searing into her skin. "I'm going to get you all killed."

"*We* turned you, little regina. Therefore, it's our responsibility to ensure *your* safety. You don't owe us anything. Not even our lives," Orion said. "I speak for all of us."

Nyx wanted to protest but her metaphorical hackles lowered as she focused on Niko and her father, her eyes zeroing in on an envelope resting on his lap. "What's that?" she whispered.

Before Niko could grab the letter, she moved and was by his side. She plucked the object from her father's lap, tearing into it with trembling hands. A glossy photo lay within and dread gripped her heart. The room in the picture was unfamiliar. Lavish and too white for the blood-staining the tiles, collecting beneath the chained figures whose wrists were bound above their heads from the high-arched ceilings. And, despite everything that bellowed and rioted against her turning the picture to see its back, she knew there would be something attached.

There was *always* something attached.

Qadira's elegant scrawl across the photo's backing:

'Two birds ... one stone. Better luck next time, Night.'

There wouldn't be a next time, not now, Nyx thought. They'd crossed a line, and now ... Nyx would ensure they died regretting it. Her simple refusal to lose anyone else was its own consequence. She flipped the photo and her thumb brushed over the twins she called her brothers, silently promising them, *I'm coming for you.* She envisioned Phaelyn and Qadira, envisioned their hearts ripped from their chests, warm and dripping blood through her fingers as she stared down at their unblinking gazes. She'd make them regret knowing of her existence—make Leon regret it too—if it was the last thing she did.

Two birds, one stone.

Two unmarked graves, one fallen sire.

One avenged death, five free wolves.

A prophecy to some, a *promise* to Nyx.

Death would come knocking on Phaelyn, Qadira and Leon's door, but it wouldn't be a man cloaked in shadows. It would be his wolves—his *helvíti* hounds. A wolf tethered by a leash was still a wolf.

The light of the moon caught Nyx's face, turning her visage into something terrible. Her smile was resignation and requital. Nyx, Orion, Kotori, Niko and Kade would delight in ripping their foes apart to free themselves, bringers of death and carnage amid the shadows.

In the shadows of their vengeance.

LXI

Tobias

D*rip-drop, drip-drop, drip-drop.*

The patter of blood from Alexander's weeping wound echoed in the lavishly decorated entryway, collecting in a crimson puddle beneath his Conversed feet. But Tobias was more concerned about the ashen quality of his brother's skin. Grisly slashes across his chest, courtesy of Phaelyn, and the way he blearily blinked, relying heavily on chains attached to the high-arched ceiling to hold himself up. "Alex," he called, urgently when Alexander took too long to reopen his eyes. "*Look at me*. You have to stay awake, okay?"

"I'm trying, Bias … but it's hard," Alexander murmured, resting his temple against his bicep as he shuffled his feet and tried to roll his shoulders, the ripped front of his shirt shifting with the movement.

"That's all I ask. *Try*, because I can't lose you."

Alexander's hazel eyes sparked with fiery determination. "You won't. I promise."

Tobias opened his mouth to respond, short-lived relief swirling as his dark stare settled on Phaelyn and Qadira. The pair sauntered into the room with twisted grins. The metallic cuffs at his wrists bit into his skin as he angled his body toward them, trying to block Alexander. They'd taken a particular interest in him, apparently deeming him easier to crack or maybe enjoying the way Tobias tried to lunge for them, he didn't know, nor did he want to understand the women before him.

"So, are we feeling more *talkative*?" Qadira drawled, manicured nails drumming against her leather-clad hips as her crystalline gaze burrowed into him.

"It depends on what you want to know," Tobias said, wincing as his bruised ribs smarted with his slight shift.

Phaelyn cocked her head, silvered stare filled with unseemly intentions as she pulled a knife from the holster strapped to her thigh, thumbing the blade with fanatic reverence. "Don't play coy, *Tobias*. You know what answers we're after … or do we need to ask Alexander again?" she said.

"If you touch him—" Tobias started, stepping toward the women who could kill him as easily as they breathed.

"You'll what?" Qadira mocked, stalking toward him before she gestured to the chains secured to the ceiling. "I don't know if you've noticed but you can't stop us. You're a human. *Expendable*."

"We'll ask once more, yes?" Phaelyn crooned, eyeing Alexander over his shoulder as she sidled up beside Qadira, polishing the steel of her knife with the hem of her obsidian tank top. "What does Nyx know about killing a sire?"

Tobias plastered an expression of utter boredom across his face, eyes devoid of emotion despite what he knew. Orion had informed him and Alexander two days earlier, bringing Nyx's notepad notes on Asher's journal for them to cross reference with vampiric lore. He didn't know for sure but he suspected it'd been days since they'd dragged them here, to this windowless entryway. It reminded him of a sitting room, fancy tables with antique vases of flowers placed beneath abstract art pieces, the french doors cinched shut, heavy curtains blotting out light and, two fainting couches of deepest emerald pushed against the opposing doorway.

He lied as he clutched the knowledge of Leon's weakness—Nyx's blood making her the tainted link—to his chest. He met their searching gazes, his voice as dark as night, uncaring of the repercussions. "We don't know. Orion doesn't trust us enough to let Nyx tell us that." He tossed a glance toward Alexander to ensure he was still conscious.

"And … you expect us to believe that?" Qadira said, readjusting the leather holsters crisscrossed over her sapphire-blue shirt, the long sleeves covering much of her pale skin.

"It's the truth," Alexander murmured, shaking his head groggily. "All of this has been for nothing."

All of this for Nyx, Tobias mused, wondering how much more they could endure to keep her secrets safe. *She owes us* ... big *time.* But Tobias knew, despite the constant fear in his chest whenever he looked at his brother and the bleeding wound on his chest, that he'd continue to lie for her—that they both would. It was a fact of their loyalty to the girl they called their sister. As stupid as it might have been, they loved Nyx too much to care.

Tobias knew he could have saved himself and Alexander from this pain and fear if they'd cut ties with Nyx then, once they'd realised she'd become entangled with the rulers of Celacali, but they hadn't. And he knew Alexander would never let them give up on her, not even if it saved their lives. Not even after Phaelyn and Qadira had jumped them in their own home or forcibly shoved them into the back of a darkly tinted car. Not even in the wake of the Fates' scales tipping, maybe not in their favour. As Phaelyn had carved a jagged cut down Alexander's chest and his bellow of pain echoed like a phantom in Tobias' head, he held on and closed his eyes.

They *wouldn't* give up on Nyx. Not now. Not ever.

Not for their lives.

As stupid as that might be.

"I wouldn't say it's been for nothing," Phaelyn said, pointedly glancing at the wound on Alexander's chest.

Qadira feigned contemplation before a feline-like grin grew across her face, the blond tresses of her hair brushing her shoulders as she turned to Phaelyn. "I think Tobias needs to learn why he shouldn't lie, don't you?" she drawled.

Phaelyn stepped closer to him, twirling her knife with depraved excitement in her eyes. "I think you're right, sis. Where? I'd hate to ruin his pretty face," she crooned, trailing the blade edge against his jawline.

"Then don't. There's plenty of flesh to choose from," Qadira said, uncaring.

Phaelyn's eyes flitted to him and away from his arm. "This will hurt."

And, quicker than Tobias could comprehend, she shredded the sleeve of his hoodie, brandishing her knife and its intricate hilt before carving a series of quick slashes to his bicep. *One. Two. Three. Four.*

A white-hot, burning agony bloomed in his mind, wrenching a strained groan from his lips as he refused to falter—to show the pair his pain. Instead, he held Qadira's gaze, his warm blood trickling down his arm. He sucked in a ragged breath as the metallic rattle of chains to his left captured his attention, Alexander's expression was livid despite the clammy sheen of his skin before Phaelyn struck again, carving criss-crosses into the flesh nearest his elbow—nearest the veins, inches below. He tugged weakly against his restraints with the little strength he had left.

Tobias tried to block Qadira's path to Alexander as her interest locked on him, ignoring the agony of Phaelyn's ministrations with gritted teeth, everything in him bellowing its need to protect his brother—his *twin*. "No. Alex," he said, pulling against the bruising grasp Phaelyn had on his shoulder to ensure her slashes were precise.

"On the contrary, yes, Alex," Qadira purred, tossing a glance at Tobias before she rounded his shoulder and wandered to Alexander, her attention on him. "All this can stop if you tell us what we want to know. It's that simple. Tell us, stay alive. Continue to lie and you'll leave here in a casket. Which will it be?"

Alexander's amber gaze flickered and locked on Tobias as he responded, "I *can't* tell you that. *Anything* else, but not that."

Qadira hummed in acknowledgement. “Are you sure?”

“Yes,” Alexander said; no room for argument laced throughout his voice.

Silence stretched across the room for a moment as Qadira surveyed Alexander, her head dipping in the next breath. “Okay,” she murmured, holding his gaze, her lips twitching into a salacious grin. “*Phaelyn*.”

The air in Tobias’s lungs lodged itself in his chest, constricting his breathing as Phaelyn shifted beside him, her knife swiftly tucked back into its holster. Her grip tightened while one of her hands forcibly angled his head to bare his throat. Terror clouded his mind as he recalled the vampiric lore—that a vampire could control the flow of blood, killing him slowly or quicker than humanly possible. He felt fear and finality as Alexander began anew on his restraints, shouts echoing in the lavish room.

“No!” Alexander screamed.

“Tell us what Nyx knows,” Qadira retorted as Phaelyn’s silvered gaze bled white-gold.

Alexander’s gaze darted to Qadira, directing his words at her, “*No*.”

Tobias pulled against Phaelyn’s grip, his brother’s voice drifting in and out of his focus as terror gripped his heart and his eyes darted between the chains keeping him prisoner and Phaelyn. Her face was all sharp edges and rutted bone structure, canines and incisors elongated as he helplessly fought to free himself—to get away from her. To save himself and his brother.

Phaelyn’s fangs pierced Tobias’ skin, sinking into the junction of his throat as a pained sound tumbled from his lips and he screwed his eyes shut, hoping it would end. Though Tobias knew a vast amount about vampiric lore and their abilities, *nothing* had prepared him for the harrowing agony of a vampire’s bite, and nothing could have. It was as if a thousand knives carved and pierced his skin. Like a branding iron pressed into his flesh, its brand glowing white-hot. Like a shark shredding into the carcass of a whale, tearing away fragments of his sanity as easily as the fish tore flesh from the bone. It was all of those sensations combined, a mind-numbing blend of agony unlike any Tobias had felt before. He yanked at the bindings keeping him in place, automatic hope draining his strength with every mouthful Phaelyn swallowed of his blood.

Tha-thu ... mp, tha-thu ... mp, tha-thu ... mp.

Black spots danced behind his eyelids, appearing in quick succession. Knowing the unsteady beat of his heart was a by-product of Phaelyn’s actions, he knew he had under a minute to survive if she didn’t stop. She readjusted her grasp, pulling more of his blood from his body until he couldn’t hear anything over the rushing in his ears and the terror in his veins. He couldn’t die like this. He couldn’t die knowing Alexander would live with that anguish, with the memory of his death carved into his skull. He *couldn’t*.

He *wouldn’t*.

Tha-thu ... mp, tha-thu ... mp, tha-thu ...

PART FOUR

Blood, vengeance and death. Oh my!
Don't be afraid … your end is nigh.

LXII

Nyx

Three days, she repeated like a broken mantra in her head, pacing beneath the sunlight pouring into the sunroom of her family's home. *It's been* three *days and nothing. Absolutely nothing. Not one word on the twins' safety.*

Nyx shoved her thoughts to the depths of her mind, continuing to fret for Alexander and Tobias as Azeil re-entered the room. Blueprints, maps, case files and photos were cradled in his arms before he deposited them on the glass table in the middle of the room. If not for Orion reminding her that acting without thought would kill her, she would have torn Celacali apart to find her brothers.

Not that it mattered now. Her black tennis skirt brushed her thighs and she was, somewhat, content to bide her time to ensure the twins' return was swift and unchallenged. She could quash the instincts that bellowed at her to act first and think later. She could do that for the twins, even as she worried for their safety. Even as her mind tossed unbidden imagery before her eyes, flashes of blood and harrowing wounds blurring into a cornucopia of unwanted visions.

Three days.

How had three days passed and not one of them—not Orion, Kotori, Niko or Kade—had found anything to point them in the right direction? Not even her father, with his seemingly endless supply of connections, could pinpoint *where* Alexander and Tobias were. How could two women evade them all? How could they disappear so easily? And *why* had they finally fallen silent? Nyx wasn't foolish enough to convince herself that this was over. That would be too easy. And if Nyx had learned anything since the day she'd moved to Celacali, it was that *nothing* was ever that easy.

Azeil broke the rocky silence, eyebrow quirked before he peered down at his watch, gaze lifting a moment later, "Alyvia and Xander, they should be here right about … now."

The front door opening and closing drew Nyx's attention to the sunroom's doorway, and as Azeil's words hung in the air, Alyvia and Xander came into sight. Nyx's eyes lit up at the sight of her mother and adopted brother, a brilliant grin stretching her lips as she hurried to them. She wasted no time in pulling her mother into a hug, basking in brief comfort and happiness before she stepped from her mother's embrace and into Xander's; his lips twisted in an adoring smile.

Xander's arms banded around her in a bear hug, an elated laugh tumbling from her mouth as she returned his embrace. After a moment, she pulled away enough to peer up at him. His shoulder-length hair was contained in a messy bun, stray mouse-brown tresses wisping against his face.

His hazel eyes were alight and careworn. "I've missed you, Night," he said, hugging her again. "It hasn't been the same without you in Malor."

"Celacali hasn't been the same without you either," Nyx admitted, glancing at her mother, whose curls hung freely down her back. "It hasn't been the same without the both of you."

It wasn't lost on Nyx, as her gaze swept across the room, the tension that stretched between Alyvia and Orion, Kotori, Niko and Kade. Despite her mother's understanding and open-hearted assurances to Nyx three months ago. Nyx suspected that Alyvia was still wary—terrified even—of the men she'd once known. She watched her mother as Alyvia twisted the fabric of her flowy, white skirt in her hands. The way she smiled softly at Xander when he resituated himself beside her, brushing a comforting hand down her arm.

Orion's orotund voice filled the room, laced with goading, cigarette perched between his gloved fingers, "Aw, don't I get a hug?"

Alyvia's cocoa-brown eyes narrowed on him, her arms folding tightly over her beige long-sleeved shirt. "I have half the right to smack sense into you, *Orion*. After everything you put Nyx through. It would only be fair," she quipped.

Orion arched his eyebrows in slight surprise, a slow smirk crawling over his face. "I sense a 'but' to that statement, and you always liked those," he said.

"*But*" Alyvia started, "that decision lies with Nyx. Not me."

"I think that's enough posturing to last a lifetime," Azeil said, glaring pointedly at Orion as Niko and Kade hid their grins behind their hands. He shifted his gaze to Nyx, who saw how he stared longingly after her mother, like he regretted everything that had happened between them before their divorce. "Let's get back to why we're really here," he said, inclining his head to Orion.

With a soft sigh, Nyx turned to Orion as Kotori resettled by her side. "Orion, let's be *rational*," she said, parroting similar words he'd spoken to her.

Orion's eyes sparked with devilry, head cocking. "Rational *is* my middle name."

Kotori released a doubtful sound. "Right."

"As you all know, Alyvia and Xander were once closer to Leon than we were," Kade began, "and because they were mortals when our *sire* found them … he entrusted certain information to them, believing they were too foolish to understand it." Kade chuckled lowly with a bitter shake of his head. "Of course, he was wrong."

Nyx pivoted toward her mother and Xander, irises sharp with interest. "Information? Like where-Tobias-and-Alexander-are information or killing-Leon information?"

Xander rested his jean-clad hip against the glass table. "Killing-Leon information."

The pair meandered to Azeil's side, crowding around the table, and began sifting through the assortment of paperwork spread across the glass surface. Nyx caught a proud glint in Niko's eyes as he tracked Xander. Niko's expression reminded her of the way Asher used to look at her—the look of a proud uncle spread over his broad but chiselled features—as she came to her family's side, her gaze roving over the content Azeil had spread across the table. Nyx furrowed her brow with confusion, looking at Orion. "Didn't we get Asher's journal for that information?" she said.

"We did," Orion confirmed. "But we need someone *mortal,* with … *first-hand* knowledge to confirm or reinform us of the truth. We needed the mortals who helped Asher confirm parts of his research."

Azeil nodded his approval—an action that stumped Nyx for a moment as she glanced between the two men—before he retrieved the copy of *The Wizard of Oz* with Asher's journal hidden inside and flicked to the page he was looking for. He paused on the page containing the information on how to kill a sire and break their bonds to the pack members, angling the book toward Xander and Alyvia who skimmed Asher's handwriting and the sentences Nyx had hastily jotted. Nyx waited with bated breath as they read Asher's notes, flicking through the pages of information before they shared a look and Alyvia dipped her head in curt nod, her gaze sweeping across the room.

"It's the truth," Alyvia said, thumbing through pages covered in Asher's handwriting with a reminiscent gleam. Like she missed Asher as much as Nyx did.

"Leon once mentioned a fragment of lore that told of killing a sire *and* shattering the ties connecting them to their pack. Something about tainted blood being able to kill them. I suspect that's why the twins were taken … he is running out of collateral," Xander explained.

Nyx shared a look with each of her men as Alyvia's gaze locked on Nyx, a smile tugging her lips. "Thank you," Nyx murmured, looking between her mother and Xander in turn. "Thank you for helping us when you didn't have to."

"Anytime, Night. We'll be in Celacali for however long it takes this mess to get cleaned up. You know I'm only a call away," Xander said, pressing an affectionate kiss to her forehead.

Alyvia's fingers tucked a stray curl behind Nyx's ear as her dimple-fused smile brightened her oblong features. "I'm glad you figured out what you wanted in Celacali—from the world—my little shadow. You look good with them," Alyvia murmured, brushing a thumb affectionately against her daughter's cheek. "Stay safe and trust your men. Trust in yourself. I'll see you soon."

With a last brush of her thumb, Alyvia released her hands and made her exit from the room. Azeil and Xander followed. They had much to talk about. The soft snitching of the door closed a circle in Nyx's mind, one she hadn't known had been left open. Not really, as Kade came to her side, draping an arm over her shoulders.

"She's right you know," he said.

Nyx shifted, meeting his stare. "About what?"

"That you look good with us. You're more at home in your own skin now … more than you were when you moved to Celacali."

A distracted smile wavered over her face. "I know. And despite … everything. I wouldn't trade it for the world."

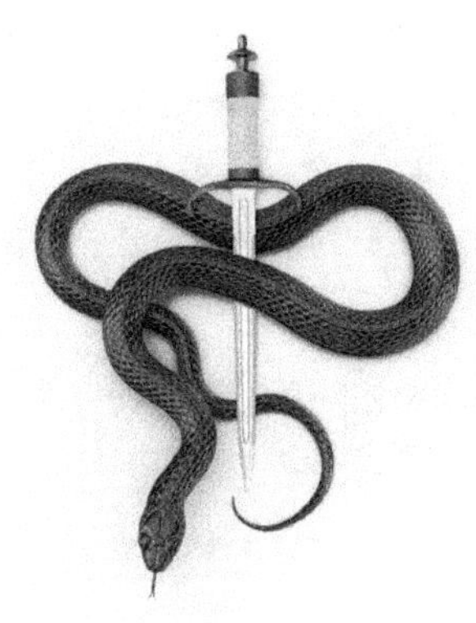

LXIII

Nyx

Golden rays of sunlight cascaded in through the high-arched windows of Alexander and Tobias's home above the comic bookstore. It was the following day as Nyx leaned against the window frame, observing the boardwalk-goers who continued their lives so obliviously. She paid her father, Kotori and Niko little mind as they prowled the two-bedroom, one-bathroom apartment in search of *something* that would point them in the right direction. Her ring-clad fingers toyed with the zipper of Niko's leather jacket slung over her shoulders, booted foot tapping anxiously against the floorboards.

As she continued her silent appraisal of the tourist-busy boardwalk, she tried to purge the image of the lounge room's disarray from her skull, knowing the scattered comics, leather-bound hardbacks, odd trinkets and upturned furniture were the aftermath of a struggle. Nyx knew the twins hadn't been prepared for it and couldn't have been, not even if they'd tried. Her gaze flitted to the shattered glass of 'holy water' and the handwritten label, their beloved comic books scattered across the room, a static buzz emitting from the TV.

It was a quiet sort of agony, standing in the ruins of a place she knew to be a sanctuary, and it did little to calm her restless nerves whenever her mind drifted to them. Wondering if they were okay or if Phaelyn and Qadira had harmed them, the latter filling her with bouts of nausea. Wondering how much of Xander's words had been truth, if the twins were collateral, a bargaining chip, they were running out of time. She couldn't focus as her mind tugged her down a dozen paths of teenage memories. A perpetual mask frozen in terror, the raspy crackle of Ghostface's voice echoing in her ears. The terrified beat of her heart, her bruised flesh in the mirror of their bathroom, a vehement vow uttered for no one but herself. Childish screams of elation as their younger selves were delighted by the Twirling Teacups ride. Asher's mirthful nickname for them uttered after he'd finished scolding them for running amok on the boardwalk, the trio sharing mischievous looks. Their attentive care and brotherly concern, taking her in and watching over her after Azeil fled town and Leon's attempted murder of her.

"Nothing," Niko said, breaking her from her thoughts as he wandered to her side and curled an arm around her waist, pulling her into his side and pressing a kiss to her temple. His lips brushed her skin as his voice lowered so only she could hear him. "We'll find them, chica. I promise."

"It's been four days, Nik," she murmured, a betraying sliver of doubt in her tone.

"And we'll find them. Orion and Kade are turning the city upside down, and you've seen the growing body count of the Ivory Skulls. We'll find them," he assured.

Azeil purposefully cleared his throat, drawing the pair's attention to where he stood beside the overturned coffee table. A flash of silver caught her eyes as Azeil revealed two stainless steel bracelets, a grim set to his jaw and a darker look to his slate irises. "Not nothing. Just nothing that we didn't already know," Azeil said.

Nyx rounded on her father, a burst of anger lashing her insides. Her lip curled, irises flaring white-gold as frustration wrapped around her throat, choking her in a tide of emotion she'd fought since learning of Tobias and Alexander's disappearance. It mattered little to Nyx that it wasn't Azeil's fault. In that moment, she only had rage to guide her and she recalled the night he'd kicked her out. A foolish thing to focus on with everything that was going on, but … a thousand unsaid words stretched between them.

"You have more connections than I know of and what are you doing with them? *Nothing*!" she snapped.

Azeil's eyebrows lifted in surprise at her outburst. "Night—" he began.

"No," she said, cutting him off as she drew closer. "You've been applauded for being a *renowned detective* for years now, but do they know about your corrupt connections? Do they know about the lengths you'll go to? Because I do. I've heard the whispers." She laughed without amusement. "I've been the reason why *Azeil Monroe* had to use those connections—couldn't have my reputation staining yours. Imagine what that would've done, if people knew about what I'd done to Kai in Malor? It would've ruined you." Her words fell like stones.

A low whistle tumbled from Niko's lips, his shoulder leaned into the window frame she'd once occupied, his Guns N' Roses tank top cropped over his midriff, dark ripped jeans hugging his thighs as he slowly shook his head. "It seems you're not quite the saint you've tried to tell yourself you are. Isn't that right, Azeil?" he chimed in.

Azeil held her gaze, unwavering in the swell of her anger and unwilling to deny her accusations. "I'm not a great man, Night, but I did those things for you and everyone I care about. I won't apologise for them either. Even though some parts of my career have been wrong, they've been done for all the right reasons."

She opened her mouth to rebut his words but, before she could, Kotori came to her side and his deeply timbred voice sent a shiver down her spine. "That's enough, kleintje. Arguing about the past won't help us now and neither will letting your anger cloud your mind. We must do better than *them*," he said.

For a moment, silence cloyed thickly in the air between them. Nyx's gaze locked on her father's. Azeil was unwavering and straight-spined, his posture relaxed as he folded his arms over his white dress shirt, dark jeans and shoes perfectly in place, unlike his naturally tousled head of curls. *Breathe and think rationally*, she thought. Something she knew was lacking in the days that had passed since Alexander and Tobias went missing, she was *lacking* her unfazed and *rational* thoughts, swept away the moment her brothers were taken. "I'm sorry," she exhaled, raking her fingers through her curls as she tried to dispel everything she felt. "I shouldn't have—"

"No, Night. Don't apologise. You didn't say anything that wasn't true and I'm not mad," Azeil said, chuckling softly as Kotori glanced between them. "I'm proud actually."

"Proud?" she parroted, doubt etched in her eyes.

Azeil's lips pulled into a soft grin, his eyes shining with mirth and adoration. "You're *exactly* who you're supposed to be … you're exactly who Asher hoped you'd be, who I hoped you'd be," he said.

Nyx blinked with confusion that matched the look in Kotori's eyes, staring at her father like he'd grown two heads as the front door swung open. It took a moment for her to register who stood in the twins' home, but she realised she recognised the champagne-blond man with Argentine eyes. *Donovan Carter,* she reminded herself.

"I've got it," Donovan exclaimed, a happy glint to his features before he seemed to pause, glancing between Niko and Kotori with uncertainty.

Nyx turned to her father questioningly. "What's Donovan doing here?" she said.

"Yes, why *is* he here?" Niko said, eyeing the blond with dark interest.

Azeil sighed, the picture of a fed-up father sick of his squabbling children. "He's got information on the whereabouts of Tobias and Alexander from one of my connections. And if his entrance was anything to go off, he got it," he explained.

"That doesn't explain *why* he's helping or why you trust him with this," said Kotori.

Donovan straightened the fabric of his inky shirt, the sleeves rolled up to his elbows. "I owe Azeil," he said, simply.

Nyx frowned. "Owe him? What the hell does that mean?"

"I killed someone," Donovan stated bluntly, ensnaring Nyx, Niko and Kotori's attention. "I had a one-way ticket to *any* forensics position I wanted but … I was a reckless person. I spent two months in jail for manslaughter and drunk driving, my sentence was shortened because of Azeil."

"Did you …?" Nyx murmured.

Donovan nodded solemnly. "I did. I killed my sister. I owe Azeil for saving my career."

Azeil brushed Donovan's words aside, "And I've told him that the debt has been paid but he insists not. So instead of being a lackey, Donovan has been a long-standing friend for several years." He looked to Donovan with an air of authority. "Did you get it?"

Donovan's expression brightened, a brilliant grin stretching across his face as he pulled a file from his leather satchel. "The vipers' den has been found."

Azeil shook his head with mirth, accepting the file the blond passed him, thumbing through the contents with a pleased smile. "This is why we've stayed friends for this long. You never disappoint."

Donovan tossed Azeil a playful wink. "I aim to please."

Nyx huffed a soft laugh and peered down at the information within the cream-coloured file. Her tone squashed the lightness in her chest, hoping he had the insight she needed to find her brothers. "Where are they?" she said.

Donovan gestured to the map of the city, trailing his finger to the lavish part of the city. "Northern Celacali. White house with serpentine statues lining the gate," he said.

Her brows knitted together as recognition plunged her senses and she glanced at Niko and Kotori for a moment. She remembered that house. She remembered its serpentine gates as she'd driven past with Niko, Kotori, Orion and Kade by her side, before they'd hidden their bikes in the shrubbery bordering the gates and the next door's property. Her voice was a disbelieving whisper even as she knew it to be true, "That's the house next door to Cassia Dawson … I mean, before we killed her."

Donovan blinked in shock, his head snapping towards her. "You—what?"

She shrugged, eyes dark and unflinching. "We needed to send a message."

"Okay, and?" Donovan prompted.

"Cassia *was* the message … just as Phaelyn and Qadira will be the next one."

LXIV

Nyx

Time passed in a fitful haze, seeming to drag on or dart past her eyes as Nyx, Orion, Kotori, Niko and Kade constructed their plan to rescue the twins, breaking it down and straightening it out, melting the serpentine blade and reforging it with her blood encased in the silver until Orion gave the go-ahead … but that had been a day ago. Nyx reasoned with as much serenity as she could muster that Alexander and Tobias were okay. She was on edge, feeling like a thousand ants crawled over her skin.

The greying hue of twilight dappled the sky as her ears homed in on the slightest sounds, doing little to ease her discomfort and racing thoughts. But the harder she tried to hear something, the quieter it seemed. Northern Celacali was quieter in the lavish part of the city, every abstract house and driveway illuminated by fanciful light fixtures while some were bathed in darkness like the residents already slumbered. Their decision to leave their bikes on the outskirts of Northern Celacali had been a wise one, lest the rich of the city called the police and created an unwanted problem for them to fix.

Kotori's ring-clad hand gently squeezed hers in a gesture of silent reassurance and Orion paused before a set of looming, black-iron gates embellished with serpents. He outstretched his hand, and touched the metal. A sharp string of curses followed as he wrenched his hand away, shaking it.

Electrified ... and cattle-grade at that. Annoying but not life-threatening, she mused as the blueprints and information they'd gathered on the property darted across her mind. The white marble of the house glared back at her from the opposing end of the paved driveway, hedges manicured and shaped to resemble serpents like the ones on the gates that obscured their path to the lavish home. "Why would you touch it? We know the gates are electric," she said with an exasperated tone.

Orion arched his eyebrows, glancing pointedly at the gates. "So … you want to *trust* the information Phaelyn and Qadira might have planted?"

"And … was it misleading?"

"No."

"Well, there you go," she uttered dryly. Nyx waited a moment before she wedged her foot into a groove in the cobblestone and grasped the jutting stone, climbing the wall with an ease that left her child-self speechless. The thought elicited a smile as she climbed the remaining metres and pulled herself atop the wall. There, crouching above Orion, Kotori, Niko and Kade, she took stock of the building below, the breeze gently ruffled her unbound curls.

Then, tossing a cheeky wink down at the quartet, she turned and steadied herself, rising enough from her crouched position that she could jump from the cobblestone wall as smoothly as possible. Without letting herself process the six-metre drop, she jumped. Her legs absorbed a little of the impact before she rolled and her shoulder met a manicured lawn, ensuring her head and neck were positioned correctly to avoid serious *mortal* injuries. She righted herself in the next breath, stabilising with preternatural swiftness.

For a brief moment, she wondered what Azeil, Alyvia and Xander were doing to pass the time as they waited at the vacant residence of Cassia Dawson in Xander's Impala for Kotori and Kade to bring the twins to them. Nyx knew her father itched to be a part of the action as she rose and brushed the grass from her dark-washed jeans, knowing he'd want to protect her from the women loyal to Leon, but she couldn't let any more of her loved ones get hurt. She had promised herself that much, that her loved ones would stay safely away from Leon and his perimeter while she disposed of the women endangering them. From there, Leon would die as surely as Phaelyn and Qadira.

Nothing but their memory and the blood that would stain her hands would be left.

But first, before any bloodletting could begin, they needed to split into two groups; Niko and Kotori as one, herself, Orion and Kade as another. Then they needed to infiltrate the lavish, white-stone house that was a perfect blend of cottage and villa. The rest of the plan was simple: save and ensure the twins' safety by taking them to the 'getaway crew.' Kill Phaelyn and Qadira.

Nyx surveyed the maintained front yard with indifference, sweeping a long look across the paved driveway and lights dotting it as her fingertips brushed the knife-holster at her thigh. She started up the driveway as Kade lithely jumped down from the wall, followed by his companions.

She didn't have to check to see if Orion, Kotori, Niko and Kade followed her, their footfalls on the pavers like an ominous drumbeat to a great battle. She pushed a fraction of her vampiric speed into her stride, vanquishing the distance between herself and the white stone house in a matter of moments. Her dark gaze swept the slight veranda, her boots a dark blot against the white steps as she crossed to the front door and raised her hand to knock. *Foolish.* "I guess knocking *is* pointless, considering you're kicking the door in." She grinned darkly at Orion before stepping aside with a sweeping gesture.

"As much as that would annoy them, we need the sound of the door breaking to mask Niko and Kotori's entrance through the back door," Orion said.

"Now," came Kotori's voice through their shared bond as Nyx shifted closer to Kade and out of Orion's way.

As swiftly as Kotori's voice had conveyed a simple order, Orion raised his right leg and kicked the door down in one fluid movement, pieces of wood skittering across the marble tiles. Silence stretched for several moments as they seemed to bask in the brewing storm and something in her preened at the ease—strength—Orion possessed. She released a low whistle, her expression alight with avidity and excitement, Kade shadowing her shoulder as Orion turned to her with arched brows.

"Can you do that again?" she said, ignoring Kade's chuckle.

Orion rolled his eyes with mock disdain, closing the distance between them and cupping her cheek before he pressed a quick kiss to her lips. "Maybe another time, little dove. We have some … *vipers* to kill," he said.

With a sigh of feigned disappointment, she followed him across the threshold.

As much as the scent of blood filled Nyx with dread and a dizzying swell of memories of Asher, she forced herself to keep walking. To put one foot in front of the other, to find her brothers and save them from Phaelyn and Qadira. She knew Orion and Kade could hear the racing of her heart. Everything and nothing pressed upon her shoulders, careening through her bloodstream until she couldn't *think* of anything else.

She couldn't focus on the entryway they crossed, caring little for the fanciful furnishings or décor. Her heart stalled in her chest when Orion grasped the handles of a set of french doors, glancing over his shoulder to her before he pushed them open.

Her gaze settled on Alexander and Tobias strung up by chains from the high-arched ceiling of the windowless room and her eyes lingered on the crimson-stained tiles beneath them and the grisly gashes across their bodies. Without thought, she ran to them, Kotori appearing at her side to unfasten the chains around Alexander's wrists as she froze, turning to Tobias.

Silence. Not a tell-tale sound of his heart to be heard.

Niko seemed to notice what she did at the same moment, hauling her away as she released a choked sob. A sound that quaked with something breaking. A sound of anguish and horror, of doubt and denial. A pause of silence as she trembled in Niko's embrace, her stare locked on Tobias. Then, as if Kade's movement jolted her—the blond swiftly unlatching the chains from around Tobias wrists, his gaze lingered on her.

She tugged to free herself, irises bleeding white-gold as a louder, harsher shout of agony rent the room. "*Tobias,*" she cried, her voice breaking as her heart shattered. She found no comfort in Niko's arms as she struggled to get to Tobias. She whirled to Niko when he wouldn't relent, fangs cutting her bottom lip before she bared her teeth in an animalistic snarl. "No!"

The howl that erupted from her was base and terrifying in its intensity and it ripped open wounds old and new until thought seemed like an alien presence. Pain like nothing she had felt until now eclipsed her for what seemed like eternity.

Kotori hoisted Alexander in his arms, like Kade easily lifted Tobias. Together, the pair disappeared from the room as she turned to watch their retreat, taking the twins to where Azeil, Alyvia and Xander waited. As they vanished from her sight, her anger somehow vanished with them, leaving her with an emptiness she hadn't felt since she'd lost Asher.

"Tobias is … he's gone," she murmured, blinking furiously to stop the tears. Like tears mattered.

"Not everything is as it seems, little regina," Orion drawled from behind her, something in his voice making her turn.

Her irises narrowed to pinpricks. *What the hell did that mean?*

"I don't like this. Something is … *missing*," Niko said, huffing out a frustrated breath. "This isn't like them. Not one bit."

Orion lingered at the doorway before he turned to Niko, a matching look of unease in his eyes. "You're right, Nik. Find Kotori and Kade, get them to search the grounds while you check the second story. Nyx and I will cover the first floor, splitting up—"

"*Split up*?" Niko interjected, staring at Orion like he'd grown a third head.

"Yes," Nyx said, injecting as much assurance into her tone as she could muster. "We need to find them. They *need* to die."

They did. Need to die. Until that happened, she had to put all other thought and emotion to one side. Tobias—*no*, she slammed it away. Thoughts of Tobias came later.

"I understand wanting to avenge Tobias and Alexander, chica … but what if this is a mistake? What if they *want* us to split up—for you to wander into their path like a bow-wrapped present?" Niko said, lifting his hand to card his fingers through his hair.

Nyx grasped his free hand in both of hers, peering up at him with a faint smile. "You once told me that nothing good ever came without sacrifice and now, we *need* to make some of our own. We need to do this, Nik," she said.

With a great reluctance, Niko dipped his head as his gaze held hers. "Be careful," he warned.

"I will."

Niko held her stare for a long moment as Orion waited in the room's doorway, mild interest splayed across his features, before Niko shook his head and strode past Orion, from the room, disappearing down the corridor.

Where would I hide if I were vampiric henchwomen? she wondered as she turned in a slow circle, surveying the bloodied tiles and the thick curtains hanging where a window *should have* been. Her gaze caught on a faint divot peeking from behind a curtain and she hurried over to it, sweeping the fabric aside to reveal a white-wooded door. *Why hide a door?* she thought as she grasped the handle and pushed.

The door opened onto a sterile-looking office. Her instincts ran rampage beneath her flesh as she sucked in a breath and stepped over the room's threshold, approaching the desk bracketed by squared pigeonholes. A keening screech rang in her ears despite the silence and emptiness of the office with its pristinely white walls. It was almost too … perfect as she scrutinised the grey desk and the high-backed chair, typewriter and labelled folders situated neatly in its centre, four pens lying in perfect lines.

Odd, she thought as the scent of dust and disuse grappled with her senses, temples aching with the beginnings of a headache. With a soft wince, she raised her hand to rub at her forehead when a faint creak sounded and she froze, her heart drumming.

"I thought I heard a *mouse*," mused a feminine voice before a hand struck out and gripped her hair quicker than Nyx could turn, driving her face into the desk with enough force to send the pens rolling.

Pain bloomed in Nyx's nose and she reacted on instinct, ploughing her elbow into the woman's stomach and shunting them both backward to break the firm grasp on her head. She cared little for the burning pain of her scalp as she slowly pivoted to face her attacker. A faint scent of citronella rose in her nostrils as her stare locked with Qadira's and her fingers brushed her nose, blood wetting her digits. "That hurt," Nyx mused, wiping her blood on her shirt, tongue tracing her teeth.

"Did it? Because that was a warmup," Qadira drawled, head quirking as savage interest sparked in her eyes, lips twitching like a grin wished to crawl across her face.

Nyx darted forward in the same breath Qadira lunged, a startled scream tearing from her chest, eyes wide and fear laced as she realised her mistake; thinking Qadira's shift to her body's left was the direction she'd move. *Stupid,* she thought, cursing herself as Qadira's hand latched onto her throat and the desk edge collided with her spine, fingers scrambling to loosen Qadira's hold. *She played you like a fool.*

"Don't look so surprised, *fledgling*," Qadira crooned, mock disappointment echoing across the room. "I have *centuries* on your … *almost* two-decade existence. Your fight is admirable, but you're so *stupid*. Like all mortals."

"Oh, Qadira," Nyx said, forcing the words from her mouth as her lungs burned and Qadira's grasp tightened on her windpipe. "Humanity is only as *stupid* as the ones who peer down their noses at it."

"Careful," Qadira warned, a livid glint flaring in her eyes at Nyx's words. Her lips curled with an animalistic sneer, irises bleeding white-gold as she pushed Nyx further into the desk, wood pressing painfully against her tailbone.

As she held Qadira's eyes, Nyx couldn't tell what would happen next. A monster stared back at her without a trace of humanity to be seen.

"Leon needs the journal," she whispered.

"I need you *dead* more. You can't share its secrets if you're not breathing," Qadira said, silvered nails digging into Nyx's throat as her features rutted and sharpened, fangs brushing her bottom lip.

"More of us know," she managed in a strangled gasp.

"Then I'll kill you all," Qadira said giggling.

Horror dawned like a knife rammed into flesh, dragging a ragged path down Nyx's ribcage and spilling her innards for Qadira to see, damning and clarifying. Nyx's hands scrabbled against the hand around her throat as her instincts bellowed and she struck, embedding her fangs into the top of Qadira's hand, willing agony to blaze through the blonde's veins. Qadira's pained shout was music to Nyx's ears as she shoved the blonde away, spitting blood onto the tiles with satisfaction. "Careful, I bite," Nyx murmured, inching toward the doorway with a mocking smile intended to showcase her blood-stained teeth.

"So do I," Qadira snapped, lunging for Nyx in fury.

Fear and adrenaline addled Nyx's mind as she dropped to her haunches and swept Qadira's feet from beneath her, an enraged cry filling her eardrums when she made to rise from the tiles and her brown eyes clashed with blue. Anger shone like a thousand suns in Qadira's eyes as Nyx held her gaze, heart hammering when Qadira's hand shot out and grabbed Nyx's ankle, dragging her with terrifying ease.

Nails sharpened to deadly points pressed painfully into Nyx's skin as she kicked out, boot colliding with Qadira's hip before the blonde hissed and moved in a blur too fast to see. Pain rang across the back of Nyx's head as it collided with the tiles and Qadira shifted their grappling frames until she glared down at Nyx, stifling Nyx's thrashing by standing on Nyx's shins. She smiled with no emotion, one of her hands pinning Nyx's above her head and her lips brushed Nyx's ear. Dread settled itself like barbed wire in her chest.

"I think it's time I tasted your blood. After all … you tasted mine," Qadira crooned, lifting her head to survey Nyx's face as the hand gripping her chin bared the flesh to her gaze.

"I think I'll pass," Nyx quipped, bucking her hips in an attempt to free herself.

"Oh … it wasn't an option," Qadira said, her scent of citronella engulfing Nyx's senses and smarting against her temples as her breath fanned Nyx's throat.

"If you—" Nyx's words died as a harrowed scream wrenched from her lungs, instincts rioting against the white-hot agony flooding her nervous system. Qadira's fang pierced her flesh, legs flailing beneath the blonde's weight, desperate to be free of the shredding, burning bite. Through the haze of pain, Nyx hastily opened the mental connection she shared with Orion, Niko, Kotori and Kade to send a single jolt of anguish down the bond;

one she hoped they'd understand. *I* need *to fight*, she reminded herself as she tried to force the pain out, gritting her teeth. *Use your brain.*

Her eyes locked on the ceiling as her thoughts clamoured, focusing on Qadira. *Willing* the blonde's mind to believe Nyx's blood was acidic—*rancid*—as she recalled the titbit of information she'd read in a folklore book, stating vampires could manipulate the perceptions of mortals *and* vampires if they wanted to.

Myths didn't start from nowhere, a fact Nyx knew to be truer than the sun's rise and fall, but how many stories dictated and shaped the one she'd read? And would it save her from the agony of Qadira's bite or the jittery cold in her body with each mouthful of her blood Qadira swallowed? Nyx didn't know but she wouldn't let it dissuade her, imagining her blood tasted like battery acid or had the nauseating tang of rotted meat.

A garbled gag filled the room as Qadira's head raised from Nyx's throat and her blue eyes darted in confusion. Satisfaction cleaved Nyx's insides and she bucked her hips, dislodging Qadira from her body and hurrying to her feet. Nyx's hand pressed against her weeping throat as she bolted from the office and into the windowless sitting room in a burst of lightning speed. She collided with a solid chest.

"Nyx, it's me," Niko said, grasping her arm to steady her before he released her when she didn't waver, Orion, Kotori and Kade loomed over his shoulder.

"I found Qadira … or she found me," Nyx broke out desperately.

"You're bleeding," came Kade's concerned voice, rounding Niko's shoulder to survey the bitemark Qadira had left behind and the stain from her nose.

"I'm fine," Nyx assured, mustering a smile across her face she hoped they'd believe.

Suddenly, Kotori pulled her behind him. A squeal startled from her lips as a knife *whacked* into the artwork above a vase, the canvas tearing as the blade lodged into the wall. Qadira's bitter chuckle resounded across the room from the entranceway as she appeared beside her sibling, all vampiric fluidity. A glint of silver—the knives Phaelyn adored. *The vipers had arrived*, she thought with disdain, offering Kotori a grateful grin before it twisted into something else.

A dark, taunting gleam trickled across her face as she turned to face Phaelyn and Qadira. "It seems your aim is off, Phaelyn because you missed," Nyx said.

Phaelyn scowled, pulling another knife from the sheaths at her hips with an elegant twirl. "Now that I've got *all* your attention. Who am I gutting?"

LXV

Nyx

Phaelyn's words hung in the air like a dozen blades tossed in deathly circles by a juggler. Although it *should* have unnerved Nyx, Tobias's face rose in her mind. Ripping Phaelyn and Qadira to shreds for harming her loved ones was her overriding thought. *It's going to be so easy*, she thought as Orion and Niko bracketed her sides while Kade sidled to her back. *They won't stand a chance.* "Do your worst …" she whispered. "It won't do you any good."

Qadira's manicured eyebrows quirked, her scarlet-painted lips twisted in a resentful smile. "Oh, we can assure you that it'll do us plenty good," she said, pointedly glancing at the weeping marks she'd left on Nyx's throat.

Nyx keenly noted the knives strapped artfully across Phaelyn's chest and ribcage from her leather sheaths, criss-crossing over her breasts and ebony shirt, another sheath strapped to her thigh. Qadira seemed to ignore the men at Nyx's sides as she dabbed at the cut Nyx had left on her face offhandedly.

"Watch them," Orion warned in her mind, the sharpness of his tone re-instilling Nyx's unease. *"Qadira talks to distract."*

Phaelyn tutted as she wandered to Qadira's side, gaze trailing over the assorted wounds across her flesh. "It's not *polite* to have conversations in front of others … especially if it's about them," she crooned, silvered eyes filled with something ungodly.

Qadira's laughter fell into the room like a shaking of bells. "Oh, Phae', Nyx wouldn't know that. She hasn't been a vampire long enough. Isn't that right, *puta*?" she taunted.

Nyx took the derogative slur on the chin. "*Puta*?" she repeated, a humourless scoff wrenched from her lips. "Is that what we've come to? Petty slurs?"

"You don't know the *half* of who I really am," Qadira snapped, irked that Nyx and Orion, Kotori, Kade and Niko weren't rising to the bait.

Nyx nodded in agreement. "You're right. I don't," she said before she strode *closer* to the pair, ignoring the uneasy growls from Kade and Niko. "The Qadira *I* know wouldn't waste her time on pointless slurs. You cut quicker than light and struck without mercy before so … where is she? *That's* who I want the satisfaction of killing."

Qadira scoffed, "*You* think you can kill *me*? *You're* as dead they come."

"At least, when we're finished with you … you will be," Phaelyn drawled, creeping closer as Niko appeared at Nyx's side.

"Don't be like that, Niko, we had such a *good time* the last time we were together," Qadira taunted, a twisted glint in her eyes. She pouted, scrutinising the slashes left across his arms and chest.

The boast sent every one of Nyx's instincts rioting, suddenly maddened for Qadira's blood. She felt an unhinged desperation in herself to hear this woman's screams, her agonised pleas for mercy. To see the life leave her eyes became an urgent beacon. This was the goal.

To right the wrongs they'd committed for Leon.

"This is childish, even for you," Kotori said, his voice carrying level and true as he strode to Nyx's side.

"Childish?" Phaelyn parroted as though she didn't believe she'd heard him correctly.

"Isn't that what this is? A childish approach to a bloodstained end," he paused, surveying Phaelyn with scrutiny—the way he catalogued people's actions and interactions on the boardwalk. "For your … *age*, this is childish. Unbecoming of either of you."

Qadira made a slashing movement, almost too fast to see coming. Nyx's hand darted forward, snatching her knife-wielding wrist, preventing the blade from piercing her flesh as it hovered centimetres from her collarbone. Her face twisted in a grimace with the strength it took to prevent Qadira from plunging the knife into her chest. Nyx widened her stance. Qadira huffed in annoyance, ripping her wrist and the knife out of Nyx's grasp as she pulled a secondary blade from another sheath, twirling the polished steel in a ripping blur. Nyx blearily registered Qadira's swift move, ducking and sweeping the blonde's legs from out beneath her before she skittered back several paces and Qadira rose, as if from the depths of hell, blades clutched tightly in each hand, her knuckles white.

"Mark my words, Nyx. You're *dead*," Qadira spat.

Nyx watched her upper lip twitch and images of a rabid wolf came to mind. *Or a wounded one*, she thought, eyeing the older vampire with trepidation. Without warning, Qadira lashed out in a burst of speed, the tip of her knife slicing through Nyx's forearm. A ragged hiss tumbled from Nyx's mouth, teeth gritting when Qadira twirled and delivered a brutal slash along her spine, sending her to her knees. Beneath the weight of

Qadira's gaze and vicious smile shadowing her features, Nyx fought the urge to cower as her *mortal* instincts warned her of the danger stalking toward her, bellowing at her to run, to hide, to *live*.

But like so many times before, Nyx wouldn't cower. Not for Qadira or Phaelyn. Not for Leon whenever he showed his face. Not for these *monsters*. She wouldn't cower, not anymore. Not when the immortal fragments of her soul coalesced like living vengeance, craving retribution for Asher and Tobias—craving the blood of everyone who'd ever wronged her until the only name they remembered was hers.

"You already said that," Nyx murmured, her tone belying the creeping red over her vision. She eyed Qadira with unfiltered distrust. Her palm pressed against the tiles as she glared at Qadira, twirling her knives with a sick smile. Faster than a speeding bullet, she felt the frigid press of a blade against her throat. Grimly, Nyx recalled the day Amir had done the same. He too had pressed a knife to her throat. She remembered her terror and the bite of metal as it nicked her skin. She'd been down this road before and, as she refocused, she knew she could travel it again—this time, without fear.

Kade's tattooed hands grabbed Qadira's biceps and wrenched her away, pinning Qadira's arms behind her back as Nyx rose from the floor with a grimace. She pried Qadira's knives from her hands, tossing them aside and watched the woman thrash, eyes a livid shade of blue-gold. Kade dragged her floundering body toward Phaelyn—who glared daggers at Nyx, the thought alone caused Nyx to smile.

Orion was suddenly at her side. *"You did good, little regina. Exactly as we'd planned,"* he praised through their bond, emphasising his words by pulling her closer to his side.

"*You once said I was a good actress ... I guess you weren't lying*," she said, thinking of the night she'd killed Kai and what he'd said to her then.

"I've never lied to you. I was just selective."

"Ah, how you love evasion," she drawled, laughing.

His glacier gaze locked on hers as they halted before Phaelyn, something heavy and profound between them. "*Among other things."*

A darkly delighted grin uplifted Nyx's lips as she turned away from Orion, focusing on Phaelyn, whom Niko and Kotori had strung up in the chains Alexander and Tobias had been in. She watched with twisted satisfaction as Kotori moved to help Kade secure Qadira. Her struggles and sharply snapped insults echoed across the room, heels dragging in the twins' blood. It was a bittersweet justice and short-lived. Unbidden images of Tobias' lifeless body killed any joy. This was for him and Alexander, but he wouldn't know that—would never know. The thought hurt more than anything these women or Leon had done to her.

Nyx's gaze flitted from Qadira to Phaelyn, lingering on the chains keeping them in place, their efforts at breaking free useless. Their intertwined bodies and the way they fought and lashed, reminding her of serpents. Phaelyn and Qadira were like the serpents her mind drifted to, but their bites could no longer harm—their snapping was futile and impotent.

Qadira's eyes narrowed into thin slits, her irises an eerie discoloration of blue and gold. "So what? You think you've won, is that it?" she said, eyeing them all.

Niko sauntered toward her, lopsidedly grinning as he paused before her, his black mesh shirt exposing his defined body and the sprawling ink of his cheetah tattoo. "It's *almost* won," he drawled.

Phaelyn's bitter laughter filled the room as she pulled against the chains, side-eyeing Kotori when he appeared at her side and his be-ringed hand wrapped around the chains above her, staying her struggles. "You got lucky."

"Luck has nothing to do with this," Nyx said, stepping closer, a sneer curling her lips. "This is *retribution.* This is but one wrong needing to be righted."

"You might get rid of us but there's still Leon," Phaelyn said, holding Nyx's stare.

"For now," Orion said, orotund voice laced with dark promise.

Qadira eyed him incredulously. "You think *you* can kill him? He's a *sire*."

Kade stooped closer to her ear, his honeyed gaze locked on Nyx. "And even he has a weakness," he said.

Phaelyn's brows furrowed, silvered gaze darting between them as disbelief clouded her tone. "That's impossible. You're lying."

Kotori shrugged, peering down at her without emotion. "Whether it's the truth or not … you won't be here to find out."

Nyx stepped toward the bound women, to Phaelyn, and Niko handed her a pristinely-carved stake. She weighed it, twirling it artfully as Phaelyn's eyes widened and Qadira froze. Finally, the calamity of their deaths seemed to press upon them. Nyx grasped Phaelyn's shoulder, resting the stake's tip lightly against her chest and looked directly into Phaelyn's eyes. She didn't regret what she'd done as a vampire, and this would be no different. This was vengeance, cold yet sweet on her tastebuds and at the same time, more bitter than anything she'd ever tasted. It had to end.

This was for the twins.

"*Neither* of you will see the truth," Nyx breathed, refusing to tear her gaze from Phaelyn's as she drove the stake through the other woman's chest with a sickening *squelch* and the deathly point pierced the vampire's heart.

A crimson hue overtook Phaelyn's veins, webbing and forking through her bloodstream as the colour drained from her skin. Her heart stopped beating. Just like that, her life was snuffed out like a flame as her eyes stared without seeing, lips parted as though she'd been about to cry out, fangs ever-so-slightly peeking from beneath her lips; a true statue of death; both the giver and the receiver. Nyx thought it was a dark sort of irony as she gazed upon Phaelyn and the frozen aftermath of her passing—a once-vampire, slain by a stake.

Qadira's agonised shout of pain for her sister rent the room and Nyx turned to face her. She *wanted* to be the person who killed Qadira. *It was only fair*, she thought as she wandered toward the blonde who straightened, baring her fangs. She could feel the weight of four gazes watching her every move, intent on seeing her obtain her vengeance, the way she knew they revelled in—the way *she* revelled in—until mere inches separated her from Qadira. Nyx held Qadira's gaze like she'd held Phaelyn's, accepting a pale-wooded stake from Kade without looking.

"Please," Qadira murmured, her voice wavering as she begged before Death.

And, despite everything she'd done, Nyx found she wanted to give her a swift death. It was a mercy she didn't deserve but … it was the right thing to do. Nyx was not a monster, despite having hunted two. Qadira's death had ceased to be about pleasure or gain. Now, it was simply a means to an end. It must end. The anguish in Qadira's eyes gave Nyx windows into Qadira's soul, the gaping void Phaelyn's death had left behind. The shell of a sister who clung on. Maybe Nyx cared little for what would bring Qadira comfort as she plunged the stake through her chest and the *tha ... thump, tha ... thump* of her heartbeat vanished. Maybe she cared not for absolution as the crimson red of her veins pulsed over her paling skin in a ruby web, but only hurt people hurt.

It was in that final moment of decision, Nyx decided she would not allow Tobias' death to be reduced to something as trivial as revenge. As terrible as it was, it would not make her a monster. He would not have wanted that, Asher would not have wanted it. It wasn't who Nyx was meant to be. In that moment, Nyx was the executioner of hearts, for all their hearts, both still and beating.

She withdrew her hand as Qadira's face stilled.

Now she'd be reunited with her sister. Two beings frozen for eternity, side by side like the statues of men in Medusa's temple. Together even in death as they were in life.

Nyx stared for several long minutes as her heartbeat filled her ears and she realised what came next. Of *who* came next. Some part of her couldn't really believe that Phaelyn and Qadira were dead, but she knew they were. The pale-wooded stakes protruding from their chests was proof of that fact. A part of her wondered what a life of freedom would be like after everything she'd endured in the months since she'd come to Celacali. Would she find happiness with the men she loved? Would she find herself and establish that person until she knew it with every breath she took? Would she live for herself and everyone she loved?

Would she find peace in the world's darkness and her vampiric instincts?

Tha ... thump, tha ... thump, tha ... thump.

She heard her own heart beating.

Familiar applause ricocheted across the room and broke Nyx from her thoughts, mocking and entitled. Nyx didn't need to turn to know who had come. She knew. The time had come to fulfil her promise to the tawny-haired man she turned to face, half obscured by Orion and Kade's backs. Her lips twisted with disdain as her stare locked on a moss-green gaze she couldn't forget but it was with a cold calm of purpose that propelled her forward. The end had finally come.

The sire was here, and she couldn't wait to bring him to his knees.

LXVI

Nyx

Tha ... thump, tha ... thump, tha ... thump.

Clean, cold rage sliced Nyx's insides, dicing, and cauterizing chunks of her unfazed bravado away, piece by piece until she seemed to burn inside. Leon. His tawny-blond hair was as impeccably styled as she remembered, the inky fabric of his dress shirt tailored to his broad shoulders as he rubbed his hands together with the barest of glances at Phaelyn and Qadira's statuesque bodies, their loyalty as meaningful as autumn leaves. Everything about Leon was impeccable, from his unstained slacks and scuff-free dress shoes to his formidable height and unsettling gaze. Perhaps it was this which stoked her rising terror. This perfected and constructed mask which hid his true, monstrous nature. An image of immaculateness, like a skin sack over putrefaction. One so drenched in death and deeds so dire, he could only be rotting from the inside out.

Everything he—sire, controller, and captor of the men she loved—had done, to her men, *his sons*, to Qadira and Phaelyn—she could no longer doubt it—*his daughters* … to her, flicked in her mind like a simple switch. She stepped closer to Kade and Orion's backs, standing between them with her head held high. Leon wouldn't see her waver, nor would he glean a *fraction* of the terror she had once felt in his presence.

The sharpened point of a stake brushed against the bandages wrapped around her abdomen. A choked sob followed by vicious snarls. A harrowing squelch *and agony like no other.* She blinked the haze of her memories from her mind as the tension of the room wrapped around her throat, and Nyx realised that nothing would stop her from killing Leon. Like she knew nothing would stop Orion, Kotori, Niko and Kade because they'd waited, like Nyx had waited, confined to captivity and torment ordered or delivered by their sire. Haunted and tortured. Unable to fight back or protect themselves, until now.

These wolves had waited long enough. His leash had snapped along with their humanity, his death nudged forward by his sons. And now, *nothing* would save him from their vengeful maws.

Leon shifted his posture in a fluid movement so his gaze was unobscured, and he could hold Nyx's stare. He gestured airily to Qadira and Phaelyn over Nyx's shoulder. "I wish you hadn't done that," he said, tone bruised with mock disappointment. "We could have sorted this out civilly. Like *adults*."

"Like you've been doing?" Nyx said, daring him.

He shrugged, moss-green irises emotionless. "I've merely been responding in kind."

A dark grin stretched across her face. "Did you like my messages?"

Something darted across Leon's features, there one moment and gone in the next. "Was Cassia necessary?"

"Was torturing and keeping Kotori, Kade and Niko your prisoners *necessary*?" she quipped. "Were the children?"

"They needed to be taught a lesson, growing *feelings* for a mortal," he paused as his gaze swept across his sons before returning to her. "I thought I taught them better than that. I turned Phaelyn and Qadira for my eldest sons, as I would've done for Kade and Niko when they'd *matured*. And the children, well … we all have our vices." He grinned viciously.

Kade peered over his shoulder to Niko with a look that screamed, 'What the fuck!' before he turned back to his sire. "What happened to *free will*?" he asked.

Leon bristled, ignoring the question to ask one of his own. "What happened to the sons *I* raised?" he countered.

Kotori scoffed, towering over her, closing the distance. "They found someone *good* for them," he said.

As Kotori's words rippled inside her head, she glared across the room at Leon, and he glared back. She didn't like him, and he didn't like her. No love lost.

Leon stared Nyx down without concern that he was outnumbered. Like he knew he could fight them off if he had to. And maybe he could, but she knew he didn't know what they did.

"You know, I'm getting *sick* of you coming into our lives every decade or so just to remind us that you're our sire," Orion said, venomously.

Leon chortled in amusement. "But that's what I am, *boy*. I am your *sire*. I *saved* you. You're *my* protégés."

"You *were* our sire," Niko interjected, his cyanic gaze devoid of emotion.

"I *am* your sire!" Leon snapped, his mossy irises flickering gold.

Nyx caught the tangible shift in Leon, spreading through his flesh like oil atop a vast lake, tarnishing a once serene place with something horrid. It started in his eyes, leeching their forest-green hue until a nightmarish gold remained. His stance straightened as his head cocked eerily. His fingers moved to neaten his suit jacket, which didn't need neatening. *Almost like a nervous tick*, she thought.

"Oh, boys … don't tell me you think you can get rid of *me*. Vampires don't kill their sires; it goes against their instincts as pack creatures," Leon said.

Kade hummed, pretending to mull over Leon's words. "Well, you'll find *these*," he gestured to them, "vampires don't want any part of your *pack*. They've made something for themselves and intend to get rid of the issue standing in their way."

"You stupid boy," Leon sneered.

Kade shrugged, a devious grin inching across his face as he glanced at Nyx with a fire in his eyes. "Stupid but free."

Leon's gaze drifted from his youngest 'son' to the statuesque forms of Phaelyn and Qadira before resting on Nyx, eyeballs dark. "What is it that you *think* is my weakness? What did you find in Asher's journal? I'd *love* to know what had you all so confident you slaughtered my girls," Leon said.

"We don't need to tell you though, do we?" Niko said, his husky tone filled with a mischievous edge that matched the look in Kade's eyes.

"You're never going to be free of me and whatever you *think* you've found … it'll only ensure Nyx's death," Leon said, his words final.

This last comment seemed to set Orion, Kotori, Niko and Kade off as Kotori and Niko's grasps tightened upon her, bracketing her between themselves while Orion and Kade shifted. Their faces began to split, their eyes as bright gold as their sire's. Kade's lips twisted into a snarl and he bared his fangs in warning—touch my queen and die.

It pleased Nyx, as she watched through the gap between shoulders when Leon's upper lip twitched in response to their display—of their choice to defend her once again—She was theirs, and they were hers.

Her pack, *her* lovers, *her* protectors, *her* equals and … her *saviours*.

They *had* saved her in every way that a person could be saved, establishing her place with them as she warred with the right and wrong of her wants. *Encouraging* her to walk the path *she* wanted to walk. *Supporting* her decisions, no matter how dark or bloody. They accepted her, just as she accepted them. They loved her for her, cradling the pieces of her soul like diamonds.

Their *angel*, their *chica*, their *godin* and their *little regina*.

Theirs.

Now, they stood as one.

Leon looked at them with obvious disappointment, huffing an exasperated breath. His eyes returned to their mossy hue and an otherworldly edge laced his voice, "*Step aside*, boys," he ordered.

As Leon's words ratcheted off the walls, Nyx had the satisfaction of seeing his command-filled words fall short. She knew it was the first time in decades that Orion, Kotori, Niko and Kade had successfully fought one of Leon's commands and won. Once, it had been impossible to go against his commands, but it seemed their blood-bond to each other had overridden Leon's thrall. Their bond rendered the sire bond broken.

Leon watched as his control crumbled in his hands and his eyes sparked with fury, locking on Nyx as he strode toward her. "*You,*" he snarled.

Nyx grinned balefully, tilting her chin up in defiance. "What's the matter, Leon? Did the high of children's blood run out?"

"I should have ripped your heart from your chest at Chades Cove," he spat.

"Maybe you should have. It would have saved you some trouble," she drawled.

"You—your blood tainted *my* boys," he said, a golden edge to his mossy irises.

Nyx pulled a face of disbelief, eyeing him like one watched a madman. "Did it? Or did your leash snap?"

Kade's fingers wove through hers as Leon approached with the fury of a thousand suns. Orion's fingers looped possessively through her belt loops, anchoring himself to her. He and Kade stared Leon down when he halted before them, neither moving as a warning snarl reverberated from Niko. Leon's stare darted between his sons before it stuck on Nyx, the promise of her impending death etched in his eyes. It should have unsettled her, but she didn't care. She still had one more card up her sleeve.

"Move," Leon snapped, eyeing Kade and Orion in turn.

"I don't think we will," Orion drawled, making a show of turning to each of his companions before he returned his glacier gaze to Leon.

"I don't want to harm my sons just to get to *her*, but I will if you don't step aside. This is your last warning," Leon said, his tone softer than it had been before.

"Then, consider us warned," Kotori said, his deep voice like a brewing storm as Orion, Kade and Niko murmured their agreement and Leon's eyebrows furrowed.

"You would die for her?" he asked, genuine puzzlement on his face.

"We'd kill for her too," Niko said, tossing Nyx a wink when she peered up at him before she turned back to Leon with a soft smile.

Leon smoothed a hand down the front of his shirt before his eyes locked on Nyx. Then he lunged toward her. Nyx's heart hitched as Orion released her belt loops in a graceful movement and shunted Leon back several paces, the tawny-blond stumbling backward. Orion peered over his shoulder at Nyx, his steely gaze sweeping across her before he rolled his shoulders and turned back to his sire. Leon dragged his tongue against his teeth and struck Orion across the face with the back of his hand, the *crack* ringing in her eardrums.

A rage-filled snarl tore from Nyx's throat as Orion stood frozen. Kotori shifted beside her as Niko wound his arms around her waist, trapping her to his chest.

"Remember the plan, chica," Niko said as his voice filled her head through their bond.

She remembered.

Nyx watched as Kotori and Orion shared a look, Kotori's head dipping with a nod of understanding before he crossed the room and the pair started circling Leon, forcing him to continuously turn in a slow circle to keep them both in his sight. Kade tossed Nyx a look before he joined his companions. The trio worked in tandem to herd their sire, waiting for the moment Leon's self-control would waver and he'd strike, his guards lowering whenever he let his emotions show.

Leon shifted with supernatural ease, feigning left before he slipped past Kotori to come face-to-face with Orion, who blocked his path, eyes glittering. Orion easily sidestepped Leon's aggravated lunge, grabbing his arm to shift his centre of gravity before he shoved Leon toward Kotori. A deathly snarl tore from Leon's throat, his eyes bleeding golden-yellow as he lashed out and the metallic bite of blood filled Nyx's nose, and Kotori's shout of pain echoed in her ears. Niko's grasp on Nyx tightened as she made to intervene, his head shaking with a warning when she forced her eyes away from the gash down Kotori's forearm, crimson splattering the tiles.

Nyx turned to face Niko then, peering up at him as his brows furrowed and his eyes darted across her face. "*Do you trust me?*" she said into the bond they shared.

Niko's frown deepened, his stare darting to his brothers before returning to her. "*With my life.*" Reluctantly, he stepped back, nodded and grasped her hand, pressing a syringe vial into her palm. He gently curled her fingers around it. *"Don't miss,"* he said in her head.

She held his gaze

and Orion's brows furrowed, turning toward her a moment too late as Leon darted forward, grabbing Kade and hauling him to his chest. Her ears filled with a ringing sound as everything but Kade faded to nothing. She strode several paces toward Leon, willing her heart to cease its terrified patter.

"Let him go, Leon," Nyx said, her voice carrying calm and devoid of emotion as she stared the formidable man down.

A bemused chuckle rumbled from his chest, his grasp shifting on Kade as he pushed the tattooed blond to his knees and twisted his arm awkwardly behind his back. "That's not how this works, Nyx," Leon said.

"I'll join you … just don't hurt him," she said, praying it was what Leon wanted to hear. "We could be a family, all of us, together, no more hurting each other."

"Nyx, no." Orion began, stepping toward her with a frantic look in his eyes.

Leon moved swiftly, a sickening *crunch* filling her ears as he applied too much pressure to Kade's shoulder, shattering it before grasping Kade's forearm with his stare locked on hers. He twisted Kade's wrist until a sharp *crack* and Kade's anguish-filled shout pummelled her eardrums. Kade's wrist was contorted at an odd angle when Leon released him and Kade seemed to bow before him, cradling his arm to his chest, his eyes screwed shut as his jaw clenched.

"You. Dead. That's what I want. Your use to me expired in Chades Cove," Leon murmured, appearing before her in a burst of speed until she was forced to tip her head back to hold his stare.

Her tone was soft as she spoke, "I could be the daughter you've always wanted. I'm strong. Stronger than they ever were." As she said this last, she looked pointedly to where the stone bodies of Phaelyn and Qadira lay.

"Nyx," Kotori protested, moving toward her before Orion grasped his bicep, halting his stride. Kotori's gaze darted across Orion's face and his eyes widened at whatever he saw. He tugged at Orion's grasp. "No, don't do it."

Leon's grin grew as his hand shot out and wrapped around Nyx's throat, dragging her toward him with a punishing grip that drew a hiss from her lips. "You. Me. Us. One big happy family? I rather like that." Leon laughed again and the sound was hollow. "Yes. You see, dearest Orion told me that you'd all be here," he said, fingertips sinking into her windpipe. He stooped so that his lips whispered over her skin, "He brought *you* to me."

What? "He wouldn't …" she started before trailing off as her eyes darted to Orion. She searched his face for something to dissuade Leon's words and found nothing but frigid disinterest as Orion held her stare. She shook her head, refusing to believe Leon as a knifing pain plunged her chest and razored her sternum to her stomach. *He wouldn't do that*, she thought, repeating it like a mantra in her head even as her traitorous thoughts whispered that yes, *he would*. That he'd do anything to keep his companions safe, even get rid of her.

He wouldn't do that.

He wouldn't do that.

And maybe she would've believed it … if Kotori's face hadn't fallen with shock and disbelief. If Kotori hadn't whirled on Orion and shunted him back until he stumbled, advancing on Orion with a wolfish snarl. If Niko hadn't pushed himself from the floor and grasped Kotori's arms, hauling him away from Orion with a blistering glare tossed to their emotionless companion. *Maybe.*

The hurt she felt was bigger than the world—the abyss of sinking tearing the floor out from beneath her almost … welcome. She wished she didn't feel at all—as she squirmed in Leon's grasp, wincing as he dug his fingers further and her lungs started to burn from the lack of oxygen. Her teeth gritted against the burning sensation in her chest, ignoring Orion's desolate stare. She saw as Kotori, Niko and Kade clustered together, their faces stricken. Her fists clenched at her side and, for a moment, froze as the syringe vial dug into her palm. Her gaze darted to Niko and his head dipped in an almost imperceptible nod.

Don't miss.

She adjusted her grasp on the vial, thumbing the cap off the needle while her lungs bellowed their distress, and she forced the dizziness from her mind. Her fingers trembled, mind fogging as she forced herself to meet Orion's steely gaze, holding his stare. She spoke in a ragged wheeze, "If only you knew."

"Knew what?" Leon said, sounding amused as she struggled to talk.

To think. To move. To breathe.

Tha ... thump, tha ... thump, tha ... thump.

Her onyx irises pierced Orion's, conveying a message she wasn't sure he'd understand but hoped he would. "It's not the lion the wildebeest fears … it's the lioness that crushes its windpipe." With the little strength she had against a millenniums-old vampire, she gripped the syringe tight and plunged the needle into Leon's thigh, sinking her thumb on the plunger.

Surprise tore from his throat, his grasp leaving hers as he shoved her away and wrenched the hypodermic from his thigh. Sweet oxygen flooded her lungs as her knees collided with the tiled floor. Choked coughs and ragged breaths seared her tender throat, but she didn't care, she could breathe.

Orion spared Leon a frigid look before he strode to Nyx's side—ignoring Kotori, Kade and Niko's confused looks—and helped her up from the floor, winding his arm around her waist. He grinned down at her as she gazed up at him, a smile spreading across her face as he pressed an adoration-filled kiss to her lips. "Look at you, my little regina. Aren't you just the *perfect* actress?" Orion whispered.

"You're not so bad yourself," she croaked.

"What—" Leon said, whirling to Orion. "What the hell was in that vial?"

Kade leaned into Niko when he rose from the ground, wincing with a proud glint in his eyes. "That would be silver and the blood of a bonded pack. I hear it's … paralysing to a sire if it's from his bloodline *and* is mixed with one that's not," he said.

Kotori chuckled, patting Niko's shoulder affectionately before he stalked toward Nyx, pulling a familiar serpentine dagger from a hidden knife holster in his boot and handing it to her. This dagger was different. Instead of the silvered blade of polished steel, the blade had been replaced with pure silver, its centre split by a crimson-red hue that melded into the metal; *their* blood combined and instilled into the blade.

What was created from one can be undone *by blood. Condemned by the bloodline they created, vanquishable by their bloodline. A blade of tainted blood to kill the sire of immortality.*

Nyx twirled the serpentine dagger in her grasp, the reddish hue of the blade catching the light as Orion and Kotori moved in sync, grasping Leon's arms and forcing him to his knees, their hands clamped on his shoulders. Leon's stare flicked across the room like he was searching for a way to escape, struggling as Nyx halted before him.

She thumbed the blade with smouldering irises. "Remember how you said you couldn't kill a sire?" She peered down at him as Niko and Kade bracketed her back. "Well, that's not true."

"Wha—how?" Leon spluttered; his brows furrowed with confusion.

"Let's just say that we found a friend in The Wizard of Oz."

"You can't—" he protested.

Nyx laughed without amusement, shaking her head as she cut him off. "You've done unspeakable things, you've hurt those I love. You're a child-killer. You've tried … to kill me. Your time as a sire is over, our freedom begins now." She held Leon's stare as she stepped forward and rested her hand on his shoulder above Kotori's hand, tightening her grasp on the dagger before she plunged the blade into his chest with a wet *squelch*, piercing his heart.

Unlike Qadira and Phaelyn before him, Leon did not cry out. Instead, hate registered in his eyes.

Nyx would never forget the look he gave her. It was as if a century of pain and power resided behind his eyes and he clung to the sight of her until the light left them. His skin drained of colour and his veins flared crimson through his skin, webbing and stretching, his fangs protruding from beneath his lips while his body turned as statuesque as his daughters.

The resoluteness of his death registered a moment later as she stared down at him, releasing the hilt of the dagger and leaning into Kotori's embrace. It didn't seem real, this sense of serenity in the aftermath of calamity. It was over. After everything they'd done and what Leon had done to them, a part of Nyx didn't believe it was real and she'd wake up to realise it was all a dream.

She knew it wasn't, knew they were free but still …

She waited.

They were free—Orion, Niko, Kade, Kotori and herself—but she'd lost people loved along the way. She'd lost Asher and Tobias, parts of her soul she couldn't get back but she would live every day remembering them. If only to do everything they would have wanted for her, everything she would have shared with them. As the ashes of her anger subsided and a new calm settled in her mind, she knew this was how it would be.

"Dii te acriter," Kotori murmured, his chin propped upon her head as he gazed down at Leon's body.

Nyx's lips tugged into a soft smile as she repeated what Kotori said and the weight of them carried across the room, "May the gods judge you harshly."

With their words of condemnation, Nyx started through the house to a kitchen she'd glimpsed in the blueprints in Asher's journal. She made her way to the stove and twisted the dials as the hiss of gas grew louder.

"Need a lighter?" Orion drawled from behind her.

Smiling, she extended her hand palm-up to him, knowing they were all there.

"Of course," she said, weighing the silvered lighter in her palm.

For a moment, she stood transfixed by the lighter flame as she brought it to the curtains bracketing the door, enjoying the way they licked at the fabric and smoke drifted across her senses. Flicking the lighter shut, Nyx turned to her men with a malignant smile. "I think it's time to go," she mused, tucking Orion's lighter in her pocket as she started out the door.

Niko's soft chuckle filled her ears as his arm wrapped around her shoulders and he pulled her closer to his side, the group clearing much of the driveway's distance before a resounding *boom* thundered into the night. As she turned to face the once mighty estate, a deranged smugness settled inside her. They watched as tangerine flames found their way out of the building, pluming black smoke swallowing the moon and the stars.

Nyx watched as Leon's estate burned with her men by her side. She basked in the knowledge that her wolves were free of their tyrant master, the weathered chains that had once bound them were gone and *nothing* could contain them again.

In the shadows of vengeance left behind, she vowed to ensure they were never prisoners again. And if she had to kill a few people to ensure it, then so fucking be it.

EPILOGUE

Nyx

Something black flitted across the shadowed alleyway as she manoeuvred through the darkness with ease. She glanced at the Ivory Skull who followed her around the corner, eyes heavy with false interest and, like a moth to a flame, the chestnut-brown-haired man followed. Walking himself into Death's embrace. Nyx turned and a baleful smile lifted her lips when she passed Ares, who waited in the dark, guarding the entrance.

Days had passed in a daze since she'd driven the serpentine dagger through Leon's heart and watched him die with morbid satisfaction—and a moment hadn't gone by that Nyx didn't revel in the knowledge of their freedom. It cocooned her in a malignant embrace, embedding itself into her senses. Orion, Kotori, Niko and Kade, she ... they were safe. The monstrous man and his puppet strings was gone. His puppet girls were dead. She'd watched them die, she'd watched him die. Then she'd borne witness as their bodies burned like she'd watched Ryder and Amir burn. Darkness returned to the dark.

"Who's this, Night?" came a voice laced with feigned confusion as Tobias stepped out from the shadows and blocked the man's retreat. His stainless-steel bracelet glinted in the moonlight when he removed his hands from his jean's pockets.

Nyx couldn't hide her happiness at Tobias' presence. She couldn't describe the relief she'd felt when she'd learned about Tobias' '*insurance policy*' and the part Orion had played in it. She'd learned later that, in the days before Phaelyn and Qadira had kidnapped the twins, Orion had visited Alexander and Tobias to keep them in the loop, using the guise of needing confirmation about her notes on Asher's journal to slip undetected by Nyx, informing them of their plans while they searched for Leon's daughters. Little did she know what Tobias had requested from Orion in return for his, and Alexander's, silence. But Orion had agreed, nonetheless, and given him what he wanted—a vial of his blood—but not without warning them of the potency if they ingested it.

It seemed Tobias had readily grasped the olive branch Orion extended as his eyes now flickered golden-yellow, enough to send terror shooting through the Ivory Skull, a shout of surprise tumbling from his lips.

Nyx focused on the alleyway and not her thoughts. The burgundy sleeves of her flowy shirt brushed her arms, her dark-washed jeans slit along the knee as the coin charm of her necklace caught the moonlight. "A friend," she replied, her dark gaze showcasing the lie as she wandered toward the Ivory Skull.

A snicker skittered across the alleyway, capturing the man's attention. He whirled and his hazel eyes locked on Niko, who sauntered from the shadowed dead end. His stride was feline, the leather of his pants complimenting the array of bracelets stacked on his wrist. His broad features twisted with dark excitement—a cheetah in pursuit of a fleeing antelope.

His cyanic gaze flitted to her, alight and yet dark. "Aw, chica. You shouldn't have," he crooned.

The Ivory Skull frowned with confusion, wary as he looked between Nyx, Niko and Tobias. He whirled to Nyx, his hands clamped around her biceps and his nostrils flared like an agitated bull. "What's he talking about?" he snapped, gesturing to Niko with a jut of his chin.

"He's one second away from ripping your hands off. Didn't you ever learn not to touch something that isn't yours?" Kade said, appearing at Nyx's side with blazing irises—his shoulder and wrist mended—before his voice dropped several, menacing octaves. "Now, get your fucking hands off her."

In his haste to escape Kade's wrath, the Ivory Skull hurriedly dropped Nyx's arm and stumbled back, colliding with Kotori's bared chest. Kotori looked at the man with disinterest before his dark gaze flitted to Nyx and hers to the darkest depths of the alleyway. There, she knew, Orion lurked, staying out of sight.

The Ivory Skull turned in a frantic circle, his eyes darting between Niko, Kade, Kotori and Nyx. "No," he whimpered, side-stepping Kotori to come face-to-face with Tobias in his feeble attempt to shove past them and return to the safety of the boardwalk. "*Please*."

Orion's laughter split the alleyway like a flash of lightning, his intimidating presence appearing from the shadows like the answering rumble of thunder. In a heartbeat, he was there. His glacier-like irises were brightened by his dark intentions, his leather-clad fingers adjusting the cuffs of his gloves, obsidian slacks and shirt accentuating his ivory skin. The Ivory Skull's terror was apparent as the man turned to bolt. Kade and Niko snatched up his arms, pinning him between them with easy, predatory zeal.

"What's the hurry, Murray?" Kade said, belying his love for the hunt.

"Please, let me go. I won't say anything," the man pleaded.

Orion draped an arm over Nyx's shoulders as she angled her head to hold his gaze. "What do you say, little regina? Does he live … or does he die?"

"It depends," she replied, turning back to the Ivory Skull to scrutinise him like a scientist plagued by their findings.

"On?" Kotori said, a knowing undertone laced in the deep timbre of his voice.

"On whether his soul is as *tainted* as ours," she replied.

"And if it is?" Tobias asked, a new darkness Nyx had never seen before etched in his dark eyes.

"Then Celacali's monsters will claim their next victim," she said, her onyx gaze locked on the struggling man.

She knew she should have been ashamed—maybe disgusted—by her easy vocalisation of the man's death, but she also knew it was a pointless worry because he'd die as surely as every other person she'd killed. It wasn't a question of *if*, just a matter of *when*. She supposed she had Asher to thank for her way of thinking, since he'd always wanted her to pursue her goals. He'd supported her decisions while Azeil had tried to be the voice of reason, reminding her of the repercussions before she decided on which path she took. She missed Asher, and she knew she'd always miss him, but she knew she'd made him proud, choosing the path she wanted and fighting for it. Although her father seemed disgruntled by Orion, Niko, Kade and Kotori, and now Tobias, she knew he'd support her decisions even if he disagreed. Always the voice of reason and *always* supportive of her. Even if they were the men from his past that he loathed, Azeil had decided to stay in Celacali. Her mother and Xander had returned to Malor as soon as Alexander was released from the hospital and Tobias had woken as a halfling.

Alyvia had wrapped Nyx in a loving embrace before she'd left, an unspoken forgiveness of the men in Nyx's life, remnants too, of her own past. Nyx knew her mother's fear of them couldn't be forgotten, despite how well she hid it, but she tried and that was as much as Nyx could ever hope for. She missed her mother, but she couldn't blame her for putting herself first, knowing that she wouldn't spend more than a week in Celacali. Xander, however, had promised to return every fortnight, ruffling her curls before he'd engulfed her in a bear hug and Nyx had waved goodbye to them, watching until his Impala had disappeared.

As she focused on her surroundings, Nyx locked eyes with Tobias and dipped her head subtly. *"He's all yours, Bias,"* she said, catching the devious grins that split across Niko and Kade's faces as her voice carried through their bond.

"After you," Tobias said, ever the gentleman.

Nyx's lips tugged into a malicious grin as she stepped away from Orion and approached the Ivory Skull, surveying his dirt-stained pants and desolate eyes. Her fingers trailed tauntingly across the man's chest, fingertips toying with the neckline of his shirt before her eyes bled white-gold and she felt the familiar shifting of her features.

Niko stooped his head, his voice laced with an otherworldly command, "*Don't make a sound*. We wouldn't want anyone to hear you … *scream*, now, would we?"

A feeble whine tumbled from the man's throat, a constricted sound that almost made Nyx believe someone had pressed their shoe into his windpipe as she tightened her grasp and her fangs pressed against her bottom lip. She didn't spare the man another glance, using one of her hands to bare more of his throat before she embedded her fangs into his jugular. After a moment, she pulled away as Kade extended the man's wrist toward Tobias. The halfling twin wrapped his fingers around the offered appendage and sank his fangs into the man's flesh at the same time as Kade's embedded in the Ivory Skull's throat.

Niko strode toward her with a hungry look she recognised and he drew her to his chest, one hand cradling her face. His thumb collected the blood on her chin and brought it to his mouth without looking away and a jolt of lust jammed in her chest. He pulled his thumb from his mouth and connected their lips in a searing kiss, backing her into the nearest wall with the scuffling of Kade and Tobias as white noise.

"Niko," Came Kotori's exasperated voice, his boots crunching on the pavement. "C'mon, you couldn't have waited until you got back to the cave?"

Niko pulled away from her with a mock eye-roll. "*Tori*, not all of us have restraint," he gestured to Nyx and the crimson staining her skin. "Look at her. You expect me to *control myself* when she's covered in blood?"

A sickening *thump* echoed across the alleyway as Kade released the Ivory Skull and the body collided with the pavement. Nyx's gaze found Tobias as he raised his hand in a wave, and disappeared into the shadows. Kade wandered to Nyx's side, wiping the Ivory Skull's blood from his face with a tattoo-embellished hand before he grasped Nyx's chin between his fingers and pressed a bloodied kiss to her lips.

Kade's hazel eyes locked on hers when he broke the kiss. "We all know you want a taste, and Kotori? She tastes *divine,*" Kade crooned.

The coarse bricks of the wall pressed into her back as Nyx tipped her head to peer up at Kotori. His scent of freshly fallen rain and the earthy tones of a forest engulfed her as his lips brushed hers, featherlight at first before the metal of his lip ring ghosted over her lips and his tongue traced the seam of her mouth. Her lips parted without a second thought as the towering brunette *tasted* her, her hands grasping the lapels of his leather jacket.

Orion's chuckle drifted through the shadows; his voice etched with mirth. "Anyone would think you haven't seen her for *months* with the way you're acting. It's been … an hour since you last kissed her, where's your self control?"

Where Kotori had been, only moments before, now Orion's gloved hand cradled the back of her head and he kissed her with abandon. Nyx reciprocated, revelling in the undertones of sandalwood and cigarette smoke that clung to him as her hands rested against his chest.

Breaking away, Orion eyed each of his companions before he peered down at Nyx like she was the light in his life—his everything. "Let's go home," he said as Niko and Kade's hollers echoed off the alleyway.

Home, Nyx mused with a soft smile, her gaze tracking the blond duo as they strode in the direction of the carpark and their waiting bikes. She realised—not for the first time—that home wasn't a place. Niko's sharp whistle summoned Ares before the Malamute trotted happily to his side, barrelling down the alleyway with unfiltered excitement. Home had never been a place in Nyx's life, merely a metaphor for a person she'd someday find. *Home* wasn't the hideaway tucked in Elveszett Bluff, it was four men who'd turned her world upside down and then rebuilt it. It was Celacali and its bloodied enigma. It was every warped desire she had and readily embraced. It was death reigning over life, ever-patient and equally gentle, but it was also the eternity of life; a thousand lifetimes bestowed by her hand and revoked by Death's.

The City of the Dead had been ruled by monsters with golden-yellow eyes and the shadows of the night—of their vengeance—but now, it was ruled by five instead of four. The kings of Celacali had found their queen, and they'd ensure anyone who threatened their rule was dealt with.

If it was the last thing they ever did.

Also by Charlize K. Kelly

SHADOWS OF THE NIGHT DUET

Shadows of the Night

Shadows of Vengeance

Acknowledgments

Where do I begin saying thank you for a five-year-long journey? The answer is I don't know. I'll admit that I stared at this page for too long before I decided where to start because every word makes me realise that my time in Celacali—that world, its characters and the blood spill of … a lot of its pages—has come to an end.

Thank you to my editor, Agatha Whitechapel, for all her help and endless conversations where I rambled or second-guessed myself. She pushed me through my revisions and I couldn't be more grateful (they kept me sane).

Thank you to Betthina Eriella, my cover designer, for my stunning cover (all hand drawn) and the artwork of the Celacali crew for *SoV*. I'll be forever floored by everything she's created. We had one goal; make it *darker* than *Shadows of the Night*, and we did it. Easily. As always, she is a *GODDESS* when it comes to her artwork.

Thank you to my interior designer, Natalia Junqueira, for bringing *SoV* to life within its pages and its updated map! I absolutely adore the notes and darkness you brought to the interior, tying to my cover *perfectly!* I love being able to *see* my world and the places the Celacali crew travel to, each new edition such a satisfying reward.

I thank Def Leppard—Joe Elliott, Phil Collen, Rick Allen and Rick Savage—for being a mental soundtrack on my five-year-long journey. If *Shadows of Vengeance* had one song, it would be '*Women.*'

Thank you to my beta readers, who grew from three to nine. For every unhinged comment that kept me sane to every bit of carnage I put you through. I found a bunch of people who adore the villains (and vampires) as much as I do. Go *#teamvamp!* Thank you to my proofreaders – we all love a typo … especially the ones that make it to the final *published* version and Leon (said no one).

To my doggo, Satan, because Ares' tendencies, minus the homicidal parts, were inspired by my goofball. He has two thoughts—love me and pat me—and doesn't go a day without stealing my attention, nudging my hand from my keyboard until I give *him* attention. You're an absolute dork but you're my heart dog (so, it's an automatic pass).

To you, my readers, thank you for coming back for Book Two. Your candid reviews, your endless support. Without you, none of this would have been possible and I am forever grateful for your help in making this dream my reality. Your love for Nyx, Orion, Niko, Kade and Kotori, and for a little … darkness fuelled my writing. You *might* see them in the future, but only time will tell.

And now, as the sun sets and night makes its way across the sky, I hope you'll return to the City of the Dead whenever you miss it and find yourself at home there. As eternal as its rulers and as malignant as its sinners, it'll always be there, waiting …

About the Author

Charlize K. Kelly writes dark, paranormal romance with unorthodox characters and adventures of the deliciously corrupt kind. She's a villain's villain and quests for the ethereal of eighties glam rock, bridging the then and now in every chapter.

When she's not creating fictional worlds, she spends her time reading, hanging out with her dog Satan, and blasting Def Leppard, Mötley Crüe and Bon Jovi from the coast to the Wheatbelt. Charlize lives in Western Australia and dreams of the day somebody will bring the eighties back with a modern edge.

Follow Charlize K. Kelly for teasers, news and chaos!
Website: charlizekkelly.squarespace.com
Tiktok: @charlizekkelly
Instagram: @authorckkelly
Add to Goodreads: Shadows of Vengeance by Charlize K. Kelly

www.ingramcontent.com/pod-product-compliance
Lightning Source LLC
Chambersburg PA
CBHW081131300726
48982CB00005B/927

* 9 7 8 0 6 4 5 7 3 3 5 1 8 *